Dragonsbreach Mountains

Howling Falls

Bone Forest

RE...

SPIRES

Spiral Keep

...ver Province

Red Fork River

Solitary Pass

GLIMMER

Gold Fork River

Plains

Blue Hills

Ruby Fields

...Wood

34

Sun Province

Griffin Hold

Dripstone Cavern

Bounty Fields

Satyr Wood

Harvest Province

Sharptooth Mountains

...River

Rookwood

EARTHBANK

Sunset River

King's Highway

King's Highway

EASTGUARD

Boneharvest Plain

Sharptooth Pass

Sphinx River

Deep Harvest

Griffinclaw Range

PHALANX

Singing Hills

Snakewall

Sphinx Gate

Lamassu Gate

CHARIOT

GRIT

...entrywood

F G H I J

⊙ ~ City
■ ~ Town
🏚 ~ Ruin
★ ~ Gate

EVERWAY

SILVER ANNIVERSARY EDITION

1995–2020

Book 1: Players

THE EVERWAY COMPANY
everway.com

PUBLISHED BY THE EVERWAY COMPANY

THE EVERWAY COMPANY, EVERWAY, SPHEREWALKER, RUBICON GAMES, GASLIGHT PRESS, and the portrayal of the pyramid and portal are trademarks of The Everway Company, LLC

ISBN 978-1-7345856-1-2

Everway Silver Anniversary Edition Book 1: Players © 2020 – The Everway Company, LLC

Printed in China

Fall 2020

10 9 8 7 6 5 4 3 2 1

See Section 2: Fortune Guide to learn about the Fortune Deck card draws on each page!

THE DRAGON

Silver Anniversary Edition Credits

Original Design: Jonathan Tweet

Silver Anniversary Edition Design: Richard Thames Rowan and Jesse McGatha

Graphic Design, Layout, & Typesetting: Richard Thames Rowan

Setting Design Contributions: Greg Stolze

Editing: Karen Babcock

Proofreading: Jesse McGatha and Rob Barrett

Maps: Richard Thames Rowan

Production Assistance: Marcee Charlshe

Cover Art: Doug Alexander (front), Scott Kirschner (back)

Interior Art: Credited near where art appears

Special Thanks: Kat Miller and Darvin Martin for abundant feedback and playtesting

BOOK 1: PLAYERS

Section 1: Playing Guide
Design Contributions: Richard Thames Rowan and Jesse McGatha
Roundwander Setting: Jesse McGatha and Richard Thames Rowan

Section 2: Fortune Guide
Methods of Fortune Design: Richard Thames Rowan

Section 3: Vision Guide
Vision Questions: Jonathan Tweet and Richard Thames Rowan

Section 4: Quick Start Guide
Hero Creation Guide: Jesse McGatha
Reference Charts: Richard Thames Rowan

BOOK 2: GAMEMASTERS

Section 1: Gamemastering Guide
Creature Contributions: Jesse McGatha and Richard Thames Rowan
Gamemaster Contributions: Kathy Ice, Bob Kruger, Jesse McGatha, and Richard Thames Rowan

Section 2: Questing Guide
Quest Designers: Jesse McGatha, Richard Thames Rowan, Jonathan Tweet, Nicole Lindroos, and Jenny Zappala.

110. Woman and the Llama Dog – Daniel Gelon, 1310. Fortune Reader – Joe DeVelasco, 1212. Temple Statue – Doug Keith, 910. Order of the Silver Nail – Jerry Tiritilli, 511. Gamblers – Doug Alexander, 401. Skull Lord – Ed Lee

THE KING – REVERSED

Creating a new edition necessarily means changing things, and some people's work gets lost or revised. Special thanks go out to Maria Cabardo, John Casebeer, Sue Ann Harkey, Susan Harris, Steve Heller, John Scott Tynes, and Amy Weber. Their prior contributions helped make EVERWAY what it is today.

1995 Edition Credits

Design: Jonathan Tweet

Editor & Design Contributions: Jenny Scott Tynes

Realm Contributions: Scott Hungerford, Kathy Ice, Bob Kruger, Aron Tarbuck, and John Scott Tynes

Realms Research: Jana Wright

Ready-to-Run Heroes: Kathy Ice (Chance), Aron Tarbuck (Amber, Clarity, Shadow), Jonathan Tweet (Cleft, Fireson, Praise, Serenity, Whisper Walker), and Jenny Scott Tynes (Detritus, Opal, Puma)

Four Element Illustrations: Amy Weber

Art Direction & Hero Sheets: Maria P. Cabardo

Playtest Gamemasters: Ken "Panda" Bontinck, Scott C. Hungerford, Kathy Ice, Bob Kruger, Chris Lackey, Nicole Lindroos, Rachel Nation, Greg Stolze, Aron Tarbuck, John Scott Tynes, Lynne Wilson, and Teeuwynn Woodruff

The Originals: Eric Tumbleson, Greg Stolze, J'nypher Hoelter, Chris Metzl, Roger Decker, Jr., and Andy Vlack

Dedicated to Tessa Marie Tweet

Thanks To: Lee Gold, James Wallis, the huxter's room at I-Con, J'nypher Hoelter, Eric Tumbleson, Mrs. Short, Robin D. Laws, Nicole Lindroos, Aron Tarbuck, and John Scott Tynes

Special thanks to Greg Stolze. EVERWAY owes a lot to his prolific imagination.

In Memoriam

We mourn the loss of talent from the EVERWAY family over the last quarter century. Your work lives on.

Joe DeVelasco (1933–1999)
Christopher Rush (1965–2016)
Rudy Rauben (1963–2019)
Karen Babcock (1964–2020)
Martin McKenna (1969–2020)

Table of Contents

901. Red Lady – Doug Alexander

110. Lady and the Llama Dog – Daniel Gelon

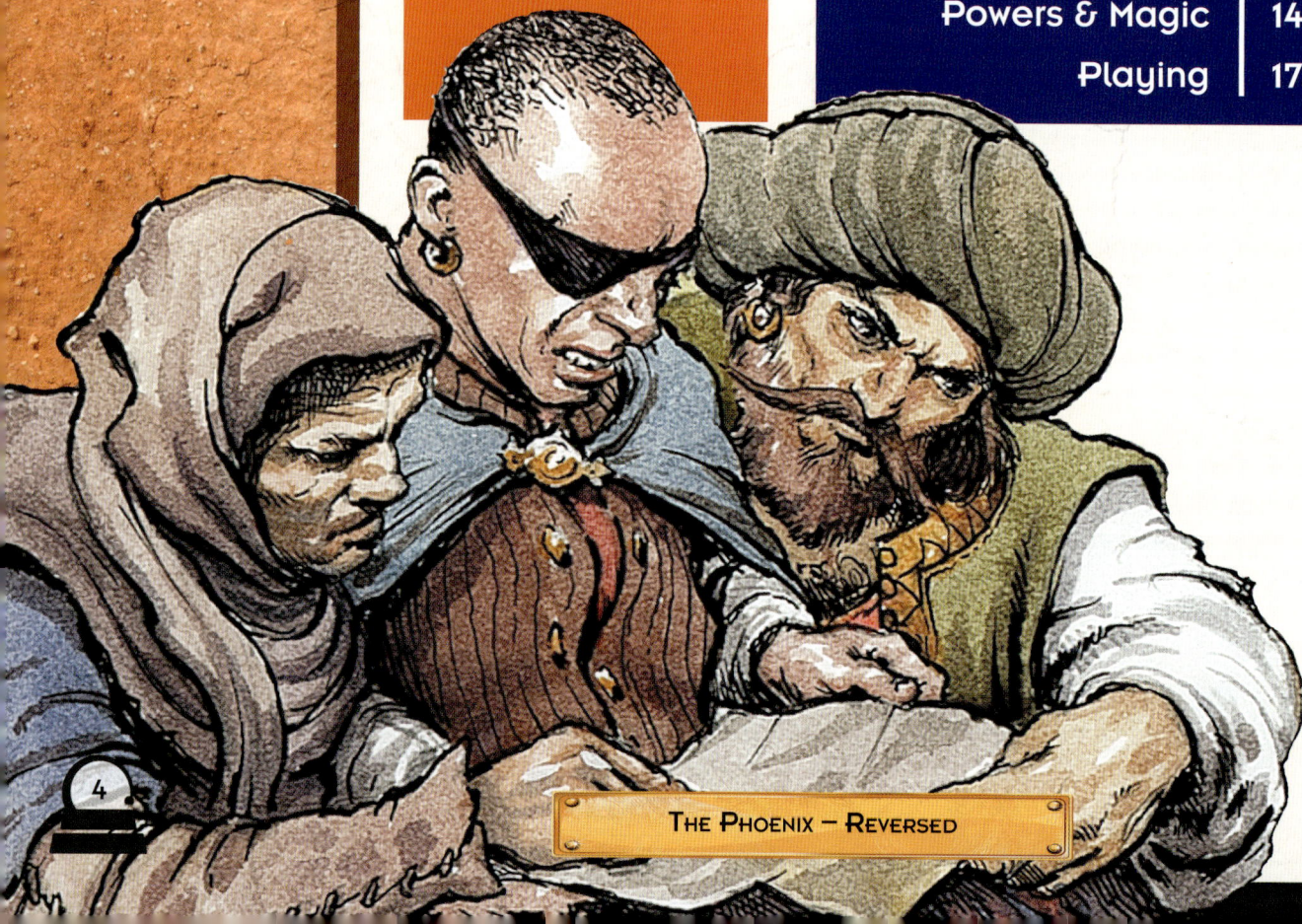

THE PHOENIX – REVERSED

4

901. Red Lady ~ Doug Alexander

SUMMER

Publisher Foreword

I fell in love with EVERWAY on August 10, 1995, the day it debuted at Gen Con in Milwaukee, Wisconsin. I had just started my first job after college working for Wizards of the Coast, and I got to help explain and promote the game to the attendees in the Wizards booth. I immediately started running my own game as soon as I got back home to Seattle.

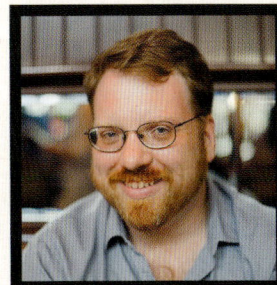

As you can imagine, I was deeply saddened by Wizards of the Coast's decision to cancel their RPG lines in 1996, but I was also excited about the possibility of acquiring EVERWAY. Jesse McGatha and I, along with a group of friends, formed Rubicon Games and were ultimately successful in our bid. I was the project manager for Rubicon's first EVERWAY supplement, **Spherewalker Sourcebook**, and helped get several other projects underway.

By early 1997, however, I left both Wizards of the Coast and Rubicon Games to go work in the videogame industry, I got married, and generally my life became overly full. Still, when I heard in 2001 that Rubicon Games was in financial trouble, I purchased the EVERWAY line again, this time from Rubicon Games. I always wanted to see it carried forward and to release a new edition and support material, but life kept getting in the way. My life has recently slowed down now that I have transitioned to being a full-time college professor. I can finally return to a game that I love, just in time for its twenty-five year, Silver Anniversary.

EVERWAY, in many ways, was ahead of its time. It was a quiet influencer of a number of games and designers, particularly in the indie RPG market. Unfortunately, it was also a victim of bad timing and a rotten string of bad luck. For a variety of reasons, only in the last couple years has a new edition become viable.

The Silver Anniversary Edition includes very nearly all the same content as the 1995 edition, but it has been substantially reorganized, expanded with new content, and converted from a boxed set to a book series. I hope you enjoy this new edition as much as Jesse and I enjoyed making it.

Richard Thames Rowan
The Everway Company

502. Toymaker – Ian Miller

THE SOLDIER – REVERSED

Designer Foreword

It's gratifying to return to EVERWAY and see how well it holds up. This game has a special place in my heart, partly because it is the only roleplaying game that I ever talked my late wife into playing. This book is where the game's heavy lifting gets done.

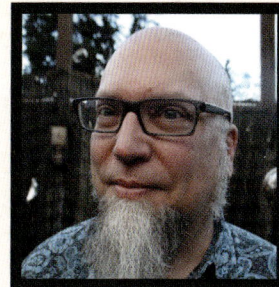

Mythic Roleplaying

EVERWAY is a game of mythic roleplaying. The players take on the role of heroes, larger-than-life figures with abilities that rise above the average person, including the ability to walk between worlds. As such, the type of stories tend to be epic, narratively driven, and deeply symbolic. When EVERWAY was first released, it often seemed strange to roleplayers, but the hobby has grown and changed since then. Some of the ideas may not seem so strange today.

For fans of the original game, the rest of this foreword describes some points where I have advised adjusting the rules and the play style from what we published in 1995. Many of these suggested changes have been incorporated into this edition's game rules.

Suggestions for Character Creation

Premise: In addition to using vision images to inspire players to invent their heroes, the group should probably start with a shared understanding of the sorts of quests and fellow heroes to expect. Sometimes this means a discussion of the sort of campaign the people at the table want to create. Sometimes it means the gamemaster stating a premise for the campaign or at least for the campaign's starting point.

Motives: The meanings of the heroes' Motives were obscure. Each of the seven Motives corresponds to a planet, as hinted at by carefully chosen words in their descriptions. It would probably be better to think of Motive as Planet and have your hero influenced by one of the seven planets. This influence could be interpreted as reflecting not just the hero's motives but also their personality traits, interests, and so on. The planets appear in the Fortune Deck, so an explicit connection to a planet might suggest personal meanings for certain Fortune Deck draws during game play.

105. Hand Stitches – Rudy Rauben (Roger Raupp)

MOTIVE	HINT	PLANET	FORTUNE CARD
Mystery	lunacy	Moon	The Priestess
Wanderlust	sun, dawn	Sun	The Fool
Knowledge	hermetic	Mercury	The Hermit
Beauty	evening star, morning star	Venus	The Peasant
Conquest	martial	Mars	The Smith
Authority	joviality	Jupiter	The King
Adversity	saturnine	Saturn	The Soldier

Element Scores: A hero's maximum Element score should be 6 and minimum 3. Scores of 2 or 7+ make the game harder to play, one way or another.

Magic: Thankfully, the new edition includes additional guidelines for spelling out what mages can do with their capabilities. In a free-form system, it takes work to agree on what a mage can do or can't do. Be sure to put in the effort.

FEARING SHADOWS – REVERSED

About the Fortune Deck

Developing the Fortune Deck was a big, collaborative accomplishment of the design team. In the end, a pattern developed out of the cards, almost as if we had discovered it rather than invented it.

The Fortune Deck has a pattern that was not made explicit in the text. See this table for the seven sets into which the cards fall, each set including two to eight cards that cohere as a group. The Usurper is alone, not part of any set. This pyramid pattern doesn't change what the cards mean, but it might help you *remember* what they mean. Sometimes, given a special context, it will be obvious that a card from among the Deities set, say, is especially meaningful for a draw, good or bad. If cards from the same set show up repeatedly in a scene, the gamemaster is probably going to interpret the subsequent draws as indicating especially broad or decisive outcomes.

	TIER	FORTUNE DECK CARDS
1	Void	Usurper
2	Duality	Creator, Defender
3	Animals	Eagle, Fish, Lion
4	Seasons	Autumn, Spring, Summer, Winter
5	Follies	Drowning, Fearing, Overlooking, Sowing, Striking
6	Beasts	Cockatrice, Dragon, Griffin, Phoenix, Satyr, Unicorn
7	Estates	Fool, Hermit, King, Peasant, Priestess, Smith, Soldier
8	Deities	Death, Fertility, Inspiration, Knowledge, Law, Nature, Trickery, War

This pattern of the Fortune Deck mirrors the unfinished Walker's Pyramid in the city of Everway, which has eight stones on its lowest level, seven on the next level up, and so on until the penultimate level with two stones. The final level, the single capstone, is still out there somewhere.

If you use the Fortune Deck for any length of time, you will get draws that fit so perfectly that it feels as though it can't just be random. You might especially get that feeling if you're playing with people that you really care about. When you get that feeling, enjoy it.

Jonathan Tweet
EVERWAY Designer

Section 1

Playing Guide

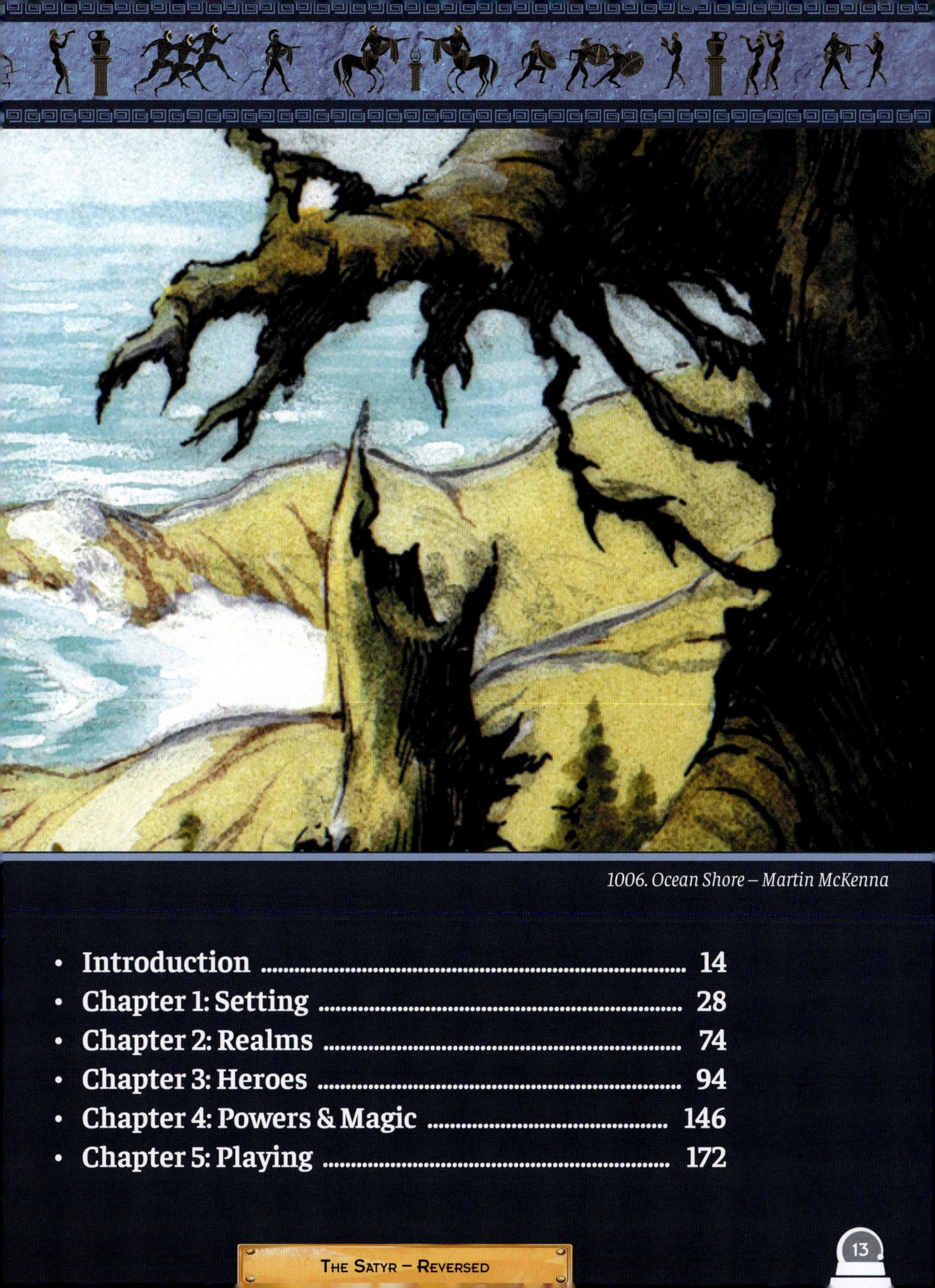

1006. Ocean Shore – Martin McKenna

THE SATYR – REVERSED

Introduction

WHAT IS EVERWAY?

EVERWAY is a fantasy roleplaying game.

What Sort of Fantasy?

EVERWAY presents a world of warriors, shamans, monks, assassins, unicorns, dragons, goblins, ghosts, temples, castles, shrines, ruins, curses, spells, prayers, and quests. The heroes of EVERWAY games travel from realm to realm. Some of these lands have knights, castles, dragons, and wizards, similar to the settings in many popular fantasy stories and games. Other realms, however, more closely match historical places and eras, such as indigenous North America, ancient Middle Eastern lands, imperial China, feudal Japan, tribal northern Europe, ancient India, the Aztec empire, African kingdoms, and so on. Still other realms contain people and cultures unlike anything that's ever existed on earth, including lands populated by societies that aren't human. The people, lands, creatures, and adventures found in a game of EVERWAY are limited only by the imaginations of those playing.

> The title of the game comes from the name of an important city that exists in the game world. Read about the city of Everway in Chapter 1: Setting.

What Is Roleplaying?

Roleplaying can mean many things, and different people have very different ideas about what is and is not included under this label. For the EVERWAY game, we mean a sort of interactive storytelling in which each player speaks out the role of an imaginary character; these characters have adventures together in worlds that are portrayed by a gamemaster.

For a taste of EVERWAY's style of fantasy, look over the images in Section 2: Fortune Guide and Section 3: Vision Guide.

Playing a character in a roleplaying game appeals to people in several different ways. One aspect people enjoy is the challenge. Their heroes clash with villains, and the wits of the players lead their heroes to victory. Though entirely imaginary, these victories feel great. Another enjoyable part of the game is portraying a character. Though the players are just sitting around a table, they "take on" the roles of fantasy heroes. Some heroes are braggarts, some buffoons, some diplomats, some ineffable magicians. Speaking out the role of someone different from yourself can be a lot of fun. Another aspect to the game is discovery or wonder. With the guidance of the gamemaster, you can imagine the strange and marvelous lands that your hero visits, worlds that you can interact with through your imaginary character. Taken together—setting, character, and action—these elements can produce memorable stories of which you and your character are a part.

Gamemastering is also rewarding. It requires more effort than playing a character because a gamemaster has to know the game, the setting, and the characters well enough to present an engaging plot and pace the action so that the plot unfolds dramatically. The gamemaster invents strange lands for the heroes to explore, exotic creatures for them to encounter, weird mysteries for them to solve, and daring quests for them to undertake. Dreaming up these imaginary people, places, and things could be a pastime in its own right, but gamemasters also get to see their creations brought to life during the game.

This book includes advice for beginning players. **Book 2: Gamemasters** contains a section for experienced as well as first-time gamemasters and ready-to-run quests. These features, and the design of the game itself, make EVERWAY suitable for people who have never roleplayed before.

To see what sorts of heroes you might portray as a player, look over the twelve ready-to-run heroes included in Section 4: Quick Start Guide. If you've never roleplayed before, see Chapter 5: Playing.

In What Way Is It a Game?

Like any game, EVERWAY has rules. These rules let the people playing know what to expect from each other and how to interact with each other. When playing EVERWAY, however, nobody wins or loses. The point is to play and to keep playing, not to end play by defeating an opponent. Since nobody's victory is riding on the rules, the gamemaster is free to change them to suit play. Indeed, many of the "rules" are simply suggestions for how to play.

During the game, the gamemaster may present the players' imaginary heroes with tough challenges. The players can use their wits and insight to solve the problems that the gamemaster presents, and when they succeed, the players feel as though they've "won." No one loses, however, when the players "win." Indeed, any victory is followed quickly by another adventure and another set of challenges,

so the story of these heroes and their adventures can go on indefinitely.

EVERWAY is also a game in the sense that "make-believe" is a game, an opportunity to play without concern for accomplishing this or that feat. Much of the joy of roleplaying comes from portraying a character or imagining new worlds and possibilities, regardless of whether the hero defeats the villains or is vanquished by them.

EVERWAY GAME SYSTEM

The EVERWAY game system includes the following:

Book 1: Players

Playing Guide: This section of this book. Gamemasters should read it, and players may read it if they wish. It covers the basics of how the game works.

Fortune Guide: Section 2 of this book, which explains how the Fortune Deck works in the imaginary world as a tool for divination and in the real world as part of the game. The Fortune Deck is a deck of thirty-six cards with images on the card faces. The gamemaster uses them to guide play of the game.

The Fortune Deck is sold separately, but this book can be used as a Fortune Deck by

> See Chapter 5: Playing for an example of the sorts of quests or challenges heroes can face. If you're going to be the gamemaster for your group, you can look at the ready-to-run quests in Book 2: Gamemasters for more detailed examples of the sorts of challenges heroes face on quests.

> Only the gamemaster should read Book 2: Gamemasters, since it contains the Gamemastering Guide and Questing Guide. Each includes information the players' heroes will not have. The gamemaster will share this information with the players as the players' heroes discover it during play.

flipping to a random page and looking at the Fortune Deck card draw at the bottom of each page.

Vision Guide: Section 3 of this book contains many images that can help players invent their heroes. Each image is accompanied by questions to help players explore their heroes' background.

Quick Start Guide: Section 4 of this book contains a condensed hero creation summary and twelve ready-to-run heroes. These heroes show what the players' own heroes could be like. Experienced roleplayers can play these heroes if they don't have time to invent their own, but inventing your own hero is a lot of fun. Gamemasters can use ready-to-run heroes as background characters. An empty full-color hero sheet is available for download from **EVERWAY.COM**. Players may print these sheets for use in play.

Browse through this book at your own pace, in whatever order you like. The gamemaster will eventually need to read through most of this material, but players can start play without knowing any of it.

Book 2: Gamemasters

Gamemastering Guide: Section 1 in **Book 2: Gamemasters** explains how to be a gamemaster. This section includes ideas that should be surprises to the players, so players shouldn't read that book without their gamemaster's permission.

Questing Guide: Section 2 contains ready-to-run quests for the gamemaster. Players should not look at this section.

911. Arctic Scout – Janine Johnston

Glossaries

These two glossaries define terms as they are used in EVERWAY. Terms in the first set are used by players but not by their heroes. Terms in the second set are used by heroes and others in the game world.

Words in Game Play

The following words are for players and gamemasters to use when they talk about the game. The fictional people in the game world do not use these terms, or at least not in the game-related sense that they are used here.

Background Character: A CHARACTER that the GAMEMASTER portrays.

Boon: Any benefit that a HERO gets from a QUEST.

Character: An imaginary persona, either a HERO or a BACKGROUND CHARACTER.

Company: A group of HEROES.

Elements: Four categories—Air, Fire, Earth, and Water—by which a CHARACTER is rated to determine that character's basic strengths and weaknesses.

Fortune Deck: A deck of thirty-six cards the GAMEMASTER uses to guide play.

Gamemaster: The person who prepares and runs the QUESTS in which the HEROES participate.

Hero: A CHARACTER that a PLAYER portrays.

Mage: Any CHARACTER who can use MAGIC. (In the game world, people who use magic are known as wizards, sorceresses, spirit doctors, and so on.)

Magic: A CHARACTER'S ability to perform a variety of supernatural feats by use of esoteric knowledge or talent.

Player: A participant in the game who portrays a HERO.

Power: A CHARACTER'S ability to perform a special, possibly supernatural feat.

Quest: A journey, adventure, or mission that the HEROES undertake.

Run: To portray a CHARACTER, as in "I enjoy running magical heroes," or to be

the GAMEMASTER for a QUEST, as in "I ran a really surreal quest last week."

Session: A meeting of the PLAYERS and GAMEMASTER to play the game. The lives and stories of the HEROES continue from session to session.

Words in the Game World

These are words that people in the fantasy world use.

Air: The element of thought, spoken wisdom, focused energy, speech, craft, skill, intellect, reason, and forethought.

Among the Spheres: A phrase that roughly means "in the universe."

Earth: The element of might, passive power, resistant integrity, endurance, security, safety, health, and fortitude.

Elements: AIR, FIRE, EARTH, and WATER—the substances that make up the physical world. Each element is connected to certain aspects of the self.

Fire: The element of action, active power, forceful energy, change, strength, speed, and vitality.

Fortune Deck: A deck of symbolic cards used to divine the future.

Gate: A connection between two SPHERES.

Heaven: A phrase used to mean the gods and goddesses collectively; also divine or cosmic forces in general.

Heavens: The PLANETS, stars, and constellations.

Planet: A heavenly body that moves in relation to the fixed stars. The seven visible, known planets are the sun, the moon, Mercury, Venus, Mars, Jupiter, and Saturn.

Realm: An area of land or other location in which certain cosmic forces hold sway; an area with a shared story. A realm is often a kingdom or other unified place.

Star River: The band of brighter stars across the HEAVENS and the twelve zodiac constellations.

Sphere: A world that contains many REALMS. Physically, almost every sphere is very much like our real world.

Spherewalker: Someone who can walk through GATES to other SPHERES.

The Tongue: The language that almost everyone AMONG THE SPHERES speaks.

Water: The element of feelings, silent wisdom, receptive integrity, intuition, and flexibility.

Important Ideas

EVERWAY uses some specific ideas and terms in special ways. These ideas and terms are described here.

Gates

A gate is a way to move from one sphere to another. When you step through a gate, you appear on the sphere to which the gate connects after a period of travel.

What do gates look like? Gates are often simple arches or portals made of stone. They can also be caves, open spaces between trees, wells, waterfalls, mist-covered moors, and so on. If the people of the area know about a gate, they may have built a temple or other structure around it.

Who can go through the gates? People who are particularly sensitive to magic and unseen forces can travel through gates to other spheres. Those who travel the gates are called spherewalkers. Some spherewalkers aren't magically sensitive but can travel the gates because of magical blessings, special training, or supernatural heritage. People who have the ability to travel the gates but never have are not called spherewalkers.

What does it feel like to go through a gate? Different spherewalkers describe the feeling in different ways. Many say it's like falling through the air on a starless, silent night. When traveling from one sphere to another, one moves between

Gate

Gates lead from sphere to sphere. Most people cannot use the gates, but those who can are known as spherewalkers. The realm of Roundwander, whose capital is the city of Everway, has seventy-one gates, far more than any other known realm. The gate in this picture leads from Roundwander to Deep Mist, a realm of cool, foggy woods and secretive people.

1201. Gate – Janine Johnston

Spherewalking

Spherewalking is tied to Water. Generally, a character with 4 Water may be able to sense a gate and walk it safely, but not "open" it. A 5-Water character can open most gates safely and guide another person, creature, or large object or two along the path. A 6-Water character can walk gates and guide a small group. And someone who has 7 Water can guide a large group safely through a gate.

Heroes are exceptions: all heroes have the spherewalking talent regardless of their Water scores. Remember that "hero" is the term in EVERWAY for the character that a player creates and plays, so your hero can spherewalk no matter what their Water score is. Plenty of background characters are spherewalkers as well, and there are plenty of "heroic" background characters who are not spherewalkers.

Someone who tries to walk a gate path without a 4 Water or stronger or open a gate without a 5 Water or stronger cannot get the gate to work. Such a person simply walks through the gate as if it were a mundane portal. If such a character goes through a gate that someone else has opened, they may "fall off the path" and be lost. They may show up at a random gate at some point in the future, or they could be lost "in between" for years. Indeed, they may never reappear. There are unconfirmed rumors of objects called journeystones that allow a non-spherewalker to travel a gate path, but not much is known about them.

(See *Chapter 3: Heroes* to read about heroes and Water scores.)

two places whose cosmic energies are different. If one travels within a sphere to another realm, the transformation is usually very gradual. On the other hand, if one travels between two spheres by going through a gate, the change is sudden and may bring visions related to the cosmic energies of the new sphere and realm.

How long does it take to go through a gate? The time varies. To the spherewalker, it may seem to take only a few moments, but days or weeks may have passed. (Most spherewalks take a few hours to a week.) Since the sun, moon, and stars are the same from sphere to sphere, informed spherewalkers can tell how long their

journeys lasted, often simply by looking at the moon's phase.

The amount of time it takes to travel the astral path between two gates varies every time, so it's impossible to know beforehand exactly when one will arrive on the next sphere. Some spherewalkers, however, are attuned to certain elements or planets, and they tend to arrive at certain times. Someone attuned to the moon, for instance, might usually arrive at moonrise, while someone attuned to Mars might arrive when Mars is at its zenith. Also, if a spherewalk between two particular spheres tends to be very short, say eighteen hours or less, the variation from walk to walk is small enough that one can roughly time one's arrival. In this example, leaving at dusk would let one arrive roughly at noon, give or take an hour or two. The longer the spherewalk is between two spheres, the greater variation there tends to be.

What happens to spherewalkers while they are between gates? The place between "earths" is impossible to understand with earthly senses. The term "astral path" is a metaphor; there is no physical path down which one walks bodily. It seems, rather, that one's "essential self" travels to the new sphere. While "between" spheres, the spherewalker remains in sync with the planets, which are eternal and universal. Thus, if spherewalkers enter a gate at noon and step out

of the connected gate at midnight, the spherewalkers feel as though it is midnight. For instance, they would be tired and ready to sleep. As the stars are linked to one's age, the spherewalker "ages" while between spheres. Fingernails and hair don't grow, but one comes closer to old age and death just the same.

How often can a spherewalker use gates? The transition to a new sphere usually causes little discomfort, but spherewalking without letting the body "settle in" between walks can be disturbing. As a general rule, spherewalkers can safely spherewalk again after being "grounded" for as much time as they were between spheres. For example, if a spherewalk takes a week, it's best to wait another week before spherewalking again. The dangers of frequent spherewalking include weakness, disorientation, illness, madness, and even, in the most extreme cases, death.

What can a spherewalker bring with them through a gate? If they choose to do so, a spherewalker can bring themselves and anything or anyone connected to them by touch that is not attached to the ground in some way. For example, a horse can be brought, but not while tethered to a tree. The number of things or people a spherewalker may bring with them is limited by their Water score (see p. 21).

Where did the gates come from? Legend says that the Walker made the gates while wandering among the spheres. It is said

that as the Walker steps from one sphere to the next, gates are created between them. Many consider the appearance of the comet called the Walker's Star a sign of the Walker's activity.

Can a gate connect two realms on the same sphere instead of connecting two spheres? Yes and no. A deity or a powerful magician could create a gate that connects two places on a single sphere. But the overwhelming majority of gates were created by the Walker, and they only connect spheres to other spheres.

A gate that connects two realms on the same sphere might work differently from one that connects two spheres. For instance, travel through this kind of gate might take no time or almost no time, and anyone, not just spherewalkers, might be able to use such a gate. These details depend on how the gate was designed.

Sphere

A sphere is an entire world. Spheres are physically similar to our real world, the same size and shape, with cold polar regions, a hot equatorial band, varying seasons, oceans covering most of the surface, and so on.

A sphere usually has hundreds of realms. Provided they have ships, vehicles, mounts, or other means of travel, people can travel from realm to realm all over the sphere. Typically, the only way to get from

Winter

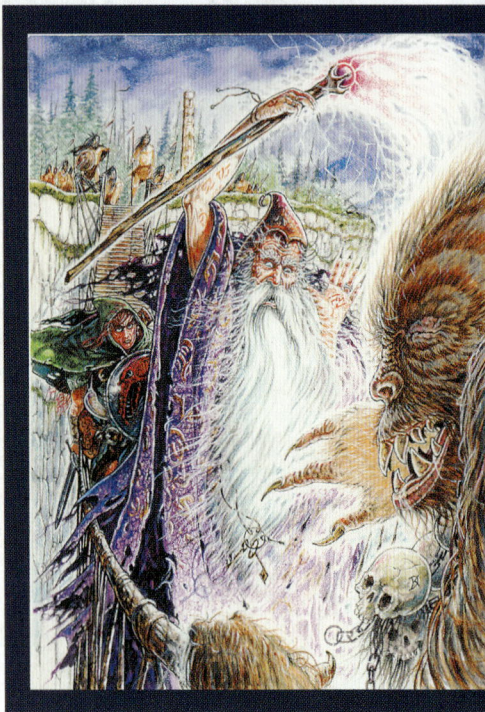

Spherewalkers

Spherewalkers travel through the gates from sphere to sphere, and the "spherewalker's code" calls on them to help those they meet during these travels. Many spherewalkers are considered heroes, following this code to aid those in whose lands they journey. Others, however, use their knowledge and powers to rob or to conquer those unfortunate enough to cross their paths.

1301. Spherewalker – Doug Keith

one sphere to another is to travel through a gate by spherewalking. If the people in a realm know about gates, they are probably in contact with people from other spheres. Most realms, however, do not know about gates and are therefore not in contact with spherewalkers.

Are spheres planets? Yes and no. A sphere fits the modern definition of a planet. Indeed, spheres are a lot like our real world: they're enormous orbs on which life exists. The societies in the EVERWAY universe, however, are much more like pre-technological cultures in our world; planets are understood simply to be special kinds of stars, ones that move across the sky. (In fact, the word "planet" means "wanderer.") The known planets are Mercury, Venus, Mars, Jupiter, and Saturn.

The sun and the moon are typically categorized as planets as well.

What do people call the spheres on which they live? They usually just call their sphere "the world" or "the earth." Most people don't even know that there are other spheres than their own.

Why do all spheres have the same stars, planets, length of year, and so on? The deities created the spheres for people to live on, and they made them fit for healthy human life. That's why the spheres have fresh air, sunlight, water, plants and animals, planets, and stars. If the deities made a sphere without a planet, it would unbalance the sphere's energy. For instance, a sphere without Mars would be lacking in energy. It might be a peaceful place, but it also might be lethargic.

Realms

A realm is an area on a sphere in which certain cosmic forces hold sway, an area with a shared story. It may encompass several kingdoms, city-states, or lands, or it can be a small area. A realm can be as big as an entire sphere, but usually realms are smaller, and there are many realms in a sphere.

What is a border between realms like? The nature of the border between two realms depends on the realms that it separates. In many areas, wilderness lies between realms. For instance, a realm might include a city-state and the sparsely populated countryside around the city-state. People who venture far enough away from the city-state may come to unsettled land, wilderness, which may or may not be very "wild" at all. Traveling further, one comes to another area of inhabited countryside and eventually to another city-state. This settled land and the city-state at its center are considered a separate realm from the others.

Other realms have more distinct borders, usually along geographical features, such as rivers (rivers often form the border between the kingdoms within a realm as well). Sometimes a realm is tied to a type of land, such as a faerie forest that is a separate realm from the kingdom surrounding it. Generally, realms are culturally different from each other.

Is every kingdom a realm? No. Often a realm covers several kingdoms, especially if those kingdoms are culturally and historically tied in some way, just as a family is made up of several related people. And sometimes a kingdom contains more than one realm. For instance, there could be a conquered land in which the conquerors and their castles or cities form one realm while the native people of the countryside are essentially another realm.

How can I know for sure what the boundaries of a realm are? Many times you can't. The concept of "a realm" is usually clear and useful, but it's still just a concept, not reality itself. Different people will use the term "realm" in different ways; just remember that there are no right or wrong answers.

Are all the realms on a sphere alike? No. Realms on a sphere can be at least as different as various cultures on historical earth have been. It is possible, however, that some overriding force on a sphere gives all the realms something in common. For example, if the sun circles a sphere's equator, none of the realms will have seasons or solstices, but such a sphere would be very unusual.

Spherewalkers

A spherewalker is someone who travels from sphere to sphere, usually through gates, though some have found other means to do so.

What makes someone a spherewalker?
Those who are sensitive to mystical things (in game terms, those who have high Water scores) can open gates and walk the paths between spheres. A few other people who aren't particularly sensitive also can open and travel the gates. Different people have this ability for different reasons. Those with even a little blood of the deities can usually spherewalk, as can those sent on missions by their deities, those who have been given special gifts by spirits or faeries, those conceived or born at propitious or magical times, and so on. Often no one knows what makes spherewalkers able to travel the gates, not even the spherewalkers themselves.

Why do spherewalkers travel the spheres? Spherewalkers offer various answers to this question. Some are seeking new lives, others are looking for adventure, and others are after fame or other rewards. It's possible to become wealthy by trading goods across the gates, though most spherewalkers have higher purposes than profit and are led by forces that they don't understand to fates that will surprise them.

Can you tell who is a spherewalker?
No, there is no distinguishing mark or characteristic tied to the spherewalking ability. Still, people can sometimes guess that strangers in their land are spherewalkers. Spherewalkers generally have exceptional abilities; they may be mighty warriors, powerful wizards, or enigmatic shamans. They often stand out by being different from the natives, such as having different clothes, features, skin colors, statures, or manners. Spherewalkers often have a broader perspective on local events because they have seen many realms and many different people.

Besides gates, how can one move from sphere to sphere? Gods, magical rituals, and powerful mystic objects can lead one from sphere to sphere. Often these means send people to specific realms. For example, a magic talisman may bring the wearer directly back to the realm of its origin, or a vengeful magician may make a scroll that transports someone to their dungeon when it's opened. Some rituals summon people from other spheres or draw spherewalkers off their paths. For instance, a priestess may be able to summon people to her temple in times of need. The people summoned may seem random, but the laws of magic dictate that it is often spherewalkers (or potential spherewalkers) who are pulled in.

How many people are spherewalkers?
It seems that very few people are spherewalkers, but no one knows the exact count. Some spheres have no spherewalkers and no knowledge of other spheres (though some people there might be able to walk through the gates if they knew about them). Other spheres have a high number

of spherewalkers, especially if people have traveled there from other spheres. In the city of Everway (see *Chapter 1: Setting*), about one in every hundred people is a spherewalker, and that's the highest concentration known.

How do others see spherewalkers?
Spherewalkers are known by different names in different realms depending on the attitudes that the natives have toward them. These include terms like "stranger," "outsider," "ghost," or "oath-breaker."

Spherewalkers are usually different from the natives in a given sphere. They may unwittingly break taboos or insult hosts. And even when they behave themselves, they still often consider themselves somehow "above" the realms they visit, and this attitude may not endear them to the natives. On the other hand, spherewalkers can bring new knowledge, crafts, goods, and magics, and they can often solve problems that the natives cannot.

1208. Tree Gate – Gerry Grace

THE GRIFFIN

506. Marketplace — Rudy Rauben (Roger Raupp)

Everway Marketplace

People from a hundred spheres meet in the city of Everway. In the market-place, they trade the rare, beautiful, and valuable goods from their homelands for wonders from other realms. It is said that one can find and obtain any-thing in Everway, if one looks hard enough and long enough, and if one is willing to pay the price.

INSPIRATION — REVERSED

Chapter 1: Setting

This chapter describes a specific setting: the realm of Roundwander and its capital city of Everway. Players may find the information in this chapter helpful in creating their heroes, but it is not necessary for them to read this material first. Gamemasters may need this information to help them create their quests.

CROSSROADS OF THE SPHERES

The realm of Roundwander is known as the Crossroads of the Spheres. Most spheres have two gates, each leading to a different sphere. The sphere of Fourcorner, however, has at least seventy-one gates, and all of them are in the realm of Roundwander. The central city of Roundwander is Everway, to which spherewalkers from hundreds of realms come to trade, learn, and settle.

Most of the realm is somewhat-tamed wilderness dotted with settlements, towns, and cities. Quite a variety of terrain exists within its borders. Far in the distant past, Roundwander was a much smaller realm than it is today, occupying only the area immediately surrounding the city of Everway, Roundwander today has six provinces: the River Province, Whiteoar Province, Tower Province, Sun Province, Harvest Province, and Starfall Province.

Roundwander can be used in several ways. It can serve as a central area where heroes from different spheres meet, as a home to which heroes return after every adventure, as a fascinating place to visit, or as a location for quests. Players may use Everway as their heroes' hometown, incorporating it into their heroes' origins and backgrounds.

THE REALM OF ROUNDWANDER

Every realm is characterized by a Virtue, a Fault, and a Fate. These concepts are described in *Chapter 3: Heroes*. Some realms are further characterized by a Usurper. This concept is explained in *Section 2: Fortune Guide*.

Virtue: Autumn (*plenty*). The place is old but still active. It is past its most energetic stage but not yet into winter. Roundwander's Autumn virtue represents not just plenty in terms of quantity but also in terms of variety. The people of Roundwander present the hundred colors of a forest in fall.

Fault: Spring—Reversed (*stagnation*). Roundwander is an old, old place, and the habits of a hundred generations are worn into the stone-paved pathways.

Fate: Cockatrice (*corruption vs. recovery*). The influx of new people, magic, and ideas could undermine what is good about Roundwander or bring it the energy it needs to overcome stagnation.

Usurper: The Pyramid (*cooperative effort vs. dissension*). This Usurper represents coming together, working together, balance, order, and progress. Reversed, The Pyramid means dissension, imbalance, conflict, and regress.

Geography: Roundwander extends over six provinces of irrigated fields, pastures, hills, and forests. The weather is warm and dry most of the year, with rains and some flooding during winter and spring. Everway, the capital city of Roundwander, sits on the northwest bank of the Sunset River (so named because it flows west, toward the sunset), where it flows into Shimmermoon Bay. Shimmermoon Bay flows into the Circle Sea and connects Everway to many distant realms by sea.

People: Roundwander is a traditional, highly ritualized, ceremonial, and prosperous society. Extended families serve as guilds or classes. The great king's scribes estimate the population at ten million, with half a million living in Everway itself and possibly half that in Strangerside. Roundwanderers are a diverse people.

Walker's Pyramid

In the center of Everway stands the Walker's Pyramid, built stone by stone by the Walker. The Walker is now wandering the spheres looking for the final stone. Some say that the Golden Age will return when the last stone is in place. The Pyramid has been here since before recorded history. On certain nights, the Pyramid glows with energy.

1104. Pyramid – Amy Weber

Clothing varies by family. Skin tones, unless noted otherwise, range from light brown to olive. City residents tend to have more body fat than rural residents.

Rule: Horizon Emerald, the great king, rules all of Roundwander from his palace in Everway, and his power is felt in surrounding realms. The Council actually has more real power than the great king.

Religion: The people of Roundwander worship countless gods and goddesses, including many whose worship was brought here by spherewalkers. The great king's family devote themselves to a deity they call "the Goddess," who is therefore especially popular among the inhabitants of Roundwander. They understand all goddesses to be manifestations of their transcendent deity.

Crafts: The people of Roundwander, especially the Everwayans, are skilled at all endeavors, from architecture to weaving to magic, though families jealously guard their secret techniques.

Tamed Animals: Dogs, oxen, mules, horses, and elephants are common work animals. Cattle, goats, sheep, and chickens are raised for meat, milk, eggs, leather, and wool. Dogs, cats, peacocks, fish, and lizards are kept as pets.

Connections: Roundwander is open to visitors from other realms. While outsiders are slow to be incorporated wholly into society, the natives tolerate them and their unusual habits very well. On the southeast bank of the Sunset, across from Everway, is Strangerside, where strangers from other spheres are welcome to settle.

Roundwander Society

For centuries, all manner of people have come to Roundwander, not only from across the spheres but from across this sphere's surface as well. People of all shapes, sizes, colors, backgrounds, and cultures mingle here. Tolerance of differences is the rule, although some groups prefer to shut themselves off from others to preserve their traditions or bloodlines.

Families

Families are the central system of ordering society in Roundwander. One is considered to be related by blood to all those whose birth name one shares. A child takes their mother's birth name, so one's

sister's children are related to one, but one's brother's children are not. A husband takes his wife's name and becomes part of his wife's family, though it is understood that he is still related by blood to his birth family. His own children, however, are not considered to be related to him by blood, as they are born with a name different from the name he was born with. Same-gender couples may choose who joins which family. Roundwanderers use the term "cousin" to mean any other person who bears the same last name. The eldest woman in a family is called Grandmother and the eldest man is called Grandfather.

One's name determines, generally, one's position in society. "Position" can be very different from "status," as "position" refers to one's role without necessarily giving any indication of how much respect or power one has. For example, members of the Stonebreaker family build structures of stone. The family leaders are respected architects who lay out plans for temples and mansions according to astronomical alignments and secret, magical formulas. They wield significant power and enjoy much adoration. Other members of the same family, however, work side by side with slaves and convicts in the quarries.

In Roundwander, all those who come from elsewhere on Fourcorner are called "Stranger," with the term used as a last name, as in "Firstborn Stranger." All those who come from spheres other than Fourcorner are given the name "Outsider." A Stranger or Outsider man may marry into a Roundwander family, taking his wife's name, but a woman cannot. If she wishes to integrate fully into Roundwander society, the best she can usually do is arrange for her sons to marry into Roundwander families and to encourage her daughters to arrange similar marriages for their sons. Under extraordinary circumstances with many immediate family members, she may be able to found her own family.

In addition to position, one's family in Roundwander largely determines one's

habits (including dinner etiquette), iconography, morality, philosophy, and secret rituals and prayers. Each family has an oral history passed down to the new generations (and, oddly enough, each family's history portrays that family as founding, saving, or somehow glorifying Roundwander). Since the family is traced along the mother's lines, women in Roundwander are the holders of family secrets, knowledge, and tradition.

People from Roundwander are used to members of other families behaving differently from how they've been taught to behave. As a result, they are remarkably tolerant of Strangers and Outsiders with different ways. It would be bizarre to a Roundwanderer to imagine that one set of standards should apply to all people.

Names usually reflect families' positions, but sometimes the connection is tenuous. A family's position results from generations of habit and tradition, traditions that usually developed after the name was established. In other cases, a family's position has changed over the centuries, resulting in a name that is imprecise or wholly inaccurate. The Stonebreakers, for example, may have originally worked only in the quarries, but in present-day Roundwander they are primarily architects, engineers, and artisans, not simple laborers.

There are nearly a thousand families in Roundwander, some with a handful of members, some with over a thousand.

Some of the more important or noteworthy families in Roundwander are described below. (Players and gamemasters can make up additional families to serve as backgrounds for heroes and background characters.)

- **Carter:** a family that maintains the roads and transports goods.
- **Crookstaff:** a family renowned for magical ability, secrecy, and strange ways.
- **Crow:** a military family commanding armies, training troops, and competing in the Arenas.
- **Digger:** historically, a family of miners. Now, however, they're mostly moneylenders, but they still maintain a monopoly on mining.
- **Emerald:** royal family of Roundwander.
- **Ferry:** family of ferry and barge operators that also deliver messages.
- **Fleet:** sailors and fishermen that run the navy of Roundwander.
- **Harvest:** an agricultural family that also brews ale and raises horses.
- **Host:** a family that offers hospitality to travelers in its family members' houses. Some host only the most important visitors, while many will host just about anyone. Visitors who offend the Host family are hard-pressed to find a place to stay in Roundwander.
- **Jade:** workers in precious metals and gems. Their skin is tinged yellow because this family was founded by a yellow-skinned Stranger.

When the original Stranger applied to be recognized as the head of a Roundwanderer family, she had to agree that her family would never sell their products for less than three gold hefts so they would not compete with the Smith family for the market in less expensive goods. The Jade family has a tradition of inviting men from their homelands across the sea to come and marry into the family.

- **Keeper:** the black-skinned family that maintains the gates, guarding roads to and from the gates, posting guards at gates through which dangerous people might come, and so on.

- **Mask:** a family that, officially, provides amusements and diversions. Unofficially, they are involved in various illicit and even illegal activities.

- **Moondance:** a family of priestesses and cousins who support them. Moondances are found in temples dedicated to many different deities.

- **Mother:** midwives and healers. In this family, the family name precedes the personal name, as in Mother Joy or Mother Firstborn. They worship Parvati of the Hindu pantheon.

- **Mudbank:** leatherworkers and river tenders. They are responsible for removing dead animals from the streets. The odor that follows them is often joked about.

- **Plume:** imperial guards. They mostly protect only the royal family, court officials, and provincial governors.

- **Scratch:** scribes, scholars, and bureaucrats.

- **Smith:** smiths, metalworkers, armorers, and weapon-makers.

- **Snakering:** courtiers, ambassadors, and functionaries. They were once a powerful family, but now they work at the behest of others.

- **Stonebreaker:** architects and engineers who construct stone structures, especially large monuments and buildings.

- **Sun:** a family that guides pilgrims and travelers among the spheres.

- **Tender:** those who prepare bodies for burial and bury them. They are considered too holy to touch.

- **Tower:** a former royal family that are now hunters, woodsmen, and carpenters.

- **Wailer:** ceremonial specialists. Public ceremonies, as well as many private, familial ones, require the Wailers to participate. Some Wailers are made mute so that they are unable to reveal the secrets they learn by participating in secret ceremonies. It is considered a sin for a Wailer to work for a living.

- **Watcher:** city guards. They keep the peace, or at least keep trouble from threatening important families. They wear armor made of steel plates sewn onto long shirts, and they carry long spears.

- **Weaver:** historically, a family of weavers and dyers, but they now do all manner of trades. They are particularly friendly to Outsiders (and the new skills and techniques they bring), but they are regarded by some as troublemakers for slighting tradition.

Fashion

Long, loose garments draped over the body are the most common. They can be white or tan, or they can be bright and colorful. Many people wear rings, earrings, bracelets, and anklets that have special meanings within their families. These meanings may be public or private. Dressing properly is a sign of status. At social functions, people often wear elaborate, impractical clothes.

Both men and women use makeup, wear jewelry, and groom their hair to increase their beauty. Since a man must be accepted by a woman's family to marry her, men go to great lengths to look good. Standards of modesty vary from family to family and also according to status. High-status men and women sometimes dress provocatively as a triple display: of one's physical beauty, of the wealth and leisure it takes to dress and groom carefully, and of one's confidence in one's guards.

Most men are clean-shaven. In some families, it's traditional for men to trim their facial hair in certain ways, such as a mustache but no beard, a goatee, a beard only on the chin, a beard only under the jaw, and so on.

Rule

The Emerald family rules Roundwander, with the great king holding the highest title. Kingship passes to the great king's eldest sister's eldest son. The great king cannot marry, as that would mean that he had joined another family. He may have progeny through concubines, but they bear their mothers' names, and so they are not considered royal. (Indeed, he's not considered to be related to them by blood.)

When referring to the great king, one says "Great King Horizon" or "His Imperial Majesty." To refer to the great king as "the

601. Skin Scribes – Mark Tedin

king" or "a king" is considered an insult. When addressing the great king directly, one refers to him as "Your Imperial Majesty," never as "you." Certain families maintain traditions of using other terms as well. For instance, members of the Crookstaff family refer to him as "His Imperial, Majestic Wisdom." Ambassadors from other lands are required to use certain forms of address that reflect their lands' relations with Roundwander. For instance, "His Imperial, Conquering Majesty" or "His Generous, Imperial Majesty" are common. (Learning the proper forms of address for the great king, members of the Emerald family, ambassadors from other lands, and important functionaries in the government is an important task for a new courtier. It can make the difference between a good courtier and a dead one.)

As solidly entrenched as the Emerald family may be in Roundwander, most true power resides in the Council and to a lesser extent the provincial governors. Centuries ago, the leaders of prominent families formed the Council as a way to relieve the great king of an endless stream of mundane decisions and obligations. The Council members would make decisions among themselves and enforce them independently so that the great king would not have to be bothered with every minute issue of policy. Over the centuries, the Council has taken on more and more duties until now it is indeed

THE HUNDRED FACES OF EVERWAY

Everyone who comes to Everway gets a different impression of the city. Ambassadors who come from distant courts and receive the great king's hospitality may leave with the impression that Everway is a thoroughly prosperous and beautiful city, with well-scrubbed servants and endless diversions. Lone wanderers, however, may wind up in the shadier areas around the Gaming Houses or Strangerside, where they are exploited, cheated, and manipulated. They may leave believing Everway is a giant cauldron of vice, greed, deceit, and crime. Newcomers may find themselves bedazzled by the lively customs, colorful festivals, and busy marketplaces. They may leave Everway thinking it is an ever-changing jumble of random events. Scholars come to the Library of All Worlds and find the city to be the best-educated, most cosmopolitan city they've ever visited (provided they avoid the Court of Fools). The face of Everway that heroes see depends on the motives and actions of those heroes and on the gamemaster's designs.

the prime originator of law and policy in Roundwander. This function frees the great king to play a largely ceremonial and spiritual role, while still allowing him to intervene in the Council's decisions during the inevitable conflicts that prevent consensus.

The families with representatives on the Council include Crookstaff (mages), Crow (soldiers), Digger (moneylenders), Moondance (priestesses), Scratch (scribes), Snakering (courtiers), and Stonebreaker (architects and builders). In addition, a place is symbolically reserved in the Council for a representative from the Whiteoar family, whose last members died hundreds of years ago in a civil war. It is conceivable that another family could gain a seat on the Council, but this could only happen if all the current representatives agree. As each new representative reduces the power of the current representatives, few families bother trying to gain a seat.

The laws of Roundwander cover property crimes and violent crimes, but personal vices, such as gambling and prostitution, are considered matters of family or personal concern. In fact, even violence and theft seldom reach the attention of the authorities, as individuals and families often execute justice on their own. Families often punish criminals among their own number in order to see justice done and to preserve their family honor.

Economy

The city of Everway thrives on trade and expertise. Traders can take portable valuables, such as tea, spices, tobacco, gold, silver, gems, and steel goods, through the gates, making Everway the hub of profitable trade.

The basis of any civilization, of course, is agriculture, and irrigated fields throughout the realm of Roundwander provide grains and vegetables for Everway. Fishing also brings in plenty of food.

PRICES IN ROUNDWANDER

Prices are always subject to haggling.

Food, Drink, and Tobacco

- bread, stewed vegetables, and tea — 6 beads
- a meal with meat — 1 heft
- a gourmet meal — 5 hefts
- a dozen tobacco cigars — 3 hefts
- a day's food and lodging — 5 hefts

Weapons

- a small knife — 10 beads
- a steel-tipped spear — 5 hefts
- a steel sword — 10 hefts
- iron armor — 60 hefts

Clothes and Accessories

- an elegant set of clothes — 8 hefts
- an elegant set of jewelry — 50 hefts
- fancy perfume and makeup for an evening — 3 hefts
- incense as an offering — 12 hefts

Animals

- a mule — 40 hefts
- a horse — 200 hefts
- an elephant — 3,000 hefts

Services

- a night's lodging at a Host family dwelling — 3 beads
- a day's labor — 4 hefts
- a day of a sage's consultation — 12 hefts
- a day of a doctor's care — 40 hefts

Houses

- a wood and stone home in Strangerside — 1,000 hefts
- a stone house in Everway — 20,000 hefts
- a stone estate in Everway — 200,000 hefts

Throughout Roundwander a silver coin of about a quarter ounce is used as the standard currency. The coin is called a "heft," which is also used as a measure of weight. Thus a knife might weigh "a fiftyheft" (about a pound) and cost "a five-heft." The Digger family controls exchange of foreign coins, which are common in Everway.

For smaller purchases, Round-wanderers use pea-sized beads of copper, with holes that allow them to be strung on lines for easy keeping. Twenty-four beads are valued at one silver heft, though this exchange rate can change. Some merchants consider it beneath them to accept beads, or they do so only at steeper exchange rates. It's also possible to cut hefts into fourths or even eighths to make small purchases.

For large purchases, especially between families or royal courts, people use gold. A heft of gold is worth twenty-four silver hefts.

Most business, however, does not involve the use of coin. For example, laborers hired to work the fields around Everway typically live on the estates where they work, getting food, clothes, lodging, and a few coins in exchange for their

labor. Professionals generally work the same way. Families, for instance, often house and provide for doctors who see to the families' health. People frequently trade goods and services rather than using coin.

Religion and Magic

Everway has been called "the City of a Thousand Gods." Divine images are everywhere in the city, representing deities from across the spheres. Each family has its own spiritual traditions, and many families are particularly devoted to certain deities. The royal Emerald family is devoted to "the Goddess," whom they consider the transcendent deity of whom the various more individual goddesses are manifestations. Because of the royal family's support for the Goddess, goddess images are popular in art, architecture, and personal adornment. The great king is spiritually linked to the prosperity of Roundwander, and he is the chief participant in Everway's solstice and equinox rituals.

Traditional magic takes three general forms in Roundwander: religious, familial, and transcendent. Religious magic is the magic of temples and priests, and it is tightly tied to the deities. In most temples, this magic mostly means religious prayers and rituals, while in some it involves an intellectual study of magic as well. Familial magic is the magical techniques and secrets of the various families. Among their secret rites, most families have spells, wards, and charms. Some of these magics are tied to the families' specific missions, but often they're simply powerful secrets they keep to themselves. Transcendent magic is the way of the lone magician, a path that takes the mage out of their family and social circles. For some, the point of the path is great power; for others, power is merely the side effect of greater wisdom. Transcendent magicians are accorded respect, and others often fear them.

In addition to the three types of traditional magic practiced in Everway, Outsiders have brought dozens of other styles of magic. Natives rarely practice them, but they have been known to avail themselves of the services of Outsider mages.

Strangers and Outsiders

In Roundwander, the terms "stranger" (meaning someone from another realm on this sphere) and "outsider" (meaning someone from another sphere) are used as family names and are thus capitalized. Strangers and Outsiders, paradoxically, are welcomed because they are kept at a distance. The natives tolerate them but keep their distance socially. Since Strangers and Outsiders can only really enter Roundwander's society through marriage, they are not a threat to tradition and can be welcomed without fear.

Roundwander

SNOWCAP

Dragonsbreach Mountains

Dragonsbreach Pass

Scale Isles

Stone Lands

Troll Hills

City of Shades

Murkwater

Cockatrice Fens

Lost Home Tower

ANCHORVIEW

Whiteoar Province

Turtle Bay

Mirror Lake

Stonebreaker Hill

Heartwood

Phoenix Rock

Owlwood

Emeraldcloak Forest

Clearpoint Lighthouse

Sentinel Forest

EVERWAY

Boarwood

King's Way

Charmwood

Walker's Causeway

River Province

Strangerside

Valley of the Walker

CIRCLE SEA

Shimmermoon Bay

Chime Forest

Centaur Ridge

Memory Fields

HAVEN

Harrow Island

Unicorn Forest

Sword Downs

Three Sisters

Starfall Province

Starfall Lake

Raven Heights

Spirit Lake

Holy Tears

White Ferry

White River

0 10 20 30
Miles

A   B   C   D   E

THE FOOL – REVERSED

Roundwander Map – Richard Thames Rowan

REFLECTION

Dragonsbreach Mountains

59
Howling Falls 7
71
Bone Forest
SPIRES
50
21
36
Tower Province
Spiral Keep
47
14
Red Fork River
Rust Plains
Gold Fork River
Solitary Pass
8
Blue Hills
GLIMMER
70
Goddess Wood
27
Ruby Fields
49
34
Bounty Fields
60
Sun Province
Sunset River
7
Griffin Hold
2
Satyr Wood
61
15
Dripstone Cavern
Sharptooth Mountains
52
37
5
Rookwood
EARTHBANK
3
Sunset River
44
King's Highway
EASTGUARD
57
64
King's Highway
10
3
Boneharvest Plain
Sharptooth Pass
17
28
Sphinx River
Deep Harvest
Griffinclaw Range
PHALANX
18
32
Singing Hills
42
Snakewall
Sphinx Gate
CHARIOT
Lamassu Gate
Gentrywood

⊙ ~ City	
■ ~ Town	
~ Ruin	
★ ~ Gate	

F   G   H   I   J

GRIT

Provinces of Roundwander

Roundwander contains six provinces that were once independent realms in the distant past. While they have long been integrated, traces of their original character still remain.

Harvest Province

Harvest Province is an agrarian land of pastures and fields. It provides a plentitude of grains and produce for the whole realm of Roundwander. While the cheerful inhabitants are gregarious and welcoming, many residents are covertly fond of gambling, beer, and darker vices.

History

Harvest Province joined Roundwander nearly two thousand years ago to seal an alliance against the raiders from beyond Sharptooth Pass. It has remained under an unbroken chain of governorship by the Harvest family, the original royal line of the province. Hundreds of years ago, satyrs arrived in Harvest Province, it is thought from the realm of Hedge Maze, settling in the Satyr Wood. They have been a subversive influence on many of the people of the province ever since.

Geography

- **Bounty Fields & Earthbank Fields:** These fields grow much of Roundwander's produce. [F-3/G-4]

- **Deep Harvest:** The rolling hills hold crops of mysterious, magical, and possibly dangerous plants. The residents are secretive, unwelcoming, and territorial. [G-2]

- **King's Highway:** This wide stone road is the main highway across Roundwander. [F-3/H-3]

- **Satyr Wood:** This twisty wood hosts many magical creatures, including a small enclave of satyrs. [G-4/H-4]

- **Singing Hills:** Some say the whistling wind is the singing of a creature, but others say it's the hills themselves. [F-1/F-3]

- **Sphinx River:** This seldom-navigated river is one of only a few somewhat safe overland routes to the neighboring realm of Chariot. [F-4/G-1]

- **Snakewall:** This seventy-foot bluff covered in ancient arcane petroglyphs marks the border between Roundwander and Chariot. [F-1/G-2]

Background Characters

- **Dawn Harvest:** Dawn Harvest is the grandfather of the Harvest family, and he has been the governor of the province for nearly 150 years. He rules with his husband, Chalk.

- **Felicity Mask:** The diminutive representative of the Mask family within Earthbank is well-connected to nearly all the city's vices.

- **Silvertongue Carter:** Silvertongue is the grandmother of the Carter family. The Carter family maintains the roads and bridges of Roundwander and transports goods within the realm.

- **Temperate Host**: This laconic man represents the Host family in Earthbank, ensuring there are places for visitors to stay during events.

Connections

- **Racing Circle:** This Harvest family organization hosts the annual Spring Races, drawing entries from other realms and spheres.

- **River's Edge:** Harvest trades food and crops extensively with the distant spherewalking center of River's Edge by way of the gate to Stormsong.

- **Temple of the Mother:** The identity of this goddess is a secret known only to initiates and the Harvest family. The priestesses of the temple are Moondance family members, but they operate largely independently. The Temple is connected with dozens of other Temples of the Mother among the spheres, but they have no spherewalkers of their own.

Harvest Province

The Satyr – Scott Kirschner

⚥ EARTHBANK

Earthbank is the principal city of Harvest Province with about 25,000 residents. The city is surrounded by a tall earth mound nearly twenty feet high, topped with a wooden palisade. Earthbank is the hub of food production for Roundwander. Inside the city, vast warrens of underground storage chambers spread for miles under the city. The city hosts the annual Harvest Festival, which is known for its many foods, beers, and horse races. Each spring it hosts the Spring Races, a prestigious week of horse racing. Both events draw attendees from across Roundwander, Fourcorner, and other spheres.

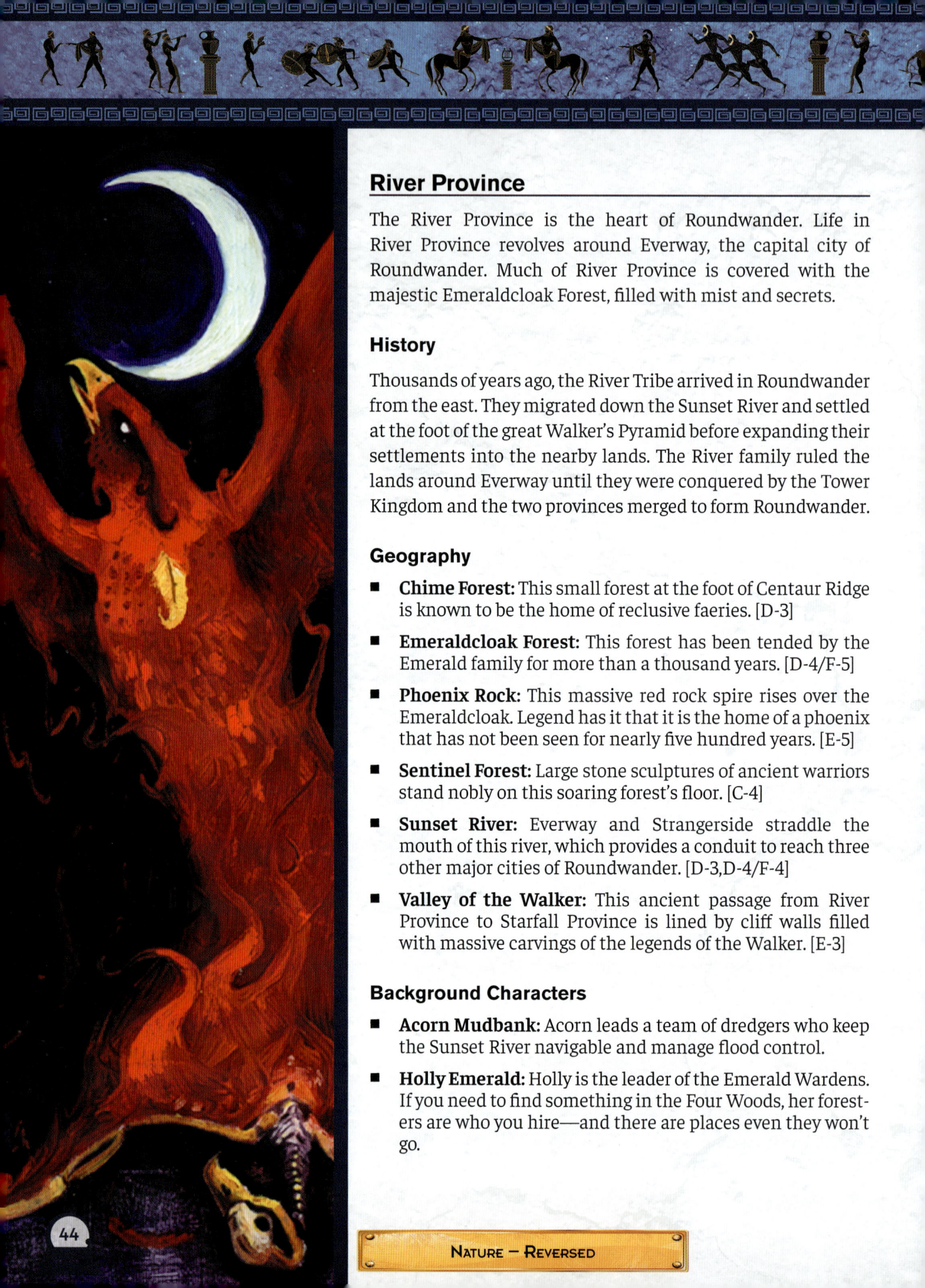

River Province

The River Province is the heart of Roundwander. Life in River Province revolves around Everway, the capital city of Roundwander. Much of River Province is covered with the majestic Emeraldcloak Forest, filled with mist and secrets.

History

Thousands of years ago, the River Tribe arrived in Roundwander from the east. They migrated down the Sunset River and settled at the foot of the great Walker's Pyramid before expanding their settlements into the nearby lands. The River family ruled the lands around Everway until they were conquered by the Tower Kingdom and the two provinces merged to form Roundwander.

Geography

- **Chime Forest:** This small forest at the foot of Centaur Ridge is known to be the home of reclusive faeries. [D-3]

- **Emeraldcloak Forest:** This forest has been tended by the Emerald family for more than a thousand years. [D-4/F-5]

- **Phoenix Rock:** This massive red rock spire rises over the Emeraldcloak. Legend has it that it is the home of a phoenix that has not been seen for nearly five hundred years. [E-5]

- **Sentinel Forest:** Large stone sculptures of ancient warriors stand nobly on this soaring forest's floor. [C-4]

- **Sunset River:** Everway and Strangerside straddle the mouth of this river, which provides a conduit to reach three other major cities of Roundwander. [D-3,D-4/F-4]

- **Valley of the Walker:** This ancient passage from River Province to Starfall Province is lined by cliff walls filled with massive carvings of the legends of the Walker. [E-3]

Background Characters

- **Acorn Mudbank:** Acorn leads a team of dredgers who keep the Sunset River navigable and manage flood control.

- **Holly Emerald:** Holly is the leader of the Emerald Wardens. If you need to find something in the Four Woods, her foresters are who you hire—and there are places even they won't go.

NATURE – REVERSED

Everway and the Emeraldcloak — River Province map

- **Redmane Carter:** Redmane is the bridgemaster who raises and lowers the Threshold Bridge crossing the Sunset into the Emeraldcloak.

Connections

- **Emerald Wardens:** Emerald family members not in the line of succession oversee the Emerald Wardens of the Emeraldcloak. This organization accepts outcasts from other families and even Strangers and Outsiders to care for the Four Woods.

- **Ferry Family:** The Ferry family runs a barge and message service up and down the Sunset River, particularly to the cities of Glimmer and Spires.

- **Triple Kingdom:** A dizzying array of trade goods travel the Great Way from the Triple Kingdom to Everway via the gate to The Market.

21 EVERWAY AND THE EMERALDCLOAK

The Emeraldcloak Forest, also called the Four Woods, is a massive forest in River Province just north of the city of Everway (see p. 55). The Owl Woods primarily contains sycamore trees, the Heartwood is mostly oak, the Boarwood is mostly maple, and the Goddess Wood is mostly aspen, although oaks appear throughout the Emeraldcloak. Parts of the Emeraldcloak are thickly obscured by understory trees and brush. Eerie mists often crawl through the forest at night, and rumors of magical creatures hiding deep in the forest abound.

The Phoenix – Scott Kirschner

Starfall Province

Starfall Province is a magical land of quiet meadows and misty forests. Exotic creatures and enigmatic beings pass their solitary lives deep in the wilderness. Despite this, Starfall Province has almost as many towns as River Province, the heart of the realm. In part this is because it is the largest of all the provinces in Roundwander. Scholars, priests and priestesses, mages, and miners have settled in the city of Holy Tears.

History

In the distant past, a falling star struck the province, forming Starfall Lake. Scholars theorize that the abundance of magic and divine influence in the province traces back to this event during the dragons' War Against Heaven.

Starfall Province joined with Roundwander to defend the land against the dragon Omeryx during the Dragonbreach War.

Geography

- **Harrow Island:** Ghosts haunt this lonely island. [B-2/C-2]
- **Memory Fields:** These meadowlands are known for inspiring visions in travelers who pass through it. [E-2/E-3]
- **Raven Heights:** This forested hill region is known for the giant ravens that nest among its many ancient ruins. [C-1]
- **Spirit Lake:** Naiads and sylphs live around this lake. [D-1]
- **Starfall Lake:** All manner of creatures and strange encounters have been reported in the Starfall Lake area. [E-2]
- **Sword Downs:** These rolling hills became a battlefield between highwaymen and Roundwander forces. [B-2]
- **Three Sisters:** These three fify-foot megaliths are rumored to move at certain times of the year. [F-1/F-3]
- **Unicorn Forest:** This majestic, giant beech forest with a vaulted canopy is filled with mythical creatures. [D-2/D-3]

Background Characters

- **Purity Digger:** As the governor, Purity mediates conflicts between the needs of her towns and the wild, magic places.
- **Sincerity Moondance:** Sincerity, an elder of the Moondance family, has lived in Holy Tears for all her ninety-two years.

SOWING STONES – REVERSED

Starfall Province

Shimmermoon Bay

Centaur Ridge

Valley of the Walker

Memory Fields

Sphinx River

Harrow Island

Unicorn Forest

Sword Downs

Three Sisters

Starfall Lake

Singing Falls

Spirit Lake

Raven Heights

Holy Tears

Snakewall

White Ferry

Lamassu Gate

CIRCLE SEA

White River

Gentrywood

- **Temerity Scratch:** Temerity operates a research site in Holy Tears for the Library of All Worlds.

Connections

- **The Architects:** A retreat for scholars and engineers lies just past the Lamassu Gate in Chariot.

- **Autumn Court of Gentrywood:** This gentry court shares a festival with Starfall Province once every five years.

- **Blackwand Centaurs:** An elusive centaur band known for their mages lives in the hills of Centaur Ridge.

- **Sanctum:** The gate to Temple is the starting point for pilgrims to Sanctum, a distant center for the study of countless religions.

C HOLY TEARS

The city of Holy Tears and the White River both get their name from the diamonds found in the river valley. The city began as a mining and gem-cutting settlement. Mystics, priests, and scholars discovered the diamonds of this area had magical traces of the Goddess and began to flock to the settlement. Some speculate that the diamonds were the tears she shed over her slain children. The city today still feels like a small town despite its size of approximately 16,500 residents. Life moves languidly in Holy Tears, and the people are very social, despite the dangers that lurk in the wilderness.

The Unicorn – Scott Kirschner

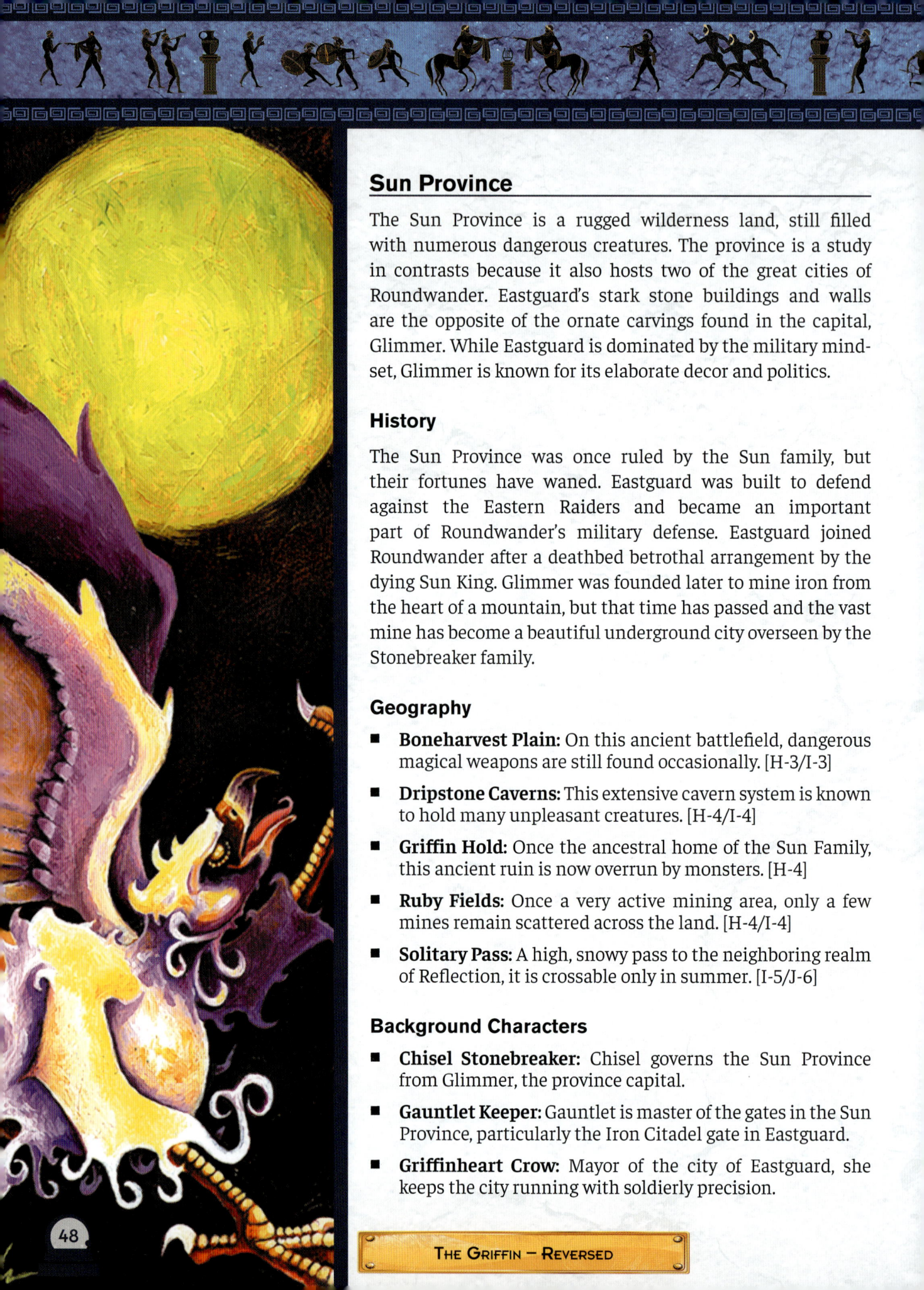

Sun Province

The Sun Province is a rugged wilderness land, still filled with numerous dangerous creatures. The province is a study in contrasts because it also hosts two of the great cities of Roundwander. Eastguard's stark stone buildings and walls are the opposite of the ornate carvings found in the capital, Glimmer. While Eastguard is dominated by the military mindset, Glimmer is known for its elaborate decor and politics.

History

The Sun Province was once ruled by the Sun family, but their fortunes have waned. Eastguard was built to defend against the Eastern Raiders and became an important part of Roundwander's military defense. Eastguard joined Roundwander after a deathbed betrothal arrangement by the dying Sun King. Glimmer was founded later to mine iron from the heart of a mountain, but that time has passed and the vast mine has become a beautiful underground city overseen by the Stonebreaker family.

Geography

- **Boneharvest Plain:** On this ancient battlefield, dangerous magical weapons are still found occasionally. [H-3/I-3]
- **Dripstone Caverns:** This extensive cavern system is known to hold many unpleasant creatures. [H-4/I-4]
- **Griffin Hold:** Once the ancestral home of the Sun Family, this ancient ruin is now overrun by monsters. [H-4]
- **Ruby Fields:** Once a very active mining area, only a few mines remain scattered across the land. [H-4/I-4]
- **Solitary Pass:** A high, snowy pass to the neighboring realm of Reflection, it is crossable only in summer. [I-5/J-6]

Background Characters

- **Chisel Stonebreaker:** Chisel governs the Sun Province from Glimmer, the province capital.
- **Gauntlet Keeper:** Gauntlet is master of the gates in the Sun Province, particularly the Iron Citadel gate in Eastguard.
- **Griffinheart Crow:** Mayor of the city of Eastguard, she keeps the city running with soldierly precision.

THE GRIFFIN — REVERSED

GLIMMER

Glimmer is a city built inside a mountain. The eighteen levels of the city are home to just over 14,000 residents. Shafts bring sunlight to the central arcade and the Abyss leading downward to the lowest levels of the city. Only the top eight levels are occupied by the residents. The four levels below that are workshops and factories. In the lowest levels, Digger family mages work with the Glimmer automatons to mine emeralds and rubies. The Stonebreakers govern the city but have reserved access to the lower levels for the Digger family's operations.

- **Lightarm Digger:** Lightarm is master of the mines of the city of Glimmer.

Connections

- **Glimmer Automatons:** Deep in the mines of Glimmer, the Glimmer automatons have begun asking spherewalkers to join them for some unknown purpose.

- **Glorious Empire:** This distant spherewalking empire can be reached by way of the Iron Citadel gate in Eastguard.

- **Phalanx:** This warlike realm remains stiffly at arm's length with Roundwander. They send diplomats to Everway every three years to inquire if Roundwander is ready to join the empire.

- **Reflection:** The reclusive neighboring realm of Reflection can be reached via the winter-impassible Solitary Pass.

Sun Province

The Griffin – Scott Kirschner

EASTGUARD

Eastguard is a military city of about 12,500 that was built to fill Sharptooth Pass from cliff face to cliff face with high stone walls. Eastguard protects the only road to the large, expansionist empire of Phalanx, which is the greatest threat to the security of Roundwander. A circular wall inside the city encloses the gate to Iron Citadel, another warlike realm. Iron Citadel used to send assassin spherewalkers through the gate in the past, although tensions are much eased now. It is not unusual to find masters of various martial skills in the city, training those who will pay.

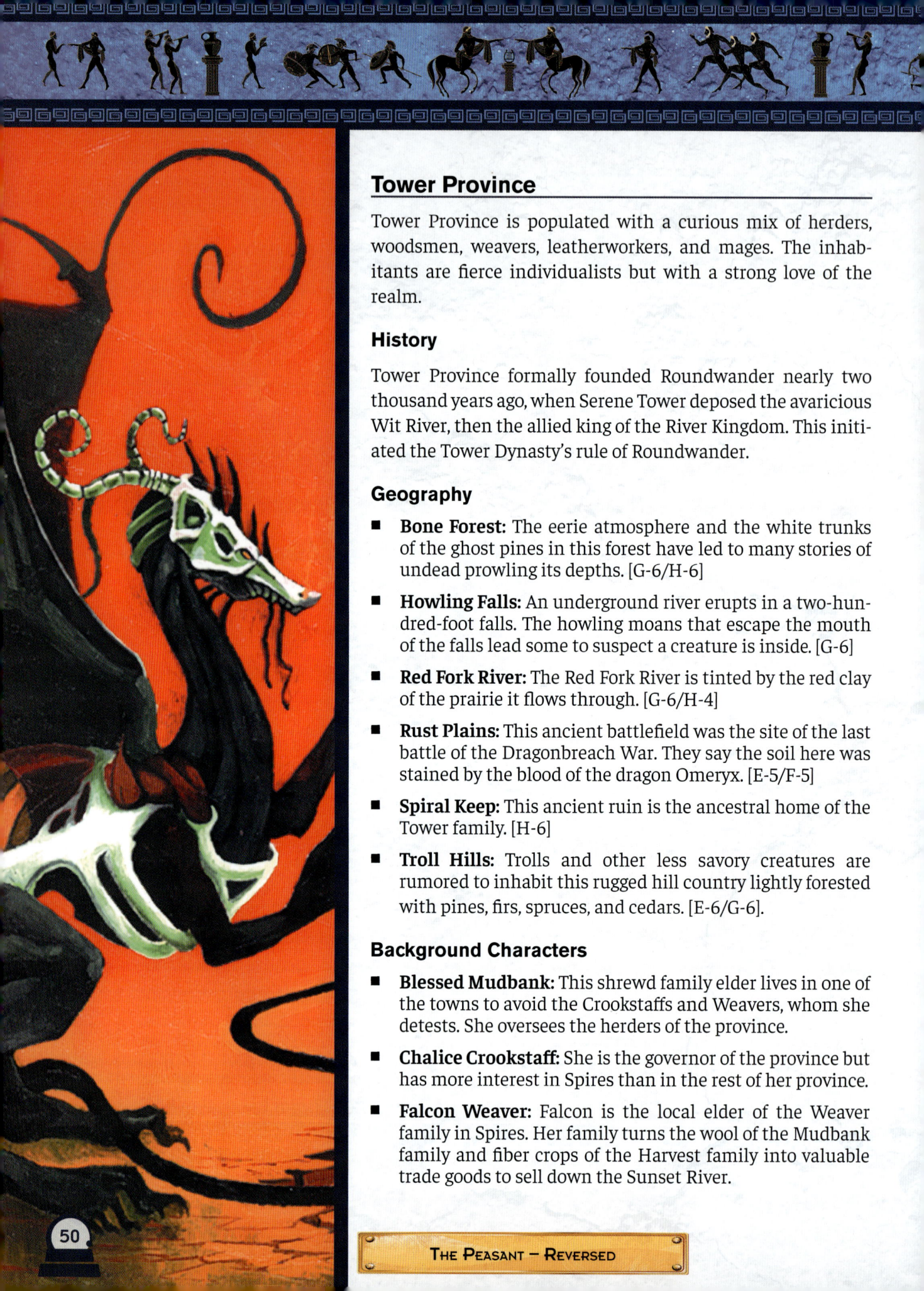

Tower Province

Tower Province is populated with a curious mix of herders, woodsmen, weavers, leatherworkers, and mages. The inhabitants are fierce individualists but with a strong love of the realm.

History

Tower Province formally founded Roundwander nearly two thousand years ago, when Serene Tower deposed the avaricious Wit River, then the allied king of the River Kingdom. This initiated the Tower Dynasty's rule of Roundwander.

Geography

- **Bone Forest:** The eerie atmosphere and the white trunks of the ghost pines in this forest have led to many stories of undead prowling its depths. [G-6/H-6]

- **Howling Falls:** An underground river erupts in a two-hundred-foot falls. The howling moans that escape the mouth of the falls lead some to suspect a creature is inside. [G-6]

- **Red Fork River:** The Red Fork River is tinted by the red clay of the prairie it flows through. [G-6/H-4]

- **Rust Plains:** This ancient battlefield was the site of the last battle of the Dragonbreach War. They say the soil here was stained by the blood of the dragon Omeryx. [E-5/F-5]

- **Spiral Keep:** This ancient ruin is the ancestral home of the Tower family. [H-6]

- **Troll Hills:** Trolls and other less savory creatures are rumored to inhabit this rugged hill country lightly forested with pines, firs, spruces, and cedars. [E-6/G-6].

Background Characters

- **Blessed Mudbank:** This shrewd family elder lives in one of the towns to avoid the Crookstaffs and Weavers, whom she detests. She oversees the herders of the province.

- **Chalice Crookstaff:** She is the governor of the province but has more interest in Spires than in the rest of her province.

- **Falcon Weaver:** Falcon is the local elder of the Weaver family in Spires. Her family turns the wool of the Mudbank family and fiber crops of the Harvest family into valuable trade goods to sell down the Sunset River.

THE PEASANT – REVERSED

The Dragon – Scott Kirschner

- **Hart Crow:** She is charged with keeping the wilderness creatures away from the settled parts of the province.

- **Longwalk Tower:** He is the grandfather of the remnants of the ancient Tower family. In the current age, the Towers are foresters once again.

Connections

- **Celestial City:** Sages in Spires often correspond with the distant Celestial City universities by way of the gate to the realm of Heaven.

- **Tower Family:** This once-royal family of woodsmen is rumored to hold ancient histories and secrets.

- **Sun Province:** The Tower Province maintains strong bonds with the Crow family in Eastguard for defense.

SPIRES

Spires was founded by mages banished from Everway by the impetuous King Wit River. The Crookstaffs reached out to Grandmother Hawthorn Tower to seek re-settlement in Tower Kingdom. The city was so successful that it became the seat of government for Tower Kingdom. After Serene Tower consolidated the River and Tower Kingdoms into Roundwander, the Crookstaffs returned to Everway, but they remain a strong presence in the city they built to this day. The city is now known for its mages, scholars, and textiles and has about 20,000 residents.

Whiteoar Province

Whiteoar Province used to be a bounteous province, built partially on a dark past of piracy. Centuries ago, cockatrices began to flourish in the Green Fens, fouling them. Now the people of Whiteoar Province live a harsh life amidst dangerous creatures, ruled from the raucous city of Anchorview.

History

Whiteoar Province was originally a realm ruled by the pirates called the Redsails. Twelve centuries ago, the Redsails sacked parts of Everway, which roused Roundwander to war. The Whiteoar family betrayed the other Redsails to forestall their own doom, subjecting Whiteoar Province to Roundwander rule. A century later, a Whiteoar was named heir to the throne when the Tower family abdicated. The Whiteoar reign became more corrupt over the centuries, and eventually the Whiteoars were expelled in a civil war, giving rise to the Emerald Dynasty.

Geography

- **Charmwood:** People make wishes on charms and hang them from the trees in this birch forest. [B-4]
- **City of Shades:** Once the capital of the province, the city was abandoned after the catacombs started releasing wraiths awoken by the corrupted land. [D-6]
- **Cockatrice Fens:** Formerly the Green Fens, this marsh became foul and corrupted by cockatrices. [B-6/C-5]
- **Dragonbreach Pass:** This narrow pass is the only pass through the Dragonbreach Mountains into Snowcap. [D-6]
- **Mirror Lake:** This enchanted lake is said to reflect truths of the viewer's past and visions of their future. [B-5/C-6]
- **Stone Lands:** Boulders migrate around the landscape in this region, preventing anything from growing. [A-6]
- **Stonebreaker Hills:** These hills with many marble quarries form part of the border with River Province. [B-5/E6]

Background Characters

- **Halcyon Fleet:** Halcyon Fleet is the governor, and his family is staid compared to the wilder residents. His family does an adequate job of collecting taxes, letting Everway turn a blind eye to the lawlessness of the province.

THE CREATOR

The map shows Whiteoar Province with locations including: Scale Isles, Stone Lands, Dragonsbreach Mountains, Dragonbreach Pass, Cockatrice Fens, City of Shades, Murkwater, Lost Home Tower, ANCHORVIEW, Turtle Bay, Clearpoint Lighthouse, Mirror Lake, Sentinel Forest, Charmwood, Stonebreaker Hills, Heartwood, Phoenix Rock, Owlwood, Emeraldcloak Forest, Boarwood

Whiteoar Province

- **Dill Snakering:** Dill leads the local Snakerings filling most administrative roles. They are well known for their petty corruption.

- **Moonlight Mask:** Moonlight runs an underground gambling house in the city and is aware of most events in the province.

Connections

- **Dexter City:** The gate to Merryflag leads to this distant city of thieves.

- **Haven:** Anchorview trades extensively with the realm of Haven.

- **Northdawn Raiders:** The Fleet ships repulse the pirates from Northdawn.

- **Omeryx Cultists:** Dragon cultists in Snowcap raid over Dragonbreach Pass.

ANCHORVIEW

Anchorview is a boisterous city of merchants and fishermen. Fully half of the city is built on pilings out into placid Turtle Bay. The city of about 33,000 residents teems with activity day and night. Fire is forbidden, so magic lanterns float amid the channels to illuminate the wooden decking. The residents are generally happy on the surface but with the grim and desperate knowledge that their province is slowly falling into decay. Many residents are just trying to make enough to survive until they can relocate elsewhere. Much of the province has fallen into ruin.

The Cockatrice – Scott Kirschner

54

THE USURPER

THE CITY OF EVERWAY

Everway is a huge, ancient city, home to half a million people. This section describes features of the city, but the only way to appreciate the city in full detail is to explore it.

The Walker's Pyramid

At the center of Everway in the Stonefast district is the Walker's Pyramid, a large, stone structure without a capstone. It is a round step pyramid with seven tiers. Each block is about thirty feet high, and the Pyramid is about two hundred feet tall and some five hundred feet in diameter at the base. The Walker's Pyramid dominates the skyline as the city's tallest structure.

Legend has it that a deity known only as the Walker (no one knows the Walker's name, sex, or gender) built the Pyramid stone by stone. The footsteps the Walker left as they traveled from sphere to sphere are the gates that now connect the spheres for mortal travel. It is said that the Walker is out among the spheres now, searching for the capstone that will complete the Pyramid. The comet known as the Walker's Star is said to presage his return. No one knows what will happen when the Pyramid is completed. Some say all the spheres will come to an end. Others say that the web of spheres will advance to the next stage in its evolution, an era of peace and prosperity. Some say nothing ever really changes.

Around the base of the Pyramid, visitors find temples, wandering mystics, and booths that sell magical goods and items for offerings. A group of "pyramid priests" tend to the Walker's Pyramid and to the pilgrims who come to visit it. They take the offerings that people leave and store them away; their intent is to present these to the Walker personally when they return with the Pyramid's capstone. Where they store these treasures and how much they've accumulated is a secret of the Moondance grandmothers.

In religious art, the Walker is pictured in many different ways. No one know what the Walker looks like or even, as mentioned earlier, whether the deity is male, female, or neither. Indeed, many people hold that the Walker takes different forms to make traveling among different spheres easier.

Architecture

The great buildings of Everway are made of stone, soaring structures with tall arches, daunting pillars, and narrow spires. The faces of gods and goddesses, monsters, spirits, people, and beasts peer out from the stonework. On the most celebrated buildings, not one square foot is left unadorned.

The older buildings in Everway record the architectural styles of ages past. For instance, buildings that date from

101. Pyramid Priest – Rudy Rauben (Roger Raupp)

GREETINGS

It is the custom in Roundwander to greet others by placing one's palms together in front of one's mouth, bowing slightly, and saying "a thousand times" (or "thousand" or "thou" for short). This phrase refers to the inhabitants' belief in reincarnation and is meant to remind the speaker of the good things that the greeted person has done for the speaker in countless past lives. A more formal greeting specifies the actions referred to, and each family or individual chooses which action is recalled. For instance:

A thousand times you have borne me in your womb.

A thousand times you have nursed me at your breast.

A thousand times you have tutored me.

A thousand times you have tended me in my illness.

A thousand times you have comforted me in prison.

A thousand times you have fed me when I was starving.

A thousand times you have buried me with tears.

1,300 to 1,700 years ago often have sun images or solar motifs. During that era, the Tower family was the royal family of Roundwander, and they were as devoted to the sun as the Emerald family is devoted to the Goddess. Buildings from 2,300 years ago often have a unique pink and green marble worked into them. When these buildings were built, the Stonebreaker family had recently discovered a vein of this marble, and it was very popular. After the vein was depleted, however, the Stonebreakers never again found marble like it. Stonebreakers can often tell the date of old buildings by noticing even more subtle details than these. The very oldest buildings around the Walker's Pyramid bear the tortoise motif of the River family dynasty.

The estates of wealthy Everwayans are also made of stone, with generous use of wood shipped down the Sunset from forests upstream. The faces of these buildings are also carved, often with the likenesses of ancestors and other images important to the families. An estate is typically a large, parklike, walled area with several houses and open-air patios inside. The estate is home to the extended family, and many areas are open only to family members.

The poor live in houses made of adobe and scraps of stone. Tarps often serve as shutters, doors, and even roofs. Some of Everway's poor live in ancestral homes, but they are more likely than the wealthy

to live in newer homes. Everway is so old that pieces of rubble from once-glorious temples and palaces can be found throughout the city. The poor sometimes use this rubble to hold down tarps, build steps, or otherwise improve their homes; it's not unusual to find a piece of an ancient statue used as an ordinary rock.

The Stonebreaker family has masterminded the construction of great stone aqueducts and cisterns that supply a series of fountains with fresh, clean water throughout the city, and they are popular in the homes of the wealthy as well.

Stone walls encircle the city of Everway proper (not including Strangerside) for protection. Many new homes are found outside the walls because Everway has not had to defend itself from direct assault for hundreds of years.

The streets of Everway twist and turn. Each is known by an informal, descriptive name, such as Three Trees, Old Temple, Stone Mask, and so on. There is no official designation for any street so there are about twenty streets in Everway known as Old Temple Street. A long street with several landmarks may have several names, each applying to the section of the street nearest that landmark. For instance, a minor street leading away from the Court of Fools, past a black statue of an ancient great king, to a square fountain is known as Long Fool Street, Black Man Street, or

Square Water Street, depending on which section is being referred to. The exception to all these general rules is the Walker's Way, a straight thoroughfare that leads directly from the Imperial Gate to the Walker's Pyramid. The Imperial Gate and Walker's Way are wide enough so that, upon returning to Everway, the Walker will be able to carry the final stone to the Pyramid.

Three large bridges span the Sunset, connecting Everway to Strangerside. These are the Fool's Bridge, the Dusk Bridge, and the Mercy Bridge, named for the centers they are near (see below). Another bridge in the wharf district crosses to Fleet Island.

Centers of Everway

Around the Walker's Pyramid are several centers of interest. Each center is large enough that it could be considered a separate, albeit small, city. Each supports a different sort of business and attracts a different sort of visitor.

West of the Pyramid are the GAMING HOUSES, where fortunes change hands over rolls of the dice. Other amusements of questionable morality can also be found nearby. Strangers find themselves welcome in this part of town. The Carter and Mask families have their principal estate near the gaming houses.

Northwest of the Pyramid is the LIBRARY OF ALL WORLDS, a collection of large buildings filled with scrolls holding knowledge and wisdom collected from a thousand spheres. The Chamber Platinum is a group sponsored by the Library who explore new realms and spheres. The Crookstaff, Keeper, and Scratch families have their head estates in this center.

North of the Pyramid is the COUNCIL HOUSE, where the Council meets and addresses the great king, who rules Everway and the surrounding realm of Roundwander. The estates of Everway's wealthiest families are all in this area, as is the great king's palace on the overlooking hill. The Emerald, Host, Plume, and Snakering families all have their head estates near the Council House.

Northeast of the Pyramid are the GARDENS, which contain various temples to deities of nature and the earth. Exotic animals and plants from other spheres can be found here, if one knows where to look. The air is filled with the smells of blossoms. The head estates of the Digger and Stonebreaker families are close to the Gardens.

Knowledge, Nature, Fertility, Death, War – Scott Kirschner
Law, Inspiration, Trickery – Jeff Miracola

To the east is the TEMPLE OF MERCY, with several associated temples and charities around it. Here one finds poorhouses, hospitals, orphanages, and temples to deities of fertility and healing. The poorer inhabitants of Everway live in the shadows of the city walls. The Mother and Wailer families have their head estates here.

To the southeast are the HOUSES OF DUSK, where the dead are prepared for their final journeys. The people of Everway traditionally place their dead on rafts that are left to float out to sea, but the Houses of Dusk include many family memorial mausoleums and can accommodate many other cultural funeral practices. Artisans, laborers, and those who attend the Houses of Dusk live in the area. The Moondance, Ferry, and Tender families also have their head estates here.

To the south is the COURT OF FOOLS, a large plaza where entertainers of all types demonstrate their arts. Mixed in among the buffoons and jugglers, one can sometimes find prophets and seers. All are welcome at the Court of Fools, if they can amuse or be amused. This is the city's principal market. The Jade, Mudbank, Smith, and Weaver families have their head estates in this area.

To the southwest are the ARENAS, where gladiators fight and martial families demonstrate their skill and courage. Rough sports are popular here, as are contests of weapons. Fights to the death are rare; confrontations are always meant to settle some point of honor or vengeance, never merely to please a crowd. Temples to the deities of war are here, and the Crow, Fleet, and Watcher families have their head estates here.

Strangerside

The "south bank" (actually the southeast bank) is the home of Strangers (those from other realms on Fourcorner) and Outsiders (those from other spheres). This area probably has as many people as Everway proper, but no census has ever been taken here.

Strangerside is a dynamic, crowded, colorful, and sometimes dangerous mix of people from distant lands and other spheres. Newcomers attract vendors, thieves, beggars, wanderers, and recruiters for legitimate and illicit jobs, all of them want to see what they can get out of those who set foot in Strangerside. On one hand, Strangerside's experience with

Sights in Everway

In every part of Everway, a visitor may see a thousand different sights.

Sights Around the Arenas

- Warriors of the Crow family staging an exhibition fight (with practice weapons).

Sights Around the Gaming Houses

- A wealthy envoy from another land, accompanied by a large entourage, losing piles of silver at games of dice. Shady figures tail the group through the night; they are criminals who are there to see that no harm comes to the envoy. (Injury to an official would bring retribution and would dissuade other officials from visiting the gaming houses and losing their wealth there.)

- A wealthy young woman selling jewelry to raise money to get back into a dice game.

- A spherewalker being beaten for using magic to influence the roll of the dice.

Sights Around the Library

- A humanoid dragon, a guest of the Library, teaching the language of the dragons.

- A sage demonstrating her body control by doing a one-handed handstand.

- Two scholars engaged in a slapping duel over their different interpretations of an epic poem.

THE CREATOR – REVERSED

Sights Around the Council House

- Great King Horizon Emerald, touring the city atop a covered platform on an elephant's back.
- Brightly bedecked guards of the Plume family keeping a close eye on Strangers and Outsiders.
- A dozen people bearing a flower-strewn idol through the streets to celebrate one of the city's countless holy days.

Sights Around the Gardens

- Spherewalkers leading a wagon that carries a giant, spotted cat in a cage. They are taking it to one of the gardens.
- An old woman selling all manner of herbs and dried plants. Some are in a wicker basket, while others are pinned to her clothes.
- A thin, dirty, wild-looking face peeking over the wall that encloses a large garden.

Sights Around the Temple of Mercy

- White-robed, barefoot monks visiting the sick and needy. (Monks can be either men or women.) They carry begging bowls, which they hold out to all they meet. Those with something to give are welcome to place it in the bowl, and those in need are welcome to take from it.
- A Mother leading a group of young orphans on a walk. ("Mother" is a family name; the adult could as easily be male as female.)
- A leper clapping stones together to warn others of their presence as they walk down the street.

Sights Around the Houses of Dusk

- A file of mourners walking silently, several of them carrying a dead body wrapped in tan shrouds. They are taking the deceased to one of the Houses of Dusk, where it will be prepared for its journey out to sea.
- A small group of Wailers in gaudy ceremonial costumes squatting in a circle behind a House of Dusk. They're playing dice, drinking strong tea, and laughing while they wait for their next assignment.
- Black birds circling above a House of Dusk. All at once, they flock down and out of sight onto the roof. They are feeding on the a corpse of a Stranger whose tradition requires this ceremony after death.

Sights Around the Court of Fools

- A woman costumed as a high priestess of the Moondance family performing a bawdy, impromptu dance and making lewd suggestions to passersby.
- An engineer testing their latest contraption: a giant construct of gears and levers that, if it works, will walk under its own power.
- A holy woman who has taken a vow never to let both her soles leave the ground. She is sleeping, hanging in a sling that leaves her feet resting on the ground.

newcomers means that their needs can be accommodated no matter what they are. On the other hand, some use this same experience to exploit, trick, mislead, or rob newcomers. Those who visit Strangerside are wise to remember that the people of Strangerside are much more experienced at dealing with newcomers than newcomers are at dealing with Strangerside.

Officially, Strangers and Outsiders are considered visitors in Roundwander, even though some trace their ancestry back to Strangers and Outsiders who came to Roundwander hundreds of years ago. In order for Strangers or Outsiders to become accepted as residents of Roundwander, they must either marry into Roundwander families (possible only for men) or start their own families (possible only for women). The prosperous Jade family is an example of a family started by a Stranger.

Strangerside is home to numerous enclaves of like-minded people or people from the same cultures. These groups, which range in size from single houses to sprawling, walled estates, have no legal status, but the larger ones do wield some clout in Everway society.

Wandering about Strangerside, one may encounter any of the following:

- A walled, closed community of well-dressed, black-skinned Outsiders. One can gain entrance only by showing proper deference to the exiled noble who lives within.

- A large, stone estate now completely overrun by people who would otherwise be homeless. The inhabitants don't seem to care who else comes and goes. Rumors in Strangerside say that one of the inhabitants is a notorious, hardhearted mage who is hiding from the Watchers.

- A narrow alley in which several short, light-skinned, brown-haired merchants ply visitors with a bewildering array of small, exotic goods. They refuse beads, insisting on being paid in silver, gold, or (preferably) gems.

- A large, two-legged bearlike creature wearing a harness. It's sitting in the shade, swatting flies that buzz about it. It watches passersby with intelligent eyes.

- The mortal remains of an Outsider who tried to make it in Strangerside on their own.

- Bedraggled refugees from a distant realm who have come here to find champions to bring justice to their homeland.

- A mighty warrior spending his latest plunder and attracting a crowd of temporarily loyal hangers-on.

- A one-armed opportunist trying to persuade a group of spherewalkers to act as bodyguards on an expedition to another sphere to trade steel to the inhabitants of a primitive realm in exchange for huge amounts of gold.

- A band of troublemaking kids, some homeless and others just running with the gang for kicks.

- An elegant home where a necromancer lives. The servants that come and go on errands are all animated corpses.

- Two mages engaged in a staring contest that's gone on for hours. The contest is probably also a magical duel.

Coming to Everway

When coming to Everway, especially for the first time, each visitor or group of visitors may have a different experience. Still, some events occur commonly enough to note. Gamemasters and players may find these ideas interesting as they help set the stage for heroes' travels.

On the Other Side

To arrive in Everway, one usually travels from a connected realm through one of Roundwander's seventy-one gates. The realms that have the most ready contact with Roundwander, and the ones through which the spherewalkers are most likely to travel without incident, include Crisscross, Heaven, Iron Citadel, The Market, Merryflag, Midlands, Roundhome, Seashift, Stormsong, and Temple.

While in realms connected to Roundwander, spherewalkers often meet people who have traveled there or even natives of Everway. They can learn much about the city from these fellow spherewalkers (though travelers have been known to exaggerate).

> See Chapter 2: Realms for more information about the spheres adjoining the realm of Roundwander

Getting Through the Gate

Every gate leading to Roundwander is different, depending mostly on the realm it is in. The spherewalkers may have to get permission to use a gate, pay a toll, or wait their turn in a long line of travelers. Sometimes a gate is fortified to prevent dangerous people from entering the realm from Roundwander. These gates are "reverse fortresses," built to keep travelers in Roundwander, rather than to keep invaders out.

Some gates are guarded by members of the Keeper family of Everway or by those in the Keepers' employ. The guards stop and question all who want to use the gates to get to Roundwander. Guards are traditionally armed with spears, iron scale armor, and steel helmets, though sometimes the Keepers retain the services of local warriors who use their standard armaments. The guards are serious but not hostile; they know that Everway benefits greatly from the goods and knowledge that spherewalkers bring.

It usually takes a few hours to a week to travel the astral path from gate to gate. Those who watch the skies can tell how much time has passed by the phase of the moon; a week is enough time for it to go through a quarter cycle, such as from first quarter to full. (The skies among spheres are synchronized, so it's a full moon on the same night in every realm.) Spherewalkers may arrive at any time, day or night.

While there may or may not be Keeper guards at the gate in the other realm, there are usually some at the gate where spherewalkers arrive in Roundwander. Spherewalking parties may find themselves ringed in by walls, within a fortification. Here, Keeper guards question travelers, even if they've already been questioned on the other side. Usually, the guards let spherewalkers past, and visitors may find themselves beset by children, officials, beggars, messengers, and people offering their services, especially guidance to a city or to respectable lodging.

Coming to Strangerside

Unless visitors have business in Everway proper, guides and passersby direct them to Strangerside. The journey from the gate to Everway takes anywhere from a few minutes to a week, depending on where the gate is located. If the travelers need to find lodging before they reach Everway,

THE SOLDIER

guards, guides, and passersby can usually direct them to a Host's home in one of the provincial cities or local villages.

Visitors may travel overland to Everway or take a boat down the Sunset. In either case, they are likely to see Everway well before they arrive. While the towers, palaces, and temples are impressive, the mighty Walker's Pyramid dominates the scene.

About half the gates are on the south side of the Sunset River, and about half are to the north. Getting to Strangerside on foot from the north means crossing the Sunset at one of the many bridges.

Once in Strangerside, newcomers are confronted on all sides by vendors, would-be guides, beggars, and others offering services to or asking things of the spherewalkers. With luck and patience, newcomers can find a Host's home without incident. Different Hosts maintain homes offering different levels of comfort. It is impossible to get into the nicest homes without class. An exiled and penniless king is more likely to be welcomed in finer homes than a barbarian offering to pay a fortune. Those who prefer not to stay with a Host can often find lodging set up by competing

Strangers or Outsiders, but they do so at their own risk.

> See the map of Roundwander for the location of each gate.

Staying in Everway

Unless a Stranger or Outsider can marry into an Everway family (and only men can do so) or establish a newly recognized family (and only women can do so), the newcomer cannot buy property within the walls of Everway proper. To live in Everway proper, a person must persuade a family to let them live on family property. Some families maintain quarters separate from their estates for just this purpose.

More likely, a newcomer will settle in Strangerside or in the less densely inhabited lands surrounding Everway. There are no legal restrictions on either action. In Strangerside, choosing one's neighbors can be difficult, though entertaining. Some neighborhoods are simply motley mixes of Strangers and Outsiders, while others have definite cultural and ethnic identities.

THE POINT OF EVERWAY

The city of Everway serves several purposes. Gamemaster and players should keep these purposes in mind when they use Everway in their games.

First, Everway provides a starting place for gamemasters and players who want cultural background on which to base their quests and heroes. My original idea was to have no background at all in EVERWAY, relying on players and gamemasters to make up any sorts of backgrounds they wanted. A game without a setting, however, works for some people but not for everyone. For those who want to create their heroes and quests in a cultural context, Everway is here for them. A gamemaster can state as a premise that the heroes are from Everway, or players can choose such a background for their heroes.

A setting to serve an open-ended game such as EVERWAY has to be flexible. Everway, therefore, provides plenty of room for gamemasters and players to invent details to their liking. If a player needs to invent a family to serve as a hero's background, there's still room for many new families in Everway. If a gamemaster needs to invent a new subculture tucked away in Strangerside, there's room for numerous little enclaves that most people haven't heard about before. I made Everway big and varied so that you would feel free to add the details that you wish to add. In this way, Everway provides the benefits of background without restricting your imagination too much.

Third, Everway provides a number of "jumping-off-points," ways in which heroes can get involved. They can explore spheres for the Chamber Platinum of the Library of All Worlds; investigate strange occurrences in Strangerside; or involve themselves in the political struggles among the Emeralds, Snakerings, and other elites. Heroes can find plots within the city itself, a nearby city or town, or they can find reasons to explore other realms.

Finally, Everway includes a few magical patterns that aren't explicit. You can enjoy Everway without finding out all of its secrets, but they're here for those of you who like a little mystery.

— Jonathan Tweet

Sphere of Fourcorner

Fourcorner gets its name from the four major continents surrounding the Circle Sea. The sphere has two other oceans, the deadly Storm Sea in the north and the southern Trackless Sea. A long archipelago of wild, magic-filled, volcanic islands called the Rift Islands separates the Trackless Sea and the Storm Sea.

Myriad

The western continent is less ancient than the rest of Fourcorner. It is filled with a hundred small realms all churning with agriculture, industry, and invention. The coastal realms are Roundwander's chief trading partners on Fourcorner, bringing exotic foods, spices, and crafts to the markets of Everway and for trade via the Great Way.

Northdawn

The northern continent of Fourcorner stretches into the arctic regions of the sphere. It is named for the beautiful nightly shows of bands of color across its sky. Its temperate southern lands host multiple settlements but its wild lands host many warlords, brigands, and hardy settlers. Pirates hide in its many offshore islands.

Veilmist

The southern continent of Fourcorner is a land of great mystery. It once held mighty empires that fell in antiquity. Any settlement on this continent over the last thousand years has disappeared without a trace, and no one knows why. There are rumors of fabulous treasures of ancient times on the continent, but it is widely considered to be cursed or taboo to visit.

Crossroads

The eastern continent of Fourcorner is host to the two strongest military powers on Fourcorner, Roundwander and Phalanx. While Phalanx dominates much of the land, Roundwander has a dominant naval force. A few lesser realms continue to survive in the shadows between these two military powerhouses. Crossroads is most known for the many gates in Roundwander.

Neighbors of Roundwander

Roundwander shares a border with four other realms and has strong trade relations with a fifth on an island in the midst of the Circle Sea. These neighboring realms are described briefly on the following pages.

Realm of Chariot

The realm of Chariot is a realm of wandering horsemen, with the exception of a few fortress towns and the capital city of Arcade on the coast. Chariot has a cordial relationship with both Roundwander to the north and the realm of Grit to the south. The rugged terrain prevents much interaction with its eastern neighbor, Phalanx. Chariot is known for its military might and the engineering of its majestic monuments, particularly along the Sphinx River.

Geography

Chariot is mostly steppe land, with the notable exception of the faerie Gentrywood. The people of Chariot stay out of the forest, content to let the faerie gentry there live in peace. The gentry likewise rarely venture out into the steppe. The rolling grasses are ideal for the horse-centric culture of the Charioteers.

People

The citizens of Chariot are intelligent, hard-working people. They do not accumulate possessions, focusing instead on the fantastic engineering of their stalwart fortresses, impressive monuments, and elaborate temples. Scholarship is also a popular vocation. Royal army forces run drills in the summer months in cavalry, chariot maneuvers, and archery. Despite Chariot's constant military readiness, they have not been in any serious conflict for centuries.

Rule

Chariot is ruled by a hereditary Scholar-King, currently his Majestic Wisdom Strongwind March. The Scholar-King is advised by two bodies, the Martial Senate, composed of the top military generals, and the Sage Council, composed of respected scholars and engineers.

FATE — War

War
(great effort vs. effort misspent)

VIRTUE — The Eagle

The Eagle
(the mind prevails)

FAULT — Overlooking the Diamond

Overlooking the Diamond
(failing to see opportunity)

The Fish, Drowning in Armor, Law, Striking the Dragon's Tail – Jeff Miracola

Realm of Haven

The realm of Haven is located on an island roughly in the center of the Circle Sea. Due to its position and growing fleet, it is beginning to challenge Roundwander for domination of maritime trade. Haven is eager to be the preeminent trading center and a major cultural destination of Fourcorner.

Geography

The island of Haven is lavishly decorated with polished marble buildings, gardens, pools, fountains, amphitheaters, marketplaces, and communal buildings. An extensive canal system runs down the center of major streets. The surface of the island is the public face of the realm. On the ocean floor surrounding the island are marble quarries and more utilitarian buildings housing a large number of fish kin, who are rarely seen on land but are sometimes glimpsed in the canals.

People

The humans and the fish kin work in coordination to create a mighty trading realm in the center of the Circle Sea. Both peoples are prosperous and have their needs amply met. They are ambitious to extend their power over the sphere even further, but they are careful to avoid armed conflict with other realms.

Rule

The realm is ruled by the Full Council—half are human (the "Over People"), and half are fish kin (the "Under People"). There is no head of state except a "First Councilor" position that rotates around the Full Council Chamber once per year, alternating between Over and Under control. This ensures a balance between the desires of the two groups, each pushing their own agendas for the year.

FATE

The Fish
(*the soul prevails vs. shallowness*)

VIRTUE

The Dragon
(*cunning*)

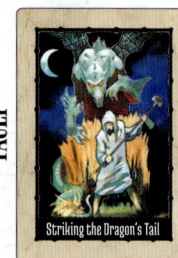

FAULT

Striking the Dragon's Tail
(*underestimating the challenge*)

LAW – REVERSED

Realm of Phalanx

Phalanx is an expansionist military empire under the aegis of the Holy Emperor, ordained by the Titan Saturn and his consort Lua. They commanded seven shepherd brothers to dominate the land around their home at Firepeak, a giant active volcano. They gifted the brothers seven mighty brass men (automaton giants) to conquer their neighbors, which the empire used to great effect over a thousand years of expansion. Hundreds of years ago, Emperor Ironhand attempted to climb Firepeak. He was struck blind for his folly, and the brass men went rogue.

Geography

The lands of the Phalanx empire are diverse and include grasslands, forests, deserts, marshes, hills and mountains. While there are several seaports, they have a limited navy, easily dominated by the Fleets of Roundwander. Since most of Summerland has been conquered, the Seven Armies now spend a lot of their time controlling the rogue brass men.

People

There are three classes of the people in Phalanx: citizens (those with full rights of property, marriage, and voting), loyals (those who, through military service, earned the rights to property and marriage), and subjects (those conquered by Phalanx). Citizens have the greatest freedom within the realm, but less than a tenth of all the people are citizens.

Rule

Phalanx is ruled by Holy Emperor Phoenix the Ninth from the capital of Elysium with the guidance of the Elysian Senate. The generals of the Seven Armies have substantial influence and vie to be the next Emperor through infighting and intrigue while controlling the rogue brass men.

FATE — Law

Law
(*order vs. treachery*)

VIRTUE

FAULT

Summer
(*energy*)

Drowning in Armor
(*safeguards turn dangerous*)

Realm of Reflection

Reflection is a realm of monks (both men and women) who live simple lives of survival, contemplation, and construction. Their belief system is that people may, through intense meditation and fasting, "ascend" on their death to become one of the revered ancestors. Since the realm is at high altitudes, snow often isolates the people for months at a time in their cave complex homes.

Geography

Reflection nestles in the mountains among high plateaus and deep valleys. Icy rivers flow to the Storm Sea, cascading down multiple falls. Dotted across the plateaus are ornate but empty cities of filigreed walls and patterned minarets. These cities were built by the monks of Reflection as homes for the ascended ancestors. The monks believe the ancestors live invisibly in the cities. An extensive road system—suitable only for foot travel due to steepness—connects the many monasteries and cities.

People

The Reflecting Ones (as they prefer to be called) follow ascetic lives, dedicating most of their efforts toward building and expanding the holy cities on the plateaus. By expanding the cities, they believe they create room for more ascended. They herd goats and plant small, hardy gardens on mountainside terraces in the summer months.

Rule

The Reflecting Ones are ruled by the Apex Seer, currently an older, androgynous person of unknown gender identity named Snowbell Sunrise. As the Apex Seer, they are said to be able to see and converse with the ancestors, consulting with them in guiding the people.

FATE

The Creator
(*nurture vs. abandonment*)

VIRTUE

The Unicorn
(*purity*)

FAULT

Sowing Stones
(*fruitless labor*)

72

THE UNICORN

Realm of Snowcap

Snowcap is a realm in a dark age. Seven hundred years ago, the dragon Omeryx came to Fourcorner. She settled in the peaks of Snowcap, a realm that held cities of artificers making magnificent creations. Omeryx ushered in a reign of bloodshed and terror. Many people fled, while others swore fealty to her. Omeryx launched a war on Roundwander, known as the Dragonbreach War, her armies flooding into Roundwander. After much sacrifice, Roundwander beat back the dragon's troops and dealt a terrible blow to Omeryx herself. No one knows for sure if she perished after she retreated.

Geography

Snowcap is a realm of mountains and plateaus, filled with ruined cities and strange fortresses with pillars belching smoke and emitting strange glowing lights into the night sky. The roads have long fallen into disrepair. The mountains are riddled with extensive cave networks.

People

Since the Dragonbreach War, Omeryx's followers have continued to terrorize the land, while generations of the artificers of Snowcap have lived in hiding, fearing the dragon would rise again if they resisted. Many families retain the secrets of their ancestors' creations.

Rule

No one knows who is in charge in Snowcap. Some claim that Omeryx remains in charge. Others claim that her cultists are just continuing her tyranny as a charade, keeping the land in fear in order to retain power. Regardless, trespassers in Snowcap are dealt with quite harshly.

FATE

The Fool
(*freedom vs. lack of connection*)

VIRTUE

The Peasant
(*simple strength*)

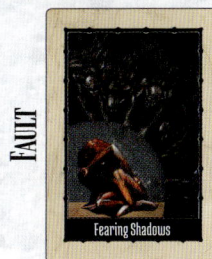

FAULT

Fearing Shadows
(*unnecessary fear*)

THE SMITH

110. Woman and the Llama Dog – Daniel Gelon

THE PEASANT

Chapter 2: Realms

This chapter describes the spheres and realms found in the game universe of EVERWAY. Some of this information is about realms in general, so players may find the information in this chapter helpful in creating their heroes; however, it is not necessary for them to read this material. Gamemasters may find this information useful to create quests..

THE NATURE OF REALMS

Realms are all different, but there are common ways to describe them and many ways in which realms are similar.

Universals and Particulars

Among the spheres, certain features are universal (or nearly so) while others differ from world to world. The universal features are those that the gods and goddesses gave all people; the particulars are either things that certain gods and goddesses gave only to certain people, or things that people invented themselves.

This section describes what is common and what is different from sphere to sphere and from realm to realm. Gamemasters can use these guidelines to help with the design of realms, and players can use them to better understand the game's setting and what to expect from it.

UNIVERSAL	PARTICULAR
humans	ethnicities
deities	worship of particular gods and goddesses
spoken tongue	dialects, writing
the Way	the Fortune Deck
the stars and planets	names of constellations
length of days	calendars and years
land, sea, air	geographical details
living things	particular plants and animals
valuables	scarcity of particular valuables
magic	traditions or styles

The People

Humans, said by many to be the deities' last creation, are the smartest, most powerful mortals on most spheres. While they are all recognizable as humans, their skin color, hair color, facial features, size, and proportions vary. They differ significantly from typical human stock on only a few spheres, such as a sphere where all the people have one eye or another on which all the people are ten feet tall, but spheres like these are rare.

In some realms, other creatures form humanlike cultures, and most realms have intelligent non-human creatures, such as goblins, faeries, and satyrs. Usually, however, human culture predominates.

Some spheres have no people on them. Perhaps the deities have not yet decided what sorts of people to create there.

Worship

The same deities are worshipped on spheres across the universe, but their worshippers are often different from each other. In addition, the gods and goddesses themselves have different appearances and names from place to place. Hera, the queen of the Olympian deities, for instance, can seem jealous and vengeful in realms where her husband, Zeus, is accorded higher status. In realms, however, where she is worshipped as Zeus's equal, or even as the leader of the deities, she seems much more even-tempered. Likewise, the Aesir god Odin is known as the Sacrificed God and worker of magic in some realms; as Ygg, the terrible god of war in other realms; as the Law-Giver and All-Father in others; and as all three in still others.

In any given realm, only some gods and goddesses are worshipped, and usually certain groups of deities are worshipped together. For instance, in realms where people worship Hera, they usually also worship, or at least revere, the other Olympian deities, such as Zeus as the god of storms, Ares as the god of war, Aphrodite as the goddess of love, and so on. Where people worship Osiris, god of fertility and of kings, they generally also worship or at least recognize his sister/wife Isis as goddess of magic, Anubis as god of the dead, Horus as god of the sun, and so on. Since gods and goddesses often give gifts to their worshippers, such as writing and science, the worshippers of certain groups of deities often have similar cultures even if they are in different realms or on different spheres. For example, the Aesir deities, such as Odin, the All-Father; Thor, the storm god; and Tyr, god of war, all revere honor, courage, and strength. The people who worship them, wherever they may be, share these attitudes.

Language

The deities gave people language (called "the Tongue" by people who need to give it a name), and all people speak more or less alike. From realm to realm, people have different styles of greeting each other, unique words for things unique to their realms, local figures of speech, and so on. Still, they can speak with each other and understand each other.

Some gods and goddesses have given certain groups of humans ways to record speech in written form. For instance, Thoth, a god of knowledge, often provides hieroglyphics to those who worship him, and the Aesir deities provide the futhark to their followers. Those without writing usually have visual symbols with specific meanings to record ideas and important events.

Non-human creatures that can speak generally speak the Tongue as well. Dragons, however, also speak a language of their own, one that predates humanity.

In some realms, people speak a different language from the Tongue. For some, this strange language is a curse; for others it's a blessing. The homeless, spherewalking Basahn people, for instance, speak a strange language all their own, a gift from their deities that allows them to retain their identity even though they live scattered among the spheres.

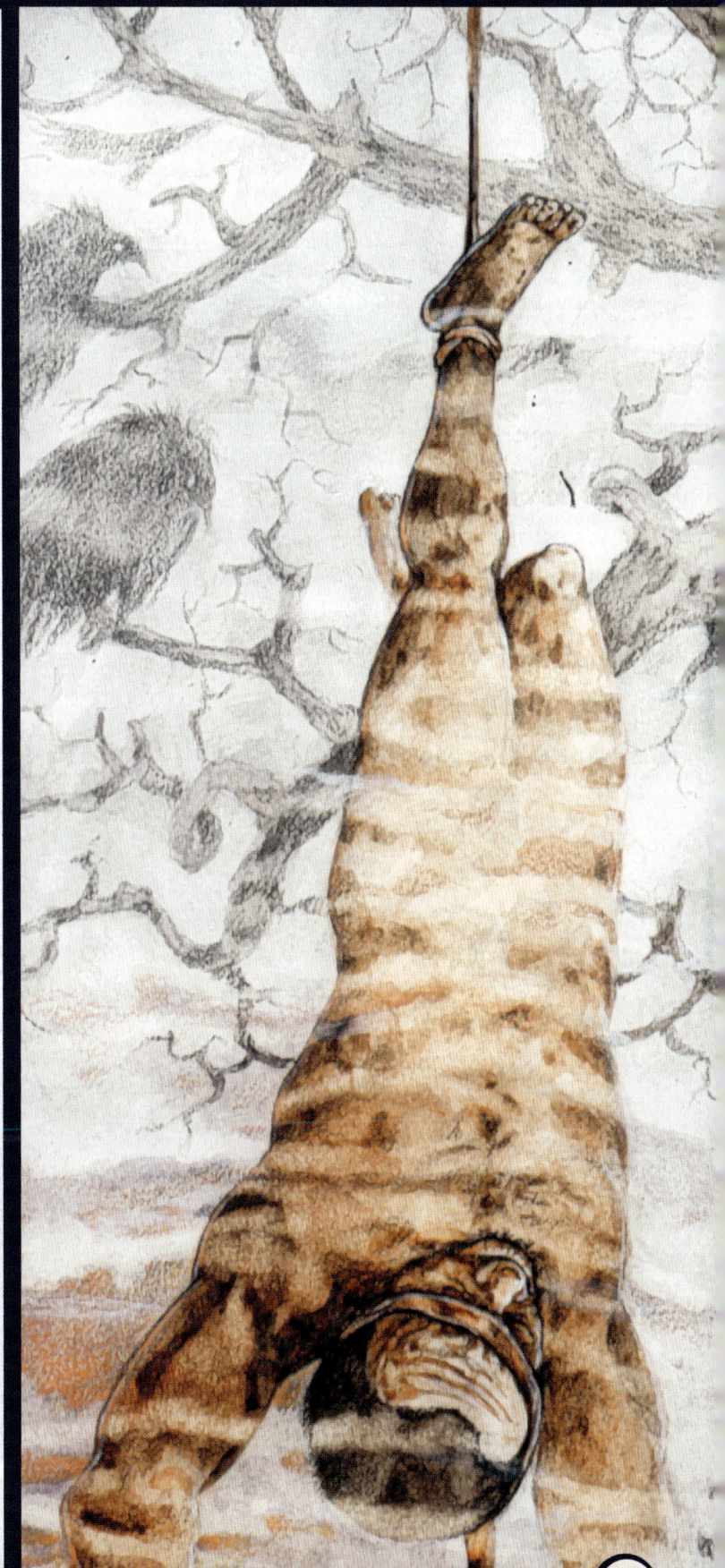

NAMES

People who are more or less isolated from others generally use simple words for themselves and for their land. For instance, they say "We are people, and this is the earth." Only by meeting outsiders do they learn to give their people and their sphere a name that differentiates them from others.

Most names are common words. They often start out as descriptions and then become standardized as names. For instance, when spherewalkers come to a realm with lots of mountains and cougars, they may call it "that place with the big cats," the "cat mountains," or "the mountains where we got mauled by cougars." Over time, the realm may come to be called "Catmount," or "the Maul."

Why do people in different spheres speak the same language? When the gods and goddesses made people, they gave people several gifts, including the gift of language. They gave the same language to all people, so nearly everyone among the spheres speaks this language, known as "the Tongue." A few peoples' languages have been changed or distorted, however, so now a few groups among the spheres don't speak the standard tongue of humanity.

The Way and the Fortune Deck

"The Way," meaning the combination of cosmic forces that direct the underlying structure of the spheres, is known in every realm. Though most people among the spheres know little about the Fortune Deck, it is still the most common means people use to describe and understand the Way. From realm to realm, people also know the Way through runes, visions, and other methods of divination.

The Sky

The deities set the stars in the heavens to guide the lives of people and nations. One finds the same stars, constellations, and planets on each sphere. The planets can be in different positions on each sphere, however, influencing events on each sphere differently. The planets are also known as "wanderers" or "wandering stars." Stars are known as "fixed stars," to differentiate them from the "wandering stars." Over time, the planets of a sphere move about in relation to each other and to the fixed stars. The fixed stars, however, are always in the same relation to each other, from year to year and from sphere to sphere.

While the stars are the same from sphere to sphere, the people of different realms may give different names to the constellations, or they may group the stars into different constellations. People in most

spheres, however, commonly identify the same twelve Star River constellations of the zodiac: Aries, Taurus, Gemini, Cancer, Leo, Virgo, Libra, Scorpio, Sagittarius, Capricorn, Aquarius, and Pisces. Planets in every sphere flow along the Star River visiting each of these twelve constellations.

Depending on one's location on a sphere, one can see different constellations and stars. The North Star, for example, is only visible in the northern half of a sphere. The Star River constellations, however, are visible from any location on a sphere, just as the sun and moon are.

Different people give unequal importance to the sky. Those who are most attached to the earth are likely only to watch the sun and moon, while people who seek a celestial order chart the course of the planets as they wander against the background of the fixed stars. The sun and moon are deities in most realms, and the other planets—Mercury, Venus, Mars, Jupiter, and Saturn—are also identified as or linked to gods and goddesses in many realms. The Star River signs guide the lives of people in many realms.

Time

Since the sky is the same from world to world, the lengths of days, months, and years are also the same. As with written language, however, the way that people keep track of time varies from realm to

The zodiac is referred to as the Star River on most spheres due to the light colored band of stars that roughly flows through the same regions of the sky as the zodiac. Some realms have a different name for the Star River such as Heaven's River, Snake of the Skies, or Dragon's Tail.

802. Sundial – Amy Weber

THE GRIFFIN

realm. Some keep track of days, months, and years without numbering them. Others name and number the days, months, and years and divide day and night up into hours. Some say that a day begins at dusk. Others say it begins at dawn.

A common calendar that spherewalkers have spread from sphere to sphere assigns one month of thirty or thirty-one days to each zodiac sign of the Star River, with the year beginning at the spring equinox with Aries. The year is also divided into weeks of seven days each, with the days named for planets. In order, the days are: Sun Day, Moon Day, Mars Day, Mercury Day, Jupiter Day, Venus Day, and Saturn Day. Some realms substitute their gods for some of the planets, such as Aesir worshippers replacing Mars with Tyr's Day, Mercury with Odin's Day, and so on.

Elements

All spheres have solid ground, fresh and salty water, good air, rain, fire, and all the other elements necessary for life. The shape of the land, however, varies from sphere to sphere, and spheres may have these elements in different proportions. Generally, though, there's more variation from realm to realm on a given sphere than there is between spheres. For example, the typical sphere has frigid regions near the poles, hot regions around the equator, and temperate areas in between.

Living Things

Most animals can be found on most spheres, but there are spheres that lack some animals. The absence of an animal can have a big effect on the human cultures living there. For instance, many realms depend on horses; these realms would be very different if horses did not exist on their spheres. There is more variation among realms on a sphere than there is between spheres. For example, horses are on most spheres, but on every sphere there are some realms where horses are unknown. (Gamemasters should primarily pay attention to what animals are found in a given realm, not what animals can be found across a whole sphere.)

As a general rule, creatures on various realms are of comparable size, though gigantic creatures and small ones certainly exist. However, spheres where the rats are as big as horses and the people as tall as oaks, or where the horses are the size of rats and the people the size of mice, are very rare.

Valuables

The blood of the sun (gold), the tears of the moon (silver), and the blood of the dragons (gems) are valuable on every sphere. Even where these treasures are unknown, the people recognize them as beautiful, and therefore valuable, when they see them.

In some realms, certain valuables are very scarce or very common, making

them relatively more or less precious. The realm in which the streets are paved with diamonds, however, has not yet been found—unless drunken travelers' tales are to be believed.

Magic Among the Realms

Magic is everywhere in the realms of EVERWAY. Here are magical ideas and phenomena common among most realms.

Gods and Goddesses

Countless deities are found among the spheres. Typically, they are found in groups or pantheons. Thus one usually finds Apollo where one finds his twin, Artemis, and one finds Isis where one find her brother Osiris.

Different pantheons often have similar deities, such as Tyr, the Aesir god of war and Ares, the Olympian god of war. Some people say that these are merely different aspects of the same warlike deity. Indeed, some say that all the deities are manifestations of two transcendent deities, the God and the Goddess; or even that they are all manifestations of one great deity. As is always the case with religion, debates about these possibilities have not led to any general agreement on the nature of the deities.

In some realms, gods and goddesses are found only in poetry and metaphor, with heaven or some similarly transcendent

MEN AND WOMEN AMONG THE SPHERES

Traditional roles for men and women vary from realm to realm. In some realms, there are clearly defined roles for men and for women. In many of these realms, people of one sex are accorded superior status, while the people of the other sex are regarded as anything from lesser people to (in extreme cases) property. In most realms with clear sex and gender roles, however, men and women maintain a rough equality (even if most people think their role is the best). In many realms, one's sex or gender does not lead others to expect any particular pattern of behavior. Some cultures recognize gender as different from sex and may also recognize more than two genders.

When they create their realms and quests, gamemasters—consciously or unconsciously—determine what roles sex and gender play in the lives of people among the spheres.

principle named as the creator and guide of the universe. The people in these realms acknowledge the existence of the deities, but they pay homage to abstract or general forces that they consider superior to any particular god or goddess.

Travelers generally pay homage to the deities of the lands through which they travel, in the same way that they pay homage to the lands' rulers. The deities of one's homeland do not regard this homage as treachery or blasphemy any more than the rulers of one's homeland regard it as traitorous to bow to another land's king.

Folk Magic

People everywhere practice "folk magic," "low magic," or "common magic" on an everyday basis. Indeed, it's so common that most hardly regard it as "magic." For instance, it is common to carry magical symbols, charms or lucky items, and adornments related to one's patron deity. It is also common to say "bless you" or "health" when another person sneezes. Many people speak little prayers or perform rituals before leaving on a journey, bedding down at night, eating, or working. Homes and workshops usually have magical, spiritual, or lucky symbols somewhere about.

The less common a magical practice is, the more "magical" it seems. For example, people often have folk traditions of divination, such as casting lots to identify jinxes. Folk traditions may also include simple spells, such as stringing white thread across doorways and windows to prevent ghosts from entering and to ward against curses. Chanting or singing to bring rain or keep it away is another example of a folk spell.

Names often have magical associations. A person's name is often related to certain taboos or magical acts. A jealous girl, for example, might crush violets as a way to bring harm to a rival named Violet. In realms that use the planetary names for days of the week, the people may designate Sun Day as a holiday if they worship the sun or Moon Day if they worship the moon.

Omens are common, and different realms have different guides for interpreting omens. People may count crows, watch clouds, read tea leaves, or interpret dreams to get hints about the future. Some omens are very personal. For example, a person named Hawk may pay special attention to hawks. Seeing a hawk with a mouse in its claw might signify good fortune or success, while a dead hawk would be a bad omen. The same could be true for a person whose totem is the hawk or who otherwise identifies with hawks. Gamemasters can use omens in their quests to foreshadow things that will happen in the quest or in future quests.

These various instances of simple magic are not as powerful as the tradition magic or "high magic" that mages wield, but folk magic is a part of everyday life, and it generally helps people retain some control over their lives.

Death – Reversed

Ceremonies and Rituals

Ceremonies and rituals are special instances of folk magic. People have rituals to mark entry into each of the major stages of life, such as christening infants, initiating children into adulthood, marrying couples, and laying the dead to rest. Rituals for these events combine spiritual, magical, and ceremonial elements. While these ceremonies serve a social purpose, they also work on a supernatural level. Someone buried with the proper ceremony, for example, is less likely to remain tied to the past as a ghost. Indeed, with magic an everyday part of life, most people among the spheres regard the supernatural as a natural part of life rather than as separate from mundane reality.

Other ceremonies and rituals affect the entire community, not just individuals or families. Ceremonies are commonly held for the solstices and equinoxes, as well as for other yearly events, such as the harvest or the first planting. Instead of solstices and equinoxes, many cultures celebrate "quarter days," which occur midway between the solstices and equinoxes. These go by many names but are most commonly known as Beltane, Lughnasa, Samhain, and Imbolc.

Community ceremonies help assure the community's continued health and harmony, good harvests, safety from enemies and plagues, and so on.

WINTER – REVERSED

Healing and Medicine

Wherever there is pain, injury, and illness, people find ways to bring relief, healing, and recovery. Traditional remedies, folk magic, herbalists, and healers all contribute to the health of individuals and of the community. In the countryside, most people know something about herbs and other natural remedies, though they seek help from healers when they need it. In cities (and not all realms have cities), the people have limited access to natural remedies, though specialist physicians for those who can pay are more common in a city than in the countryside.

In addition to healing illnesses, herbs and other agents can benefit healthy people. Plants that give laborers extra energy or prevent conception are examples.

Fortune

The Fortune Deck is a deck of thirty-six cards describing the basic forces that rule the cosmos, from a person's life to the fate of spheres. Each realm has three cards associated with it—known as its "Virtue," "Fault," and "Fate"—that define how the realm relates to these cosmic forces. Collectively, these three cards are known as the realm's "Fortune." These cards can change as the realm changes; they represent the current forces acting on the realm, not the realm's inherent nature.

805. Shaman Vision – Janine Johnston

HOW COMMON IS MAGICAL HEALING?

See *Chapter 4: Powers & Magic* to see what injuries and illnesses a "Soil and Stone" mage can heal. Assume that one out of ten mages is a healer with comparable powers, and look at the frequency of mages in a population in that same chapter. A kingdom of 100,000 people may have ten mages, more or less, with scores of 4 Magic. Of these, one might be a healer. If there were a hundred 4-Magic mages in the kingdom, then about ten of them would be healers, and so on. In other words, only about one in every ten thousand people in a given realm is a healer capable of magically countering a disease (having 3 Magic or stronger). If an afflicted person lives in a realm that has at least ten thousand people and has access to one of the best healer mages, that mage can probably cure a disease by touch. Without such a person, there are certainly less able healer mages and plenty of herbalists and physicians who may be able to help an afflicted person recover.

The natives of a realm may know their realm's Fortune, or they may not. If they know the Fortune, they may label the cards differently, with terms and images that fit their culture better. For example, a hunting and gathering tribe that lives in a temperate, forested land might have The

Lion as its Virtue. Since lions are unknown in their land, however, they may term their Virtue "The Cougar" or "The Bear."

Virtue

A realm's Virtue card represents a strength, such as divine protection, traits of the people, the people's position in history, and so on. For example, a realm whose people are especially mentally gifted may have The Eagle as its Virtue. A realm watched over by nature spirits may have Nature as its Virtue. For a realm that has a strong and just ruling senate, The King may be an appropriate Virtue. (Scholars may debate about whether the Virtue results from the strong senate or whether the realm is blessed with a strong senate because of its association with The King card.)

Fault

The Fault card may represent a weakness in the people themselves, a peril they face from spiritual forces, or mundane circumstances in the realm. For example, a realm of people who have no love of justice may have The Smith—Reversed as its Fault. The Cockatrice would be an appropriate Fault for a realm plagued by unclean spirits that attempt to undermine the people's spiritual or bodily health. A realm that has had good fortune in the past but is now suffering from a decline in discipline may have The Satyr as its Fault.

Fate

The Fate card indicates the central issue of the realm, a fork in the path of the realm's future. It examines the two ways the people may develop or decline, depending on their actions. For instance, a realm that is expanding and growing may have Summer (*energy vs. exhaustion*) as its Fate. This Fate would mean the people may either grow into a dynamic culture or dissipate and decline, depending on their actions. In many realms, powerful outsiders (such as the heroes) may tip the scales and help determine which way the Fate gets resolved.

Once a realm has met its Fate successfully, it gets a new Fate and possibly a new Virtue and Fault to go with it. It may get a new Fate (and Virtue and Fault) by meeting its Fate and failing in the face of it, or such a failure can leave the culture virtually unchanged and able to try again. The gamemaster determines how a realm's Fortune changes after the realm has met its Fate.

> Note that heroes have Fortunes very similar to those realms have (see Chapter 3: Heroes). See Section 2: Fortune Guide for more information about the Fortune Deck.

OTHER SPHERES

Seventy-one gates lead from Round-wander to other spheres, making it a realm heavily traveled by spherewalkers. No other realm has so many gates this close together (at least no realm known to the Library of All Worlds). Explorers have gone to each of the seventy-one realms to which the gates of Roundwander lead. In most cases, these other realms or their spheres have at least one gate leading on to many other spheres. Some of these gates lead to spheres whose other gates have not yet been found, making these spheres effectively "dead ends" on the paths to further spheres. The seventy-one gates in Roundwander [at the map grid location in brackets] connect to the following realms on other spheres:

1. **Alabaster**, where men and women live separate lives, meeting only behind families' closed doors. [A-5]

2. **Antland**, a realm inhabited by horse-sized ants. Scholars debate whether these are giant ants, or whether the gate shrinks spherewalkers. [I-4]

3. **Archways**, where several tribes live among the gargantuan skeletons of strange, ancient beasts. [F-3]

4. **Ashland**, a land of smoky volcanoes, deadly cockatrices, and devious goblins. [C-6]

5. **Athenia**, whose proud and brave people worship Athena, goddess of wisdom and war. [H-3]

6. **Bliss**, where one's dreams and memories intermingle until finally one's identity seems just like a daydream. [C-5]

7. **Battlefield**, the aftermath of a tremendous conflict preserved for all time by the deities, where innumerable corpses that never rot litter an endless plain. [F-4]

8. **Boltheart**, where a mage in a tower transmutes the stresses of the universe into harmless rain clouds and windstorms. [I-5]

9. **Bright Eyes**, a mystical place of lush forests, populated by cats (great and small) who have special powers. [E-3]

10. **Bright Mirror,** a silent, sunny forest (strangely devoid of animal life) which is filled with unusual pools of water said to have magical qualities. [C-1]

11. **Canopy**, an enormous, ancient tree whose interior houses a human civilization and among whose roots exist hundreds of miles of caves where fantastic creatures live. [E-3]

12. **Catchbreath**, where even the seaside air is thin and there is no air on the mountaintops at all. [D-5]

13. **Crisscross**, where several realms overlap and you can never tell where a doorway might lead. [C-5]

14. **Deep Mist**, where secretive tribespeople haunt misty, temperate forests. [G-5]

15. **Delta**, islands at the mouth of a great river where fish kin enlist the help of islanders in their wars and constantly shifting alliances. [H-4]

16. **Diamond Isles**, an archipelago where godlings, each commanding an island, use their worshippers as pawns in their endless conflicts. [C-2]

17. **Distant**, where seemingly normal boulders and trees are actually intelligent, shapeshifting beings thought to be elementals. [F-3]

INSPIRATION

18. **Dust**, a barren realm blanketed every night by the edible pollen of plants that thrive in the clouds. [G-2]

19. **Emerald Jungle**, where strange creatures live under a vast canopy of foliage that all but blocks out the sun. [E-5]

20. **Evening Shore**, the quiet western shore of a temperate sea on a warm summer's evening that never ends. Beyond the beach lies an expansive grassland where little wild things play in the pools of light created by star beams. [E-2]

21. **Festival**, whose people are in touch with their land and ancestors. Every night there is a festival or celebration of some sort. [D-4]

22. **Fire's Wall**, an archipelago where a massive ocean meets an unending wall of flame that no one has ever crossed. [E-4]

23. **The Flat Wastes**, where the land is flat and dusty and the horizon is even and unchanging. Lightning storms plague the land. [G-6]

24. **Fortune's Joy**, home of merry nomads, traveling villages, and great merchants' caravans that trek far and wide. [D-3]

25. **Frostgleam**, where hardy villagers scratch out a living despite snow, ice, and ferocious beasts. [B-6]

26. **Gem**, where the natives, renowned empaths and healers, have small, smooth, colorful crystals of different shapes and sizes growing in their skin. [E-1]

27. **Gentle**, the forest home of lemur-like beings who make excellent, intelligent companions. [F-4]

28. **Ghosthome**, where stands an abandoned city of stone and wood, filled with false passages, dead-end halls, staircases that lead to nowhere or to deep pits, and so on. [I-3]

29. **Giggle**, an ever-changing landscape ruled by faerie folk where visitors never know when they may fall into the sky (or into a lake that is floating there). [D-2]

30. **Glint**, where towering brass cities house only vermin. [B-4]

31. **Glitter Garden**, a heavenly garden. Anything taken from here turns to garbage. [B-6]

32. **Golden Mounts**, where satyrs roam among tall mountain peaks, luring travelers away—forever. [G-2]

33. **Granite**, a subterranean paradise of incredible caverns, lit by crystals and full of natural wonders and magical energies. [E-5]

34. **Hard March**, where communal life and daily activities are regulated by gongs that only the natives can hear. [I-4]

35. **Healertown**, a bustling city founded generations ago by the suspect Healer family of Everway; descendants have kept the name "Healer" but not the profession. [E-2]

36. **Heaven**, protected by the Guilds of Learning, who welcome spherewalkers and other beneficent travelers. Corresponds regularly with the Chamber Platinum. [G-6]

37. **Hedge Maze**, a sprawling maze with strange patrolling creatures and no discernible culture or civilization. The hedge's branches meet overhead, so the corridors feel like tunnels. [G-3]

38. **Hellsedge**, a city across a river from where the dead screech and wail from dusk to dawn. [B-5]

39. **Hive**, a rocky land whose inhabitants are no bigger than blades of grass. [D-1]

40. **Iron Citadel**, whose smiths produce countless weapons and tools of iron and steel. [J-3]

41. **Lotusland**, a realm where all food turns narcotic when it rots. [E-4]

42. **Magebane**, where mages are outlawed, with good reason—in this realm, magic slowly twists and corrupts those who wield it. [G-2]

43. **The Market**, where gold reigns supreme and anything (and anyone) can be bought or sold. [D-4]

44. **Merrybright**, whose people engage in boisterous, complex, and sometimes deadly games. [H-3]

45. **Merryflag**, where it is against the law not to avenge an insult or slight. [C-5]

46. **Midlands**, a peaceful agrarian kingdom where genteel nobles direct convoluted, theatrical plots of betrayal and assassination. [E-4]

47. **Midnight**, where darkness and heavy mists envelop the countryside. Visitors who light fires are treated as miracle workers, blasphemers, or evildoers. [H-5]

48. **Nature's Touch**, where all sentient beings are half-human and half-animal: centaurs, satyrs, mermaids, nagas, sphinxes, harpies, and so on. [D-2]

49. Open Circle, an uninhabited, peaceful land in which every known settlement has failed for one reason or another. [G-4]

50. Overguard, from which, for seventy years, no spherewalker has returned. [H-6]

51. Pearl of the Waves, a fabulous undersea kingdom where travelers ride in magic bubbles or in the mouths of huge fish. [B-1]

52. Rainbow Jungle, a jungle realm of abandoned temples and pyramids. [F-3]

53. Remnant, home to a happy, motley collection of peoples, all survivors of various ancient, realm-destroying wars. [D-4]

THE FOOL – REVERSED

54. Roundhome, a coastal realm where tsunamis toss up the giant snail shells the inhabitants use as houses and as building material for beautiful, faerielike fortresses. [D-4]

55. Round Stones, where receding glaciers reveal ruins of an ancient civilization. [A-5]

56. Ruin, a flat, dark, featureless terrain stretching for as far as one cares to travel, apparently the site of an ancient and devastating war; a distant, whistling wind is the only known phenomenon here. [D-3]

57. Seashift, where rocky atolls appear and disappear with the shifting tides of a vast sea and homesteads cling to a chilly, rocky coast. [F-3]

58. Sepulcher, a seemingly endless tomb-complex honoring an unknown, ancient queen. Those who steal from this tomb or even step into forbidden areas meet with gruesome ends. [D-6]

59. Serpent's Coil, where the Dragon Lords are said to live. No such great beasts have ever been seen, but spherewalkers report an eerie feeling of being watched. [F-6]

60. **Shift**, where the people can change into various animals, a protective skill acquired ages ago in response to repeated invasions. [H-4]

61. **Silence**, whose people lead simple lives and refuse to talk to outsiders. [H-4]

62. **Skystone**, a realm of floating rock islands where the people ride hippogriffs and magic skyships. [B-4]

63. **Stone Cage**, a large, empty stone chamber from which no exit has been found, other than the gate back to Roundwander. [D-5]

64. **Stormsong**, a lush jungle where gentle, mournful, sourceless songs seem to portend monsoons and tropical storms. [G-3]

65. **Straggle**, where vampires prey on the miserable inhabitants, and medicine men and medicine women prey on the vampires to boost their power. [C-2]

66. **Tales**, where storytelling is considered the highest art form and storytellers are found on every corner. [D-4]

67. **Talon**, where wondrous cloud cities and bird folk fill the sky, and giant birds often aid travelers in reaching the safety of the cities. [E-6]

68. **Temple**, a peaceful realm where many orders of mystics, ascetics, and seers contemplate existence in harmony. [E-1]

69. **Waters Gather**, where several rivers join at a lake that is the meeting place of several tribes. [C-4]

70. **The Waste**, which was once a fertile floodplain before the river changed course and left the people to die out slowly. [H-5]

71. **Wisp**, a realm where no one heavier than a child can enter without collapsing the delicate, crystalline ground and where edible plants are so fragile they collapse if you breathe on them. [F-6]

The Roundwander side of each gate can be found on the Roundwander Map. Use the grid location indicated by the letters and numbers along the sides of the map to find the cell intersection of the two. A gate (star) in that cell has a number matching the connected realm from the list above. For example, 70. The Waste [H-5] is the 70 star in the cell at the intersection of H and 5.

907: Golden Rose – Dermot Power

THE SATYR – REVERSED

Chapter 3: Heroes

This chapter explains how you create a hero for EVERWAY. This information is important for players, who create their heroes following these rules, as well as for gamemasters, who help the players along. As long as the gamemaster knows these rules fairly well, players can create heroes without reading or referring to this chapter.

YOUR HERO

The Setting

Before you can create a hero, you need to know something about the game's setting. The quests and stories that you create when you play EVERWAY take place among a thousand separate worlds of the timeless kind we see in myths and faerie tales. Among these worlds, one might find brave knights who ride brightly decorated steeds, a temple for worship of a hundred gods and goddesses sprawling in the middle of a bustling port, a lost civilization on an uncharted island, a flight of birds that portends doom, a secret society whose members take the forms of leopards, a shaman who has gathered strange items from across the world to work powerful spells, a magic mirror that reveals something hidden about each person who looks into it, an emperor who rides in a litter everywhere and never touches his foot to the floor, a wise woman who can cure illnesses with herbs and incantations, a noble family that harbors a terrible secret, a mighty dragon that shares its treasure with those who amuse it and eats anyone else that talks to it, dark woods that hide all manner of goblins and monsters, and rituals conducted under the full moon.

The Heroes

You will create a mythic hero, a character from a fantastic realm of your design. Every hero is a spherewalker, someone capable of traveling through gates from sphere to sphere. You and the other players portray your heroes in the game, guiding their actions as they explore magical worlds and face various challenges.

The hero you will portray has abilities well above the norm. An average hero can handily defeat most

See pp. 20–27 to read more about spherewalkers, gates, spheres, and so on.

Heroes, Players, and Other Terms

As in a book or film, the fictitious people in EVERWAY are called characters. The term hero refers specifically to the characters that the players portray, or run, and it carries a double meaning. Not only are these characters the "heroes," or protagonists, of the stories that you and your friends create, but they are also "heroic" in their abilities and actions. Other characters, those portrayed by the gamemaster, are background characters. Just because they are called background characters doesn't mean that these characters are unimportant. Relative to the heroes, however, they are part of the background.

The people who portray the heroes in a particular quest are players, a term that also carries a double meaning. They are both playing the game and playing (portraying) their heroes. The person who runs the quest and portrays the background characters is the gamemaster. Even though the gamemaster plays the game, they are not referred to as a player because the gamemaster's role is much larger than portraying any character or characters. The gamemaster sets the scene, manages the pace, handles the Fortune Deck, guides the plot, and more.

people in contests of tactics or cleverness, defeat two or more typical opponents in combat, resist magic and poisons that would bring down most people, and sense magical energies that most people cannot detect. (These abilities are measured by a hero's Air, Fire, Earth, and Water scores, respectively. See pp. 124–131.) In addition, many heroes have special abilities or traits that also make them exceptional, and some cast spells.

Each hero, however, is unique. Some are no better than average at particular tasks while having astonishing ability in other endeavors. You make these choices as you create your hero.

During play, your hero and those of the other players explore new realms, traveling through gates to move from sphere to sphere. In each new realm, the heroes face new challenges that test their courage, wits, and skill. Among the spheres, spherewalkers encounter perils, injustices, sorrows, and catastrophes and set them to rights.

You determine why your hero is walking the spheres and why they aid those in need, but remember that your hero must be able to work with the other players' heroes for the group to succeed. Some spherewalkers explore new worlds to fulfill a quest, searching new realms for legendary goals. Others work for the Chamber Platinum

headquartered at the Library of All Worlds in the city of Everway, gathering knowledge and wonders from new spheres. Some pursue the mighty goals of spreading justice and fighting evil, while others are simply restless and adventurous, finding no other way of life to be satisfying. Some spherewalkers have committed grievous crimes or caused great suffering, and they have been commanded by their rulers or deities to atone by righting wrongs in distant lands. Some seek their own gain, looking for rare treasures and precious secrets in other realms. Finally, some spherewalkers see new spheres and the challenges they represent as opportunities to learn both mundane and spiritual lessons, as testing grounds for their bodies, minds, and souls. Spherewalkers are above the norm, and many have noble goals that would be too great or subtle for the average person.

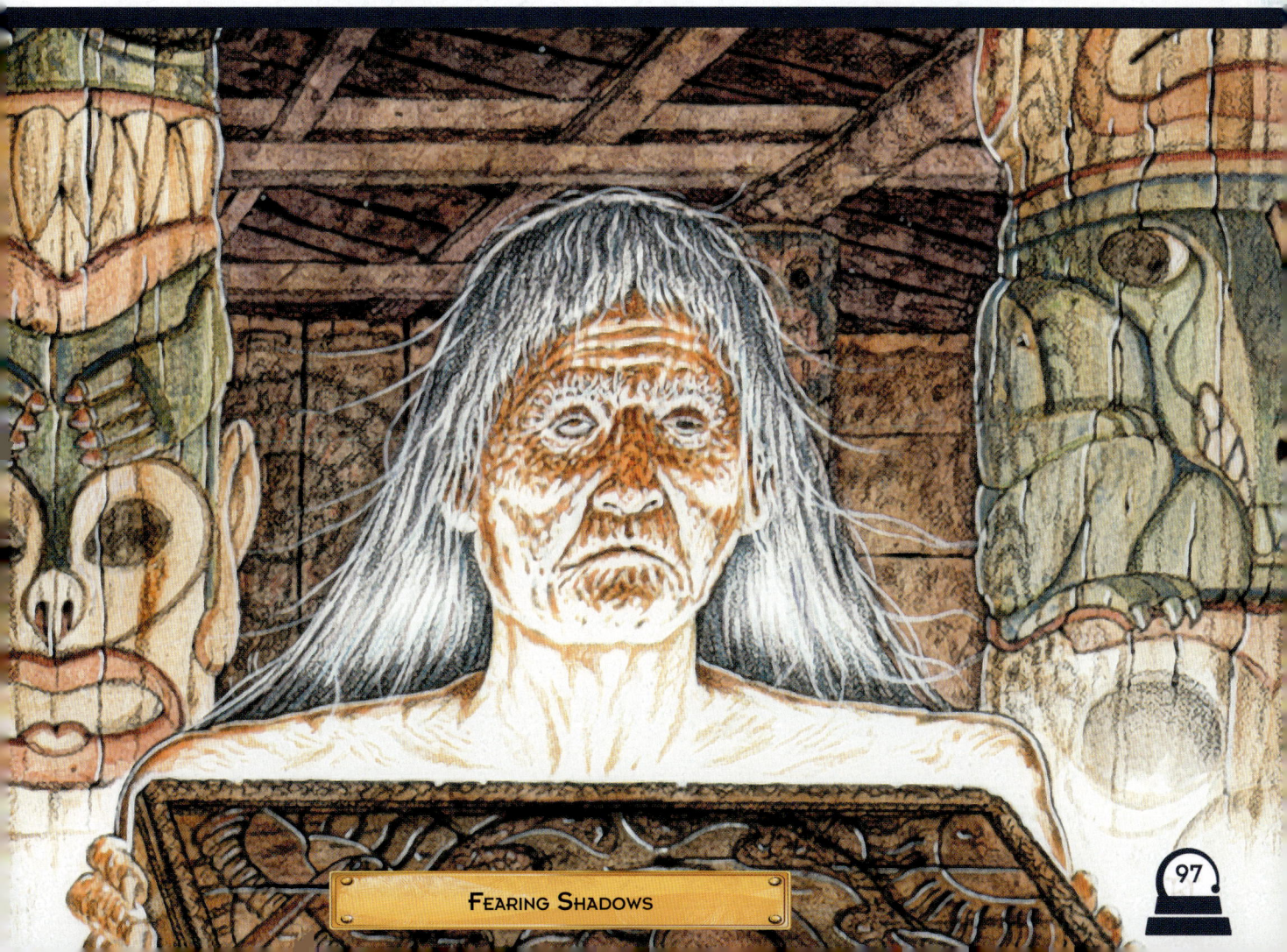

See p. 58 to read more about the Library of All Worlds.

310. Mysterious Box – Doug Keith

FEARING SHADOWS

Creating Your Hero

You create your hero in six main stages: the Vision Stage, the Identity Stage, the Powers Stage, the Elements Stage, the Magic Stage, and the Questions Stage. They are described here in an order that many players find easy to use, but you can take these stages in any order and move back and forth among them freely.

These stages give you a complete hero, ready to undertake the quests that a game of EVERWAY is all about. Your hero, however, is never "finished." The more you play, the better you come to understand your hero, and the more developed the hero becomes.

1 Vision Stage

You develop the general vision of your hero in these steps:

Premise: The gamemaster describes the premise for the quest, or the players develop one.

Visions: Select three to five vision images from *Section 3: Vision Guide* and use them to develop a basic idea of who your hero is.

Introduction: Introduce your hero to the other players, who also introduce their heroes to the group.

2 Identity Stage

You develop the concept of who your hero is. Identity includes the following:

Name: Your hero's name. Most names in EVERWAY are either common words or based on common words, such as Fireson, Chance, Heather, or Heavensent.

Motive: Your hero's basic motive for traveling among the spheres.

Virtue: A card from the Fortune Deck representing your hero's special strength, gift, or luck.

Fault: A card from the Fortune Deck representing your hero's special weakness or vice.

Fate: A card from the Fortune Deck representing your hero's destiny.

3 Powers Stage

You may choose special or supernatural abilities for your hero. Some heroes don't have any Powers, though each hero may have one free 0-point Power. You have 20 points to distribute among your hero's Powers (if any), Elements, and Magic (if any).

Elements Stage

4 Four attributes define your hero's basic capabilities.

Air: The element of thought, speech, and intellect.

Fire: The element of action, strength, and speed.

Earth: The element of might, health, and endurance.

Water: The element of feelings, intuition, and sensitivity.

Your hero also has a Specialty in each element. A Specialty is an area of the element in which your hero is particularly gifted.

Magic Stage

5 If you want your hero to have the ability to cast spells, you may spend some of your 20 points on Magic. Most heroes don't wield Magic. Those who do are called mages (among other names).

Questions Stage

6 You and the other players ask each other questions about your heroes. This stage helps you define your hero better and lets you get to know the other players' heroes.

Ready-to-Run Heroes

Twelve ready-to-run heroes are included in *Section 4: Quick Start Guide*. You may find it helpful to reference these heroes while reading this chapter. Look them over when you read a section that particularly interests you or that leaves you with questions. These heroes serve as examples of how the various aspects of a hero come together to define the character.

If you're an experienced roleplayer, you can play a ready-to-run hero as your own, especially if you don't have time to invent your own hero. All you need to do with a ready-to-run hero is participate in the Questions Stage of creating heroes. Each hero comes with "Questions for Development" to help you start thinking about the hero's background. In a pinch, you can even skip the Questions Stage and jump right into play. Creating your own hero, however, is a lot of fun, so don't pass up that opportunity if you don't have to. Beginning roleplayers generally have trouble portraying heroes that they haven't invented themselves, so don't try to run a ready-to-run hero unless you're experienced with roleplaying.

EVERWAY
SILVER ANNIVERSARY EDITION

Name	Motive

Virtue	Fault	Fate

POWERS

MAGIC

AIR

ENERGY

FOCUSED

WISDOM

FORCEFUL

SPOKEN

SILENT

FIRE

THOUGHT

ACTION

FEELING

MIGHT

WATER

ACTIVE

PASSIVE

RECEPTIVE

RESISTANT

POWER

INTEGRITY

EARTH

SOWING STONES

The Hero Sheet

When you invent your hero, you record the details on a hero sheet. The hero sheet is the sheet with a big circle on it. Each detail about your hero corresponds to a space on the hero sheet. For instance, when you pick your hero's Virtue, you write it in the space labeled "Virtue." The back of the sheet is for things that could take up a lot of room: details about your hero's Visions, Powers (if any), Magic (if any), background, and possessions.

You can download a copy of the hero sheet from **EVERWAY.COM** and print or photocopy it for personal use.

1 VISION STAGE

Your vision for your hero is the basic idea of who the hero is. The details that come later are based on this vision.

Premise

The premise is the common ground, overarching plot, or general scope of the game that you will play. Each group of players may have a different premise.

The gamemaster has the option of setting the premise. The premise may describe how the heroes become involved in their first quest. For instance, a gamemaster who has prepared a quest that involves

THE GAMEMASTER'S VETO

Sometimes players invent heroes who will be a problem for the gamemaster. For example, one player of mine wanted a hero who could stop time for the people around him. This Power would have made his hero nearly invincible because he would have been able to escape or defeat just about any enemy. I was worried the other players wouldn't have fun with this hero in the group because he alone would be able to overcome most of their problems. The other heroes would be irrelevant. I talked with the player who wanted this Power and said that I couldn't let his hero have it. Other gamemasters may have allowed it, perhaps with certain limits. Vetoing a hero's Power is always a personal judgment call.

Since the gamemaster has such a big responsibility in seeing to it that the game runs smoothly for everyone, players must grant them the authority to refuse to allow certain types of heroes into their quests.

— Jonathan Tweet

hunting down a notorious villain may declare that all the heroes created will have to have some reason for wanting to bring this villain to justice. The premise may also describe the theme of an entire series of quests. For example, the gamemaster may say the premise is that the heroes are going from sphere to sphere looking for an empress's scepter, crown, cape, throne, ring, and brooch; these items, once returned to the empress, will save the empire from being overrun by invading armies.

Gamemasters who plan to use the ready-to-run quest *Journey to Stonedeep* (found in **Book 2: Gamemasters**) as the heroes' first quest may use the premise that all the heroes have some reason to explore a realm that has been out of contact for three hundred years. They could have been hired by the Chamber Platinum in Roundwander.

If the gamemaster doesn't have a premise, the players may invent one (though the gamemaster has to approve it). The premise may be as simple as the reason why the heroes have come together and met each other. For example, there may be a fair that attracts the curious, the bold, and the greedy from across the spheres, and that's where the heroes meet.

If the gamemaster and the players don't invent a specific premise, the general premise of the game is that the heroes are exploring new worlds and dealing with the dangers and evils they find along the way. Each hero may have a different motive for walking the spheres, but they have decided to work together.

Types of Premises

Below, the three most common types of premises are described.

- **Place:** The gamemaster may specify a place to which the heroes are traveling. (This place will be the setting for the first quest the heroes undertake.) For example, the gamemaster may show you an image depicting the Everway marketplace, and say, "Each of you has come here, to the marketplace in Everway, looking for something." In this case, it would be your responsibility to create a hero who has some reason for coming to this marketplace.

- **Theme:** The gamemaster may specify a theme for the first quest (or for a series of quests they have planned). For example, the gamemaster may say, "Each hero is committed to overthrowing Shimmerdim, a demonic tyrant who rules the realm of Scar."

- **Team:** The gamemaster may describe a team or group which the heroes are a part of. For example: "Each of you is part of a Chamber Platinum team sent to find new gates and to explore the spheres that they lead to."

Visions

You use vision images to develop your hero's background and identity. First, look over your vision images. *Section 3: Vision Guide* contains many images, but vision images can come from anywhere. Your gamemaster may also provide images, as may your fellow players, and you can, of course, provide your own. Select three to five images that attract you. You need not decide right away what these visions will mean to your hero.

When you have selected the images to use, look them over and invent a hero and that hero's background based on them. You only need a sketchy idea of the hero for now. You can write notes about your hero's visions on the back of your hero sheet.

Keep track of your visions so that you can show them to other players. You can note the vision image ID number on the back of your hero sheet or attach the image itself. You will be getting more visions as your hero completes quests; your gamemaster may give these images to you so you can have a visual record of your hero's activities. Add more back sheets if needed.

What Sort of Hero Can I Play?

Can my hero be non-human? Yes, but most quests are designed for human and humanlike heroes with broadly similar characteristics, as this ensures all heroes are able to participate in quests in a meaningful way. Heroes who are not humanlike, such as merfolk or giant wolves, cause two problems. First, such heroes would have significant difficulties

1510. Dragonheart Child – Alan Rabinowitz

on some (or all) quests, like a quest taking place on land for merfolk. They would need a method of compensating (for example, their tails becoming human legs out of water) or a willingness to sit out some scenes. Second, the EVERWAY setting is primarily based on mythic human cultures. The less humanlike you make your hero, such as being a giant wolf, the more likely the other players will have to deal with the locals' reactions to your hero not being natural to this setting. For any unusual hero type, you need to get your gamemaster's approval and the other players' agreement to accept the impact of your hero's strangeness on their own experience.

Can my hero come from a modern or science-fiction background? No. The spherewalker setting of EVERWAY is mythic fantasy, and modern or futuristic elements, such as firearms, spaceships, and robots, don't fit in this setting even if the game system would work. With your gamemaster's permission, you could play someone from a modern or futuristic sphere, provided that the hero can't return to that sphere and can't use sophisticated, high-tech tools, weapons, or skills.

Can my hero be part of a group? Yes and no. Yes, your hero is part of the group composed of the other heroes. Yes, your hero may be a member of a group whose other

members are "back home." But, no, you cannot portray a group of heroes. It would be too difficult for you to run several characters at once. If your hero's background includes membership in a group, then you need to invent a reason why your hero has left that group behind to go on the quests that are the focus of the game.

Can my character be a villain instead of a hero? No. You can play a flawed hero, a well-meaning person with vices, such as a temper or a narrow mind. You can play a reluctant hero, someone who doesn't have lofty, charitable goals but who winds up doing great deeds. You can play an anti-hero, a selfish person who, through fate or circumstance, performs heroic deeds. But your character would cause too many problems in the game if they were truly a villain.

Can my hero be a character from myth or fiction? No. EVERWAY is about your imagination, not someone else's. You can create a hero who is like a character from myth or fiction, but you can't actually play that character.

Ultimately, however, EVERWAY is a game of consent, not dogma. If the other players and the gamemaster don't mind, you're free to play heroes who don't fit the guidelines outlined above.

THREE RULES FOR HEROES

When you start developing your hero's personality and background, keep three rules in mind.

1. **The mind is sacred.** Hard feelings can develop between players when one player's hero can read or control the minds of other heroes. Players want the freedom to play their heroes as they wish, without another player interfering. Likewise, gamemasters hate to see their mysterious plots ruined by a hero who can casually read the minds of treacherous villains. To avoid these problems, don't make a hero who can read minds or control other characters.

2. **Interaction is important.** Much of the fun of a quest is having your hero interact with the other heroes and with background characters. If your hero doesn't interact with many people, you might not have fun running that hero for long. Curious, friendly, helpful, talkative, confident, active heroes are usuallly more fun to play than apathetic, disdainful, quiet, shy heroes.

3. **Everything changes.** Develop a hero who has room to grow. You could even give your hero faults or vices, such as stubbornness or naiveté. Not only can imperfections be fun to roleplay, but they give the hero room to develop.

These rules will help you avoid creating a hero that doesn't work well in the game.

Introduction

Now you introduce your hero to the group and learn about the other players' heroes. Describe what you've already decided about your hero to the other players. Show them the vision images that you've chosen and describe briefly what these images mean. Don't worry if your concept for your hero is still vague; the process of introducing your hero to other players often helps you get a clearer picture of your hero.

At this point, the gamemaster and the other players ask questions about your vision for your hero. These are general questions regarding who the hero is. They'll have a chance to ask more detailed questions later. The questions help the other players get a better sense for who your hero is, and, as mentioned earlier, they may help you as well. They are not a test of any kind; if you can't think of an answer yet, or if you want to change an answer later, that's fine. Example questions might include:

"Why are they walking the spheres?"

"What sort of realm do they come from?"

"How well do they fit into new societies?"

"How much experience do they have spherewalking?"

Sometimes two heroes have similar visions. When that happens, the questions can help distinguish between them.

If the heroes in the group have a limited range of abilities or personalities, you can alter your hero's vision during the introduction stage to fill an empty niche. Consider the following potential situations:

- The group has three rude, gruff mercenaries and one reserved scholar. This means no one in the group is good at talking with strangers. One player might volunteer to alter their vision of their hero to include the ability to negotiate, speak well, and so on.

- The group has several scholars, mages, and wanderers, but no warriors. One player might offer to alter their vision to include skill with weapons in order to give the group better odds should they get forced into a fight.

- A female hero hates all men, and a male hero hates all women. These attitudes will likely lead to conflicts between the heroes that could detract from the game. The players may agree that for some reason these two heroes have taken a liking to each other (though neither will admit it).

Doing the Questions Stage Now

You may wish to skip ahead to the Questions Stage of creating heroes (see p. 138). Some players like to establish the details about their heroes through freeform questions and then add the rules-related details. If that's true for you and your group, you can ask questions back and forth until your heroes' identities are quite well established and then come back to the Identity Stage. Doing the Questions Stage first is an especially good idea for beginning players. Other players prefer to get to the rules first to see how the game system works and to get an idea of the limits on heroes' abilities. Then they feel more confident inventing answers to the questions that other players pose in the Questions Stage. If that's true for you and your group, go ahead with the Identity Stage now.

DEVELOPING A HERO ALONE

If you develop a hero alone, leave some details unfinished. When you get a chance, have another player ask you questions about the hero so you get input from others before finalizing the hero (see *Questions Stage*, p. 138). You can even talk with another player remotely as long as you can share the images with them.

Example Vision: Fireson

Throughout this chapter, I'll use the ready-to-run hero Fireson as an example of how to create a hero. Fireson really is my hero, one of the first I invented. At this stage, you probably don't have a name for your hero yet. I didn't either when I was this far along. But since you and I both know his name wound up being Fireson, I'm just going to call him that from the start.

Vision 101 shows Fireson. This scene is from his earlier years, when he was a respected priest and powerful person in his realm.

From the visions, I developed a concept for the hero: a fallen priest who retains some priestly abilities even though he has been stripped of his status and position. He is a wanderer who has seen a lot, someone who has known both luxury and hardship. The visions portray a hot, dry land, so it came to me to make him a priest of a fire deity. This outline is still sketchy, but it's enough to work from. The details of Fireson's life and abilities will come later. (If you have more details for your hero at this stage, that's all right.)

— Jonathan Tweet

Vision 1102 is some sort of ritual or test Fireson was in.

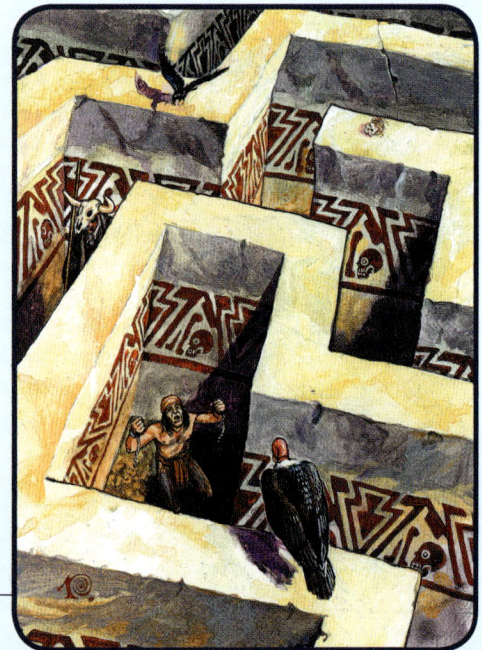

Vision 1007 shows the desolate wasteland into which Fireson was banished for blasphemy.

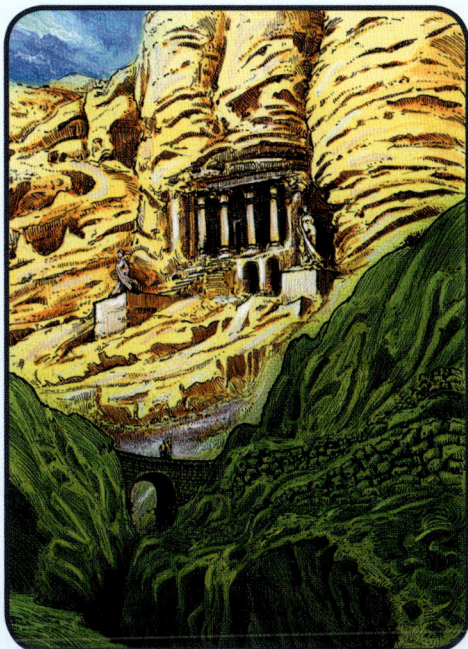

Vision 1011 shows a temple he visited in his travels.

Vision 1009 shows Fireson, now dressed in rags, coming to an oasis. Perhaps this is the first oasis he came to after his journey through the desert.

1007. Desert Wasteland, 1011. Cliff Temple – Ian Miller
101. Pyramid Priest, 1102. Labyrinth, 1009. Oasis – Rudy Rauben (Roger Raupp)

2 IDENTITY STAGE

The aspects below help define what sort of person your hero is. They help you decide how to portray your hero, but they do not define your hero's specific abilities.

Name

A hero's name is not a trivial matter. A name is often part of others' first impressions of a hero. In the imaginary game world, naming is also a central part of magic, and a baby's name may be a blessing, a curse, a prayer, or a promise. Adults may also choose new names to represent where they have been in life's journey, where they are, or where they're heading.

Choose a name for your hero. You may choose a name at any point in designing your hero. Some players think of names right away; others start the game without being quite sure of what to name their heroes. Write the name in the space provided on the hero sheet.

Names in the worlds of EVERWAY generally mean something in everyday speech rather than being merely traditional. A name may refer to the hero's traits or attributes, the hero's reputation, the attitude of the hero's parents when the hero was born, the parents' hopes for the child, and so on.

Your hero's name may be more or less normal, such as Heather, Ruby, Dawn, Robin, Jay, or Victor.

The name may relate to the hero's birth. For instance, a hero whose mother died in childbirth might be named Sorrow, and one who was born into a dying tribe may be named Hope.

The name may relate to the hero's personal history. A hero who has been exiled may take the name Outcast.

The name may refer to the hero's characteristics, such as Mighty, Persistence, or Swift.

The name may refer to special traits, such as Firedancer or Thunderfist.

The name may be prophetic and enigmatic, even symbolic, such as Earthcradle or Sparkbringer.

A name can tell something about the hero's culture or upbringing. Those who live in cities in a realm of commerce and knowledge may choose more abstract names such as Faithful or Lightson. Those who live the farming life may choose more nature-related or earthy names, such as Strongarm or Lark. Those who live in tribes may have names related to wild animals, such as Bearbrother or Wolfrunner.

Fanciful Names

Your hero may have a name that would draw little attention in the real world, such as Faith, but they may also have a very unusual name. Names such as "Keeper of Hidden Lore," Feet-of-Antelope, Mighty-Spear-of-Ishtar, Sun Killer, and so on are all possible. The hero may choose to use part of the name, such as Keeper, Antelope, or Spear, for general use if the whole name is too long. In fact, different people may know the same person by different parts of the name, so that "Keeper of Hidden Lore," for instance, might be known to different people as Keeper, Hidden, and Lore.

Multiple Names

Depending on your hero's culture (which you invent or choose), your hero may have more than one name. Some cultures use a parent's name to identify someone, such as Trueheart Gentlesdaughter, which means "Trueheart, daughter of Gentle."

The name of a family, tribe, town, or land may be part of your hero's name, especially if your hero has left their homeland.

For instance, a hero may be known as Righteous Miracle, identifying them as part of the Righteous family or tribe. Or if they're from the town of Skybright, they may be known as "Miracle of Skybright."

In some lands, children have several names, each given by a different person or group. A child might have the names Joy, Wonder, Hunter, First-Grandchild, Mighty-Shield, and Waterdark, with these names given by the mother, father, mother's parents, father's parents, village headman, and village shaman, respectively. The hero would claim all these names, probably in no particular order. The hero could choose which name to go by when meeting new people.

A hero may have a public name and a private name. (You may wish to remember the secret name but not write it on the hero sheet, in order to keep it especially secret.) The secret name may be used for rituals, or it might simply be a private matter.

Nonsense Names

While they are uncommon, nonsense names, such as Azavar, Raysa, and Melnon, are also known among the spheres. They may arise from particular traditions in the culture that the hero comes from. Gods and goddesses have personal, unique names (though they are often known by common titles, as Poseidon is called

1306. Words of Creation – Doug Keith

Earth-Shaker), and parents may give their children unique names to make them stand out or to connect them to a hero, deity, or ancestor who had that name.

Heroes with uncommon names may find that others confuse or distort these hard-to-remember names. After all, most people among the spheres don't read and write, so names are passed along only by word of mouth. It's easy for names to be changed as they are passed along since almost no one writes them down. For example, Raysa may find herself called "Razor."

The mystic language of Cleacuun uses words that are different from the Tongue, which is the language most mortals speak. A mage parent who knows a little of Cleacuun may use words that sound like Cleacuun to name a child. The actual Cleacuun word, however, is more than its pronunciation. The name "Rana-kai" may sound like the Cleacuun word that means "eternal vigilance," but you cannot actually say the word without truly understanding it, without its being a part of you.

The hero may come from a land whose language has been unnaturally altered so that the people there no longer speak the Tongue. In this case, the hero may have a name that sounds like nonsense but that actually means something in their homeland's special language.

Place Names

Like names for people, names of places usually have a common meaning, such as Greendale, Snowpeak, Great Salt Sea, Cemetery Road, Dimdwell Forest, Highthrone, Marketmeet, and so on. Place names may be part of a personal name, such as "Lightstep of Stonekeep."

Motive

There are seven general motives that spur heroes to walk the spheres, each tied to a planet. Choose one of these motives for your hero, or invent your own.

Wanderlust (Sun)

The hero wanders the spheres with little or no care for a purpose. Wherever the sun rises and sets is called "home," though no one place is home for long. While the wanderer feels no overriding purpose, one may dawn on them some day

Mystery (Moon)

The hero seeks no mundane goals but wishes to confront mysteries on other worlds. They seek a secret or subtle understanding, though others may label such stuff mere lunacy. The hero may be guided by signs to which others are deaf and blind.

Knowledge (Mercury)

The hero seeks knowledge to be found in new realms and new worlds. The knowledge sought may be mundane or hermetic. The hero may seek to share knowledge with those they meet or may simply wish to gather knowledge. Some spherewalkers work for the Chamber Platinum, a group sponsored by the Library of All Worlds in the city of Everway. They are charged with exploring new worlds and reporting their findings to the Library.

Beauty (Venus)

The hero seeks to share or to experience that which is beautiful: art, music, romance, poetry, aphrodisia, and more. No one world or realm alone can sate their appetite for the beautiful. For some seekers of beauty, the evening star heralds pleasure and delight. For others, the morning star portends a day of fresh possibilities.

Conquest (Mars)

The hero lives for challenges and loves to exert power. The hero may be a master of martial abilities or may enforce their will through trickery, wordplay, or magic. The hero may be dedicated to battling evil and serving justice, may simply take pride and pleasure in using their talents, or may be seeking fame and fortune.

Authority (Jupiter)

The hero is the hands, the eyes, the mouth, or the sword of some authority, such as a deity, ruler, or holy order. They may take the role of arbiter or lawgiver, eager to bring justice and right-thinking to realms plagued by tyranny or corruption. While the hero takes this role seriously, they may also display the joviality of a confident person in power.

Adversity (Saturn)

The hero is under some compulsion to walk the spheres. Perhaps they are atoning for a crime committed against a deity or monarch, or perhaps no realm feels like home, and the hero must keep moving in search of contentment. Such a hero may have a saturnine disposition, though they punctuate this gloom with energetic revels.

> The phrase "as above, so below" acknowledges the relationship of the heavens to the lives of people.

Estate Fortune Deck Cards – Jeff Miracola

Virtue

Your hero's Virtue represents some way in which they are particularly gifted. A card from the Fortune Deck represents your hero's Virtue.

Choosing a Virtue

Look through the list of cards in *Section 2: Fortune Guide*, select a card that represents your hero's Virtue, and note if it is reversed.

Your hero's Virtue may be related to the Virtue of the realm from which they come (as may the hero's Fault and Fate). For example, an intelligent, well-educated hero from a realm where learning is highly valued may have The Eagle (*the mind prevails*) as their Virtue, the same as the realm from which they come. Write the card's title (and its meaning, if you wish) in the space labeled "Virtue" on your hero sheet.

What Is a Virtue?

A Virtue can mean many things, depending on what fits your hero.

- **A Personal Trait:** You could choose The Priestess (*understanding mysteries*) as your Virtue to mean that your hero is in touch with unspoken mysteries. In this case, their Virtue represents a special trait.

1203. Earth Tusks – Mark Tedin

- **A Magical Gift:** You could choose The Eagle (*the mind prevails*) as your Virtue to mean that your hero is gifted with forethought. Instead of being simply a personal trait, this Virtue could be a connection to the spirit world or a gift from a deity. For instance, if your hero's totem is an eagle, they may be gifted with intelligent insights because of this spiritual connection.

- **An Aspect of Fortune:** You could choose The Creator (*nurture*) as your Virtue to mean that your hero is fated to find good luck in nurturing situations. A hero can have a Virtue that affects their life even if the hero has no personal traits or spiritual ties that connect to that Virtue.

Fault

Your hero's Fault is a way in which they are particularly weak or vulnerable. A card from the Fortune Deck represents your hero's Fault.

Choosing a Fault

Look through the list of Fortune Deck card meanings in *Section 2: Fortune Guide*, select a card to represent your hero's Fault, and note if it is reversed. Write the card's title (and its meaning, if you wish) in the space labeled "Fault" on your hero sheet.

What Is a Fault?

A Fault can represent many things, including the following concepts.

- **A Personal Trait:** You could choose The Lion—Reversed (*weakness*) as the Fault, meaning that your hero is physically weak and vulnerable. Note that some physically weak people can compensate for this weakness well, but choosing it as your Fault specifically means that your hero's weakness makes them vulnerable and can sometimes lead to their downfall. (You may wish to select a weak Fire score, a weak Earth score, or both, to fit with this Fault; see pp. 126–129.)

- **A Magical Curse:** You could choose The Dragon—Reversed (*blind fury*) as the Fault and define it as a curse put on your hero. Perhaps it's a curse that causes them to fly into a rage, a curse put on the hero by someone they harmed in anger. A strong Fire score would match this image, though someone with a weak Fire score and placid spirit could also be cursed with unusual bouts of wrath.

Example Identity: Fireson

I chose the name "Fireson" to indicate my hero's connection to fire. The term "son" shows that he feels deeply connected to fire and to his deity. While a son may be not as wise, as powerful, or as mature as a parent, the son and the parent are the same type of being. Fireson, likewise, identifies with fire and with his deity, not as a follower or servant, but as a potential equal.

Fireson's Motive is Adversity because he has been cast out of his comfortable life and forced into a life of wandering.

I chose The Lion (*the body prevails*) as his Virtue because I see him as a physically powerful man. He is tied to Fire, the element of action, so I pictured him as a man of action.

For his Fault, I chose Death—Reversed (*stasis*) to indicate his closed mind. As a man of high status in his former culture, he regards his culture as superior to the others through which he's been forced to travel.

For Fireson's Fate, I looked for a card that would reflect his having failed in his duty and having been cast out of his land by his deity. I looked for a fortune card that would relate to this conflict. The Cockatrice (*corruption vs. recovery*) made some sense, but it didn't seem to fit because I didn't see Fireson as corrupted by an outside force, or even really corrupted at all. He just hadn't done what he was supposed to do. The Creator (*nurture vs. abandonment*) seemed to make sense, too, as heaven had abandoned him to some degree, but it wasn't Fireson who'd abandoned anyone or anything, so this card didn't seem personal enough. Finally I settled on The Soldier (*duty vs. blind obedience*). I wasn't sure where the blind obedience fit in, but I knew that his destiny was tied up in duty somehow.

As it turned out, this Fate fit Fireson better than I first imagined. See *Chapter 5: Playing* to find out how he resolved this Fate.

— Jonathan Tweet

- **An Aspect of Fortune:** You could choose The Cockatrice (*corruption*) as the Fault, defining corruption as the weakness that the hero is destined to face. The Cockatrice could have nothing to do with the hero's traits or spiritual connections; it could simply be part of their destiny.

Fate

The Fate is your hero's current challenge, where the hero is in their life's story. A card from the Fortune Deck represents your hero's Fate. The Fate is temporary; it is a stage. When your hero has completed that stage, fulfilled that potential, or faced that destiny, they will move on to a new Fate.

The Fate card is neither upright nor reversed. One might say it is "sideways," to show that no one knows which way the hero's Fate will turn out. Your hero's actions will determine their Fate and which of the possible outcomes indicated by the card's meanings finally comes to pass.

To represent your hero's Fate, select one card of your choice from the Fortune Deck. Choose a card that relates to something at once important and uncertain about your hero. For example, you could choose War (*great effort vs. effort misspent*) as your hero's Fate, indicating that the hero must face the conflict between a great effort and that effort going awry. Perhaps the hero is on a mighty undertaking that may be all for naught. Perhaps the hero is very powerful but not very wise, so that being misled is a constant danger. Maybe you don't even know for sure why this Fate fits, but you sense that it does. With time, you'll learn what your hero's Fate means. Record your hero's Fate (and its upright and reversed meanings, if you wish) in the space labeled "Fate" on your hero sheet.

1402. Harp of the Hidden City – Janine Johnston

3 POWERS STAGE

You can invent magical, psychic, or unusual Powers for your hero. While these Powers give your hero advantages, you must pay for them with elemental points that you would otherwise distribute among your hero's Elements (see the *Elements Stage* section on p. 120). That means that having Powers makes your hero stronger in some ways and weaker in others. Even so, each Power is linked to an Element based on its effect.

Record the total number of points you spend on Powers in the hexagon labeled "Powers" on your hero sheet and write about the Powers on the back of the sheet in the area labeled "Powers and Magic."

The space for points spent on Powers is a hexagon to remind you that spending more than 6 points on Powers might be a bad idea; spending more than 6 points doesn't leave many points for your Elements.

Powers are limited in scope and have specific effects. If you wish your hero to wield magic, which implies a more general knowledge and ability, see the *Magic Stage* section (p. 136). You can skip ahead to that section now if you want to see how Magic differs from Powers.

Types of Powers

You can give your hero just about any kind of Power you think fits their background or that interests you. The more powerful your hero's Powers are, however, the lower their Elements (see p. 120) will be. Powers can include healing, flying, singing enchanted songs, changing shape, and so on.

It's possible for a Power's advantages to come from some object or creature rather than from the hero directly. For instance, your hero may have a familiar animal, a wand with magical properties, a flying boat, or the like.

Cost of Powers

The more useful a Power is, the more elemental points you have to give up in order for your hero to have it. Each hero starts

THE UNICORN

with 20 points to allot among Elements. Having Powers reduces this number. A hero with Powers can do special things, but their Elements are weaker.

To determine how many elemental points you need to give up for a Power, determine whether or not the Power is frequent (often useful), major (having a big effect on play), and versatile (useful in several ways). For each of these factors, the cost of a Power is 1.

- A frequent Power, a major Power, or a versatile Power costs 1 point.

- A frequent and major Power, a frequent and versatile Power, or a major and versatile Power costs 2 points.

- A Power that is frequent, major, and versatile costs 3 points.

Determining whether a Power is frequent, major, or versatile is always a judgment call. The gamemaster approves all costs and always has the final say. If you, as the gamemaster, are uncertain about how to rate a Power, just use your best judgment. Nothing terrible will happen if you rate a Power differently from how another gamemaster would rate it.

Free Powers

Each hero may have one free Power that is not frequent, major, or versatile. For instance, the Power to make an instrument play by itself fits none of these categories, so you can give such a Power to your hero without spending any elemental points. Note that a free, or 0-point, Power can be something that the hero uses often provided that it doesn't often make a difference in play. For example, "Winning Smile (Air)" counts as a 0-point Power. A hero with this Power may use their winning smile all the time, but it's rarely, if ever, going to make a real difference in the hero's capabilities, so it is not categorized as frequent.

For any Power past this first free one, however, you must pay at least 1 point for each 0-point Power. You cannot have more than one 0-point Power at no cost.

The following are examples of free Powers:

- **Bird Tongue (Air):** The hero can talk to birds.

- **Friend to Fire (Fire):** The hero is unharmed by fire.

- **Friend to Water (Water):** The hero can breathe water.

- **Horse Friend (Earth):** The hero befriends horses automatically.

> You have 20 elemental points that you use to determine your hero's Powers, Elements, and Magic. They are called "elemental points" because you spend most of them on Elements. You may spend them on Powers and Magic, but you don't have to. In fact, most players spend no points on Magic for their heroes and only a few points on Powers.

- **Marching Song (Fire):** The hero can walk and sing indefinitely, provided they do them both at the same time.

- **Phantom Musician (Air):** The hero can make a musical instrument play by itself.

- **Riding Master (Fire):** The hero can ride any sort of mount without training.

- **Sight of the Soul (Water):** The hero can tell by sight whether a person is awake, asleep, or dreaming.

- **Universal Reading (Air):** The hero can read any alphabet (but not any language, only the Tongue).

See the ready-to-run heroes in *Section 4: Quick Start Guide* for more examples of free Powers.

SPHEREWALKING

Every hero has the ability to spherewalk, meaning that they can all successfully walk the astral paths that connect gates to each other. If you want your hero to be able to guide other people along these paths, then the hero will need a Water score of 5 or stronger. (A score of 5 Water lets someone guide one or two people, 6 Water can guide a small group, and 7 Water a large group. Stronger scores are needed to guide large contingents of non-spherewalkers along the astral paths. Starting heroes are limited to 6 Water.) Alternately, a 1-point Power lets a hero guide up to large groups regardless of their Water score, and a 2-point Power lets a hero guide large contingents.

> **IMPORTANT:** For more information on Powers and example Powers, see Chapter 4: Powers & Magic.

---

4 ELEMENTS STAGE

The four Elements—Air, Fire, Earth, and Water—represent four basic aspects of your hero. The gamemaster uses them to determine what your hero is capable of and what happens when your hero takes various actions.

Look at the large circle on your hero sheet. Each quarter of the wheel is for one Element. You will give your hero a rating for each Element, a quantitative measure

of their strength or ability in that area. You have 20 elemental points with which to grant your hero Powers, Elements, and Magic. The points that you have not devoted to Powers and that you don't plan to use for Magic are what you use to rate your hero's Elements. Choose a score between 3 and 6 for each Element such that the four Elements, plus the points for your Powers (if any), plus the points for your Magic (if any) total 20.

A perfectly balanced hero has 5 in each Element, though any hero with Powers or Magic will have a weaker average score. An average hero's scores are usually between 4 and 5, as most heroes have 1 to 4 points devoted to Powers or Magic. A hero's minimum score in each Element is 2, and the maximum is 9, but anything outside 3–6 for a beginning hero may be unbalancing and requires gamemaster approval. The following pages describe all scores from 1 to 10 because some creatures or very rare background characters can have scores that weak or strong. It may also be possible for heroes, through extraordinary fortune or tragedy, to achieve a score of 10 or to drop to 1 point in an Element.

A hero, remember, is an exceptional person. An average person has Elements that total 12, not 20, so a well-balanced average person with no Powers or Magic has a score of 3 for each Element.

Record each Element's score in the corresponding quarter of the circle on your hero sheet.

Example Powers: Fireson

As a priest of fire, Fireson needed some fire-related abilities. First, I gave him the Power "Sweat Fire." I wanted something flashy but not too powerful, so I defined the Power as frequent but not major (or versatile): a 1-point Power. Then, to make him a priest and not just a "fire-guy," I gave him "Priestly Rites." While this Power is major and versatile, I wanted to make it a 1-point Power on the basis that it was part of Fireson's past, something he'd hardly ever use now. John, however, who was the gamemaster, said I should pay the full 2-point cost, as that would add some teeth to the idea that Fireson had fallen from grace and paid a price for it. While I groaned at John's ruling, I knew he was right. I also chose a free Power for Fireson that was related to fire: "Friend to Fire," invulnerability to heat and flame. In play, I use this Power as a gimmick, as when Fireson delights children by juggling live coals. If I'd turned it into a weapon, say by having Fireson repeatedly swaddled in oil-drenched cloths and igniting himself, the gamemaster would have been right in finding some way to penalize me for getting a frequent, major effect out of a 0-point Power.

— Jonathan Tweet

The Four Elements

Air: Thought, focused energy, and spoken wisdom.

Fire: Action, forceful energy, and active power.

Earth: Might, resistant integrity, and passive power.

Water: Feelings, receptive integrity, and silent wisdom.

Using Scores

When your hero opposes another character or some force in the game world, the gamemaster uses your hero's scores to judge whether they succeed. For instance, when two characters or creatures fight, the one with the stronger Fire is likely to win (other factors being equal). You can think of each elemental point increaase as "doubling" the previous rank, though this is not literally true.

Each Element covers a broad range of activities, and heroes are generally assumed to be equally good in all the activities covered by a single Element. For example, strong Water means a hero is sensitive to magical energy, deception, others' feelings, the presence of spirits, and so on. Of course, not everyone who is sensitive to magical energy is equally sensitive to deception, emotions, and spirits. You can use Powers and Specialties (see p. 134) to make your hero's abilities more precise. For example, if you want a hero who can see and talk to spirits but who isn't particularly sensitive otherwise, you can take Speak to Spirits as a 1-point (major) Power and give your hero an average Water score. If you want someone who's sensitive in general but particularly sensitive to deception, you can take a Specialty to reflect that special sensitivity, and give your hero a strong Water score.

You and the gamemaster can also take into account your hero's background to determine what the hero can and cannot

do. For instance, a 6-Air hero from a literate society can almost certainly read and write, while a 6-Air hero from an oral society almost certainly cannot.

Careers and Elements

Below are some roles heroes typically fill depending on their strongest Elements. Your hero is not limited to the listed roles. Instead, this list simply gives you some ideas of what Elements might be important to your hero and demonstrates how the abstract Elements are made concrete in the careers of characters.

- **Air:** Scholar, preacher, alchemist, engineer
- **Air and Fire:** Orator, leader, general, messenger
- **Air and Earth:** Magistrate, inquisitor, lawgiver
- **Air and Water:** Poet, physician, singer, teacher, trader, counselor
- **Fire:** Warrior, acrobat
- **Fire and Earth:** Athlete, soldier, smith
- **Fire and Water:** Hunter, dancer, thief, scout, spy, negotiator, diplomat, courtier
- **Earth:** Guard, crafter, laborer, farmer
- **Earth and Water:** Healer, priest, sea captain
- **Water:** Mystic, artist, seer, prophet

THE SEMICIRCLES

In addition to looking at each Element individually, you can look at how your hero's Elements balance when they are paired up to create semicircles. The semicircles usually have no effect on play, but they can help you get a feel for your hero's capabilities.

Wisdom and Power

The Air–Water semicircle represents wisdom. Air represents spoken wisdom, while Water represents silent wisdom. The Fire–Earth semicircle represents power. Fire represents active power, and Earth represents passive power.

Wisdom reflects the sense of what to do while power reflects the ability to take action.

Energy and Integrity

The Air–Fire semicircle represents energy. Air represents focused energy, and Fire represents forceful energy. The Water–Earth semicircle represents integrity. Water represents receptive integrity, and Earth represents resistant integrity.

Energy represents dynamic adaptability while integrity represents the ability to endure.

Will and Charm

The cross-semicircle of Air–Earth represents will. Air represents mental strength, and Earth represents physical tenacity. The cross-semicircle of Fire–Water represents charm. Fire represents active influence, and Water represents passive allure.

Will represents persistence while charm represents persuasiveness.

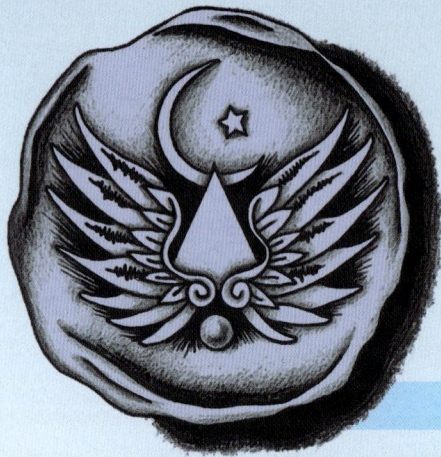

AIR

Air determines intelligence, speech, thought, logic, analytical ability, oratory, and knowledge. A hero with a strong Air score knows a lot, speaks well, and can figure things out easily. Someone with strong Air may be "swift" or "inspired."

Someone with strong Air but weak Fire can speak eloquently but is unable to put "fire" into their speech, limiting their effectiveness as a leader. Someone with strong Air but weak Water understands logic and science but is blind to the unspoken world of emotions, limiting their abilities as a singer or poet. Someone with strong Air but weak Earth can have great ideas and insight but lack grounding in practicality or the fortitude to follow through or defend their ideas.

Your hero's Air score determines how well they can communicate, work with letters and numbers, make plans, and solve problems. Air rules reading, writing, geometry, and mathematics, but these skills are only found in certain realms; a strong Air score only means your hero is good at these skills if the hero has been trained in them. Formalized types of magic require a strong Air score, as do other sciences. Each score on the next page includes brief descriptions of a character with that score and an example of how well they can understand, use, and create tools.

If a character's Air score is... the character will be:

1 Dim. The character cannot understand, develop, or communicate thoughts well: mostly instinctual.

Example: The character can use simple tools if trained to use them. The character could probably sew but not use a loom.

2 Simplistic. The character uses words and ideas but not easily or well. A hero may not start with a score of 2 or weaker in any Element.

Example: The character can use the tools of their trade but cannot use them in new ways. A character who is a weaver can use a loom but cannot envision new and imaginative patterns for their weavings.

3 Average. The character can think and speak well but misunderstands some things and believes some things that are false.

Example: The character can use the tools of the trade competently and can pick up other skills with some practice.

4 Bright. The character is well-spoken and knowledgeable. This is a weak-to-average score for a hero.

Example: The character can figure out how to work tools they haven't used before. A character with this score who's never used a loom could figure it out.

5 Brilliant. The character may have a gift with language and be a noted storyteller, or they could possibly be a scholar, philosopher, or engineer. This is an average-to-strong score for a hero.

Example: The character can figure out how to use complicated tools and how to follow complicated procedures. With time to experiment in a smithy, the character could forge simple iron implements without training (provided the character's from a culture that works iron). With some time, the character can figure out how complex tools or machinery they have never seen before works.

6 Ingenious. The character is renowned for their genius. This is normally the maximum for a human.

Example: The character knows how to use most tools and make most things in the character's culture, even if they have never done so before. The character can engineer new structures or invent new tools to meet new demands.

7 Legendary. The character has deep insight. A hero may not start with a score of 7 or stronger in any Element.

Example: The character can easily figure out how to use any culture's tools or machinery, showing an understanding of these devices that even those who work with them regularly don't have.

8 Prescient. The character can administer crumbling empires, conceive of new types of machines, found schools of philosophy, and so on.

Example: The character can construct devices, compound medicines, or refine substances to meet most special circumstances.

9 Inscrutable. The character has phenomenal insight, incredible intelligence, and a vast amount of knowledge.

Example: The character has a thorough understanding of all artificial creations. With time, they can invent machines, forge tools, compound medicines, and refine substances as if trained to do so.

10 Divine. The character is a godlike philosopher, scientist, or sage.

Example: The character has complete understanding of all artificial creations and is capable of creating new devices, medicines, and substances as if they had been trained to do so from birth.

FIRE

Fire measures vitality, force, courage, speed, and daring. Heroes with strong Fire scores are energetic and capable in physical activities. A hero with a strong Fire score might be "fiery" or "hot-headed."

A hero with strong Fire but weak Air may be a powerful warrior but could never be an effective general; the weak Air score would keep the hero from being able to inspire troops through speech or to make superior plans. A hero with strong Fire but weak Earth may be deadly in combat but unable to withstand wounds or to endure in a long-lasting battle. A hero with strong Fire but weak Water may act quickly without understanding the wisest course of action or the consequences of their actions.

Your hero's Fire score determines in general how good the hero is at sword fighting, sprinting, climbing walls, dodging spears, throwing spears, breaking down doors, and so on. Each score on the next page includes a general description of a character with that score and an example of how capable in combat a character with that score might be.

If a character's Fire score is... the character will be:

1 **Feeble**. The character is weak or listless and has difficulty moving around or exerting any force.

Example: The character is helpless in combat.

2 **Lethargic.** The character is lacking energy. A hero may not start with a score of 2 or weaker in any Element.

Example: The character can easily be defeated by an average person in a fair fight.

3 **Average.** The character displays a typical human level of ability and is capable of brief bursts of energetic activity with periods of rest.

Example: The character may win or lose a fight with an average person, depending on other factors, such as Earth scores, weaponry, training, and so on.

4 **Energetic.** The character is a dynamic, active individual. This score is weak-to-average for a hero.

Example: The character can usually defeat the average person in combat.

5 **Vital.** The character is boisterous, fit, and full of energy. This score is average-to-strong for a hero.

Example: The character can defeat an average person even if the opponent is better armed. Given equal armaments, the character can defeat four average opponents.

6 **Mighty.** The character is possibly a powerful warrior. This score is normally the maximum for a human.

Example: The character can kill, disable, disarm, pin, throw, or otherwise vanquish an average warrior at will, despite armaments and most other advantages. In a fair fight, the character is the equal of eight average opponents.

7 **Legendary**. The character has legendary physical power. A hero may not start with a score of 7 or stronger in any Element.

Example: The character can face mighty creatures like dragons and giants, though to vanquish such an opponent they may need some advantage, such as a ruse or knowledge of the creature's weakness.

8 **Boundless.** The character is filled with relentless energy.

Example: The character can face mighty monsters as equals.

9 **Unstoppable.** The character is overflowing with power and energy.

Example: The character can defeat numbers of mighty monsters and can challenge the mightiest creatures if they are able to get some sort of advantage.

10 **Divine.** The character has godlike energy capable of incomprehensible physical feats.

Example: The character is the equal of the mightiest mythic beasts, such as ancient dragons and gigantic sea serpents.

EARTH

Earth governs a hero's health, endurance, fortitude, determination, and resilience. Heroes with strong Earth scores can withstand damage, shake off the effects of poisons, and resist magic. Someone with a strong Earth score may be "earthy" or "grounded."

Someone with strong Earth but weak Fire is tough but unable to act quickly or forcefully. Someone with strong Earth but weak Water is insensitive to the nuances of positive energies, such as emotions, and neutral energies, such as magic, as well as from negative energies. Someone with strong Earth but weak Air is relentless and unwavering, but may be stubborn and difficult to reason with.

Earth determines your hero's ability to suffer damage and keep going, to recover from wounds, to endure without getting tired, to resist magic, and so on. Each score on the next page includes a short description of a character with that score and an example of how that character could withstand being poisoned. (The first seven examples are based on a strength 2 Poison (death). See Book 2: Gamemasters for more information on poisons. Poison of this strength is common in snakes and the most venomous spiders; it's dangerous but not usually deadly unless the character has a weak Earth. Poisons of different strengths would have different effects than those in the examples here.)

If a character's Earth score is... the character will be:

1 Sickly. The character is bed-ridden or fragile.

Example: The mere smell of the poison makes the character ill.

2 Frail. The character is unhealthy or easily tired. A hero may not start with a score of 2 or weaker in any Element.

Example: The poison kills the character unless medical attention is given, in which case the character may live, though it will take weeks for a full recovery.

3 Average. The character is healthy but has all the ills, aches, and fatigue of a typical human.

Example: The poison makes the character sick, weak, and helpless. It may kill them if they get no medical attention.

4 Robust. The character is only occasionally sick, recovers faster than normal from injuries, and has notable endurance and strength. This is a weak-to-average score for a hero.

Example: The poison weakens the character, but they can still act. Medical help would assure a strong recovery.

5 Tough. The character rarely falls ill or gets injured. When injured, they recover very quickly. This is an average-to-strong score for a hero.

Example: The poison slows the character down. Medical help would speed recovery, but the character will recover quickly even without it.

6 Enduring. The character is strong and apparently tireless. This is normally the maximum for a human.

Example: The poison gives the character a headache and may make them feel a little light-headed.

7 Legendary. The character is renowned for their immense strength and endurance. A hero may not start with a score of 7 or stronger in any Element.

Example: The character doesn't notice the effect of a typical poison. If the poison tastes good, the character could use it to flavor their food.

8 Indomitable. The character is vital, tireless, impervious to pain, and able to go without sleep indefinitely. The character can go without food for a month with no ill effects, survive without food for a year, survive for a month without water, and hold their breath for two hours.

Example: Only a super-potent, magical poison, such as alchemically refined dragon venom, can kill the character.

9 Indestructible. The character can go without food for an entire season with no ill effects, survive without food for years, survive for a season without water, and hold their breath for several hours.

Example: Only super-potent, magical poisons can weaken the character or knock them out for a short time.

10 Divine. The character needs no food or water, can hold their breath for a day, and is almost impossible to kill. The character will recover from any wound that is not instantly fatal.

Example: No poison has any effect on the character.

WATER

Water governs intuition, sensitivity to that which is unseen and unspoken, receptivity, psychic potential, and depth of feeling. Heroes with strong Water scores are good at sensing lies, feeling magic, intuiting hidden emotions, adapting to new social situations, and so on. Someone with a strong Water score might be "deep" or "fluid."

A hero with strong Water but weak Air can sense things but has a hard time putting them into words and explaining them to others. A hero with strong Water but weak Earth can sense forces and energies but is unable to withstand those energies if they are strong. A hero with strong Water but weak Fire can sense energies or forces but not know how to react to them.

Since Water rules the unspoken and the nonverbal, strong Water alone never lets one "read" another's mind. "Reading" relates to words, and Air, not Water, rules words. (Besides, you should not give your hero the ability to read minds, as this ability causes problems during play. See p. 105.) A strong Water score can allow one to tune in to others' emotional or spiritual states, since they are nonverbal. Having this empathic ability does not usually ruin plots because the information gathered tends to be vague.

The Water score determines your hero's ability to sense emotions, feel magical forces, understand "unwritten rules" of different communities, and so on. Each score listed on the next page includes a brief description of what a character with that score is like and an example of what a character with that score could intuit about a specific social situation. In this case, the example describes a character speaking with a husband and wife about affairs in their realm.

If a character's Water score is... the character will be:

1 **Oblivious.** The character is disconnected from emotions and social norms, as is typical of extreme recluses.

Example: The character doesn't even realize that the man and woman are married.

2 **Insensitive.** The character is awkward with animals, children, and social situations. They may lack spiritual or artistic insight. A hero may not start with a score of 2 or weaker in any Element.

Example: The character understands the facts of the others' statements, but that's all.

3 **Average.** The character is aware of social, spiritual, and internal energies but is sometimes distracted, biased, and self-centered.

Example: The character can tell that the wife is troubled by something.

4 **Perceptive.** The character notices emotional undertones and persistent energies. This is a weak-to-average score for a hero.

Example: The character can tell that the wife secretly resents her husband.

5 **Sensitive.** The character is able to sense strong energies and nuanced emotions. This is an average-to-strong score for a hero.

Example: The character not only sees that the wife secretly resents the husband but also senses some sort of evil energy at work.

6 **Empathic.** The character can sense nearby emotions and understands feelings, basic motives, and intents, regardless of language. This is normally the maximum for a human.

Example: The character intuits that the wife has an evil energy invading her psychically, causing her to resent her husband. They also sense that the husband is pulling away from her emotionally to protect himself but is not aware of either his unconscious self-defense or her resentment.

7 **Legendary.** The character is deeply intuitive and can understand the desire, intents, and feelings of even animals and can sense moderate energies. A hero may not start with a score of 7 or stronger in any Element.

Example: As above, plus the character can feel that the energy affecting the wife is growing in power.

8 **Mystical.** The character can sense weak energies, such as energies that used to be powerful in a place and are now gone or traces of powerful energy on people who have been exposed to it.

Example: As above, plus the character senses that the energy is coming from a relative of the wife.

9 **Transcendent.** The character can sense weak energies without even trying. They know most people better than the people know themselves.

Example: As above, plus the character sees the energy is coming from the wife's brother and will culminate in the wife murdering the husband within a week.

10 **Divine.** The character is constant commune with natural, social, and spiritual environments. They are selfless and nearly returned to cosmic consciousness.

Example: As above, plus the character senses that the brother's evil magic is part of a growing influence created by someone from another sphere and that this influence will corrupt this realm within a year if it is not stopped.

THE ELEMENTS

	Air	Fire	Earth	Water
1	dim	feeble	sickly	oblivious
2	simplistic	lethargic	frail	insensitive
3	average	average	average	average
4	bright	energetic	robust	perceptive
5	brilliant	vital	tough	sensitive
6	ingenious	mighty	enduring	empathic
7	legendary	legendary	legendary	legendary
8	prescient	boundless	indomitable	mystical
9	inscrutable	unstoppable	indestructible	transcendent
10	divine	divine	divine	divine

Example Elements: Fireson

I'd spent 3 of Fireson's 20 points on the Powers Priestly Rites and Sweat Fire. I didn't intend for Fireson to have Magic, so I had 17 points to use for his four Elements.

I decided his most important Element was to be—can you guess?—Fire. After all, his name, his deity, and his Virtue are all tied to fire. (Actually, the Fortune Deck card The Lion is tied to both Fire and Earth.) I wanted this Element to be quite high so it would really stand out.

Fireson's second most important Element, I decided, was Water. As a priest, he would need to be sensitive to spiritual energies. Many months after I invented Fireson, I realized his Fault is a reversed card tied to water. If his Water represents his priestly nature, then having a reversed water card as a Fault fit him, as a failed priest, very nicely. I didn't make this connection, however, when I first chose the Fault.

I also wanted Fireson to be a good speaker (strong Air), because he would have needed that skill as a priest, and a tough fellow (strong Earth) because he's been through a lot.

In my dreams, Fireson would have been 7 Fire, 6 Water, 4 Air, and 4 Earth. But that added up to 21, and I only had 17 elemental points left. I decided I could live with lopping 1 point off each Element to meet the 17-point limit. I really wanted to keep the 7 Fire so he'd be superhuman, but that would have meant having a 2 in Air, a 2 in Earth, or a mere 4 in Water. I decided that I couldn't live with any of those scores, so I dropped his Fire to 6, his Water to 5, and his Earth and Air to 3 each. (Since that early playtest, all Elements have been limited to 3–6 anyway.)

In terms of the game world, Fireson still has a tremendous amount of physical energy (6 Fire), meaning he can outsprint, outfight, outdance, and outjump most people. His average endurance (3 Earth), however, means he's likely to tire himself out quickly. His sensitivity (5 Water) indicates he's able to read unspoken hints, sense strong magical energies, and so on. His average intelligence and speaking ability (3 Air) mean he can get along in conversations but not much more. (In play, I had to be careful to use simpler words and phrases than I'm used to; I usually play well-spoken characters. Sometimes fancy sentences would slip out of my mouth. I'd say, "Certainly Your Majesty recognizes the danger inherent in delay" when Fireson should have been saying something more like, "But, King, if we don't act now, we're dead!")

— Jonathan Tweet

Specialties

Each hero has four Specialties, one for each Element. These Specialties describe areas in which the hero is especially capable. For instance, the Specialty "Stealth" indicates the hero is stealthier than their Water score alone would indicate. Generally, a Specialty allows a hero to perform an act as if the Element score were 1 point higher than it is.

The most common type of Specialty relates to the actions that the Element rules. For example, the Specialty "Oratory" is related to the element Air because Air rules speech. That is, your hero's Air score determines how well the hero speaks in public. In the same way, the Specialty "Archery" would generally be tied to Fire because Fire rules action in general and especially combat. If your hero has 4 Fire and a Specialty in Archery, the hero uses a bow and arrow as well as if they had a 5 Fire.

Cross-Specialties, however, relate to the physical element that the Specialty interacts with. The Specialty "Archery" could be tied to Air as a Cross-Specialty because arrows fly through the air. In this case, the hero's ability with Archery is rated as the hero's Air score plus 1. A hero with 6 Air and the Archery Cross-Specialty would shoot arrows as well as a 7-Fire archer, even if the hero's Fire score were very weak. In the same way, Swimming usually relates to Fire because it's a physical activity, but it could be tied to Water as a Cross-Specialty. Pottery would usually relate to Air because it's a craft, but it could be tied to Earth. Resisting Heat is normally tied to Earth because it's an aspect of fortitude, but it could also be tied to Fire.

Specialties (including Cross-Specialties) must be specific. For example, "Climbing" is a fine Specialty, but "Athletics" is too general. If you want your hero to be a good athlete, they need a strong Fire score (and secondarily a strong Earth score).

Specializing in a magic tradition, like "Flux Magic", allows you to raise your Magic score 1 point beyond the linked element (Fire). It does not affect your hero's Magic ability (see *Magic Stage*).

Record each Specialty in the quarter of the wheel that corresponds to the Specialty's Element.

Below are example Specialties listed for each Element. For Cross-Specialties, the normal Element for that Specialty is shown in parentheses.

Example Air Specialties

- Archery (Fire)
- Herb Lore
- Lying

- Occult Lore
- Oratory
- Singing
- Smooth-talking

Example Fire Specialties

- Archery
- Climbing
- Jumping
- Running
- Smithing (Air)
- Swordfighting
- Withstanding Heat (Earth)
- Wrestling

Example Earth Specialties

- Farming (Air)
- Mining (Air)
- Resisting Magic
- Resisting Persuasion
- Resisting Poisons
- Tireless Stride
- Thick Skin

Example Water Specialties

- Diagnosing Illness
- Sensing Ambush
- Sensing Death
- Sensing Divine Energy
- Stealth
- Swimming (Fire)
- Tracking

EXAMPLE SPECIALTIES: FIRESON

For Fireson's Fire Specialty, I wanted something that referred literally to fire, not to physical activity. After all, he's a fire priest. I could have taken "Withstanding Heat," but Fireson's free Power is Friend to Fire, which makes him invulnerable to heat anyway. I decided to make his Specialty "Fire Magic," meaning knowledge of magical connections to fire: fire symbols, fire spells, legends about fire, and so on. Note that this Specialty is simply knowledge, not practice. Fireson could use this Specialty to identify a spell to summon fiery spirits but not to cast the spell , which would require a Magic score. Since this Specialty refers to knowledge, it would normally fall under Air, but I took it as a Cross-Specialty. Since Fireson's Fire score is 6, his knowledge of fire magic is effectively 7.

I wanted Fireson's other Specialties to relate to his training as a priest. Even if these Specialties might not be as useful as Specialties related to exploring realms, dealing with people, fighting monsters, and solving mysteries, they helped to define Fireson's identity. For his Air Specialty, I chose "Speaking to Crowds." For Earth, I chose "Maintaining Vigils." For Water, I chose "Sensing Divine Energies." These Specialties all represent activities that Fireson undertook as a priest.

— Jonathan Tweet

MAGIC STAGE

Magic is the ability to wield supernatural energies in order to cast spells. Most heroes do not know magic, though they may have supernatural abilities because of their Powers. The term "mage" covers all characters who use magic, though specific terms such as "healer," "shaman," "spirit doctor," and so on may be more appropriate for certain practitioners of magic.

If your hero knows magic, then you must allot elemental points to give your hero a score in Magic. Record the points spent on Magic in the space labeled "Magic" on the front of your hero sheet. Your hero's Magic level is typically no more than 5 (6 if specialized in their magic tradition).

Select their magic tradition (see *Chapter 4: Powers & Magic*) or create your own. Indicate your hero's tradition and associated Element in the space labeled "Powers and Magic" on the back of your hero sheet.

Magic is a tricky art for players and gamemasters to use well. You must look to your gamemaster to establish the limits of what your mage's spells can accomplish. Your gamemaster is the final arbiter of what your character can do, so be sure that you make yourself clear about what you expect your hero to be capable of. You may need a higher Magic score than you expected for your mage to be able to do the sorts of things you want. Even if you and the gamemaster agree at the outset, problems may arise during quests when you think your mage can do something and the gamemaster disagrees. If you are not ready to concede to the gamemaster's judgment, don't run a mage.

Gamemaster's who don't feel comfortable adjudicating the flexible and open-ended nature of magic may disallow creating heroes that are mages.

KNOWLEDGE – REVERSED

Your mage cannot have a Specialty in Magic, but you can have a tradition Specialty in a linked Element that allows a Magic score to exceed a linked Element by 1. The tradition Specialty has no other impact on magic effectiveness.

Magic Level

Each mage has a Magic score representing their level of ability with magic. The knowledge and practice of magic is defined by a magic tradition that describes how the mage accesses their magic ability. A magic tradition is expressed through a specific Element, and a hero's Magic score is linked to that Element. A hero's Magic score typically cannot exceed a linked Element score.

Magic ability level is described on a 10-point scale. While creatures, background characters, and experienced heroes may achieve higher levels of magic, a starting hero is normally limited to 5 Magic since they start with 20 elemental points. For example, a hero with the Flux tradition of magic can have 5 Magic, 3 Air, 5 Fire, 3 Earth, and 3 Water with 1 point left over. The player can only add this point to Magic if they also add a Fire Specialty in Flux Magic (+1 Fire for Flux Magic).

IMPORTANT: For more information about Magic and example traditions, see Chapter 4: Powers & Magic.

205. Scroll Library – Martin McKenna

MAGIC SCORE

If the Magic score is… the character will be:

1 **An Apprentice:** A beginner, capable of both modest tricks and catastrophic mistakes.

2 **A Weak Mage:** Capable of a decent spell or two; has an understanding of magic as a science.

3 **An Average Mage:** A humble practitioner with some impressive powers in their area of specialization but not one to tackle great magical challenges. A town of a thousand people might have one such mage.

4 **A Gifted Mage:** A talented spellcaster with a good grounding in magic and some real promise. A city of ten thousand people might have such a mage.

5 **A Powerful Mage:** A practitioner well above the average that is capable of facing powerful magical threats. A kingdom of a hundred thousand people might have one such mage. A beginning hero cannot have a higher level than this.

6 **A Mighty Mage:** The mightiest living mage most people have ever heard of, a master of magic. A realm of a million people might have one such mage.

7 **A Legendary Mage:** The most powerful mage from sea to sea. A continent of ten million might have one such mage.

8 **A Supreme Mage:** A sphere of a hundred million people might have only one such mage.

9 **An Archmage:** Most spheres have no one this powerful living among them.

10 **An Avatar:** Such a mage has channeled so much magic that they are no longer human. The mage has become a force of nature or even of supernature. They are incredibly powerful but also beyond mortal understanding.

6 QUESTIONS STAGE

In the Questions Stage of creating heroes, you and the other players ask one another questions to help develop more details about your heroes. You learn more about the other players' heroes, and the other players inspire you to invent details about your own hero. For many players, this is the most enjoyable part of creating a hero.

Generally, if your group is small (four or fewer players), you can all participate in one group. If the group is larger than four, split into groups of two, three, or four. (If the group is too big, the pace can get too slow.) If possible, split into groups so that the players whose heroes are likely to know each other best are together. That way you, as a player, get to know the heroes that your hero might also know.

The players again show their vision images to each other and explain what they mean, as they did in the introduction stage. Then each player asks questions about the others' heroes. You can each ask a single question at a time, or you can ask several at once. You and the other players take turns asking questions. The goal is to develop a good sense of who your hero is and who the other players' heroes are. You may of course volunteer information the other players don't ask about. Their role is to help you develop your hero, not to restrict you.

The players ask questions for any length of time. Generally, the gamemaster determines when this process has gone on long enough. The Questions Stage, however, never really ends. At the beginning of every session, you can start out with a few minutes of questions to help the players remember who the heroes are and to develop them further. You can also ask questions at the end of a quest, to understand how your heroes might have changed as a result of the events in the quest.

Types of Questions

You can ask various types of questions for different purposes.

Character Questions

You can ask questions as though you were asking the hero, not the player. When you answer questions, you can answer them as your hero would. This practice is often best because it involves you more immediately in the heroes' lives and lets you practice taking on your hero's role.

Out of Character:

First Player: "Where does your hero live?"

Second Player: "She lives in an imperial capital, a really big city where all sorts of things are always happening. It's not a perfect place, but she thinks it is."

The Cockatrice

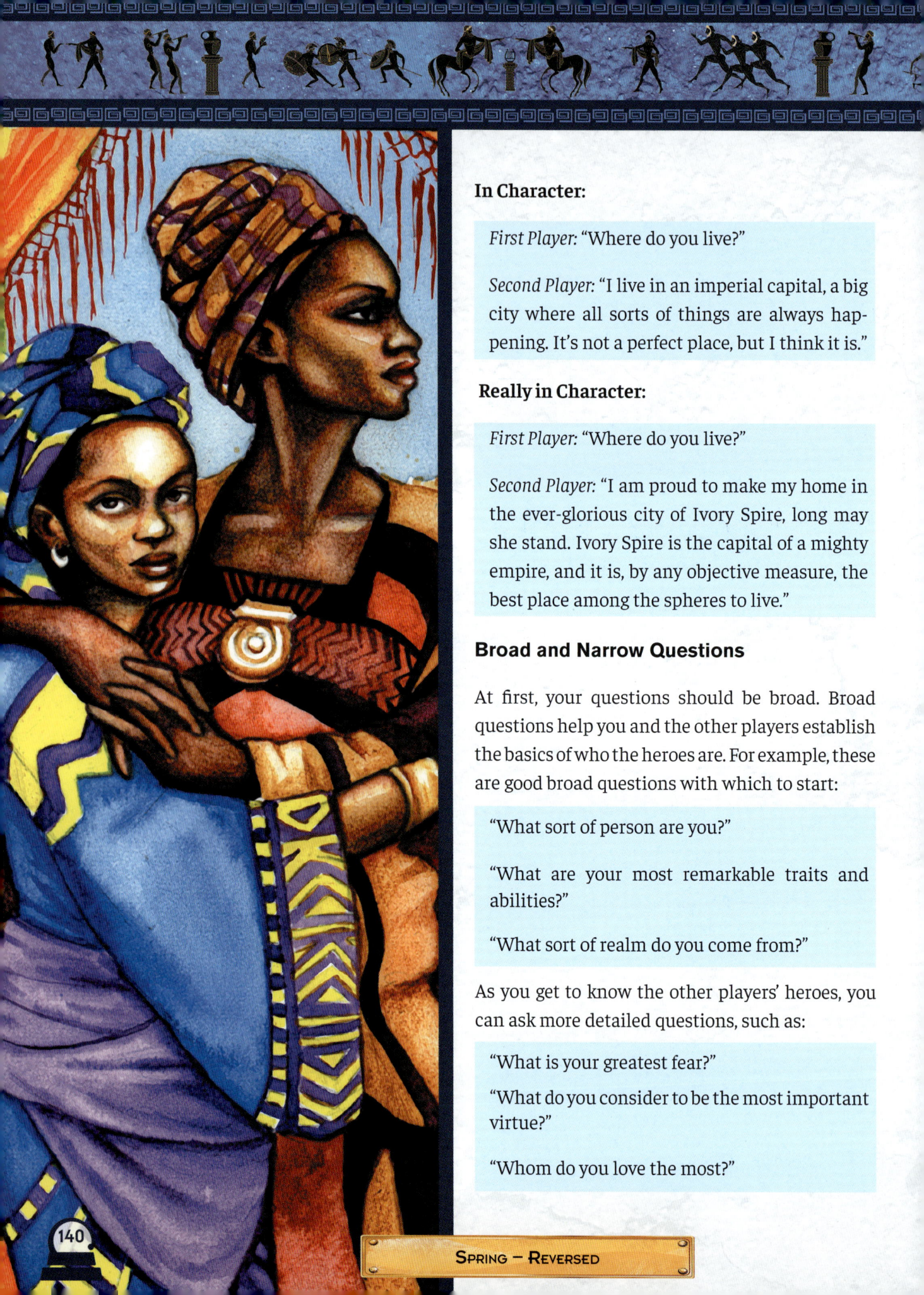

In Character:

First Player: "Where do you live?"

Second Player: "I live in an imperial capital, a big city where all sorts of things are always happening. It's not a perfect place, but I think it is."

Really in Character:

First Player: "Where do you live?"

Second Player: "I am proud to make my home in the ever-glorious city of Ivory Spire, long may she stand. Ivory Spire is the capital of a mighty empire, and it is, by any objective measure, the best place among the spheres to live."

Broad and Narrow Questions

At first, your questions should be broad. Broad questions help you and the other players establish the basics of who the heroes are. For example, these are good broad questions with which to start:

"What sort of person are you?"

"What are your most remarkable traits and abilities?"

"What sort of realm do you come from?"

As you get to know the other players' heroes, you can ask more detailed questions, such as:

"What is your greatest fear?"

"What do you consider to be the most important virtue?"

"Whom do you love the most?"

Pretty soon you can ask specific questions about particular heroes. For example:

"What was the happiest event in your apprenticeship?"

"How did your family react when you renounced the throne?"

"Why did you run away from the invaders instead of staying to fight?"

Questions About Vision Images

You can ask questions based on the visions that describe the other heroes, such as:

"Who is this person in the background?"

"Is this fancy clothing typical for these people, or is this some sort of festival?"

"What happened when you met that mermaid?"

"What the heck is that?"

The vision images in *Section 3: Vision Guide* have questions next to them that you can use to inspire you to think about the images.

Breaking Character

Sometimes it's appropriate to "break character" and ask questions that the player can answer but the hero cannot. For instance:

"What do you know about your hero that she does not know about herself?"

"In what ways is your hero lying to himself?"

"What lessons in life does your hero still need to learn?"

These kinds of questions help establish the hidden, secret, or unknown sides of the hero. They also make room for the hero to grow as a person. By establishing things that a hero doesn't know, these sorts of questions help the player invent things the hero can discover during play.

Joint Character Questions

Once you and the other players know each others' heroes well enough, you may want to ask questions about heroes' interactions with each other.

"I usually can't stand nobles, but you are different somehow, and I find myself liking you even though you have noble blood. Did your parents bring you up differently from how other noble children are raised?"

"When I brag about my exploits, how do you react?"

"If I showed up at your cottage asking for shelter, how would you treat me?"

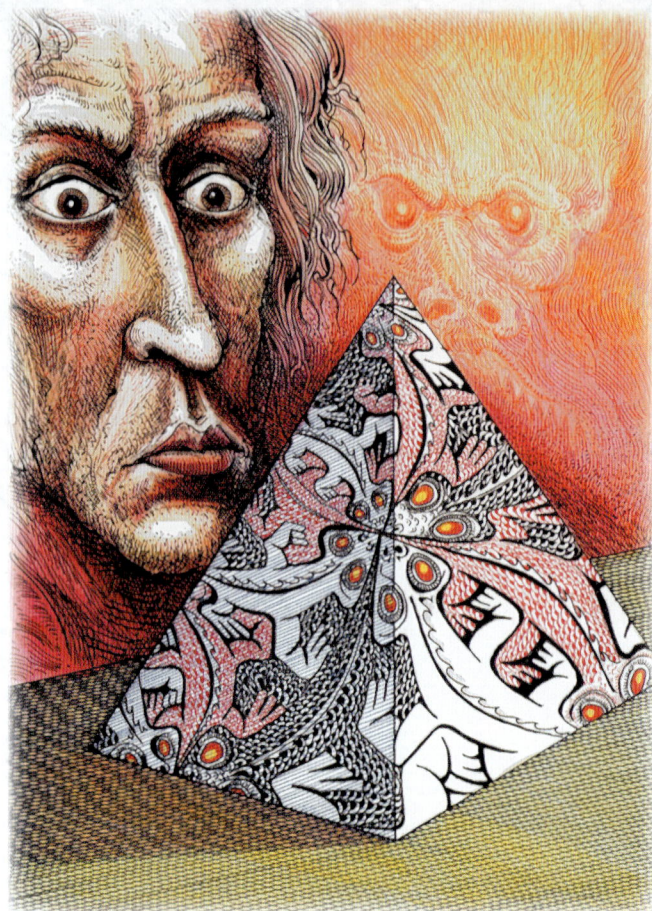

Answers

Answering Tough Questions

Sometimes other players may ask you questions that you don't know the answers to. If a question is important, you need to make up an answer. For example, if someone asks you what weapons, if any, your hero carries while traveling, you ought to have an answer because you should probably know that before you begin play. If you don't know, you need to invent an answer. Otherwise you'll probably end up making the answer up on the spot during your first quest. For less important questions, however, it's OK not to know the answer. Tell the player who asked the question that you don't know offhand, and then think about it. When you decide what the answer is, whether that's in a few minutes or a few weeks, let the other players know.

What the Heroes Don't Know

By asking questions about the other players' heroes, you will learn a lot about those heroes. Remember, though, that your own hero won't know everything you know. For example, another player may run a hero who pretends to come from a noble family although they were really abandoned at birth and raised in a temple. You, the player, may learn the hero's true history even though your hero doesn't. Part of playing your hero is keeping straight what your hero knows and what your hero doesn't know.

You can use the secrets you know as a player to make roleplaying the characters more fun. For example, during a quest your hero could ask the hero who is pretending to be of noble birth about their childhood. You know that the details that the other player's hero provides are all part of an elaborate lie, but your hero doesn't. An exchange like this lets the other player ham it up for a bit and helps to define the other hero.

POSSESSIONS

Whether anyone asks you or not, you should decide what possessions your hero owns. These possessions will be important in determining what you can do on a quest, and they also help you to develop your hero's background.

Your hero can have any possessions suitable to their background. A warrior may have weapons, armor, and perhaps a steed. A mage may have a wand, potent herbs, and possibly a scroll or two containing arcane lore. A wanderer may have a walking staff, snares and traps for catching food, tools for surviving in the wilderness, a bedroll, and maybe a tent. If your gamemaster thinks your hero is carrying more than their Fire and Earth scores would allow, they may require you to trim your list of possessions.

Less practical items are common, too. Your hero may have a musical instrument, a gift from a loved one, a pet chipmunk, or some other diversion.

Heroes may also have some valuables for trade, such as gold coins, gems, furs, salt, spices, or other easily portable items.

Experienced spherewalkers usually carry a variety of small, precious valuables for trade in new realms.

In addition to items carried, a hero may have other possessions stored somewhere else. Many heroes have permanent homes somewhere, usually inhabited by their extended families, where they may store things. For instance, a scholar may have a library, a sorcerer may have a study full of equipment, and a warrior may have a collection of war trophies.

You must get your gamemaster's permission to have any possessions that might interfere with the game. For instance, a harquebus (a primitive firearm dating from A.D. 1400) might work for some gamemasters, but others may feel that even primitive firearms change the tone of the game and therefore disallow them.

If any possessions are powerful enough that they duplicate powers or magic, then you'll have to pay for them as Powers or Magic. For instance, if your hero has a ring that lets them fly, then you have to buy it as a 2-point (frequent, major) Power.

1709. Pyramid Lizards – Ian Miller

What the Players Don't Know

Sometimes players leave "blank spaces" in the stories of their heroes. You might, for instance, decide not to detail what your hero's childhood was like at first. You can come back and fill in details later on, when you know your hero even better. If players ask you about parts of your hero's background that you don't want to invent yet, it's okay to tell them that you don't know the answers yet.

You might also want to include things that neither you nor your hero knows. For example, the hero who's pretending to be a noble doesn't know who their parents were. The player running the hero might know or might not know. If the player doesn't know something, then the gamemaster might invent details the player doesn't know about. For example, the gamemaster might invent a quest in which the hero who pretends to be a noble finds out who their true parents are.

What Gamemasters Need to Know

Sometimes your gamemaster needs to know details about your hero in order to know how your hero will fit into a quest or what capabilities your hero has. If you don't have an answer ready, your gamemaster can insist that you come up with one. If the gamemaster needs to know the answer, the game won't run smoothly without that information. For example, a gamemaster who's planning to run a quest involving elves and other faeries might need to know what a forester hero's experiences have been with these creatures.

Changing Your Character

As you develop your hero, through questions or just through play, it may turn out that the details you've chosen, such as the Virtue, Powers, and Elements, don't match your new vision of your hero. It's all right to go back and alter these details to fit your developing image of the hero.

YOUR HERO AT A GLANCE

1607. Prison Cell – Ian Miller

Name

Names in EVERWAY are almost all based on common words, such as Miracle, Glamourbright, Heather, or Victor.

Motive

A hero's Motive is the general reason the hero has undertaken a life of adventure, representing the hero's general attitude toward their journeys.

Virtue, Fault, and Fate

A hero's Virtue is a card from the Fortune Deck that represents a special gift, strength, or blessing. A hero's Fault is a fortune card that represents a special lack, weakness, or curse. A hero's Fate is a fortune card that represents the central issue, dilemma, or challenge that the hero will face. You know your hero's Fate, but your hero may not.

Powers

Powers are special abilities of your hero. You must pay for Powers with elemental points. Each hero gets 20 points for Power, Elements, and Magic.

Magic

Magic is the ability to flexibly create supernatural effects by manipulating general laws of magic. Each type of magic is usually linked to an Element. A score of 3 represents average ability.

Wheel of Elements

The four Elements—Air, Fire, Earth, and Water—describe your hero's basic capabilities. An average person's Element scores are each 3, whereas heroes' scores average around 4 or 5. A score of 6 is the strongest score people other than heroes can have, while 9 is the strongest score a hero can ever attain (a hero's strongest starting score is 6). Air represents mental ability, Fire represents physical ability, Earth represents mental and physical fortitude, and Water represents psychic and emotional sensitivity.

Your hero has a Specialty in each Element. When taking actions related to that Specialty, your hero is as capable as if the Element were 1 point stronger. For example, if your hero has 5 Fire, and your Specialty is "Running," your hero runs as well as someone with 6 Fire.

Visions, Powers & Magic, and Possessions

The back of the sheet is for details about the hero's visions, powers and magic, and possessions.

1512. Dragon Uprising – Andrew Robinson

THE FOOL

Chapter 4: Powers & Magic

This chapter explains in greater detail how Powers and Magic work in EVERWAY. This information is important for players adding Powers or Magic to their heroes during hero creation. This chapter is also essential for gamemasters, who help the players along. As long as the gamemaster knows these rules fairly well, players can create heroes without reading or referring to this chapter.

POWERS

Powers are a great way to make truly unique heroes with supernatural abilities. Powers allow you to create almost any type of effect you can imagine, but they are more specific than Magic. Understanding Magic implies a more general knowledge and ability than Powers. If you want a flexible range of abilities, you should read the *Magic* section of this chapter. You can skip ahead to that section now if you want to see how Magic differs from Powers.

Types of Powers

Powers can be almost anything you can imagine, ranging from an ability to step through shadows, to changing their skin to stone, to channeling fire, to a sleep gaze where the hero can cause others to become very sleepy if they look into your hero's eyes (this cannot force the character to fall asleep, just get sleepy if not otherwise stimulated). The only restrictions on the kind of Powers you can give your heroes are the number of elemental points you are willing to spend on them and the gamemaster's approval. Each Power is linked to an Element based on the nature of its effect.

Powers may either be intrinsic to your hero or could come from an external object or creature. In general, Powers that are not intrinsic to your hero cannot be lost, but they may become inaccessible for a time as a consequence of choices made during gameplay. For example, if your hero chooses to burn their magical harp that always plays beautiful music, afterward they might hear faint strains of music from time to time until one day they receive a gift of a magical music box that plays whatever harp music the hero wishes. Your gamemaster will find a way to return your hero's Power to you through play, but perhaps not immediately, depending on the circumstances of how the Power was lost.

Cost of Powers

The cost of a Power during hero creation is determined by how useful it is during play. The cost is determined by three factors:

- **Frequent:** Often useful

- **Major:** Has a large impact on play

- **Versatile:** Useful in several ways

Each of these factors increases the cost of the Power by 1 elemental point. If you're not sure what a Power should cost, consult with the other players and the gamemaster. You might want to conduct a Questions Stage around the Power itself to understand how it would be used in gameplay and what its effects would be. The gamemaster must approve the final Power description and cost.

Below are examples of frequent, major, and versatile Powers. These examples use three specific Powers to demonstrate what the labels mean:

- **Fast Healing (Earth):** The ability to recover quickly from wounds.

- **Spell-Reversal (Earth):** The ability to cause spells cast on the hero to affect the caster instead.

- **Magical Singing (Air):** The ability to sing with magically enhanced effect, altering the mood of the audience.

Is It Frequent?

If the Power is something that often makes a difference in play, the Power is called frequent. For example, Fast Healing is a frequent Power because it comes into play often. Since traveling among the spheres and doing heroic things is dangerous, heroes routinely get hurt.

Spell-Reversal is not frequent because the Power is only useful when a spell is cast on the hero. This Power would be frequent if the hero could reverse all sorts of magic, not just spells cast on them personally.

Magic Singing is not frequent because affecting the mood of an audience isn't helpful in many situations. A hero may sing almost all the time, but since the Power rarely affects play, it is not labeled frequent. Charging lions, falling rocks, dungeon doors, and unhappy ghosts don't care to listen to songs. If the player defined the Power as capable of working on charging lions, falling rocks, dungeon doors, and unhappy ghosts, then it would indeed be frequent.

Most abilities are frequent. After all, most players invent Powers that will often make a difference for their heroes.

Is It Major?

If the Power has a big effect, especially on another character, it is considered major. Count as major anything that greatly changes the hero's capabilities. The ability to reverse a spell back on the caster is major because it has the powerful effects of protecting the hero from magic and harming those who cast destructive spells upon the hero. Sometimes the Power will have a minor effect (such as when the original spell is minor), but since Spell-Reversal is capable of a major effect, it's a major Power.

Fast Healing is not major because it doesn't greatly change the hero's capabilities. It doesn't help the hero fight enemies, solve mysteries, or perform other important tasks. If the player defined the Power as working instantly, so that wounds disappeared in a heartbeat, then it would be a major Power because it would greatly help the hero in dangerous situations.

Magical Singing is not major because altering the mood of an audience is not a powerful effect. If the player defined the singing ability as capable of, for example, stopping charging warriors in their tracks, then it would indeed be major.

Note that if the Power is major in two or more ways, the gamemaster may assign the "major" cost two or more times. Thus a Power can cost more than 3 elemental points.

Is It Versatile?

If the Power can be used in many different ways, it is called versatile. Magic Singing is versatile because the hero can alter moods to produce a variety of effects. The hero can raise people's spirits, soothe bad feelings, stir a crowd to action, and so on. The player could define the musical ability in a much more limited way, such as only causing sadness, in which case the Power wouldn't be versatile. It would then be a 0-point, free Power (see p. 119).

Fast Healing is not versatile because there's only one thing a hero can do with it: recover from wounds quickly. If the player defined the Power as helping the hero recover from everything quickly—illness, drunkenness, heartache, sleep, confusion, enchantments, and so on—then the Power would be versatile.

Spell-Reversal is also not versatile because there's only one thing a hero can do with it: reverse spells. If the hero could reverse all manner of energies—magic, emotions, heat, and so on—this Power would be versatile.

Extraordinary Powers

If a Power doesn't have any drawbacks or weaknesses that naturally belong to it, or if it is especially powerful, the gamemaster may assign a higher cost to it. For example, Invisibility is generally a 2-point Power because it's frequent and major. Invisibility, however, has drawbacks. Guard dogs can smell an invisible intruder, and people with keen hearing can locate invisible people. If the player decides the hero not only can't be seen but also can't be heard or smelled, then the gamemaster should require the player pay an extra point for it.

Does My Power Work?

As with any other action or contest of ability, your hero's Elements and a draw from the Fortune Deck determine whether your Power works. If your hero sings a magic song to soothe an angry dragon, the gamemaster may compare your hero's Air score (which determines vocal ability) to the dragon's Earth score (which determines its resistance to being swayed). Unless your hero's Air score is at least as strong as the dragon's Earth score, it will take a very good draw from the Fortune Deck for the hero to succeed.

Your hero may also have to contend with background characters who are protected from the hero's Powers. For instance, since monarchs among the spheres have to protect themselves from magical threats as well as from mundane assassins, most of them have means to detect magic and resist spells. Just as the gamemaster may assume a queen has someone to taste her food for poison and someone to guard her chambers at night, they can assume she has mages or enchantments to protect her

from supernatural threats. If you think your hero can get away with anything by being invisible, you're in for a rude surprise.

> See pp.124–131 to read more about Elements. Gamemasters can refer to Book 2: Gamemasters to read more about using Elements and the Fortune Deck to determine whether specific actions succeed or fail.

Example Powers

Each Power can have several costs depending on how you define it. Below are general categories for Powers followed by some specific Powers within each category. Note that these are just examples, not a list from which you have to select. For more ideas, look at the Powers of the ready-to-run heroes in *Chapter 8: Quick Heroes*.

Companion

- **Pet Viper (Fire):** 3 Poison (*weakness*). A large, venomous viper has befriended the hero. All it can do is strike those who threaten it or the hero; its poison sickens and incapacitates the average person (3 Earth). The viper's elements are 1 Air, 2 Fire, 2 Earth, 2 Water. **Cost: 1** (major)

- **Cat Familiar (Water):** An intelligent cat is the hero's devoted companion. It can talk to the hero (and only to the hero), and it is as intelligent as a child. It has no other special abilities. The cat can spy, carry written messages, stand guard, and so on. The cat's elements are 2 Air, 3 Fire, 2 Earth, and 4 Water. **Cost: 2** (frequent and versatile)

- **Wolf Companion (Fire):** A clever, loyal wolf is the hero's constant companion. It can do a few specific tricks, but it's just a clever animal; it does not have humanlike intelligence. The wolf can fight, follow people by smell, stand guard, hear faint noises, and so on. The wolf's elements are 3 Air, 4 Fire, 4 Earth, and 4 Water. **Cost: 3** (frequent, major, and versatile)

- **Ape Sidekick (Earth):** A talking ape is the hero's companion. It can speak and use tools as skillfully as most people, and it is very strong. The ape's elements are 3 Air, 4 Fire, 5 Earth, and 3 Water. **Cost: 4** (frequent, twice major, and versatile)

Create Fire

Your hero's Fire score helps determine how effective these Powers are.

- **Sweat Fire (Fire):** The hero can make fire come forth from their skin. The flames are small enough that they do not improve the hero's combat abilities much (though they may be very useful against monsters vulnerable to fire). **Cost: 1** (frequent)

- **Throw Fire (Fire):** The hero can produce fire from their bare hands. The fire can be formed into balls and thrown, and these large, hot flames can also be used to increase the hero's combat ability. **Cost: 2** (frequent and versatile)

- **Mastery of Flame (Fire):** The hero can create heat, light, and flame at will. The flame can be used as a weapon in hand-to-hand combat as well as over a distance. **Cost: 3** (frequent, major, and versatile)

Healing

Your hero's Earth score determines how well they normally recover from wounds.

- **Fast Healing (Earth):** The hero recovers from physical wounds seven times as fast as normal, so a day's rest is as good as a week's would be for the average human. **Cost: 1** (frequent)

- **Instant Healing (Earth):** The hero's wounds close nearly instantly, so that no wound lasts for more than a few seconds. A blow that kills the hero immediately, however, is still fatal. **Cost: 2** (frequent and major)

Immortality

Earth can help determine how well your hero resists wounds and other forms of harm.

- **Ageless (Earth):** The hero does not age. While this ability may eventually be very useful, it has little direct effect on play, so it counts as a free Power. **Cost: 0** (free)

- **Unkillable (Earth):** The hero cannot be killed, though they can still be hampered by wounds, sickened by poison, knocked down by blows, weakened by disease, and so on. Spherewalkers' quests often bring them into danger, so this Power is frequent. It is major because it changes the hero's abilities dramatically. **Cost: 2** (frequent and major)

- **Invulnerable (Earth):** The hero cannot be wounded or poisoned by normal means, though they can still be struck down by forceful blows, knocked unconscious from lack of air, or killed by hunger or thirst. **Cost: 3** (frequent and twice major)

Invisibility

Water, because it rules stealth, can help determine how effectively and easily a hero becomes invisible.

- **Standing Unseen (Water):** The hero can become invisible but must remain still and silent or be revealed. **Cost: 1** (frequent)

- **Walking Unseen (Water):** The hero can become invisible and can move about without breaking the spell. **Cost: 2** (frequent and major)

Persuasion

For persuasion Powers, the hero's Air score, the Earth score of the person the hero is persuading, and the context of the situation help the gamemaster determine whether the hero succeeds.

- **Winning Smile (Air):** The hero's smile is charming. It helps the hero stand out and may make some people more favorably disposed toward them, but it won't sway the hearts of enemies and such. **Cost: 0** (free)

408. Lupine and Serpentine – Ian Miller

- **Persuasive Voice (Air):** The hero has a soothing voice that can sway the hearts of others. It will not, however, sway those who are hostile to the hero. **Cost: 1** (frequent)

- **Charming Voice (Air):** The hero can win the affection of those they can talk to at some length. It will not work on those who refuse to listen, and those who have been charmed may realize what's happened when they're away from the hero. (The gamemaster may restrict you from choosing such a Power unless you promise not to use it against other heroes. Manipulating other heroes is a fast way to ruin a game.) **Cost: 2** (frequent and major)

- **Dominating Gaze (Air):** By speaking firmly and gazing into a person's eyes, the hero can exert some control over the other character's will. The weaker the target's Earth score, the more the hero can get them to do. This control is usually unpredictable, and it's possible for a controlled character to snap out of the spell. (The gamemaster may restrict you from choosing such a Power unless you promise not to use it against other heroes.) **Cost: 3** (frequent, major, and versatile)

- **Instant Control (Air):** A Power that would give a hero instant and complete control over other characters would ruin too many plots, so it is not allowed. **Cost: –** (not allowed)

Priestly Powers

Most elements affect priestly Powers, but Water determines how open one is to divine messages. Earth may determine how well-grounded one's rituals are. Many priests and priestesses are mages, in which case their Powers are covered by the rules for Magic (see p. 136) instead of by these rules.

- **Priestly Rites (Water):** The hero can lead worship services and divine ceremonies to channel energy. Effects that fall within the scope of Priestly Rites include binding oaths, blessing unions, bringing fertility to crops, improving an army's fortune in war, and so on. The hero's abilities depend on having a congregation to lead, and their abilities are at their peak on holy days. **Cost: 2** (major and versatile)

- **Invocation (Water):** The priest or priestess, apart from any worshipping congregation, can invoke the power of deities to bless people, sanctify oaths, provide guidance, and so on. This Power is frequent because the hero can use it without relying on a congregation. Magical abilities that are even more directly under the hero's control count as Magic (see p. 136), not as a Power. **Cost: 3** (frequent, major, and versatile)

Shapechange

Shapechanging is related to more than one Element, though Water is the most

important in determining how easily one can change forms.

- **Werewolf (Water):** The hero can turn into a powerful wolf who is immune to normal (nonsilver and nonmagical) weapons. If the hero can only become a wolf on nights of the full moon, then the Power is major but not frequent. Cost: 2 (frequent and major)

- **Bird Form (Water):** The hero can turn into a particular type of bird, such as a crow or hawk. Cost: 2 (frequent and major)

- **Werehawk (Water):** The hero can turn into a powerful hawk that is immune to nonsilver, nonmagical weapons. The Power is "twice major" because the hawk can fly and is immune to most weapons. Cost: 3 (frequent and twice major)

- **Shapeshifting (Water):** The hero can take the shape of any natural creature up to the size of a horse and use any abilities this form provides. For example, as an eagle, the hero could see well; as a snake they could be venomous; and as a hound they would have

1411. True Pearl's Bonds —Rudy Rauben (Roger Raupp)

a keen sense of smell. Shapeshifting is a frequent Power because the hero will often find a new shape to be handy. It is major because the hero can use deadly and powerful abilities thanks to these forms. It is versatile because the hero can take on a great variety of shapes, and thus a great variety of skills. (By severely limiting the range of shapes, the player could make this Power no longer versatile. For example, if the hero can change only into different types of house cats, the Power is no longer versatile. If the hero can turn into lions, leopards, house cats, lynxes, and so on, then the Power is still versatile because the hero can use the Power to gain fighting ability, night vision, leaping ability, extraordinary hearing, small size, an innocuous appearance, and so on.) **Cost: 2** (frequent, major, and versatile)

Speech

Your hero's Air score helps determine how well they can use these Powers.

- **Bird Tongue (Air):** The hero can speak to and understand birds. Birds, however, don't necessarily want to talk to the hero, and the hero may find that they have little to say. **Cost: 0** (free)

- **Speak to Animals (Air):** The hero can speak to and understand all manner of animals. This Power, however, doesn't mean the animals want to talk to the hero, or that they have much to say. Animals in general may have a lot to say about their lives, but they're not likely to know much about the world of humans. For instance, if your hero asks a fox to describe the humans it saw lurking in the woods, it may reply, "It walked on two legs instead of four." **Cost: 1** (frequent)

- **Shadow Whispers (Air):** The hero can speak to and understand the dead (though some ghosts are in no shape to hold a conversation, and some simply don't want to talk). **Cost: 1** (major)

Visions

Your hero's Water score helps determine how strong these visions are.

- **Glimpses of the Future (Water):** During times of stress, the hero gets visions of the future. These visions are not consciously controlled and are usually hazy, general, or incomplete. **Cost: 1** (major)

- **Visionary Ritual (Water):** The hero can perform rituals to gain visions of the future, though the visions are usually hazy, general, or incomplete. **Cost: 2** (frequent and major)

- **Glimpses Through Time and Space (Water):** During times of stress, the hero gets visions of the future, of the past, or of distant places. These visions are not consciously controlled and are usually hazy, general, or incomplete. **Cost: 2** (major and versatile)

- **Mystic Eye (Water):** The hero can concentrate to gain visions of the future, of times past, or of distant places. The visions are usually hazy, general, or incomplete. **Cost: 3** (frequent, major, and versatile)

- **All-Seeing Eye (Water):** The hero can get clear visions of the future, the past, or remote locations that would ruin plots that depend on mystery. Such a Power is not allowed. **Cost: –** (not allowed)

Magic

Magic is much broader than Powers and much less specific. Your hero can adapt their magic to meet the demands of the moment rather than being limited to one particular ability.

Types of Magic

There are many different types of magic, most linked to an Element. The linked Element typically must be equal to or greater than your hero's Magic level. You can invent your hero's type of magic or use one of the examples provided here. Types of magic are variously known in the game world by terms such as "paths," "schools," "arts," "styles," and "traditions."

Mages of different realms study different types of magic. Your mage may study a type of magic that is common in their realm or may study an unusual type.

Five examples of types of magic are described on pp. 162–171. You can use one of these for your mage, or you can invent your own. Each type of magic is listed with the Element it is linked to, a general description of what that type of magic does, and examples of what the mage can do at each level of magical ability. In addition, the four ready-to-run mages each use one of these four elemental types of magic. The specific abilities of each ready-to-run mage are explained beside that type of magic.

Note that most effects of magic require the presence of the mage for maximum effect. For example, a mage who uses Words of Power can inscribe

158

THE UNICORN – REVERSED

a door with a magical binding, but it won't be nearly as powerful as a spell the mage holds and presents personally. To work permanent enchantments of any power, a mage must sacrifice something: magical materials, a great length of time, or even a bit of themselves. Permanent enchantments are therefore rare.

Mages and Elements

A mage's Elements are important to the use of magic.

Air: Mental strength and intellect are important to mages, especially those who work with magic words and formulas. A mage with strong Air may specialize in mental magic—communication over great distances, speech, and so forth—or in air- and weather-related magic. A mage with weak Air may not have the mental ability to master complicated magical formulas.

Fire: Forceful energy is important to mages, especially those who use violent spells. A mage with strong Fire might specialize in spells related to fire, heat, light, destruction, change, and action. A mage with weak Fire may cast spells without much force behind them.

Earth: Inner strength is important to mages, especially to healers. A mage with strong Earth might specialize in fertility, healing, and earth-based spells. A mage

803. Bell Walkers – Scott Kirschner

PRIMAL ARTIFACTS

The only known magical objects of seemingly unlimited power are a trinity of primal artifacts: the True Pearl of Making, the Mirror of Shadows, and the Edge of Light and Darkness.

The True Pearl of Making embodies the power of creation, the Mirror of Shadows embodies the power of utter destruction, and the Edge of Light and Darkness embodies the line dividing the two.

It is believed these are the very objects the deities used to craft all the spheres of creation.

with weak Earth may be easily influenced or manipulated by outside forces. As with physical tasks, a mage's Earth also determines a mage's endurance; magic is a demanding art, and a mage with weak Earth gets tired after casting a few big spells. A mage's Earth is the primary determinant of how much magic the mage can use before becoming worn out.

Water: Intuition and a connection to the unconscious are important to mages, especially to seers and clairvoyants. A mage with strong Water may be a psychic, a sensitive, or a specialist in water magic. A mage with weak Water is closed off to unconscious and unspoken forces and thus in danger of being misled.

FERTILITY – REVERSED

Ready-To-Run Heroes and Their Elements

Praises Be's average Earth score (3) means that he tires after doing any significant magic. His Magic score is so strong he can quickly fatigue himself into unconsciousness if he casts powerful magic too fast. His average Water score means he's no more sensitive than the average person, though his Specialty, "Sensing Magic," at least gives him a hint when powerful magic is in the works.

Whisper Walker's Earth is 4, stronger than average but not spectacular. She can handle the rigors of calling spirits into herself better than most could, but it usually leaves her drained, and a powerful spirit could drive her to unconsciousness. Her 5 Water score means she is very sensitive; since her Magic level is weaker than the Element to which it's linked, Whisper Walker has untapped potential. (That is, if she could find a way to improve her Magic level, she could do so without first having to raise her Water score.)

Transforming things is hard work, but Serenity's strong Earth score (4) allows her to cast a fair number of spells before wearing herself out. Her average Air and Water scores mean she's no wiser or more perceptive than average; she may well wind up misusing her power if she is not careful.

Cleft's strong Earth (5) means he can use his magic for long periods before wearing himself out. His other Elements are average, so he's unlikely to be capable of doing much outside his field. When it comes to identifying magic runes, dealing with spirits, and so on, he's basically no better off than anyone else.

Magic Power in Perspective

Magic is an ability that can be used in countless ways. Its limits can be tested only in play itself; neither the gamemaster nor the players will know from the start what a given mage is fully capable of doing. It is therefore important that the gamemaster and player agree on as much as they can before play begins and that the player is willing to let the gamemaster be the final judge of magic's effect. If you are not comfortable with the gamemaster being the arbiter of your mage's capabilities, you should not play a mage.

Semicircle Test

What is too powerful for a given Magic level, and what is not powerful enough? To answer these questions, apply the Semicircle Test. What could a hero do with two Elements equal to the mage's Magic level? For example, to imagine what a mage with 6 Magic can do, imagine what a hero with 6 Fire and 6 Earth (power semicircle) could do. Such a hero would be a mighty warrior, able to handily defeat several average warriors. It is fair, then, for a mage with 6 Magic to have equivalent effects. A mage using Words of Power with a 6 Magic, for example, can kill a person with a word. While this is less valuable than 6 Fire and 6 Earth when the mage is being rushed by eight warriors (as some of the warriors are bound to reach the mage before they are all killed), it's more useful

when attempting a discreet assassination, so it's about equally valuable to a combat-oriented spherewalker.

Imagine what a hero with 6 Water and 6 Air (wisdom semicircle) could do. Such a hero could sense the underlying emotions in another person and talk smoothly and persuasively enough to get most people to do what the hero wants them to do. Similarly, a Words of Power mage with a 6 Magic can say a word and hold back a group of warriors who would otherwise attack. Each of these abilities is useful in different circumstances, but they are roughly equivalent in overall usefulness.

Limiting Magic Power

Sometimes a mage's abilities get out of hand. If at any time a mage's abilities begin to ruin quests, the gamemaster has the right to restrict or reduce the mage's magical abilities below what they used to be capable of in play. For example, if a mage has the ability to make people invisible, and the heroes defeat almost every obstacle by being invisible, then the challenge and fun of the game are in peril. The gamemaster can limit this magic power directly, such as by imposing a limit on the amount of time or number of times a hero can be invisible, or indirectly, such as by creating quests in which invisibility does little good or is even useless. (For example, enemies with strong Water scores, good senses of smell, or magical wards might be able to detect invisible heroes.) Remember, magic is never an exact science, and the gamemaster is free to change the rules to preserve the spirit of the game.

WORDS OF POWER

This form of magic uses spoken and written words to affect living things, spirits, and magical forces. The mage can inscribe charms with magic words and symbols, but the charms don't have the same effect as a directly spoken word. This form of magic is very versatile, but it is especially useful for binding spirits, summoning objects, banishing creatures, compelling lesser creatures to obey, and striking down opponents with power words. If a spoken word has a lasting, rather than immediate, effect, then speaking another such word of power negates the first one. For example, if a mage compels a cat to go into the next room and scratch the first person it comes across, and the mage uses another word of power before the cat has completed its mission, then the spell on the cat is lifted. As sound is the sense connected to Air, this magic works through the mage's words.

At this Magic level… a Words of Power mage can:

1 Inscribe charms to bring (slightly) good luck; command bugs by voice.

2 Command domesticated, peaceful animals to do simple tasks.

3 Inscribe charms for various minor purposes; force back wild animals.

4 Bind spirits; misdirect mortals; inscribe charms for protection from specific dangers.

5 Force back an average person (3 Earth) with a magic word.

6 Bind powerful magics; kill an average individual (3 Earth) with a word; force back a group of average people (3 Earth) with a word.

7 Kill a small group of average people (3 Earth) with a word; force back a large beast (5 Earth) with a word.

8 Kill a large beast (5 Earth) with a word; delude a city's population through charms and words.

9 Kill a mighty beast (6 Earth) with a word; delude a realm's population through charms and words.

10 Create creatures by word; inscribe runes that shape spheres.

INSPIRATION – REVERSED

Praises Be

The ready-to-run hero Praises Be ("Praise" for short) has Words of Power Magic at level 6.

Praise's magic uses spoken and written words to affect living things, spirits, and magic. His spells fall into three general types: spoken words, rituals, and inscriptions.

By speaking magic words, Praise can compel a spirit to obey him, kill an average person (3 Earth), or force a group of average people to back away. (Average people forced back cannot approach Praise again for about a minute, but those with strong Fire scores can approach again sooner.) He can easily force back or command animals, but they are no easier for him to kill than people are. The effects of one word of power are negated when Praise utters another word of power. For instance, if he has caused bandits to back away with a word of power, and then he uses a word of power to kill one of them, the others are freed from their spell and are once again able to attack him.

Praise can inscribe objects with magic words so that the objects have magical effects. A magical inscription, however, takes a lot of time and energy to do, and it's not as powerful as a spoken word. For example, Praise could create scrolls to be used as talismans that protect their wearers from 3 Magic or weaker.

(Thus, a mage with a score of 3 would not be able to cast spells on the protected person.) If the name of the wearer is worked into the inscription, it protects against 4 Magic, and if the name of the mage whose magic is to be countered is worked into the formula, it protects up to 5 Magic (the most powerful protection Praise can offer). Praise can also craft talismans to protect people against other supernatural dangers or to have other magical effects. Depending on the strength of the talisman, it takes Praise anywhere from an hour to a day to inscribe one, with more powerful talismans taking longer. Talismans' power wanes quickly.

Praise's rituals are for major magical actions, such as imprisoning a powerful spirit, warding an area against magical intrusion, and other such feats. Praise's rituals last from an hour to a day, and they leave him weary.

Praise's average Earth score (3) means he tires after doing any significant magic. His Magic score is so high that he can quickly fatigue himself into unconsciousness if he casts powerful magic too quickly.

Praise's magic depends on his ability to speak words or to inscribe words and symbols.

H109. Praises Be – Rick Berry

FLUX

Fire magic transforms things, as fire can transform wood to ash, sand to glass, water to steam, and ore to iron. Flux magic also can accelerate or slow down natural processes such as causing a person to run faster or an object to fall more slowly. It can also cause objects to move without being touched like a fire can push objects away from it or even lift objects into the air.

As sight is the sense connected to Fire, fire magic works through the concentrated gaze of the mage.

At this Magic level... a Flux mage can:

1 Lift or slightly alter minor features of small objects.

2 Speed up, slow down, or alter minor features of small animals.

3 Levitate an object; alter the appearance or intrinsic features of average-sized animals or objects, slightly age or de-age an object (for example freshen air, rust a blade, or concentrate a poison); minorly change their own appearance.

4 Alter minor features of an average person, such as scent, facial hair, hair color, or shoe size; change the size or shape of an inanimate object; run or move at great speed.

5 Alter an average person's intrinsic features, such as height or race.

6 Transform the body of an average person (3 Earth) into that of a similarly-sized animal.

7 Transform the body of an average person into that of a very small or very large animal; transform an average person (body and mind) into an animal.

8 Transform a mighty beast (6 Earth) into another creature.

9 Transform a realm (using a months-long ritual).

10 Transform a sphere (using a years-long ritual).

SERENITY

H110. Serenity – Rick Berry

The ready-to-run hero Serenity has Flux Magic at level 5.

Serenity can transform people and things. She needs no words to do her work, but she must stare at the thing to be transformed and project her energy with hand gestures. As sight is the sense connected to Fire, this magic works through her concentrated gaze.

Serenity can easily make changes in animals and objects, altering texture, color, hair covering, and other details with hardly any effort. She can also change the size and shape of inanimate objects, though this takes more effort. All these changes are temporary, and the altered things revert to normal within a day. Certain actions, such as someone naming the transformed thing or touching the thing with iron, can make it revert to its normal form sooner.

Serenity can also alter people's hair color, skin color, facial features, height, weight, and so on, but she cannot add or remove limbs, digits, or organs. She cannot transform people into animals or non-humans, nor can she change their memory, thought processes, or sense of self. She can make a person up to a foot taller or shorter and increase or decrease a person's weight by about one-fourth. Anyone with 5 Earth or stronger, however, is hard to transform, unless the character also has a strong Water score and welcomes the change. These changes are temporary.

As Serenity's magic is linked to Fire, the least predictable of elements, her magic sometimes has unpredictable results.

Transforming things is hard work, but Serenity's strong Earth score (4) allows her to cast a fair number of spells before wearing herself out.

SOIL AND STONE

Soil and Stone magic draws on the fertile energy of soil and the enduring power of stone. A mage of this type is a healer, a ward against evil, and a source of strength and health. A Soil and Stone mage can also cause plants to grow or age more quickly or even inhibit a person from aging.

As touch is the sense connected to Earth, this magic works through physical contact, especially with the hands.

At this Magic level... a Soil and Stone mage can:

1 Aid the ill or improve crops

2 Speed healing or cause something to rot faster.

3 Counter diseases; ward someone against a particular danger or magic.

4 Bless crops with bounty; counter poisons; keep a mortally wounded person from dying.

5 Inhibit curses; let a mortally wounded person recover (slowly) from wounds.

6 Save a realm from plague; heal a dying person; destroy spirits of corruption.

7 Ward a group of people against harm.

8 Cleanse a plague-afflicted realm.

9 Bolster a realm against evil magic.

10 Raise the dead; bring health to an entire realm.

SOWING STONES – REVERSED

CLEFT

H111. Cleft – Rick Berry

The ready-to-run hero Cleft has Soil and Stone Magic at level 5.

Cleft draws on the fertile energy of soil and the enduring power of stone to work his magic. He is a healer, a ward against evil, and a source of strength and health.

As touch is the sense connected to Earth, Cleft's magic works through touch, especially through the hands. He also uses the bounty of the earth—plants, herbs, dust, and clay—to work his strongest healing magic.

In a single day, under his direct and constant care, a simple wound heals as if two weeks have gone by. If Cleft tends a wounded person daily but not constantly, the person recovers twice as fast as normal. His touch can ease pain, stop bleeding, and keep a wound clean. With great and constant effort, he can prevent a mortally wounded person from dying and nurse that person back to health. Depending on the wound, it can take days to weeks of care to heal the person to the point where death is no longer a threat.

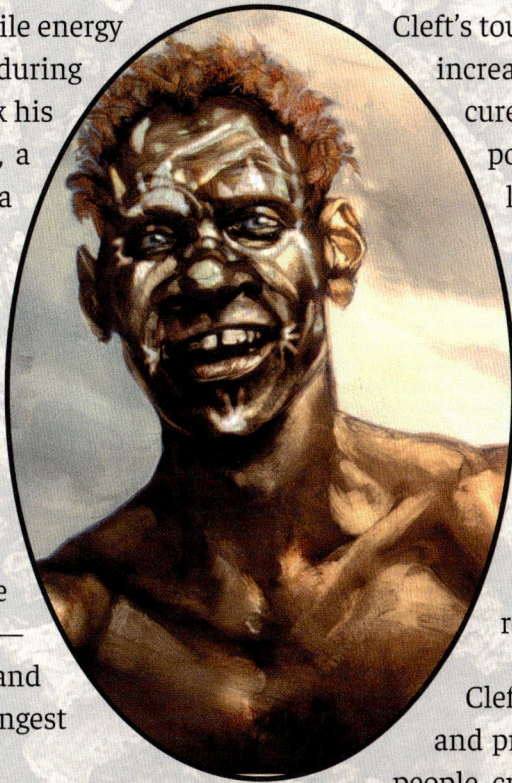

Cleft's touch and care can also (in increasing order of difficulty) cure diseases, neutralize poisons, temporarily lift curses, and banish malignant spirits. Particularly deadly or profound diseases (such as leprosy), potent poisons (such as that of the cockatrice, 6 Poison (*lethal*), powerful curses, and mighty demons can resist his magic.

Cleft can promote health and prevent harm by blessing people, crops, wagons, and so on. He can improve a person's resistance to a particular danger (such as poison, Words of Power magic, or cold), and such a blessing lasts three days and nights. (He paints a hand on the person to be protected to focus his protective power there.) He can, through a long ritual, bless fields to encourage bountiful crops. He can even give some protection to a large, unified body of people, such as an army, though only through a long and tiring ritual.

THE LION

OPEN CHALICE

An Open Chalice mage is receptive to energies, powers, and spirits. For example, a mage of this tradition can sense strong emotions in a location where they were experienced, serve as a channel for spirits to speak through, exorcise a demon, sense energies that are ruling or affecting a realm, and so on. The mage can see auras of increasing subtlety as this magical power increases, but interpreting those auras can be tricky. A new type of aura seen for the first time carries little information to the mage; only experience teaches the mage what different auras mean. The mage can allow negative energies to "pass through" without doing harm.

As Water rules intuition, this magic works mostly through the unconscious senses of the mage. As taste and smell are the physical senses ruled by Water, this magic sometimes uses magic drinks, smoke, incense, or other aids.

At this Magic level... an Open Chalice mage can:

1 Sense strong energies; bind a door shut with a weak spirit; calm emotions.

2 See strong auras; trap a weak spirit.

3 Call and channel average spirits; make a spirit visible; see auras.

4 Communicate with animals; call and channel strong spirits; weaken a magical field.

5 Communicate with plants; trap average spirits; make a target hard to notice; create a spirit-bound talisman to aid the wearer.

6 Channel powerful spirits; trap a strong spirit; weaken curse effects.

7 Sense multiple layers of magical energy; accept powerful negative energies without harm.

8 Channel and deflect powerful energies; make a target invisible; trap a powerful spirit.

9 Channel the words and powers of deities or divine powers.

10 Commune directly with heaven; trap godlings.

WHISPER WALKER

The ready-to-run hero Whisper Walker has Open Chalice Magic at level 4.

Whisper Walker can sense energies of all kinds, though particularly subtle energies may be difficult or impossible for her to identify. Negative energies disturb her, and very powerful negative energies can weaken her or even knock her out.

Whisper Walker can see unusual auras of any kind, noticing supernatural disturbances and extremes. She can tell an item is magical, a person is a mage (or is otherwise magical), an area is imbued with some sort of energy, and so on. She cannot tell if someone is lying or detect general personality traits. Only extremes of some sort are visible to her.

Whisper Walker can open herself to spirits, call them into herself, and let them act through her. (While a spirit is "possessing" her, the gamemaster runs Whisper Walker.) She can usually re-assert herself at will. She can also communicate with spirits that others cannot see or hear. Powerful spirits are likely to overcome her and may resist giving up possession of her body. The most powerful spirits may not even "fit" in her; contact with spirits of this kind can hurt or damage her. Whisper Walker's magic puts her in a dangerous position: she is advanced enough to accept spirits without always being powerful enough to control them.

Whisper Walker's magic lets her communicate with animals, but the communication is always nonverbal. (Her magic is linked to Water, not Air, so it is silent, rather than spoken.)

Whisper Walker has a special ability that she calls "Soul's Wall of Stone." It is her technique for erecting a psychic barrier to prevent intrusion. (In game terms, it's simply her Earth Specialty, giving her an effective score of 5 to resist magical intrusions.)

Whisper Walker has incense and herbs that she uses in her rituals. Some herbs she burns or crumbles into dust. Others she steeps, forming a drink. If she has time to prepare a ritual, she is more likely to meet with success.

H112. Whisper Walker – Rick Berry

STAR RIVER

Star River magic is not linked to a single Element, but rather it is made up of twelve zodiac forces, each linked to one of the four Elements. A Star River mage specializes in a number of these forces and this determines what kinds of magic they can perform.

What is Star River Magic?

The signs of the zodiac represents primal forces of magic with light and dark aspects that exert the influences of the heavens upon the occupants of the spheres. A mage can only use a few of these zodiac forces, but can use both aspects of each force.

Star River Mage Hero Creation

A Star River mage's Magic score represents both the number of zodiac forces they know how to use as well as the maximum strength of their magic effects. The player must choose their zodiac forces at hero creation.

A Star River mage's Magic score is not linked to an Element since each zodiac sign has a fixed elemental correspondence. The maximum strength of a zodiac force is the score of the Element the force is associated with; however, the Star River mage may never use a force greater than their Magic level. For example, a hero takes the Aries zodiac force (including both aspects). Since Aries is linked to Fire, the maximum Aries effect the hero can create is equal to their Fire score, or if their Magic score is less, then their Magic score.

Star River Magic Specialties

A hero may choose a Specialty of Star River magic in any Element. This Specialty increases the maximum strenth of zodiac forces related to that Element by 1 so long as it does not exceed their Magic score.

Using Star River Magic

During play, a hero must describe *what* they want to achieve as well as *how* they will achieve it using one of their hero's zodiac forces. For example, a hero might say, "I want to learn more about this town by channeling the local spirits to learn how they feel about the townspeople." The hero uses the light aspect of the Pisces zodiac force (*channel*) to achieve this magic effect. A similar outcome might be achieved using other zodiac forces, limited only by the player's creativity and the gamemaster's permission. Gamemasters should take care not to blur the distinctions between zodiac forces.

ZODIAC FORCES

	Zodiac Sign	Light Aspect	Dark Aspect	Description
Air Zodiac Forces				
	Gemini	Summon	Banish	Teleport known targets to or from known places.
	Libra	Bind	Sever	Connect two targets together or break a connection.
	Aquarius	Commune	Command	Understand motivation or compel a non-hero target to do something. *
Fire Zodiac Forces				
	Aries	Hasten	Slow	Speed up or slow down a target.
	Leo	Move	Hold	Move objects around or hold a target immobile.
	Sagittarius	Restore	Transform	Restore a target's orginal form or change it from one form to another.
Earth Zodiac Forces				
	Taurus	Grow	Wane	Enlarge or reduce in size or manipulate age of a target.
	Virgo	Ward	Bane	Protect target from or actively repel a type of creature or object.
	Capricorn	Mend	Rend	Heal a target to its former state or damage a target.
Water Zodiac Forces				
	Cancer	Reveal	Conceal	Show hidden things or hide a target from mortal senses.
	Scorpio	Infuse	Drain	Add something to or remove something from a target.
	Pisces	Channel	Seal	Allow one target to flow through another target or block passage.

* Aquarius force cannot read the thoughts of a target, nor compel them to act against their own self-interest or against an ethical or moral belief.

801. Red Priestess – Doug Alexander

THE LION – REVERSED

Chapter 5: Playing

This chapter explores how players and gamemasters work together in the game to create the events that take place in the game world. The chapter is intended for players. It also contains information the gamemaster should fully understand.

PLAYING EVERWAY

A game of EVERWAY requires one or more game sessions to complete a quest. Multiple connected quests featuring the same heroes are called a campaign.

The people who portray the heroes in an EVERWAY game are players, a term that carries a double meaning. They are both playing the game and playing (portraying) their heroes. The person who runs the quest and portrays the background characters is the gamemaster. Even though the gamemaster plays the game, they are not referred to as a player because the gamemaster's role is much larger than portraying a single character. The gamemaster sets the scene, manages the pace, handles the Fortune Deck, guides the plot, and more.

The Role of the Gamemaster

Someone in your group will need to take on the role of the gamemaster. This person can be gamemaster for a single quest or for all your EVERWAY sessions. Gamemastering is a lot of work, but it is also very rewarding. Although the gamemaster does not run a hero, they do fulfill many other roles in the game. If you are the gamemaster, it is recommended that you also read **Book 2: Gamemasters**. That book explains how to resolve actions the players take and provides advice on guiding game sessions and creating quests. It also contains ready-to-run quests to get you started.

What does a gamemaster do?

1. Knows the game

The gamemaster needs to be familiar with all aspects of the game. The gamemaster guides the players through hero creation and answers questions about how the game works during a session.

WAR – REVERSED

2. Prepares the quests

The gamemaster prepares the quests for the players before the session begins. The gamemaster creates interesting situations, realms, and background characters for the players to interact with.

3. Guides the session

The gamemaster guides the plot and pacing of the quest during a session. The gamemaster balances the players' needs and interests with the needs of the story. The gamemaster presents the scene and responds to the heroes' actions. The gamemaster also roleplays the background characters the heroes might interact with.

The Three Laws of Action

The Law of Karma

The most likely result based on a hero's Elements, Specialties, Powers, Magic, and tactics determines the outcome of a hero's action.

The Law of Drama

The needs of the plot determine the outcome of a hero's action.

The Law of Fortune

A draw from the Fortune Deck determines the outcome of a hero's action.

4. Engages the players

The gamemaster moderates the session, making sure that all players get a chance to act and to shine. The gamemaster creates a respectful and collaborative environment for everyone to contribute to the shared story and to have fun.

5. Resolves player actions

The gamemaster resolves the heroes' actions by using the three laws of action: the Law of Karma, the Law of Drama, and the Law of Fortune. The gamemaster may use any one or all of these laws to determine the result of each action a hero takes.

While combat is not the primary focus of EVERWAY, it is one example of the type of action that a gamemaster may need to resolve. A combat encounter might be treated as a single event or it might be broken into a blow-by-blow narration—it depends on the needs of the story and the needs of the players.

The gamemaster is the authority on what happens in the game, so if you're not sure if your hero can do something, just ask.

6. Listens and observes

Finally, a gamemaster listens to the players. The gamemaster watches what happens, takes note of special reactions and consequences to work into later stories, observes whether the players are having a good time, and assesses whether the players consider their judgments fair.

905. Ogun Worship – Tom Gianni

COMBAT AND WOUNDS

EVERWAY is a game that focuses more on stories than on combat, but sometimes heroes take dangerous actions and get injured. Wounds generally mark story consequences rather than having a serious impact on game play.

Wounds are a great opportunity to roleplay changes to your hero's behavior in response to being injured. There are four types of wounds:

- **Flesh Wounds:** Minor cuts or contusions that don't significantly hamper a hero and might take a week to a month to heal.

- **Disabling Wounds:** Serious wounds such as a sprained ankle, gash, concussion, or scratched eye that significantly hamper the hero. A disabling wound might take a month to a season to heal, although some of that time might not be during a quest.

- **Mortal Wounds:** Life-threatening wounds that will lead to the hero dying if not treated. A mortal wound might take a season to a year to recover from.

- **Special Wounds:** Special wound effects range from minor to significant and impact the hero's actions in various ways, such as a bleeding head wound that obscures vision.

THE DRAGON — REVERSED

How to Be a Player

This section provides some advice for both beginning and experienced roleplayers on what you need to know as a player in EVERWAY.

What Heroes Do

The adventures of your hero and the other players' heroes are what a game of EVERWAY is all about. If you don't have a hero yet, look at some of the ready-to-run heroes in *Section 4: Quick Start Guide* for an idea of what heroes are like; that will help you understand this section better.

Being a Spherewalker

All heroes are spherewalkers. In most quests, they travel together as a group to a new realm. Often, they get to these new realms by traveling through gates that connect the spheres. Each new realm presents the spherewalkers with new experiences and new challenges.

As spherewalkers, the heroes are often more experienced, more powerful, more open-minded, and more cosmopolitan than the people they meet among the spheres. They have to learn how to fit in with the inhabitants of each new realm, even though they often have a broader perspective than the locals. Spherewalkers have to be careful not to offend the locals accidentally. For example, asking to buy beef in a land where (unknown to the spherewalkers) cows are sacred could be a big problem.

Spherewalkers can expect hospitality from most people they meet, and their hosts expect them to be respectful in return. In most realms, people grow up, live, and die among people they've known all their lives. Wanderers and strangers, therefore, are very unusual, and people in most realms feel a moral obligation to help those who do not have kin and friends around. In return, strangers are expected to repay hospitality with kindness and perhaps with service

---

Heroes do all sorts of things on quests. Some examples:

- Hold a door shut against an angry mob.
- Woo a dancer.
- Impersonate an imperial official with important business.
- Engage in a drinking contest with a troll.
- Join an enemy's retinue under false pretenses.
- Debate philosophy with a guard at a toll bridge.
- Harvest beneficial and potent herbs from a meadow.

or gifts. The exception to this rule comes in the larger cities, where most people are strangers to each other. Here, outsiders can expect little hospitality unless they can pay for it or impress the wealthy.

Going on Quests

On a typical quest, your hero and the other players' heroes come to a new realm where some danger threatens the locals or the heroes. The heroes use their skills and wits to overcome the danger. If they are clever and brave, and if fortune is with them, the heroes prevail and resolve the danger. Otherwise, they may suffer defeat.

The first challenge that the heroes usually face in a new realm is to orient themselves. Where are they? What's going on around them? Whom can they trust? You can have your hero talk to the locals, investigate landmarks, or otherwise gather information to help get a sense of what the surroundings are like.

At some point, the heroes are likely to identify a conflict or problem. Sometimes the conflict presents itself immediately, while other times it takes a sensitive hero to find out that something's even wrong. Identifying a problem is the first step toward solving it. Remember, it's always possible for the problem to be more complex than it seems at first.

EXAMPLE QUESTS

Quests can involve all sorts of goals. While undertaking a quest, a group of heroes might do any of the following:

- Reunite two warring noble families that have been tricked into hating each other because of the devious dealings of a third family.

- Lift a spell that has made each village in a realm develop its own language, thus preventing trade and mutual assistance.

- Guide a repentant sultan to a hermit on a mountaintop to apologize for mistreating the poor in his lands, thereby getting the hermit to lift their curse on the sultan's family.

- Venture into a haunted swamp to retrieve the root of a magical tree that is needed for a powerful healing spell.

- Find three ritual tools that have been stolen from a city's temple by bandits and return them so the spring festival can go on as usual and bring bountiful crops.

- Rescue a town's children, all of whom have been spirited away by fun-loving but stubborn and wild goblins.

- Attend a faerie queen's ball to ask for a boon for a nearby kingdom.

The gamemaster may design a quest that can be resolved in a single session. The players gather, the quest begins, the heroes accomplish (or fail to accomplish) the quest's goal, and the game ends. Other quests may require more than a single session to play. The play session ends with the action in the game world suspended. The action resumes the next time the group meets to play. The players continue to suspend and resume play until the quest is over. Some plots have no definite ending point. Each session might be a "chapter" or "episode" in the overall plot, but the story continues indefinitely, as a TV soap opera does.

Being Part of a Group

The heroes act as a group, working together to complete the quest. When they travel to strange new realms, the other heroes are often the only people your hero can truly trust. With the combined talents, ideas, and energies of the group, the heroes can do much more together than any of them ever could do alone.

During a quest, your hero interacts with the background characters that the gamemaster portrays, but heroes also interact a lot with each other. On a practical level, the heroes often need to put their heads together to decide how to approach the challenges they face. Just for the joy of roleplaying, however, players often have their heroes banter, argue, and debate with each other. These conversations help you to get to know your own hero and those of the other players.

Sometimes two heroes have different goals, motives, or ideals. For instance, a hero who was

once held captive by satyrs may hate satyrs, while another hero in the same group may hold satyrs in awe. If the group needs to decide how to approach a band of satyrs, these two heroes are likely to have very different opinions. This sort of conflict is all right. In fact, it can be a lot of fun. Conflict drives drama. You and the other players can have a lot of fun working out your heroes' differences.

When differences become too big, heroes sometimes go in different directions. In the example above, the hero who hates satyrs might hang back while the other heroes approach the satyrs and try to talk to them. It's all right to have different heroes doing different things at the same time; you don't have to do everything as a group. The advantage of acting as a group, however, is that everyone can be involved in the action. If the heroes are all doing separate things, the gamemaster has to talk to each player in turn, and each hero spends a lot of time out of the action.

Your Hero Develops

Over time, your hero is likely to become better and stronger. With experience, you will learn more about the setting, your hero's abilities, your gamemaster's style, and so on. This increased understanding helps your hero be more effective when faced with challenges.

Your hero also gains boons from quests. A boon is anything that benefits a hero,

such as a magic amulet, esoteric training, a bonus to Element scores, healing herbs, and so on. These boons also make your hero more effective.

> Gamemasters may refer to Book 2: Gamemasters to read more about boons.

In addition to becoming more powerful, your hero also develops as a character. The more you play your hero, the better you know the hero's personality. You can invent details as you go so that, after playing a few quests, your hero has a deeper, richer personality. Your hero can also change. The dramatic conflicts that a hero faces on quests can lead to the hero changing and growing. For example, a hero who at first blunders recklessly into danger may learn to be cautious. Your hero may also change just because you want to play the hero differently.

> Heroes often change when they face their Fates. See p. 186.

Portraying a Character vs. Telling a Story

You are doing two things when you're running a hero. On one hand, you're portraying a character who has an internal logic, private motives, a history, and a personality. You can often determine what your hero will do by taking these factors into account. For instance, you might think, "Puma's never been in a tall building before; I bet she'd be nervous, but she'd try not to show it." On the other hand, you're also helping to tell a story, and you can also determine what your hero should do based on the needs of the story. For instance, you might imagine that when coming to a large city Puma would wander off on her own to marvel at the sights. Allowing her to do so, however, especially near the climax of a quest, might slow the plot down and distract from the story.

So which is more important: being true to a hero's nature or supporting the plot? Personally, I'd say that the story is more important because the enjoyment of the whole group is at stake, and portraying a hero accurately is mostly a personal pleasure. But there needs to be a balance, and everyone feels comfortable with a different one. There is no right answer. Every player answers this question differently, so bear that in mind when other players' heroes do things that you'd rather they not do.

— Jonathan Tweet

Portraying Your Hero

Once you've created your hero, you may feel you are done. You're not. Just as a character in a novel changes as the author writes the story, and changes some more as the author writes sequels, so your hero really comes to life during play. Below is advice for how to go about bringing your character to life.

Interacting With the Gamemaster

As a player, you'll spend a lot of your time interacting with the gamemaster. Together, you talk out the story that the heroes star in. Whether the heroes are battling ferocious monsters, wooing delicate faeries, drinking with rowdy goblins, or debating the nature of the Good with talking trees, in real life this all

FERTILITY

comes across as dialogue among the players and gamemaster.

For instance, the following dialogue might occur as part of quest in which the ready-to-run heroes Opal, Fireson, and Puma are looking for the soul of a prince, which an evil wizard has stolen. They have sneaked into the wizard's study.

Opal's Player: What's in here?

Gamemaster: All sorts of stuff. It's a real mess. Charts, scrolls, ink, little animal bones. And it smells. There's a writing desk, a table for experiments, and it's got bottles and twisty tubes all over it. There's a window, too, but it's shut, so it's dark in here.

Fireson's Player: I look for candles or lamps or anything, and I light them with my candle....

Gamemaster: OK. You light a lamp, and it lights up the room—

Puma's Player: And I'm closing the door. I'm pressing my ear up against it. "I'll listen in case the wizard comes back."

Gamemaster: Good idea.

Gamemaster [to Opal's Player]: What are you doing?

Opal's Player: Now that we have some light in here, I'm looking around under things, to see if there's anything hidden. I'm figuring the soul would be hidden somewhere....

Gamemaster: What's your Water score?

Before the quest, the gamemaster made notes about where the soul is hidden: in a jar in a small chest tucked away in this room. The gamemaster

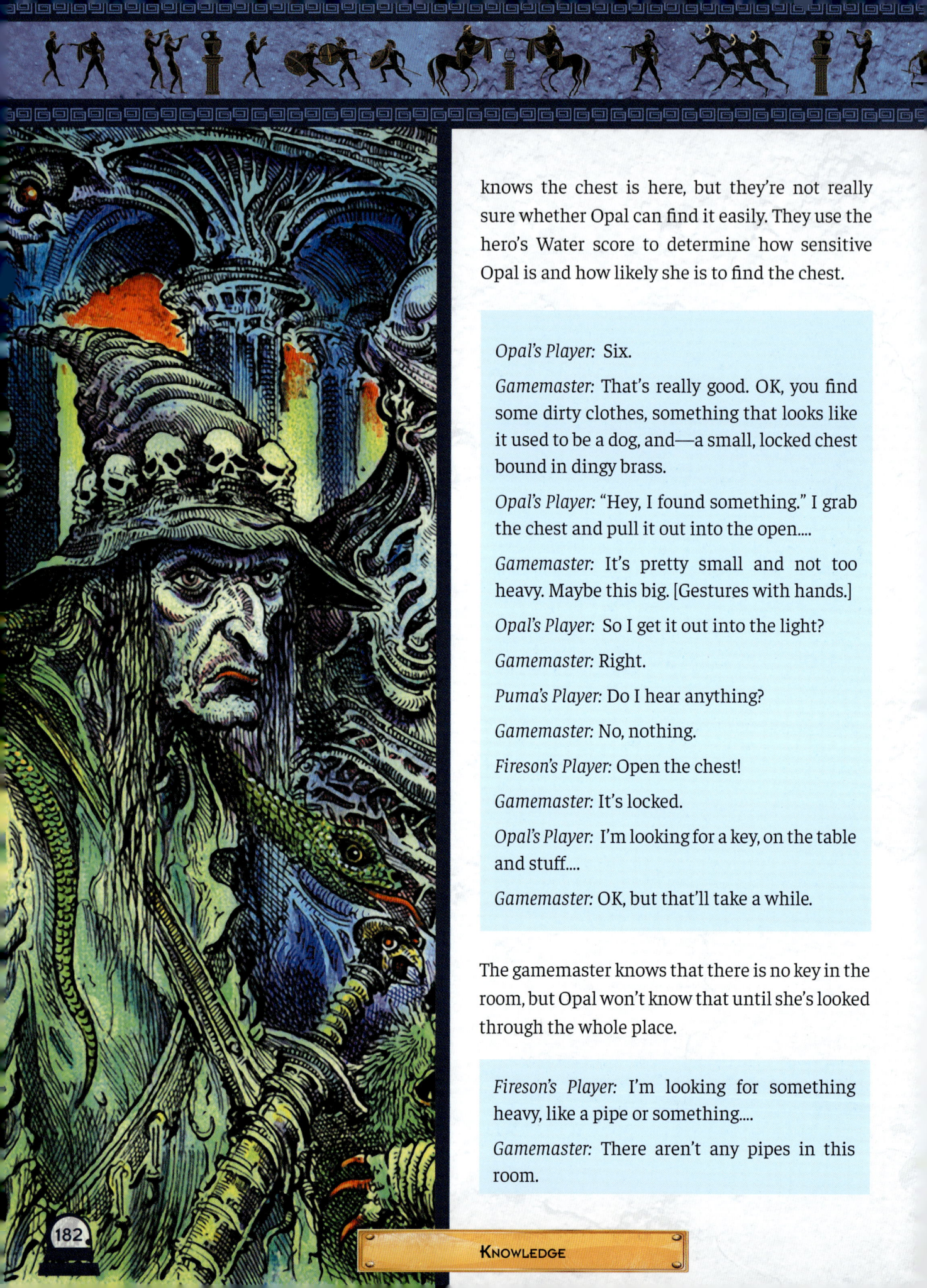

knows the chest is here, but they're not really sure whether Opal can find it easily. They use the hero's Water score to determine how sensitive Opal is and how likely she is to find the chest.

> *Opal's Player:* Six.
>
> *Gamemaster:* That's really good. OK, you find some dirty clothes, something that looks like it used to be a dog, and—a small, locked chest bound in dingy brass.
>
> *Opal's Player:* "Hey, I found something." I grab the chest and pull it out into the open....
>
> *Gamemaster:* It's pretty small and not too heavy. Maybe this big. [Gestures with hands.]
>
> *Opal's Player:* So I get it out into the light?
>
> *Gamemaster:* Right.
>
> *Puma's Player:* Do I hear anything?
>
> *Gamemaster:* No, nothing.
>
> *Fireson's Player:* Open the chest!
>
> *Gamemaster:* It's locked.
>
> *Opal's Player:* I'm looking for a key, on the table and stuff....
>
> *Gamemaster:* OK, but that'll take a while.

The gamemaster knows that there is no key in the room, but Opal won't know that until she's looked through the whole place.

> *Fireson's Player:* I'm looking for something heavy, like a pipe or something....
>
> *Gamemaster:* There aren't any pipes in this room.

Fireson's Player: Well, you know what I mean, like a crowbar.

Puma's Player: Like a rock. Hey, is there a doorstop?

Gamemaster: Yeah, it's a big, smooth rock.

The gamemaster hadn't planned for a rock to be used as a doorstop, but it is a good idea, and they decide to run with it.

Opal's Player: I'm still looking for a key....

Gamemaster: You haven't found one yet, but you've found a lot of nasty little things.

Fireson's Player: I get that rock, and I pound on the lock.

Gamemaster: What's your Fire score?

The lock can be broken, but the higher the character's Fire score, the easier it will be.

Fireson's Player: Six.

Gamemaster: Bam! With a single blow, you've knocked off the lock, and you can force the lid open.

Opal's Player: What's inside?

Gamemaster: There's a little bottle with a thin neck, with a stopper in it, and it's been sealed shut with wax.

Fireson's Player: I get it.

Gamemaster [to Puma's Player]: Something's coming down the hall....

1711. Sneaky Adventurer – Ian Miller

THE JOYS OF PIGHEADEDNESS

Everybody has a bias. Everybody sees the world a little skewed. You can use this fact to your advantage when portraying a hero. When I ran Fireson, I portrayed him as confident, good-natured, and tolerant but ultimately prejudiced against those who were different from him. In one quest, the other heroes and I met two groups of people, one group linked to the sun and one linked to the moon. Our task was to reunite the groups. The other players and I had a long discussion in character about this situation. During the conversation, I portrayed Fireson as simply assuming that the rightful place for the "moon people" was serving the "sun people." (He is a priest of fire, after all.) When the other players talked about reuniting the group, Fireson assumed they meant putting them back in their rightful relationship, with the sun people as rulers and the moon people as lessers. The other players became both more delighted and more exasperated as their heroes tried to get across to Fireson that the two groups might be reunited as equals. Finally the heroes agreed to disagree and got on with the task.

Foibles and flaws help make heroes more lifelike. Remember that even heroes are imperfect, and that just makes the game more fun.

— Jonathan Tweet

Puma's Player [in a stage whisper]: "Hey, something's coming."

Fireson's Player: [Expletive deleted]

And so the dialogue goes, with breaks now and then to get snacks or to discuss strategies or to talk about the latest movies. Eventually the action leads to a climax and a conclusion, with the heroes succeeding in their quest, or failing, or maybe doing a little of both.

Note that, as a player, you decide what your hero does, but you can't decide what the other heroes do or what the background characters do. The other players decide what their heroes do, and the gamemaster decides what the background characters do.

This is all right: "I'm going to try to sweet-talk the guard into giving me the key."

This is not: "I sweet-talk the guard, and she gives me the key."

Interacting With the Other Players

Sometimes you'll spend your time interacting with the players while the gamemaster looks on, ready to intervene, answer questions, or get the action moving should some players start to get bored. Often the quest will present a problem to the heroes, and the players will have to discuss what the heroes' response should be. Sometimes you'll discuss strategy, such as how to lure a cruel baroness out of her castle so that you can capture her more easily. Sometimes you'll discuss ethics, such as what to do with the baroness once you've got her. Sometimes you'll discuss philosophy, such as whether the baroness is truly evil, only misguided, or simply a nonconformist. If you enjoy portraying a character, especially someone different from yourself, these discussions can be lively and very enjoyable.

Point of View

Consider these two sentences, either of which could come from a player running Fireson.

In Character: "I sweat fire out of my right hand to get some light and see what's making the noise."

Out of Character: "Fireson sweats fire out of his right hand to get some light and see what's making the noise."

Both ways work; both do pretty much the same thing in terms of the plot. They affect the player differently, however. A player who refers to a hero in character as "I" identifies more closely with the hero, while one who refers to a hero out of character as "he," "she," or "they" keeps a greater distance.

Different players have different play styles. You can use whichever point of view you wish. Sometimes the game is more enjoyable if you play in character and refer to the hero as "I" because you get deeper into the hero. Sometimes you can keep a better perspective on the story, the plot, and your hero's personal development if you play out of character, referring to your hero as "he," "she," or "they." Do what you will.

Playing Your Hero's Element Points

As you are playing, you will be making many choices. What do you choose to have your hero do? How does your hero approach solving a problem? How patient is your hero? How self-controlled is your hero? Does your hero try to outsmart people they interact with? While you can choose to have your hero do almost anything, they will probably tend to act in the ways they are good at. If your hero has a strong Air score but a weak Fire score, for example, they may be someone who carefully considers their situation before acting. That might lead them to try to talk their way out of more situations. Let your hero's Element points and Specialties suggest ways they might tend to act and react. Don't treat this as a rigid rule that must be followed but rather as a general tendency of your hero. You will find that playing to your hero's strengths will more often lead to success, which will encourage you to act that way in the future—provided the ultimate consequences are good.

Playing Virtues and Faults

Keep your hero's Virtue and Fault in mind as you encounter situations in the game. Do the circumstances of play strongly relate to either their

Virtue or Fault? Let that show up in how they react. If their Virtue is Striking the Dragon's Tail—Reversed (*recognizing the larger problem*) and they are trying to talk a city guard into looking for a missing person, you might consider something like the following interaction.

> **In Character:** "I know you've got a lot of demands on your time. A lot of people don't realize just how many complaints you get that never seem to go anywhere. I understand your reluctance. This isn't something I ask lightly, but I've been around enough to know when this kind of thing may be serious. Is there any way I can help make it easier for you, clear it with the captain of the guard, go grab you some lunch, or something else?"
>
> **Out of Character:** "My hero's Virtue is Striking the Dragon's Tail—Reversed. I want to get a sense of what might be making the guard reluctant or what favor he might like so that I can convince him to help us out."

Likewise, sometimes your hero's Fault can suggest fun ways to approach a situation. If their Fault is Summer—Reversed (*exhaustion*), your hero might be more impatient with the same city guard. If there really isn't a good way to convince the guard, you can let that impatience show if you think that might be more fun for your group.

> **In Character:** "Look here, I really don't feel like trying to convince you to do your job. I see those wanted posters over there. If maybe my group went and hauled in one of those guys for you, do you think you could spend a few hours to help us find our missing friend?"
>
> **Out of Character:** "My hero's Fault is Summer—Reversed. He's getting really frustrated with this guard. So he tries needling the guard a little to shame him into helping us out."

It can be fun to play your hero's Fault—just make sure the other players are having a fun time rolling with their foibles as well.

Facing Your Fate

As described in *Chapter 3: Heroes*, each hero has a Fate, which is represented by a card from the Fortune Deck that is neither upright nor reversed. At some point in the game, your hero may face this Fate. This encounter or event is a personal climax or challenge, and how your hero handles it determines whether the Fate card becomes upright or reversed. Heroes can face their Fates in one of three ways.

Karma and Fate

"Karma" means "work." Your hero can pursue their Fate and face it because of their actions. Consider, for example, a hero with The Soldier as their Fate. The Soldier

FIRESON MEETS HIS FATE

During one quest, Fireson gave himself up as sacrifice to allow two other heroes and some smelly dwarf's daughter escape a minotaur. Fireson had a pretty good idea this sacrifice wouldn't be lethal (as the minotaur had made it sound), but he didn't give himself up until he had accepted the possibility it could mean his death, and I didn't have Fireson give himself up until I was ready to accept Fireson's demise. If Fireson was killed, it would mean I'd never play Fireson again. Fireson survived, however, and his sacrifice resolved the quest.

Fireson's Fate was The Soldier, representing a conflict between "duty" and "blind obedience." Until Fireson met his Fate, I hadn't known what this conflict meant. I thought it meant that Fireson was neglecting his duty by spherewalking and not settling down into a priest's proper role. That interpretation wasn't perfect because it's really a conflict between duty and negligence, not duty and blind obedience. After the encounter with the minotaur, I saw Fireson's Fate differently.

By giving himself up as a sacrifice, Fireson was accepting his duty. He learned he could fulfill his duty as a spherewalker, not only as a priest. The compulsion to return to the priesthood and the guilt he felt from not doing so were the real results of blind obedience, an inability or unwillingness to imagine himself leading a fulfilling life differently from how he had before.

Fireson's Fault, not coincidentally, had been Death—Reversed, meaning "stasis," or the inability to let one stage pass so a new one can begin. I had chosen that Fault to indicate Fireson has been stuck in his own culture and unwilling to accept different cultures as equal. Now, with opened eyes, I could see that this cultural pigheadedness was merely a surface symptom of a deeper stasis: the unwillingness to accept that his deity's banishment of him was not a temporary punishment but a shove into a new stage of life. Fireson's stasis had been his fixation on his role as a priest.

Fireson had changed. No longer looking to his former life as the only legitimate life for him, he had become able to accept that different cultures may hold equal value in their own right. He was also reconsidering his past. He knew that his deity banished him for questioning the deity's actions. He had assumed his doubt was blasphemy. Now he wondered whether it was wisdom.

Fireson had a new Virtue, Spring; a new Fault, Striking the Dragon's Tail; and a new Fate, The Priestess. These cards represented the new life opening up to him, with new promises and new dangers.

— Jonathan Tweet

stands for "duty vs. blind obedience." The hero may try to follow a code of honor or fulfill certain obligations without ignoring other important parts of their life. When they have done so to your satisfaction, or when they have failed substantially to do so, you can say they have met their Fate.

Drama and Fate

If, during play, the hero undertakes actions that show they have accomplished, or dramatically failed to accomplish, their Fate, you may decide that they have met their Fate. For instance, if the hero with The Soldier as their Fate were to cause great harm because they followed instructions without considering them carefully, you could declare that they have indeed met their Fate, even though they did not set out to do so. You also have the option of letting them keep their Fate so they can try again to meet it successfully.

The gamemaster may also set up a quest that lets a hero meet their Fate. The quest is usually a sort of test (though the hero and the player don't know it) to see whether the Fate will resolve itself as upright or reversed.

> See Chapter 3: Heroes for more about your hero's Fate.
>
> See Section 2: Fortune Guide for more information about specific Fortune Deck cards.

Fortune and Fate

If, during play, the gamemaster draws the fortune card that is your hero's Fate, then the gamemaster has the option of improvising an encounter between your hero and their Fate. For instance, if your hero is hunting down a mysterious spirit doctor to protect a peace-loving town from the spirit doctor's dark magic, and the gamemaster draws The Soldier (either upright or reversed), they could improvise a new plot or subplot to fit your hero's Fate. It may be, for instance, that the mage is frightening to the townspeople but has not actually committed the crimes. The test for your hero is whether the hero will attack the mage without learning more or consider the mage carefully before using violence. In other words, is the hero "blindly obedient," or does the hero fulfill their duty with foresight?

Fortune Deck In Play

During play when the Fortune Deck is used to determine an outcome, the gamemaster and the players need to roleplay the draw in game terms. Rarely does the card drawn apply directly. Usually the gamemaster will need to interpret how the card applies to the situation at hand.

Reading the Cards

Below is a sample interpretation for each card in the Fortune Deck. Imagine, for these examples, that a powerful warrior (a hero) is confronting a mighty ogre in its cave. The warrior is a better fighter than the ogre and is armed with a sword and shield as well. The ogre is stronger than the warrior but not as skilled, and it is armed only with a crude, wooden club. In game terms, the warrior has a stronger Fire score, but the ogre has a stronger Earth score. The warrior's player says, "I draw my sword and attack, raising my shield to protect myself and slashing at the ogre."

Below are thirty-six examples of how this encounter can play out, depending on which Fortune Deck card is drawn, whether it is upright or reversed, and how the gamemaster interprets the card. Based on the Laws of Karma and Drama, the gamemaster expects the warrior will defeat the ogre but will be wounded in the process. There is also a risk the warrior will be defeated, and there's always the chance some new element in the plot will arise. If the card's meaning is positive or ambiguous as to the warrior's victory, they will succeed. If it is negative, they may be badly injured by the ogre before they can kill it, or they may be defeated altogether.

Many of these examples end in the warrior's defeat. On most quests, however, heroes work together so that if one falls, the others can come to the rescue. Even when the whole group is defeated, the heroes almost always survive.

> Note that some upright cards have negative meanings, and some reversed cards have positive meanings.

THE PRIESTESS – REVERSED

Autumn

Meaning: *plenty*, a positive meaning.

Gamemaster's Interpretation: The warrior's training bears fruit. They have sown diligence, and now they reap victory.

Gamemaster: You expertly deflect the monster's heavy club and slash its belly. The thing thrashes at you as it falls.

Player: I try to block the thing while pressing my advantage.

Gamemaster: With a few thrusts, you leave it bleeding to death on the cave floor.

The Cockatrice

Meaning: *corruption*, a negative meaning.

Gamemaster's Interpretation: Corruption prevails by infecting others, not through force. Something bad comes of the warrior's victory.

Gamemaster: You expertly deflect the monster's heavy club and slash its belly. Blackish blood splashes out onto your arm, chest, and face. The ogre is falling to the ground....

Player: I step back to keep it from getting to me and hold my sword and shield ready.

Gamemaster: The ogre thrashes about on the ground, dying. Your face begins to burn....

Player: I wipe the blood off!

Gamemaster: Your wipe some of it off, but you can feel it soaking through your armor and clothes. You're feeling dizzy....

How badly the warrior is hurt by the ogre's corrupt blood depends on their Earth score and on the plot (that is, on karma and drama).

The Creator

Meaning: *nurture*, a positive meaning, but one with no direct relevance to combat.

Gamemaster's Interpretation: Nothing especially bad happens to the warrior.

Gamemaster: With your superior speed and skill at arms, you defeat the ogre, but during the battle it hits your shield so hard that your left arm is hurt.

Death

Meaning: *change*, a positive meaning.

Gamemaster's Interpretation: The ogre is killed, and something new is created.

Gamemaster: You kill the ogre. Its dark brown blood splashes over the rocks. The blood soaks into the cracks, and strange, mottled plants grow out of them. Each plant has a blood-red blossom.

These plants could have a special property, which the gamemaster can determine now or later. Some gamemasters don't like introducing new plot elements, such as these flowers, into a quest. Others draw heavily from the spontaneous inspiration the Fortune Deck cards provide.

The Defender

Meaning: *safety*, a positive meaning that relates directly to physical danger.

Gamemaster's Interpretation: The hero prevails safely.

Gamemaster: With your superior speed and skill at arms, you handily defeat the ogre.

The Dragon

Meaning: *cunning*, a neutral-to-positive meaning that applies well to an intelligent warrior fighting a less intelligent opponent.

Gamemaster's Interpretation: The more intelligent warrior prevails.

Gamemaster: With your superior speed and skill at arms, you find that the ogre falls for the simplest warrior's feints and tricks. You vanquish it unscathed.

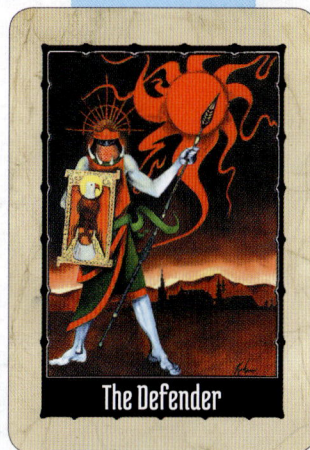

Death

The Defender

The Dragon

Death, The Defender, The Dragon – Scott Kirschner

Drowning in Armor

Meaning: *safeguards turn dangerous*, a very bad meaning for an armored warrior in battle.

Gamemaster's Interpretation: The warrior's shield and armor turn against them.

> *Gamemaster:* The ogre's blow is so fierce that it twists your shield, snapping your wrist. The force prevents you from landing a solid blow on the ogre; you cut it, but not deeply.
>
> *Player:* I try to press in so close that the ogre can't swing its club at me, and then I slash it.
>
> *Gamemaster:* The ogre drops its club, grabs your shield, and yanks on it, knocking you over. The pain from the shield, strapped to your broken arm, makes you gasp and nearly go into shock....
>
> *Player:* I try to roll out of the way.
>
> *Gamemaster:* The ogre's grip on your shield is too strong for you to get away. It slams the shield into your helmet, knocking your head against the stone floor of the cave. You sink into unconsciousness....

The hero's fate from this point on may depend on their Earth score (karma), on the plot (drama), or on another draw from the Fortune Deck (fortune).

The Eagle

Meaning: *the mind prevails*, a positive meaning for an intelligent person struggling against a less intelligent opponent.

Gamemaster's Interpretation: The warrior knows their tactics ahead of time, giving them an edge over the less intelligent ogre.

> *Gamemaster:* With your superior forethought and skill at arms, you stay one step ahead of the ogre and defeat it handily.

Fearing Shadows

Meaning: *unnecessary fear*, a very negative meaning for someone fighting a scary monster in a dark cave.

Gamemaster's Interpretation: The warrior fears the wrong thing and is thus at a disadvantage.

DEATH – REVERSED

Gamemaster: You charge the ogre, and suddenly black things come looming out of the shadows on all sides of you....

Player: I throw up my shield to protect myself and lash out with the sword to keep the things at bay.

Gamemaster: The black things rush past you, and you see that they are bats. Your sword swings through the air, connecting with nothing.

Player: Forget the bats; I'm swinging at the ogre.

Gamemaster: Too late. You lost your momentum, and now the ogre's club is already coming down on you. It smashes into the side of your helmet and collides into your right shoulder. In pain, you drop your sword.

Player: I bash the ogre with my shield, using my good arm.

Gamemaster: It's too strong. You smash into it, but it just grabs you and slams you into the wall of the cave. The world goes black....

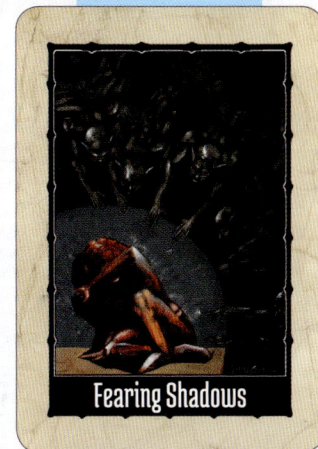

Note: If the player had said that the hero paid no attention to the bats, the warrior would have prevailed. (Karma still has effects even when the gamemaster is consulting the Fortune Deck.) The gamemaster did not simply tell the player, "Bats fly out of the shadows and scare you," because that would have made the player feel as though the hero's actions were up to the gamemaster. In order to keep control of the hero in the hands of the player, the gamemaster set up a scene in which the hero might be afraid of the bats, but it was ultimately up to the player, not the gamemaster, to determine how the hero reacted.

Fertility

Meaning: *growth,* a positive meaning but not one directly associated with combat.

Gamemaster's Interpretation: The combat goes as expected, or a little better.

Gamemaster: With your superior speed and skill at arms, you defeat the ogre, but during the battle it hits your shield so hard that your left arm is hurt.

Fearing Shadows

Fearing Shadows – Jeff Miracola

Fertility

Fertility – Scott Kirschner

The Fish

Meaning: *the soul prevails*, a positive meaning but not one directly related to combat.

Gamemaster's Interpretation: The combat turns out at least as well as expected.

Gamemaster: The ogre hits your shield so hard that your arm is hurt, but with your superior speed and skill at arms, you defeat it. It lies on the ground and, with a shudder, gives up the ghost.

The Fool

Meaning: *freedom*, a positive meaning but not one directly related to combat.

Gamemaster's Interpretation: The combat goes as expected, or a little better.

Gamemaster: With your superior speed and skill at arms, you defeat the ogre, but during the battle it hits your shield so hard that your left arm is hurt.

The Griffin

Meaning: *valor*, a very positive meaning since it is linked to Fire, the element that rules combat.

Gamemaster's Interpretation: The warrior vanquishes the ogre easily.

Gamemaster: With speed and courage, you dispatch the ogre.

The Hermit

Meaning: *wisdom*, a positive meaning for a wise person in a contest with a being that is less wise.

Gamemaster's Interpretation: The warrior does a little better than would be expected.

> *Gamemaster:* With your superior speed and skill at arms, you defeat the ogre, but during the battle it hits your shield so hard that your left arm is slightly hurt.

Inspiration

Meaning: *creativity*, a positive meaning for a creative person in a contest with a less creative being, especially in combat, as this card is tied to Fire.

Gamemaster's Interpretation: The warrior does a little better than would be expected.

> *Gamemaster:* With your superior speed and skill at arms, you defeat the ogre, but during the battle it hits your shield so hard that your left arm is slightly hurt.

The King

Meaning: *authority*, a positive meaning but not one directly related to combat.

Gamemaster's Interpretation: The warrior does a little better than would be expected.

> *Gamemaster:* With your superior speed and skill at arms, you defeat the ogre, but during the battle it hits your shield so hard that your left arm is slightly hurt.

Knowledge

Meaning: *truth*, a positive meaning but not one directly related to combat.

Gamemaster's Interpretation: The warrior does a little better than would be expected.

Gamemaster: With your superior speed and skill at arms, you defeat the ogre, but during the battle it hits your shield so hard that your left arm is slightly hurt.

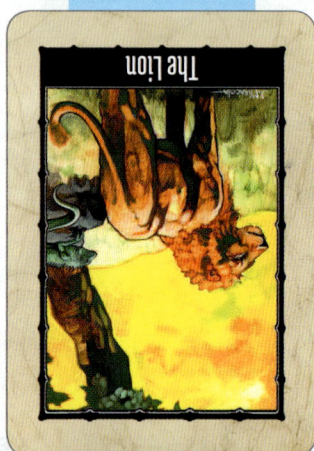

Law

Meaning: *order*, a positive meaning, but not directly related to combat.

Gamemaster's Interpretation: The warrior does a little better than would be expected.

Gamemaster: With your superior speed and skill at arms, you defeat the ogre, but during the battle it hits your shield so hard that your left arm is slightly hurt.

The Lion–Reversed

Meaning: *weakness*, a very negative meaning for a warrior engaged in battle, especially because it's tied (negatively) to Fire.

Gamemaster's Interpretation: The warrior is badly injured.

Gamemaster: Your swing hits home, but the ogre's clubs slams into your shield, and you're not strong enough to keep your footing....

Player: I scramble to stay up.

Gamemaster: Your foot catches on a large bump or rise in the cave floor, and you tumble over....

Player: I block with my shield while I back up and get to my feet.

Gamemaster: The ogre pounds you on the back while you're scrambling up. The pain's really bad....

Player: Can I keep fighting?

Gamemaster: Yes, but maybe not for long.

Player: I press the attack, then, trying to slash it and slow it down....

WINTER – REVERSED

Gamemaster: Your sword is a better weapon than the ogre's club, especially considering your training. You slash the ogre, and it falls, but not before it gets in a nasty knee shot. You're both down, but you're in better shape than it is.

Player: Can I finish it off?

Gamemaster: With a final burst of energy, you finish it, but then the pain in your arm, back, and knee get so bad that you pass out.

The hero won't die from these wounds, but they won't be fighting any big fights any time soon, either.

Nature–Reversed

Meaning: *energy sapped*, a negative meaning that is tied negatively to Earth.

Gamemaster's Interpretation: The warrior is badly drained by the fight. The reversed Earth-related card represents the negative aspects of the cave.

Gamemaster: You manage to slash the thing, but it's not perturbed, at least not yet. Likewise, it manages a few blows against you, most of which you're able to deflect almost harmlessly. Now you're breathing heavily. The dank air in the cave is oppressive. It feels bad in your lungs....

At this point the hero has a chance to draw the ogre out of its cave and into good air. If the hero takes it, the fight will still go well for them. If not, it will go badly. Thus, karma comes into play.

Player: I press on and try to finish it off quickly.

Gamemaster: You get a few more licks in, but then your sword arm gets slow. You realize that you're getting weak. And then there's this terrific pain on the side of your head, and the world goes black.

Overlooking the Diamond–Reversed

Meaning: *recognizing opportunity*, a positive meaning.

Gamemaster's Interpretation: The warrior will do well.

Gamemaster: You charge in, and the ogre raises its club up over its head, leaving itself open....

Player: With my shield to protect me, I stab at it while it's open.

Gamemaster: Before it can even get its club down, you've stabbed it, and it crumples to the floor of the cave.

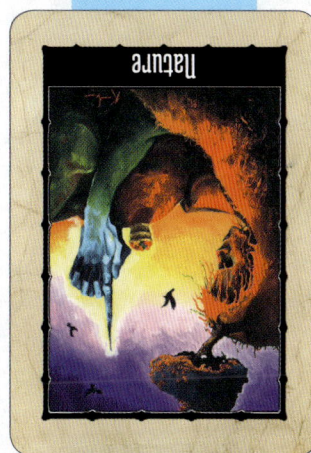

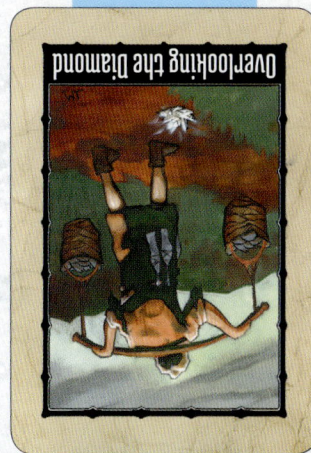

Nature – Scott Kirschner

Overlooking the Diamond – Jeff Miracola

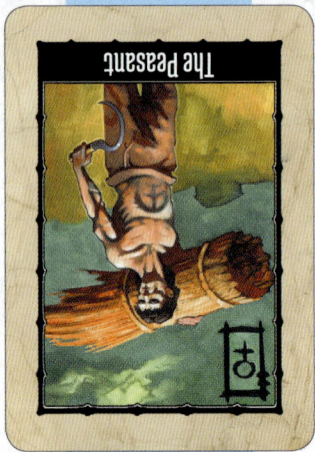

The Peasant–Reversed

Meaning: *lack of vision*, a negative meaning, the opposite of "simple strength."

Gamemaster's Interpretation: The warrior, confident in their superior abilities, fails to see how this enemy is different from those they've defeated before.

Gamemaster: Your speed and skill give you an edge, but this creature is not fazed by the nasty cuts you give it, and it pounds you hard before you finally drop it. By the time you defeat it, you're shaken, and your left arm is badly hurt.

The Phoenix–Reversed

Meaning: *destruction*, a remarkably negative meaning, especially as it's tied to Fire, which rules combat. *Section 2: Fortune Guide* says, "water quenches a fire and both are destroyed."

Gamemaster's Interpretation: The warrior destroys the ogre but is badly injured or even killed in the process. If any card means the death of the hero, this is that card.

Gamemaster: You strike the ogre and give it a mortal wound, but it stubbornly continues to fight, pounding you mercilessly as it dies. You feel bones break again and again before you finally fall senseless to the cave floor.

The Priestess–Reversed

Meaning: *impracticality*, a negative meaning, but not hopelessly so.

Gamemaster's Interpretation: The warrior's skills and tricks don't work well on the ogre, which must be faced with very straightforward tactics.

Gamemaster: With your superior speed and skill at arms, you defeat the ogre, but during the battle it sees through a feint and hits your shield so hard that your left arm is badly hurt.

INSPIRATION

The Satyr–Reversed

Meaning: *moderation*, a neutral-to-positive meaning.

Gamemaster's Interpretation: The warrior does as well as or slightly better than expected.

> *Gamemaster:* With your superior speed and skill at arms, you defeat the ogre, but during the battle it hits your shield so hard that your left arm is slightly hurt.

The Smith–Reversed

Meaning: *evil effort*, a negative meaning, especially for combat, as it's tied to Mars, the planet of war. (If it were upright, it would be very positive.)

Gamemaster's Interpretation: Some ill-advised merchant has traded iron spikes to the ogre, and the ogre has hammered them into the end of its club, making the weapon more fearsome. The warrior is badly hurt before he can defeat the monster.

> *Gamemaster:* As the club swings at you, you see large, sharp spikes sticking out from it. You cut the ogre, but the club smashes into your wooden shield and sticks into it. Against a human opponent, it would help you to have your enemy's weapon stuck like this, but the ogre is strong enough to wrench you around by your shield. With a mighty jerk, he pulls you to your knees....
>
> *Player:* I cut at its feet—no, at its legs. It can't block me.
>
> *Gamemaster:* You cut it across the shins. The ogre bears down on your shield, and since your right hand is wielding the sword, it's not there to support you. You fall under the ogre's weight, belly to the rock....
>
> *Player:* I yank my arm out of the shield....
>
> *Gamemaster:* You strain your arm doing so, but. okay, you're free.
>
> *Player:* Now I leap up and catch the ogre by surprise. It probably can't move its club fast enough to block me....
>
> *Gamemaster:* You get it between the ribs, and, no, it can't block you, but it does smash into your side with the club, to which your shield is still attached. Without the shield to protect you, you take a really bad blow, and your ribs are probably broken. You fall, but the ogre falls, too, vanquished.

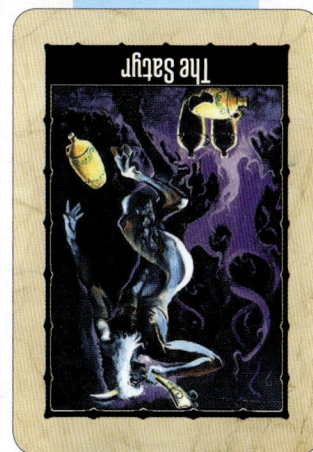

The Satyr – Scott Kirschner

The Smith – Jeff Miracola

The Soldier–Reversed

Meaning: _blind obedience_, a negative meaning. As a reversed card that's tied to Saturn (the planet of surviving adversity), it can be very bad for someone facing difficulty.

Gamemaster's Interpretation: The warrior is badly hurt by the ogre.

> _Gamemaster:_ With your superior speed and skill at arms, you defeat the ogre, but during the battle it hits your shield so hard that it breaks both the shield and your left arm.

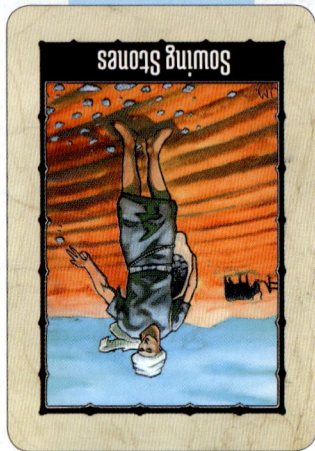

Sowing Stones–Reversed

Meaning: _ceasing fruitless labor,_ a positive meaning but not one directly related to battle.

Gamemaster's Interpretation: The warrior will have a chance to find an easy way to defeat the ogre.

> _Gamemaster:_ You slash the ogre across the belly, and it's bleeding pretty badly. It swings its club at you, but you deflect the blow. How do you proceed?

At this point, the hero can get an easy win by backing off until the ogre is weakened from loss of blood, but if they press the attack they'll be hurt. Since the outcome now partly depends on tactics, the Law of Karma is coming into play.

> _Player:_ How bad does the cut look?
>
> _Gamemaster:_ It's pretty bad. The ogre's swinging at you again....
>
> _Player:_ I'm blocking, dodging, and backing up. Does the ogre seem slowed down?
>
> _Gamemaster:_ Not yet, but it's still bleeding.
>
> _Player:_ OK, I play defensive and wait for the ogre to get tired....
>
> _Gamemaster:_ With your shield and some fancy footwork, you keep away from the thing, and it slows down. But your sword is getting heavy in your hand....

The warrior's Earth score is lower than the ogre's, so they can't fight the ogre too long.

Player: Before I get any more tired, I'm going to move in on the weakened ogre....

Gamemaster: Now that it's been softened up, the ogre falls quickly when you attack.

Spring–Reversed

Meaning: *stagnation*, a negative meaning but not one directly tied to battle.

Gamemaster's Interpretation: The warrior's plans don't work well, and they are injured while defeating the ogre.

Gamemaster: With your superior speed and skill at arms, you defeat the ogre, but during the battle it hits your shield so hard that your left arm is badly hurt.

Striking the Dragon's Tail–Reversed

Meaning: *recognizing the larger problem*, a positive meaning.

Gamemaster's Interpretation: The warrior can see the problem they're up against and has a chance to overcome it.

Gamemaster: You cut the ogre across the belly, but it swings its heavy club. You deflect the blow with your shield, but your shoulder is jarred. This thing is strong. You know that you won't be able to rely on your shield to protect you the way you can when you fight another human....

The outcome is now partly up to karma, as the warrior has a chance to come up with a good plan.

Player: I back up to get another look at this guy and see what I can do.

Gamemaster: It yells and takes a few steps after you....

Player: I'm looking for a soft spot or vulnerable point where I can get a swift kill, and I'm keeping back away from the club....

Gamemaster: The thing's stepping toward you, keeping the distance short, but you're out of the way. The monster's skin is thick, warty, and leathery, but its neck looks baggy and soft....

Player: OK, I wait for it to swing its club past me, and before it can backswing, I lunge for its throat.

WAR

Gamemaster: Like lightning, you're in and out, giving the ogre a mortal wound. It raises its club for a last swing but then drops it to the stone floor. In another heartbeat, the ogre pitches forward and lands with a thud.

Summer–Reversed

Meaning: *exhaustion*, a negative meaning, especially for a warrior engaged in battle, as it is a Fire card and Fire rules combat.

Gamemaster's Interpretation: The warrior does not have the energy or speed to overcome the ogre before it can smash them up.

Gamemaster: With your superior speed and skill at arms, you defeat the ogre, but it pounds you a few times before you take it down. Your shield arm is bruised and wrenched, and the ogre got in a nasty leg shot, too.

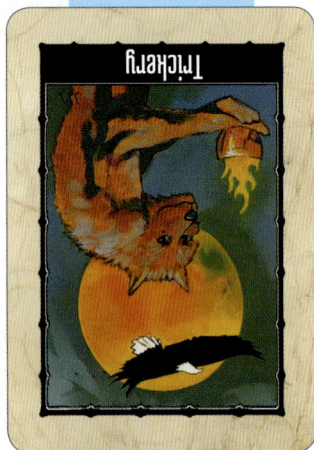

Trickery–Reversed

Meaning: *subterfuge revealed*, a neutral meaning in relation to this battle, in which the hero has superior Air and Fire (the card's corresponding elements). "Revealing subterfuge" is a good thing, but a reversed Air/Fire card is bad for combat, so the overall result is neutral.

Gamemaster's Interpretation: The warrior prevails and does as well as expected.

Gamemaster: With your superior speed and skill at arms, you defeat the ogre, but during the battle it hits your shield so hard that your left arm is hurt.

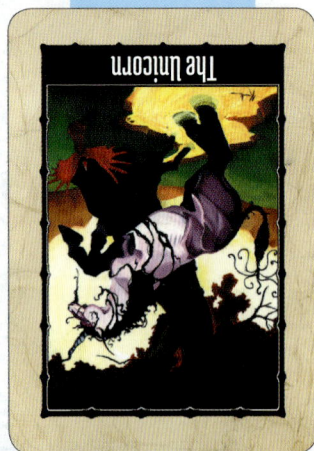

The Unicorn–Reversed

Meaning: *temptation*, a negative meaning but one without relevance to battle.

Gamemaster's Interpretation: The warrior does slightly worse than might be expected.

Gamemaster: With your superior speed and skill at arms, you defeat the ogre, but during the battle it hits your shield so hard that your left arm is badly hurt.

THE SMITH

The Usurper

Every realm has a different Usurper. It's up to the gamemaster to determine the relevance of this realm's Usurper (if any) to this particular battle.

War–Reversed

Meaning: *effort misspent*, a negative meaning, and one that is remarkably bad for battle, as it is a fiery, martial card and reversed.

Gamemaster's Interpretation: The warrior's great efforts are misdirected. Wounds that would pain, slow, or bleed a normal opponent do not faze the ogre, and it defeats the warrior.

> *Gamemaster:* You slash at the ogre and open a long cut, but its blood is so thick that it oozes out rather than pouring out. The ogre's club smashes into your shield, but you deflect most of the impact....

If the warrior backs out at this point, they'll escape. If they press on, though, they'll be defeated.

> *Player:* Then I'll go for deeper stabs and try to get at its vitals....
>
> *Gamemaster:* You score a good stab, but the ogre doesn't seem to care. With a sweep of its club, it knocks your feet out from under you....
>
> *Player:* I scramble away, using my shield to block me.
>
> *Gamemaster:* The club comes down again. Since you are against the stone floor, you can't roll with the blow. There's no give. It hits you full force, bones break, and your breath leaves you....
>
> *Player:* I roll away!
>
> *Gamemaster:* You start to move, and another blow comes down on you, and then blackness.

Winter–Reversed

Meaning: *inexperience*, a negative meaning.

Gamemaster's Interpretation: The warrior does worse than would be expected.

> *Gamemaster:* With your superior speed and skill at arms, you defeat the ogre, but during the battle it hits your shield so hard that your left arm is badly hurt.

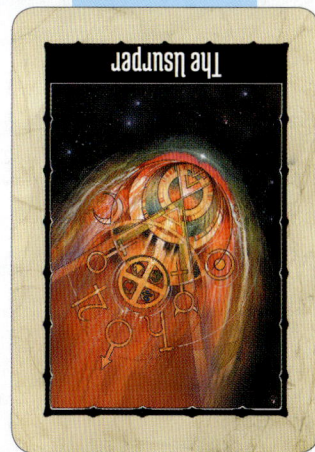

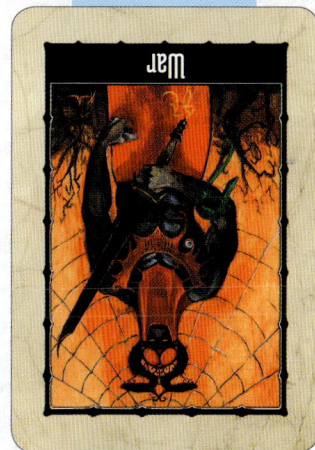

Section 2

Fortune

Guide

304. Winterwise – Rob Alexander

1310. Fortune Reader – Joe DeVelasco

Introduction

KNOWLEDGE – REVERSED

Introduction

This section of the book describes the Fortune Deck, which is central to the EVERWAY game. Both players and gamemasters use the Fortune Deck to guide the actions and progress of the heroes.

This introduction describes the Fortune Deck in the context of the mythic fantasy worlds of EVERWAY. Chapter 6 describes the various methods of obtaining a fortune reading and the meaning of each card.

Section 1: Playing Guide and **Book 2: Gamemasters** describe how to use the Fortune Deck in play.

Additional Section Credits

Using the Fortune Deck and Methods of Fortune: Richard Thames Rowan

Eight Deities of the Fortune Deck: Sandra Everingham, Tamra Fry, Daniel Gelon, Lisa Stevens, Aron Tarbuck, Jonathan Tweet, Jenny Scott Tynes, and John Scott Tynes

SILVER ANNIVERSARY EDITION NOTES

In this edition of EVERWAY, a random Fortune Deck card draw was added to the bottom of each page of the book so the book itself can serve as a Fortune Deck. New supplemental sections, *Using the Fortune Deck* and *Methods of Fortune*, were also added. The Deluxe Fortune Deck is also available separately.

AL DAVISON '95

THE FORTUNE DECK AMONG THE SPHERES

The Fortune Deck's history extends back to the creation of the spheres and of humanity, and it is now found in various forms throughout the spheres.

A Gift of the Deities

The gods and goddesses created the Fortune Deck as a guide for humanity. In its original form, it was a series of thirty-six images laid out in a specific pattern. The images detailed the evolution of the human soul from its manifestation in the world, through various lives or stages, to its eventual, inevitable perfection. Some say that the Fortune Deck, then known simply as "the Way," guided humans during a Golden Age, while others say that the Golden Age existed only in the imaginations and intents of the deities.

In any event, legend tells of the fateful action that spelled the end of, or prevented, the Golden Age. A deity variously identified as any of several gods of chaos or trickery stole one of the images and then mixed the others together so that the original pattern was disrupted and forgotten. It is because the thirty-sixth image is missing that the universe is unbalanced and imperfect. It is because the images' order is confused that human lives are in disorder.

THE FISH – REVERSED

Human sages put the remaining thirty-five images on cards to form the Fortune Deck. This deck now serves as a way to find meaning in the ever-changing universe. Some can foretell the future or read hidden forces with the cards. Others meditate on the images to gain a deeper understanding of the world. A few claim to have re-created the divine order in which the cards originally stood, but without the last card, there's little way to be sure these arrangements are accurate.

The Thirty-Sixth Card

The loss of the thirty-sixth card created a cosmic void, an emptiness the card used to fill. Sometimes in a realm, a lesser force grows to fill this void until finally it asserts itself as the thirty-sixth force in that realm. A force such as Tragedy, Despair, Vengeance, Charm, Oath, or Sacrifice, for example, may have great influence in a realm. Such a force is called a "usurper" force. Some usurper forces are positive, some negative, and still others are neutral or mixed. Inhabitants of the respective realms, however, generally take these forces for granted, considering them normal.

An accurate Fortune Deck in such a realm includes a card representing the realm's usurper force. Those who travel among realms often include a blank card in the Fortune Deck to represent the usurper force in each realm visited.

Most realms have a usurper force, but some do not. Among those that do, the force can vary from minor to overpowering in its effect in the realm. Usurper forces can also change; it is their nature to be temporal, like their realms, not eternal, like the true Fortune Deck cards.

Guises of the Fortune Deck

The most common form in which the deck appears is as a set of thirty-six rectangular cards, each with the same design, or no design, on the back and an image on the front. Each image has a particular meaning, and when the image appears reversed, the meaning is likewise reversed. Sometimes the image includes the name of the card; sometimes the reader must interpret the image alone. A few fortune cards even have brief meanings written on them.

The images and names on the Fortune Deck cards vary from realm to realm and from philosophy to philosophy. While most people claim to be using "the real Fortune Deck," every Fortune Deck is a temporal and imperfect representation of an eternal pattern. No Fortune Deck can be "the real thing"; each can only be a good model or useful symbol.

1309. Fortunate One – Al Davison

The Fortune Deck appears even in some realms where the people cannot make the stiff paper on which the cards are painted. These decks have been brought by strangers and are treasured as magic tools.

In many realms, the Fortune Deck is not known, and in most realms the common folk do not truly understand it. In all realms, however, the Way of the gods and goddesses makes itself known. In realms that do not have the Fortune Deck, diviners and wise people use magic smoke to induce visions, cast runes or lots to produce readings, interpret dreams for insight, and so on. In each case, the original forces of the Way make themselves known. The Fortune Deck has the advantage of being easy to use, but other systems of gaining insight also work for those who know how to use them.

Divining With the Fortune Deck

Diviners have developed several ways to get a reading from the Fortune Deck. The most common way is described here.

The Fortune Deck referred to throughout this book is modeled after the one that is commonly used in the city of Everway. See Chapter 1: Setting to read more about this city.

1. **The reader poses a question.** If the reader is reading the cards for another's sake, the other person poses the question. Open-ended questions are better than those that can be answered yes or no or by some other simple choice.

2. **The reader shuffles and cuts the cards.** If the reader is reading the cards for another, the other person cuts the cards instead of the reader.

3. **The reader lays two cards beside each other.** The left card is the Virtue, the force working for the questioner. The card on the right is the Fault, the force working against the questioner. Some readers prefer to interpret these as two opposed forces (known as "Rivals"), rather than as a positive and a negative force.

4. **The card representing the final result, the Fate, is laid on the top.** It is laid sideways; it is neither right-side-up nor upside-down. It is up to the questioner to determine how the result will be resolved. It will become either upright or reversed, depending on the questioner's actions (or lack of action).

5. **The reader lays out three cards in a row below the others.** These represent, from the questioner's left to

right, the Past, Present, and possible Future forces in play regarding the question posed. It is important that the reader not "right" the cards that are upside down. The orientation is part of a card's meaning.

When the process is finished, the cards look like this from the questioner's perspective.:

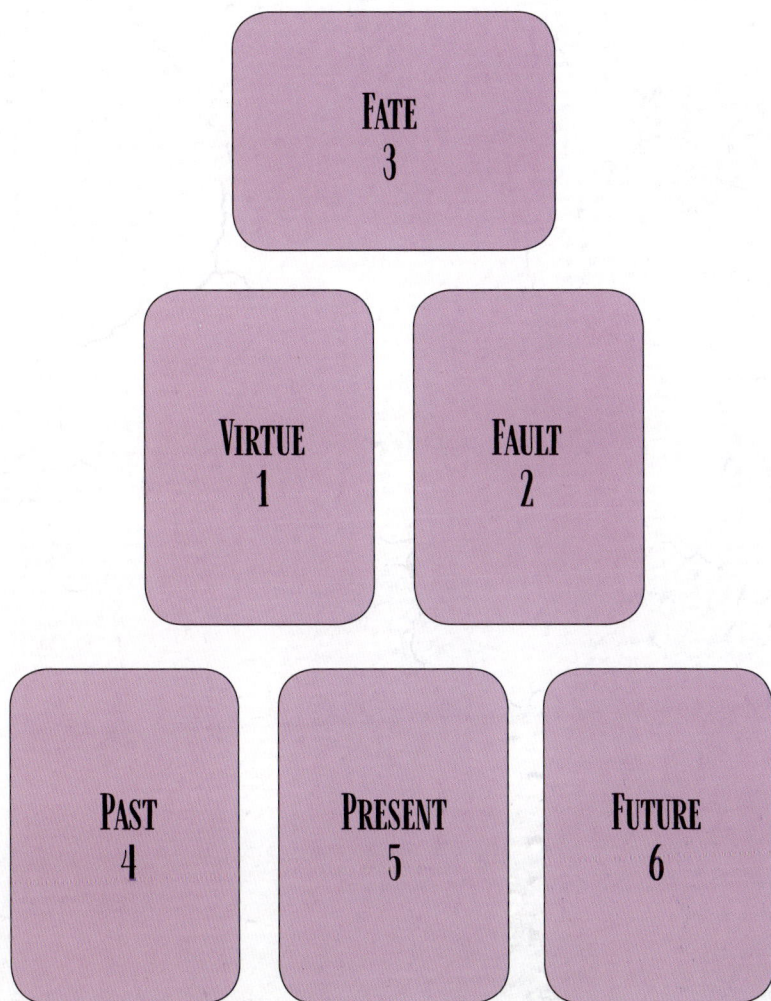

FATE
3

VIRTUE
1

FAULT
2

PAST
4

PRESENT
5

FUTURE
6

It is also possible to divine with the cards using just three: Virtue, Fault, and Fate. Such a reading provides less information, but it may focus on the most important ideas. Some diviners claim to be sensitive enough to get valuable insight from a single card, the Fate. Others say that no reading is complete without a fourth layer of four cards representing the questioner, the questioner's family, the questioner's realm or community, and the deities.

6. **The reader now interprets the cards according to their meanings and their positions in the pattern.** Different readers have different styles. Some emphasize the cards' correspondences, for example, while others work primarily with the cards' basic meanings.

EXAMPLE READING

A wanderer whose husband has been spirited away by creatures of darkness comes to a sage and asks to consult the Fortune Deck. The woman's question is: "How can I find and rescue my husband?"

The diviner shuffles the deck, the wanderer cuts it, and the diviner then lays them out as shown here:

FATE

Fertility
(growth vs. decline)

VIRTUE

The Soldier—Reversed
(blind obedience)

FAULT

The Fool—Reversed
(lack of connection)

PAST

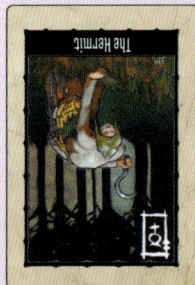

The Hermit—Reversed
(isolation)

PRESENT

The Defender—Reversed
(peril)

FUTURE

The Peasant
(simple strength)

To read more about these six cards, see *Chapter 6: Fortunes.*

THE USURPER

The Past is represented by "isolation." The diviner suggests that this card indicates some sort of isolation has brought this tragedy about. Perhaps it means the wanderer's isolation from her husband or from those around her. This card takes on special meaning when linked to the Fault card (see below). The Present card, representing "peril," is straightforward: the husband is in danger. The diviner says the wanderer should not hope that the husband is being kept safe for some future purpose; he is in danger now. The Future card represents "simple strength." This card is positive, especially because it is tied to Venus, the planet of love and fertility. This card bodes well, as the wanderer is concerned about reuniting with a loved one. This card takes on special significance when one considers the Fate card (see below).

The Virtue and Fault represent the main forces currently in conflict. On the wanderer's side is "blind obedience." How could this be positive? The diviner concludes that the beings holding the husband captive are blindly obedient and therefore able to be tricked or led astray. Working against the wanderer is a "lack of connection." The diviner says the wanderer's nomadic ways will work against her; she must strive to establish connections with others if she is to overcome her foes.

The Fate represents what hangs in the balance. Since the issue revolves around a woman and her husband, the Fertility card may literally represent offspring. The diviner interprets the issue to be resolved as whether the two will have children. (They haven't had any yet.) The diviner tells the wanderer the issue is not simply whether the husband is rescued, but whether she will bear his children. It is possible he will be rescued but that circumstances will prevent them from having children together. It is also possible the wanderer will fail to rescue the husband but will have a chance to conceive a child with him. The diviner advises the wanderer to direct her energies toward conceiving a child with the husband and to value rescuing him as secondary (though one hopes she could do both).

In sum, the husband is in danger, but the prospects of the wanderer bearing his children are good (and this probably implies rescuing him). To succeed, the wanderer should take advantage of the blind obedience under which her enemies act and strive to form strong bonds with those around her.

THE FORTUNE DECK IN PLAY

The Fortune Deck is important not only to the people in the fantastic realms of EVERWAY; the real-life Fortune Deck also guides the progress of the game.

Players and the Fortune Deck

When creating their hero, a player chooses three cards from the Fortune Deck, one each to represent the Virtue, Fault, and Fate aspects of the hero. The Virtue represents a special talent, gift, or blessing the hero enjoys. The Fault is a weakness or curse that the hero suffers. The Fate is a dilemma, issue, or challenge the hero faces or is destined to face. When a hero successfully meets their Fate, the player chooses a new one for them, including, perhaps, a new Virtue and Fault.

To read more about a hero's Virtue, Fault, and Fate, see *Chapter 3: Heroes.*

Gamemasters and the Fortune Deck

During play, the gamemaster uses the Fortune Deck to help determine how the action progresses. For instance, if a hero wrestles with a satyr, the gamemaster can use a card from the Fortune Deck to help determine which one wins. Gamemasters can also use the Fortune Deck to help them invent quests and realms.

To read more about using the Fortune Deck to determine the results of heroes' actions and using the Fortune Deck for designing quests, see **Book 2: Gamemasters**.

THE KING – REVERSED

THE GRIFFIN — REVERSED

1302. Fortune Woman –Janine Johnston

THE COCKATRICE

Chapter 6: Fortunes

This chapter describes several methods of obtaining a Fortune Deck draw, including when you don't have a physical deck in hand. Additionally, the meanings of each card of the Fortune Deck are explained in detail. This information is useful for both players and gamemasters.

USING THE FORTUNE DECK

There are many ways to use a Fortune Deck, so think about the method that you want to use and try different approaches to find the one you like the best. Some gamemasters prefer to have players draw their own card from the top of the Fortune Deck. Some prefer to fan the cards and have the player choose one. Some prefer to draw the card themselves. Any of these are possible, so experiment to find the method you and your players prefer.

The standard way to use a Fortune Deck is first to ensure that all cards are present and then to shuffle the deck. When you draw a card, do not "right" the card, as upright or reversed is part of the card meaning. As cards are used, place them on a discard pile. Continue this way until you draw the Usurper card. Interpret the Usurper card as normal, but then shuffle the Usurper, the discard pile, and the unused deck back together before your next draw. Play will always continue until the Usurper card is drawn, and you will never run out of cards to draw, as the Usurper will refresh the deck. You can also reshuffle during a significant break in the action, such as when the spherewalkers go from one sphere to another, or after a climax of some kind. Reshuffling at this point indicates that the heroes are "starting over" in some way.

METHODS OF FORTUNE

There are a couple ways to generate a Fortune Deck card draw, each described below.

Card Fortune Deck

Acquiring or making your own standalone Fortune Deck is the recommended method of playing the game. A Fortune Deck that includes all the art shown in the

The Fortune Deck is a great prop to bring to the table, as it brings an artifact from the worlds of EVERWAY right into our own!

Fortune Deck Meanings section below may be purchased separately, but you should feel free to draw your own with blank cards or to print images you own and to insert them into card sleeves. Use art that inspires you!

Book Fortune Deck

The bottom of each page in this book describes a single card draw from a Fortune Deck. Choose left or right page, then open the book to a random page and use the Fortune Deck card draw at the bottom of that page.

The advantage of this method is that you hold it in your hands right now and can start using it immediately. The disadvantage is that draws are equally likely each time you use this method, whereas in a card Fortune Deck, the card is physically removed from the deck until the Usurper is drawn. This means that it will be possible to get the same draw several times in a row. If you "draw" the same card (either upright or reversed) a second time in a row, you should try again. Additionally, if you draw the same card within the scope of a reading, you should also try again.

PUBLIC OR PRIVATE

Your gamemaster will decide if they want Fortune Deck draws to be public or private. At times they may wish to consult the Fortune Deck privately, especially in cases where they are making a decision about circumstances the players do not know about yet. Or a player may wish to consult the Fortune Deck to make their own decision. In these cases, you should reshuffle the remaining deck, including the card drawn, before continuing.

There are some real advantages to drawing cards publicly, however. If the players are aware of the card drawn, they will often better understand why the gamemaster is ruling as they are and everyone can appreciate how they work in the flavor of the card's meaning. Also, the gamemaster may invite the players to offer their own interpretation of what the draw might mean before the gamemaster makes a final judgment. This can make the players feel like they have a real influence on the direction of the game. If using this method, the gamemaster should try not to directly counter what the players suggest; instead, they should adapt the players' interpretations to include other factors that the players may not know about. They should try to use a "Yes, and..." approach to add to what the players suggested rather than to ignore their input.

PATTERN OF THE FORTUNE DECK

The Fortune Deck has a pattern of meaning when the cards are grouped into subsets of one to eight cards as shown below. It is useful to understand this pattern as another layer of interpretation and context for the role of a particular card in a reading.

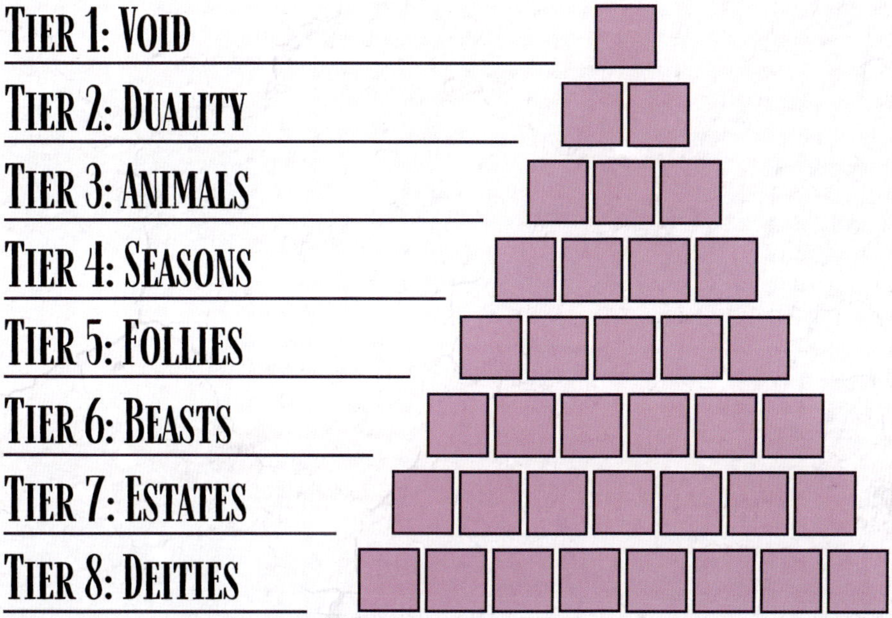

TIER 1: VOID

TIER 2: DUALITY

TIER 3: ANIMALS

TIER 4: SEASONS

TIER 5: FOLLIES

TIER 6: BEASTS

TIER 7: ESTATES

TIER 8: DEITIES

Tier 1: Void

The missing thirty-sixth card of the Fortune Deck (see *The Fortune Deck Among the Spheres* on p. 208) created a cosmic void, an emptiness that the card used to fill. Sometimes a lesser force, called a Usurper force, grows to fill this void and acts as the thirty-sixth force. A Usurper force is temporary, unlike the true forces which are eternal.

Tier 2: Duality

All things exist in opposing but complementary balance like the Creator and Defender. Each force cannot exist without its opposite because the rise of one principle necessitates the rise of its opposite. The duality cards collectively represent the principles of balance.

Tier 3: Animals

The animal cards represent the body (Lion), mind (Eagle), and spirit (Fish) aspects of mortal beings. If one aspect is weakened or damaged, the person quickly becomes unstable or even gravely ill.

Tier 4: Seasons

The seasons are an integral part of life among the spheres and represent the interconnectedness of nature through their cycling of the four Elements. The season cards collectively illustrate the passage of time.

Tier 5: Follies

The follies represent the forces of resistance that rise in natural opposition to change. The follies show the natural tendency for things to remain the same.

Tier 6: Beasts

The mythical beasts represent the six Great Morals (the principles that govern actions) and are related to the three animals, the mortal aspects of body, mind, and soul. Each mythical beast represents the two extremes of one of the Great Morals. The physical morals are Modesty (The Unicorn) and Tolerance (The Satyr). The mental morals are Prudence (The Dragon) and Resilience (The Griffin). The spiritual morals are Innocence (The Cockatrice) and Constancy (The Phoenix).

Tier 7: Estates

The seven estates represent the societal roles of humanity and are related to the planets: the artists (Fool/Sun), the spiritual leaders (Priestess/Moon), the academics (Hermit/Mercury), the physical laborers (Peasant/Venus), the craftsmen (Smith/Mars), the nobles (King/Jupiter), and the military (Soldier/Saturn).

Tier 8: Deities

The deity cards represent the Great Truths that correspond to a deity's broad domain of influence and the impact of that influence on human behavior. Each deity card depicts a god or goddess from one of the many pantheons of religious belief.

FORTUNE DECK MEANINGS

The Fortune Deck contains the thirty-six cards described here. Each card is listed with its basic meaning and an expanded meaning. When the card is upside down, the reversed meaning takes effect. Also listed are correspondences to planets, elements, and zodiac signs. Different people place more or less importance on these correspondences.

> The term "planet" in EVERWAY is used in the traditional, premodern sense. It refers to the seven heavenly bodies that are visible in the sky but that are not fixed stars: the sun, the moon, Mercury, Venus, Mars, Jupiter, and Saturn.

Autumn

Meaning: Plenty

In autumn, people harvest the earth's bounty and celebrate their good fortune with feasts.

Reversed: Want

Autumn can be a time of want if the frost comes too early, if the crop is blighted, or if anything else deprives the people of the harvest on which they depend.

Correspondences

Autumn is tied to Earth, the fertile element. The three symbols represent Taurus, Virgo, and Capricorn, the three Earth signs of the zodiac.

Autumn – Scott Kirschner

Autumn

SEASONS

The Cockatrice

Meaning: Corruption

Some say the cockatrice is born from a cock's egg hatched by a toad on a dunghill. Corruption incubates unseen and then hatches and wreaks its ruin.

Reversed: Recovery

Water and Earth, to which this card is tied, are elements of fertility. Just as waste enriches the ground, so the corruption of the cockatrice can turn to healing.

Correspondences

The cockatrice is tied to Earth and Water, two elements that, when combined, make dirty water, mud, or slime.

The Cockatrice – Scott Kirschner

The Cockatrice

BEASTS

THE CREATOR

Meaning: Nurture

The mother is the source and the supporter of all things. She brings forth life and maintains it.

Reversed: Abandonment

All children part ways with their mothers, perhaps happily, perhaps through tragedy. If the child is not ready to face the world alone, the parting can lead to destruction.

Correspondences

This card is linked to Earth and to Water, the two fertile, material elements, suggesting growth and life. Its planet is the round, full moon, representing completion.

The Creator – Scott Kirschner

The Creator

DEATH

Meaning: Change

Anubis is a god of the dead. He bears the ankh, symbol of life, to show that death is not the end of life but part of the life cycle. Death is change from the old to the new.

Reversed: Stasis

Where there is no death, stasis reigns, for the old never gives way to the new.

Correspondences

The overturned vessel represents Water, the eternal but ever-changing element of mystery and of the soul. Water is this card's element.

Death – Scott Kirschner

Death

THE DEITIES OF THE FORTUNE DECK

∼∼∼∼∼

The gods and goddesses depicted in this Fortune Deck—Anubis of Egyptian mythology, Brighid of Celtic mythology, Coyote of Native American mythology, Gaia of Greek mythology, Kuan-Yin of Chinese mythology, Odin of Norse mythology, Ogun of Yoruban mythology, and Quetzalcoatl of Mesoamerican mythology—are only a few of the countless deities worshipped among the spheres.

The sages of the Library of All Worlds in Everway selected these deities to represent the Death, Inspiration, Trickery, Nature, Fertility, Law, War, and Knowledge cards in Everway's Fortune Deck, but Fortune Decks from other realms use different deities, or even no deities at all.

807. Mirror of Souls – Joe DeVelasco

THE DEFENDER

Meaning: Safety

The father protects the family from danger. The spear represents his courage and skill, and the shield represents his fortitude.

Reversed: Peril

When people war, one family's protector is another's marauder. Times are dark when the spear is used more often than the shield. The fire that warms the home can also burn it down.

Correspondences

The Defender is tied to Air and Fire, the elements of thought, action, and energy. Its planet is the sun.

The Defender – Scott Kirschner

The Defender

DUALITY

THE DRAGON

Meaning: Cunning

The dragon is the most devious of beasts. Dragons often turn their intelligence into craftiness, guile, and treachery.

Reversed: Blind Fury

A dragon whose plans are thwarted flies into a bestial rage.

Correspondences

The Dragon's elements are Air and Earth. The dragons once flew in heaven, but many have been grounded for rebelling against the deities, unifying air and earth.

The Dragon – Scott Kirschner

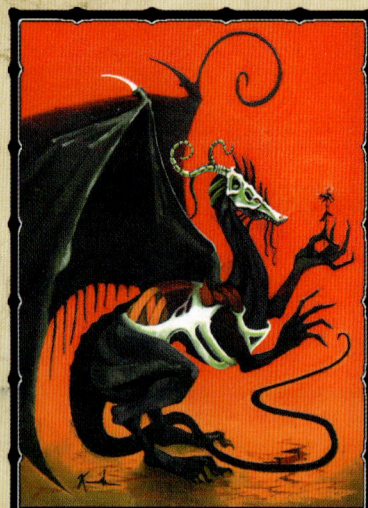

The Dragon

BEASTS

THE SMITH

DROWNING IN ARMOR

Meaning: Safeguards Turn Dangerous

A soldier may wear armor for protection in battle, but this precaution turns to doom if an armored soldier falls into the deep. Any plan made to protect people can turn against them as well.

Reversed: True Prudence

True prudence includes understanding the limits and dangers of one's defenses.

Correspondences

Water rules over this failure of intuition and anticipation that overcomes planning. Its planet is Saturn.

Drowning in Armor – Jeff Miracola

Drowning in Armor

FOLLIES

THE EAGLE

Meaning: The Mind Prevails

The eagle flies high in the air and sees to the ends of the world. The eagle represents the mind and its faculties.

Reversed: Thoughtlessness

An eagle can be carried away by the strong winds found on high. So, too, the mind can be distracted or led astray, causing one to act without proper consideration.

Correspondences

The Eagle is tied to Air, the element of thought, forethought, speech, and the mind.

The Eagle –Jeff Miracola

The Eagle

ANIMALS

FEARING SHADOWS

Meaning: Unnecessary Fear

In the dark, we are afraid of what is not really there. A little light causes frightening shadows to jump about.

Reversed: Recognizing Safety

A little light causes shadows, but a greater light banishes them so that not even the most cowardly will fear them any longer.

Correspondences

This card is tied to Fire, specifically a failure of Fire, meaning a failure to be brave or to see what's there. Its planet is Mars.

Fearing Shadows – Jeff Miracola

FOLLIES

Fearing Shadows

FERTILITY

Meaning: Growth

Kuan-yin is the goddess of mercy and the bestower of children.

Reversed: Decline

Just as the tide ebbs and flows, life comes and goes. Growth in the present is linked to decline in the past or in the future—or both.

Correspondences

The lake and the fish represent this card's links to Water, and the lotus represents the card's ties to Earth. Water and Earth are the fertile elements.

Fertility – Scott Kirschner

DEITIES

Fertility

THE FISH

Meaning: The Soul Prevails

The fish swims low, where mysteries beyond our understanding and lost cities lie. In the same way, the soul is the keeper of our former selves, forgotten but never gone.

Reversed: Shallowness

The fish can swim so close to the surface that it is dazzled by the sun. So, too, people can abandon the depths of their souls for shallow sensations.

Correspondences

The fish is tied to Water, the element of intuition, receptivity, the spirit, and the soul.

The Fish — Jeff Miracola

ANIMALS

THE FOOL

Meaning: Freedom

The fool can go anywhere and say anything. None dare strike a fool, even a fool who curses kings and queens or mocks the deities.

Reversed: Lack of Connection

The fool is also free from family, friendship, love, and community, the bonds that connect us to others. The fool's freedom can be a curse.

Correspondences

The Fool is tied to Fire and Water, the free-flowing elements, and to the sun, the planet of self-expression.

The Fool — Jeff Miracola

ESTATES

DEATH

THE GRIFFIN

Meaning: Valor

The griffin combines the features of an eagle and a lion, the two noblest beasts. Its bravery is renowned.

Reversed: Cowardice

Eventually, fear will strike every heart. Hearts that have felt fear the least often may be the most likely to succumb to it.

Correspondences

The Griffin's elements are Air and Fire, represented by its wings and its courage, respectively, like the sun in the sky.

The Griffin – Scott Kirschner

BEASTS

The Griffin

THE HERMIT

Meaning: Wisdom

Away from the demands of community, the hermit gains wisdom and inner knowledge. The hermit knows the secret mysteries of each plant in the forest.

Reversed: Isolation

The pursuit of wisdom may be an excuse to neglect one's duties to others.

Correspondences

The Hermit's elements are Air and Water, representing wisdom. It is also tied to Mercury, the planet of the mind and communication.

The Hermit – Jeff Miracola

ESTATES

The Hermit

INSPIRATION

Inspiration

Meaning: Creativity

Brighid is the goddess of inspiration, poetry, healing, and smithcraft.

Reversed: Lack of Imagination

Just as a well can run dry or a fire burn low, so, too, creative energies can wane.

Correspondences

The swan, the pool, the Perpetual Flame, and the serpent represent Inspiration's ties to Fire and Water. Creativity is the ability to balance opposites so they work together.

Inspiration – Jeff Miracola

DEITIES

THE KING

The King

Meaning: Authority

The king brings order to the kingdom, allowing his subjects to live in peace with each other.

Reversed: Tyranny

A king can become a tyrant, if he values his own desires over the good of his people. He is given the power to bring peace but can also destroy it.

Correspondences

The King is associated with all the Elements. A good ruler balances these to make his decisions. The King is tied to Jupiter, the planet of leadership and self-sacrifice.

The King – Jeff Miracola

ESTATES

KNOWLEDGE

DEITIES

Meaning: Truth

Queztalcoatl is the god of knowledge and of winds. He brings writing, the calendar, and other inventions to those he leads.

Reversed: Falsehood

The answers to some questions change in different contexts, and the more strongly one believes an answer, the harder it is to learn anything new.

Correspondences

The blue gem Queztalcoatl carries is the wind jewel, symbolizing Knowledge's connection to Air.

Knowledge – Scott Kirschner

Knowledge

LAW

DEITIES

Meaning: Order

Odin is the Law-Giver. He walks among his people and guides them with wise sayings and rules of conduct. He uses speech first and force second.

Reversed: Treachery

Treacherous people use others' faith in the law against them, violating laws that others expect them to follow.

Correspondences

Odin's ravens, Thought and Memory, represent Law's ties to Air, and thus to words and to forethought. Odin's walking stick signifies the card's ties to Earth.

Law – Jeff Miracola

Law

THE LION

Meaning: The Body Prevails

The lion is strong, fast, and powerful. It indicates a healthy body, physical power, victory in athletic contests, and so on.

Reversed: Weakness

Reversed, the card means illness, weakness, or physical failings.

Correspondences

The lion represents Fire, and the lizard represents Earth. These are the two elements that rule bodily health, strength, and endurance.

The Lion – Jeff Miracola

ANIMALS

NATURE

Meaning: Life Energy

Gaia is the goddess of the earth. The things of nature, from the animals to the trees to the hills, are her children, and they prosper from her goodness.

Reversed: Energy Sapped

Reversed, this card indicates a loss or exhaustion of energy.

Correspondences

This card is linked to Earth, the foundation of the world.

Nature – Scott Kirschner

DEITIES

Overlooking the Diamond

Meaning: Failing to See Opportunity

The peasant's labors would be over if they saw the diamond at their feet, but they pass it by, preoccupied with their load and their thoughts.

Reversed: Recognizing Opportunity

It's not too late for the laborer to stop and notice the diamond, setting down a heavy load.

Correspondences

The diamond represents Air. Failing to understand and appreciate the possibilities represented by one's circumstances is a failure of Air. Its planet is Mercury.

Overlooking the Diamond – Jeff Miracola

FOLLIES

Overlooking the Diamond

The Peasant

Meaning: Simple Strength

Kings, soldiers, and smiths all depend on the labor of the peasant, whose feet are on the earth's fertile soil.

Reversed: Lack of Vision

The peasant's connection to the earth and its cycles can be a weakness if the peasant fails to see beyond the next cycle of sowing and reaping.

Correspondences

The Peasant's elements are Earth, represented by the grain, and Air, represented by the sickle and simplicity. It is also tied to Venus, the planet of fertility.

The Peasant – Jeff Miracola

ESTATES

The Peasant

THE PHOENIX

Meaning: Rebirth

When the phoenix dies, it burns, and out of the ash it is reborn, young and pure. This card represents rebirth, a new creation emerging from the old.

Reversed: Destruction

Reversed, this card means annihilation, as when water quenches a fire and both are destroyed.

Correspondences

This card is tied to Water and Fire. Water is the element of eternity, and Fire is the element of change. The Phoenix encompasses these opposites.

BEASTS

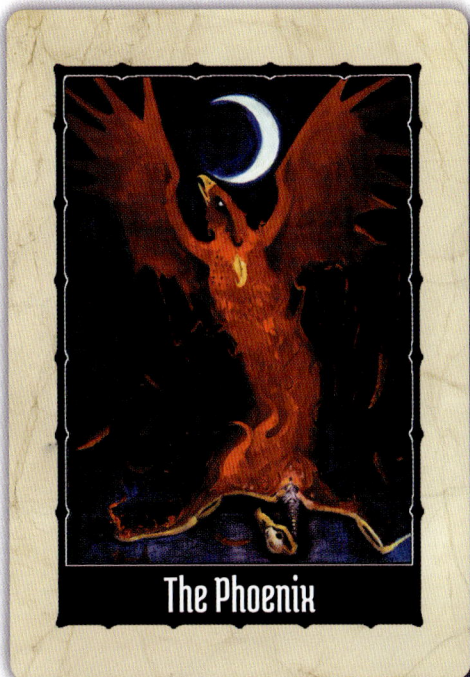

The Phoenix

The Phoenix – Scott Kirschner

THE PRIESTESS

Meaning: Understanding Mysteries

The priestess stands between the magical world of the deities and the mundane world of mortals.

Reversed: Impracticality

If the priestess delves too far into mysteries, she loses her ability to relate otherworldly wisdom to the material and social worlds around her.

Correspondences

The elements of The Priestess are Water and Earth, representing the spiritual grounded in the real world. It is also tied to the moon, the planet of mystery and emotion.

ESTATES

The Priestess

The Priestess – Jeff Miracola

THE SATYR

Meaning: Indulgence

Satyrs are renowned for their excess. Indulgence can be harmful, but a life without any indulgence is incomplete.

Reversed: Moderation

Moderation keeps one from being weakened or led astray. Even moderation, however, can be overdone.

Correspondences

The flames represent this card's ties to Fire, the element of energy and action. The satyr's goat legs represent the card's ties to Earth, the element of beasts and of primal strength.

The Satyr – Scott Kirschner

The Satyr

THE SMITH

Meaning: Productivity

The smith represents the power of directed transformation to forge new possibilities.

Reversed: Evil Effort

The smith's products may benefit others, but they may also be blades destined for the hearts of the innocent.

Correspondences

The smoke represents Air, or the ideas of what to make. The flames represent the energy and transformative power of Fire. The Smith is also tied to Mars, the planet of drive and industry.

The Smith – Jeff Miracola

The Smith

THE SOLDIER

Meaning: Duty

The safety of the land depends on the soldier's willingness to obey orders. The soldier faces hardship and risks death for the sake of his people.

Reversed: Blind Obedience

Soldiers can be put to evil use when they follow the orders of evil leaders.

Correspondences

The elements of The Soldier are Fire and Earth, represented by his spear and his shield. The Soldier is also tied to Saturn, the planet of responsibility and adversity.

The Soldier – Jeff Miracola

The Soldier

ESTATES

SOWING STONES

Meaning: Fruitless Labor

The peasant works even harder when sowing stones than when sowing seed but produces no benefit. This card represents great effort that is doomed to fail.

Reversed: Ceasing Fruitless Labor

Once the peasant realizes the error, they can drop the sack of stones and find respite immediately.

Correspondences

The card is tied to Earth, specifically the negative aspects of Earth, such as heaviness, density, and resistance. Its planet is Venus.

Sowing Stones – Jeff Miracola

Sowing Stones

FOLLIES

SPRING

🜁 ♊ ♎ ♒

Meaning: New Growth

Now that winter is over, people look ahead to the planting and harvesting that await in the year to come.

Reversed: Stagnation

Reversed, the card indicates new ideas, plans, or opportunities failing to come forth.

Correspondences

Spring is tied to Air, as symbolized by the birds. The three symbols stand for Gemini, Libra, and Aquarius, the three Air signs of the zodiac.

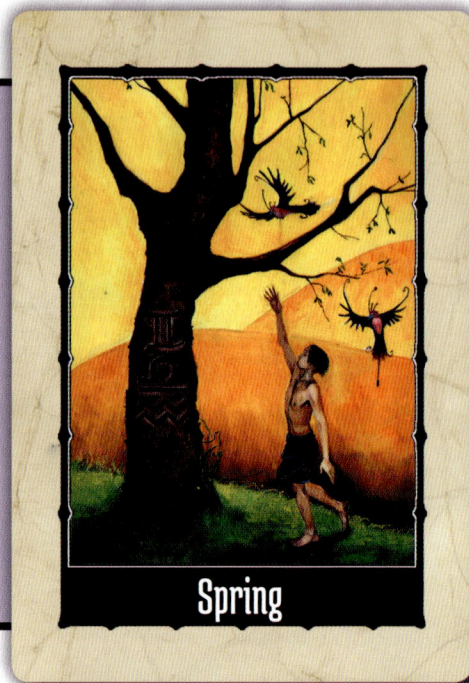

SEASONS

Spring

Spring – Scott Kirschner

STRIKING THE DRAGON'S TAIL

🜁 🜂 🜃 🜄 ♃

Meaning: Underestimating the Challenge

This card indicates a failure to understand the scope of a challenge or the seriousness of a danger.

Reversed: Recognizing the Larger Problem

If one can see the entire situation, one can usually avoid disaster.

Correspondences

The hoe represents Earth, the moon represents Water, and the dragon's wings and red eyes represent Air and Fire. This card suggests a physical, mental, or spiritual failure or danger. Its planet is Jupiter.

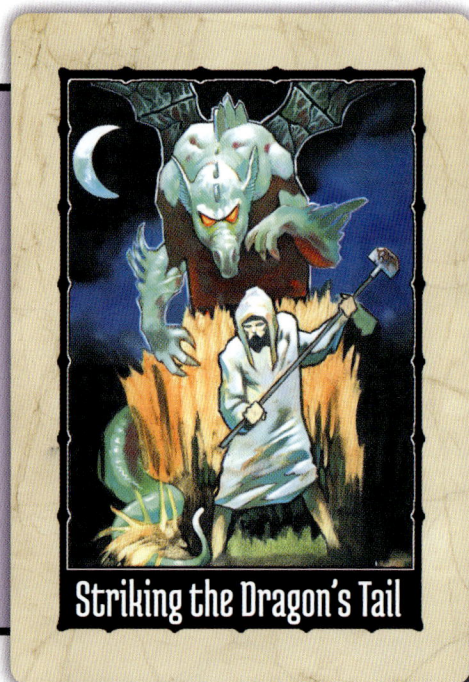

FOLLIES

Striking the Dragon's Tail

Striking the Dragon's Tail – Jeff Miracola

Summer

Meaning: Energy

The sun shines and energizes the world. Summer is the time for action: the roads are dry, and the days are long.

Reversed: Exhaustion

Reversed, the card indicates a lack or loss of energy, when great undertakings fail and new plans never become reality.

Correspondences

Summer is tied to Fire, as represented by the sun and the harnessed lion. The three symbols represent Aries, Leo, and Sagittarius, the Fire signs of the zodiac.

Summer – Scott Kirschner

Summer

Trickery

Meaning: Deceit

Coyote is the trickster. Here he is seen stealing fire. This card indicates that the subject may fall for a ruse or pretense.

Reversed: Subterfuge Revealed

Reversed, the card indicates that a scheme has been exposed or a ruse seen through.

Correspondences

The flame Coyote is stealing represents Fire, and the eagle represents Air. Trickery combines the energy and unpredictability of Fire with the foresight of Air.

Trickery – Jeff Miracola

Trickery

The Unicorn

Meaning: Purity

The unicorn is a pure and noble creature. It is so pure that it can smell the impure miles away, and it is therefore nearly impossible to catch.

Reversed: Temptation

The unicorn has a weakness: it can be tempted by purity. Some hunters use pure things as bait to lure unicorns.

Correspondences

The bird and the stream symbolize Air and Water, the two elements linked to this card. Air and Water are the elements of subtlety, speed, motion, and wisdom.

The Unicorn – Scott Kirschner

The Unicorn

BEASTS

The Usurper

Meaning: Varies

The Usurper card in Roundwander depicts the comet called the Walker's Star. Each realm's Usurper card has a different meaning based on the force in play.

Reversed: Varies

Reversed, The Usurper's meaning may be a direct opposite or an indirect one like The Dragon—Reversed.

Correspondences

The Usurper is linked to all the Elements. Like the true Fortune Deck cards, The Usurper can also correspond to planets and zodiac signs.

The Usurper – Jeff Miracola

The Usurper

VOID

WAR

Meaning: Great Effort

Ogun is the god of war and of iron. When Ogun came to earth, he cut away thick vines to make room for humans.

Reversed: Effort Misspent

Great energy and commitment can be directed toward the wrong ends, causing the double loss of both the energy wasted and the wrong deeds accomplished.

Correspondences

Ogun's smithing tools and the serpent represent War's ties to Fire, the element of action, destruction, and change.

War — Scott Kirschner

DEITIES

WINTER

Meaning: Maturity

This card indicates experience and understanding, an ability to cope and to prevail, even in harsh winter.

Reversed: Inexperience

Reversed, the card indicates a lack of experience. One is unready to face hardships, as one is unprepared when winter comes before any food has been stored.

Correspondences

Winter is tied to Water, the element of deep forces, mystery, understanding, and death. Cancer, Scorpio, and Pisces are the three Water signs of the zodiac.

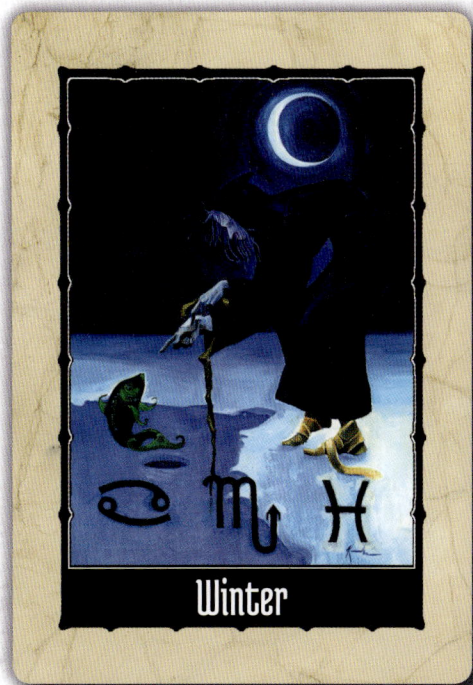

Winter — Scott Kirschner

SEASONS

Vision

Guide

240

201. *Plowed Field – Ian Miller*

THE SOLDIER – REVERSED

1008. Fish Person – Ian Miller

FEARING SHADOWS – REVERSED

Introduction

Art is an important part of the EVERWAY game. EVERWAY harnesses the inspiration art provides to spur stories in countless combinations. This section of the book presents more than a hundred vision images created by talented artists from around the world to fuel your games, whether you are a player or a gamemaster.

Players can browse through the vision images contained in this chapter to find three to five images that inspire them as they are creating their hero. See *Chapter 3: Heroes* for more on using these visions.

Gamemasters will also use these images to dream up new quests for players to enjoy. They can use these visions to illustrate the story they already have in mind, or they might let the visions spin into a story, much like hero creation. See **Book 2: Gamemasters** for more information on using these visions in creating quests.

Next to each vision image, you'll find questions intended to make you think about the art in new ways, to wonder what each character or object might have to tell you. Use these questions or your own to inspire you to look for connections that may not be immediately obvious.

Additional Section Credits

Image Questions: Jonathan Tweet and Richard Thames Rowan

SILVER ANNIVERSARY EDITION NOTES

In this edition of EVERWAY, we have included most of the original vision images from the 1995 edition, many new images from the 1996 **Spherewalker Source Cards** set, and some never-before-published art as well. This edition contains twice as much vision art as the 1995 edition. We hope you enjoy it!

1212 Temple Statue – Doug Keith

WAR

Chapter 7: Visions

This chapter provides many vision images from among the spheres of EVERWAY to inspire hero creation, realm creation, and quest creation. Each vision includes questions that can be used during the Questions Stage of hero creation and may also inspire new questions of your own.

While these images are grouped into small, conceptually related sets, you can peruse the images in any order, ignore the groupings, and mix and match visions from any set. Feel free to use photographs, personal drawings or paintings, your own images from other sources, or any other images that inspire you.

For more about using visions in hero creation, see Vision Stage in Chapter 3: Heroes. For using visions in quest and realm creation, see Book 2: Gamemasters.

ANATOMY OF A VISION

Vision Image

Title & Artist Credit

Vision ID

Development Questions

1001. Ship Upon the Waves – Janine Johnston

- Where is this ship going?
- Who is the captain of the ship?
- Who or what is in the cargo hold?
- How was the weather on this trip, and what implications did it have?
- What creatures lie in the depths below?

ELDERS AND YOUTH 1

101

- What are the pyramids for?
- Who is this man? What is his station or status?
- What is his most powerful magical or symbolic possession?
- What do his hand gestures mean?

Pyramid Priest – Rudy Rauben (Roger Raupp)

Tribal Hunter – Daniel Gelon

102

- What is this woman's community like?
- What is the purpose of the feathers near the end of the staff?
- What talents or skills does she have?
- If she could change one thing in her past, what would she change?

103

- What do this woman's headpiece and jewelry mean?
- What is she doing with the corn?
- What does the stone relief behind her mean?
- What is her position in her society?

Corn Farmer – Rudy Rauben (Roger Raupp)

FERTILITY

Plains Woman – Andrew Robinson

104

- What are the poles?
- What is this woman doing?
- Where is she?
- What do her feather and her body markings mean?

105

- What secret ability does this man possess?
- What prophesies does this man figure in?
- What caused the stitching in the man's hand?
- What is the most dangerous thing this man has ever done?

Hand Stitches – Rudy Rauben (Roger Raupp)

Tattooed and Pierced – Janine Johnston

106

- How did he get all these ornaments?
- What tattoo or piercing would he like to get next?
- What is he most proud of?
- What is the body of water behind him?

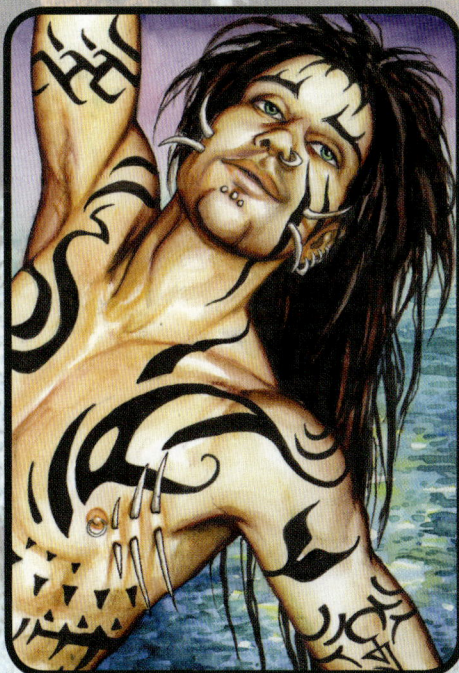

THE PRIESTESS – REVERSED

Elders and Youth 2

Fire Temple Priest – John Matson

107

- What special significance might this man's candle have?
- What is the gong behind him for?
- Who are this man's most important friends?
- What is this man's greatest hope?

Desert Rider – Janine Johnston

108

- What is the man charging after?
- What sort of weapon or tool is he swinging?
- What special traits, if any, does his mount have?
- Whom or what does he fear the most?

Medicine Woman – Janine Johnston

109

- What is this woman doing?
- What is her most potent magical tool?
- How did she learn her craft?
- What is the lizard in front of her?

Spring – Reversed

110

- What is the animal next to the woman?
- What does the sun relief mean or stand for?
- Who is this woman?
- What is her most noteworthy trait or talent?

111

- What special significance, if any, do the warrior's markings have?
- What is this man's necklace?
- What does he see?
- For what deed (good or bad) is he best known?

112

- What's happening in this scene, or what does it represent?
- How are the man and the gibbon connected?
- What do the other people in this man's community think of him?
- Is there anything special about this gibbon?

Family and Treasures 1

Plowed Field – Ian Miller

201
- What's in the treasure chest, and where did it come from?
- What's in the building in the background?
- Does the scarecrow have any special significance?
- Was the plow left there for any special reason?

Mummification – Christopher Rush

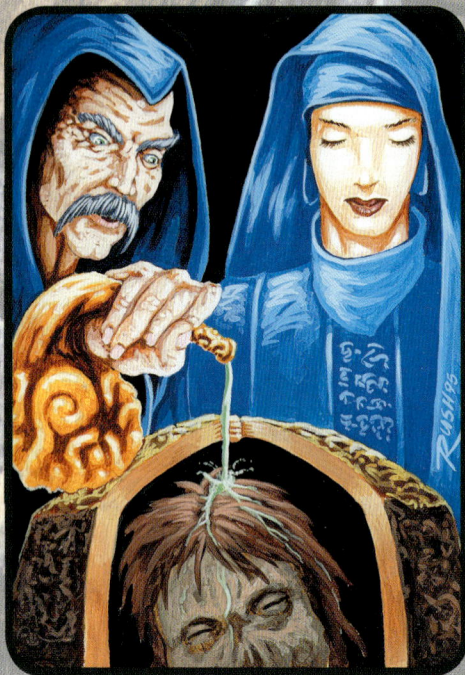

202
- What is happening in this scene?
- What is the liquid that the man is pouring?
- How are the man and woman in blue connected?
- Who is the third person?

Regal Woman with Cat – Janine Johnston

203
- What is the greatest challenge this woman has ever faced?
- How did this woman and cat meet?
- Does this cat have any special abilities?
- Do the peacock feathers in this woman's hair have any special properties?

THE GRIFFIN

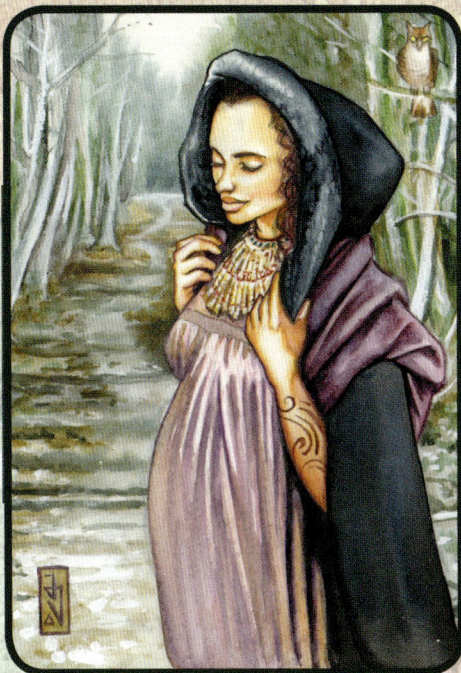
Expectant Mother – Janine Johnston

204

- Who is the child's father?
- What wishes or hopes does the woman have for her child?
- What do the markings on the woman's arm mean?
- Where does the road lead?

205

- Who owns this library?
- What sorts of scrolls does it hold?
- What's the most dangerous knowledge one can find here?
- How old are these scrolls?

Scroll Library – Martin McKenna

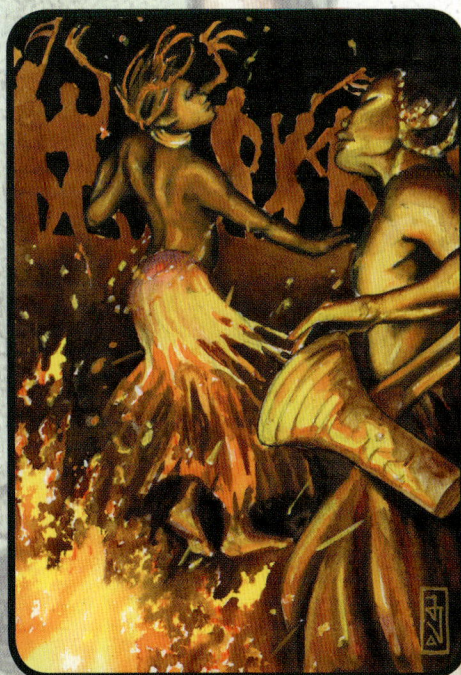
Fire Dance – Janine Johnston

206

- What sort of dance is this woman doing?
- What significance, if any, does the fire have to the dance?
- Do the people in the background have any special role in the dance?
- What is the woman's status or position in her community?

Family and Treasures 2

207

Artifact Merchant – Al Davison

- What special properties does the mask have?
- What secret does this merchant have?
- Who is inside the merchant's cart?
- Is someone watching the merchant from the rocks behind him?

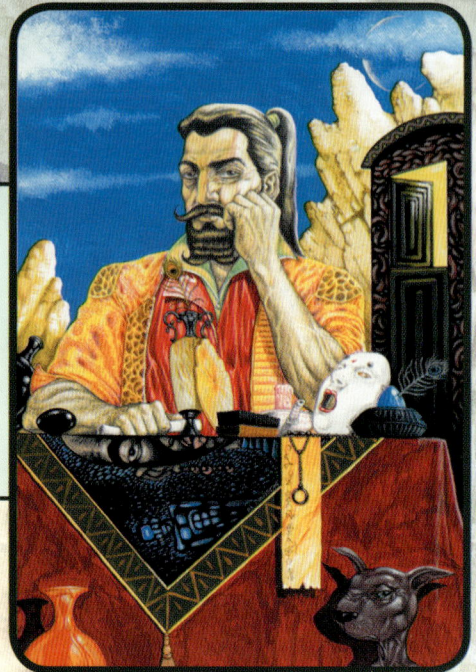

Merchant Shop – Martin McKenna

208

- Who owns or runs this shop?
- What is the shop's reputation, and is the reputation deserved?
- What's the most precious thing in the shop?
- What's the most dangerous thing in the shop?

209

Handfasting – Janine Johnston

- Who are these two people?
- What led to their getting married?
- What does the symbol behind them mean?
- What is the greatest challenge they are going to face?

The Dragon – Reversed

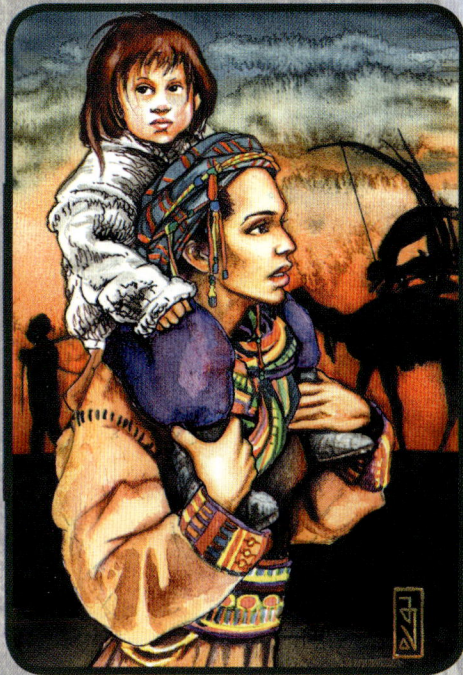

Mother and Child – Janine Johnston

210

- Who are these two people?
- What is loaded on the camel behind them?
- Why is the woman facing a different direction from the person leading the camel?
- What is the woman's biggest concern for the child?

211

- What price did the creator of this egg pay?
- Will any of the magic sigils on the pedestal have unexpected properties?
- What will this creature do when it emerges?
- Where is this room located?

Unnatural Hatchling – Jerry Tritilli

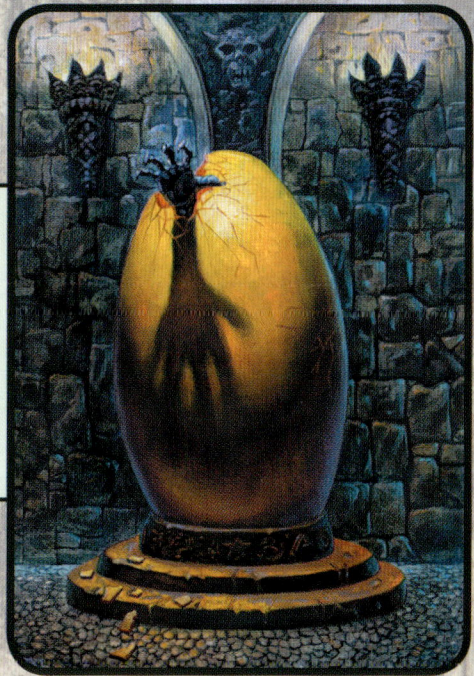

Man with a Box – Ian Miller

212

- What is in the box?
- Who is the person opening the box?
- Who is the person in the background?
- Where is this place?

Forgotten and Forlorn 1

Lost and Found – Rick Berry

301
- What is this woman's relationship with her parents?
- What tragedies have befallen this woman?
- When will this woman find what she seeks?
- What important thing has this woman forgotten?

Woman at the River – Rick Berry

302
- Whom is this person closest to?
- What is this person's greatest shame?
- Where does the river lead?
- What will happen on this day?

Undeath Totem – Ed Lee

303
- What does this totem symbolize?
- What is the significance of the triangle?
- Whom or what organization or realm is this symbol important to?
- What is the significance of eight skeletal legs?

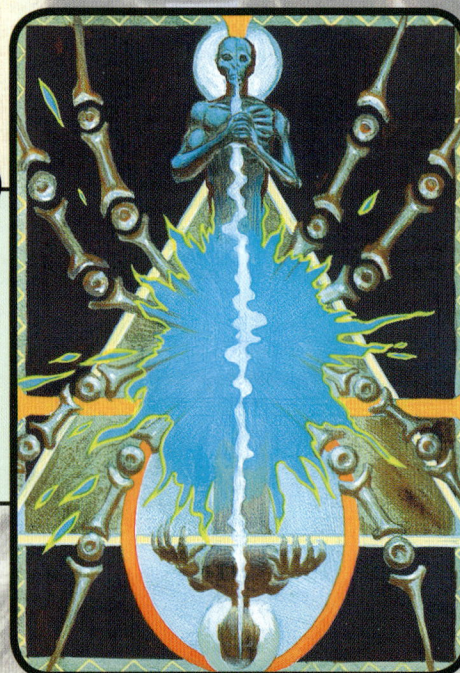

Fertility – Reversed

Winterwise – Rob Alexander

304

- Who are these people?
- What is the relationship between these people and the land?
- What do the symbols on the mask represent?
- What danger is going unnoticed by these people?

305

- Where is the herd headed?
- What other animals or people live in this land?
- What's in the hills in the background?
- What are the past and future of this land?

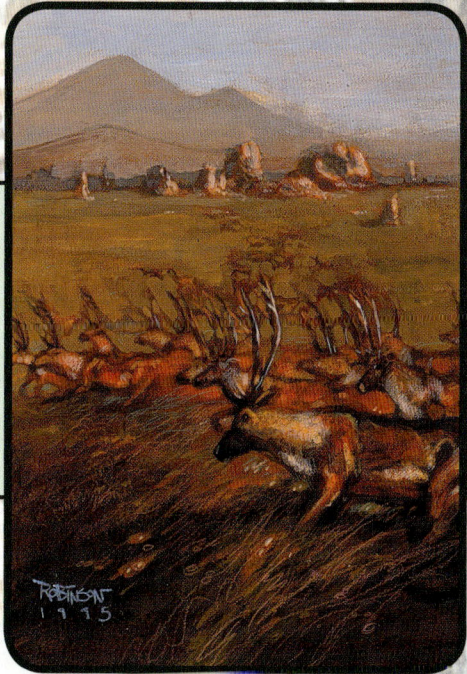

Caribou Plains – Andrew Robinson

306

- What town is this, and what are the people like here?
- Why are the dogs green?
- Who's hanging from the gibbet at the end of the street?
- What lies on the other side of the hill?

Lost Village – Ian Miller

FORGOTTEN AND FORLORN 2

307

- What destiny has been laid on this man?
- What is this man's relationship with his family?
- What is the strangest sight he's ever seen?
- What is significant about this man's blade?

308

- Who are the figures surrounding this plant?
- What conditions are needed for this plant to grow?
- What medicinal or magical properties does this plant have?
- How has this plant changed things?

309

- Who is this woman?
- Is the dress special in any way or meant for any special occasion?
- Who is the tailor?
- How might the woman and the tailor disagree over how the dress should turn out?

310

- What treasure lies inside this box?
- What do the carvings on the poles represent?
- Where is this place?
- What connection does this man have to what is in the box?

Mysterious Box – Doug Keith

311

Lost Prize – Rick Berry

- Who does this person miss the most?
- Where does this person most wish to be?
- What secret does this person have?
- What cause does this person support?

312

- Who lived here?
- Who or what destroyed this place, and how?
- Who is the figure in the distance?
- What significance do the birds in the tree have?

Desolate Ruin – Ian Miller

Inhumans and Undead 1

401

- Whose skull is on the ground?
- How can this creature be destroyed?
- What is the significance of the ceremonial armor?
- What special properties does this sword have?

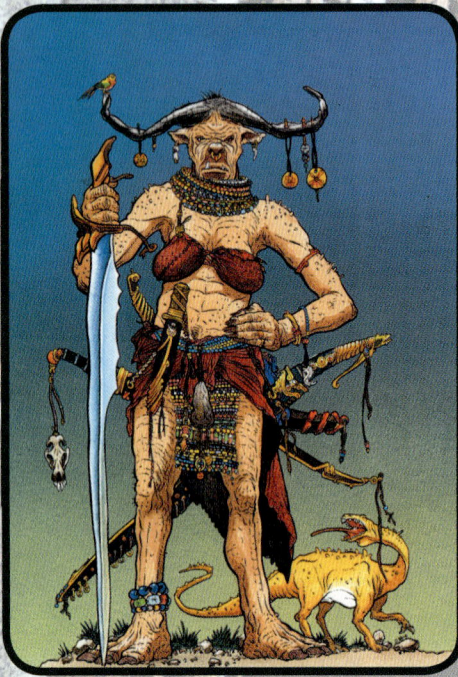

402

- What do the ornaments on this creature's horns signify?
- What is the creature in the background?
- What is this creature's greatest weakness?
- Has this creature always had a bull's head?

403

- What do the background people most desire?
- What is the shadowy creature behind the throne?
- What is the significance of the color red to this person?
- Who created these undead creatures?

THE EAGLE – REVERSED

Cutting Away the Lies – Janine Johnston

404

- Is the man or the undead creature the true form? Is the sword causing or fixing this man's condition?
- What is this place where they're meeting?
- What was the relationship between these two people?
- What are the special properties of this sword?

405

- Why are this person's eyes glowing?
- What power does this person possess?
- What does this person seek to accomplish?
- What is the relationship between these two?

Thief of Essence – Doug Keith

Ghoul Captain – Ed Lee

406

- Whom does this creature serve?
- How intelligent are the followers?
- Who is observing from the tent in the background?
- Why are these creatures camped here?

THE DEFENDER

Inhumans and Undead 2

407

- How is the tiger-headed warrior related to the creatures behind it?
- Why is the warrior drawing its sword?
- Where are they?
- What is their attitude toward humans?

408

- What is the wolflike creature?
- Why is it fighting the three-headed serpent?
- What tactics could the wolf-creature use to ensure victory?
- What is the wolf-creature's best asset, talent, or weapon?

409

- Who are these creatures?
- What are they celebrating?
- Where are they?
- Do the decorations, such as the suns and the moon, signify anything?

Temple Ruins by Moonlight – Ed Lee

410

- Who does this person fear above all others?
- Does the blade she wields have any special properties?
- What are the shadowy creatures in the background?
- Whom was this temple ruin consecrated to?

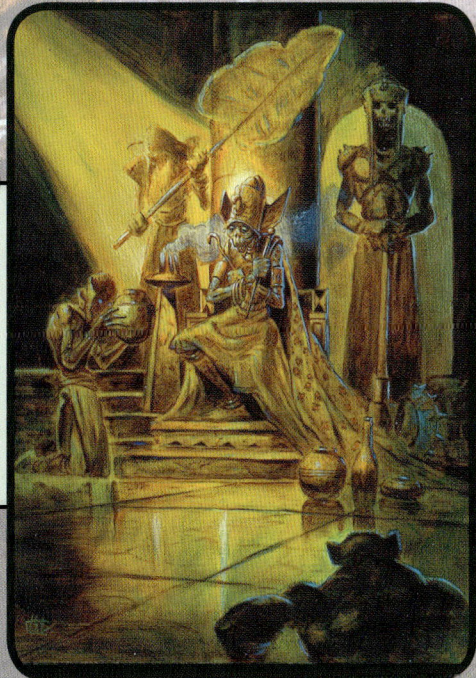

Ghoul Queen – Ed Lee

411

- What is in the jar being offered?
- How long has this person been undead?
- Does the smoke from the candles have any special properties?
- What did the most recent visitor here seek?

Dog People – Ian Miller

412

- Where are they going?
- Who is the tiny person on the shoulder of the figure on the right?
- How did the figure on the left lose its arm?
- How do these creatures feel about humans?

Labor and Leisure 1

Dancer – Janine Johnston

501

- Why is this woman dancing in the street?
- What significance might the white cat have?
- Why is no one else out in the street?
- What town is this? What is it like?

Toymaker – Ian Miller

502

- What is the bird on the table?
- What has been this man's greatest accomplishment?
- What has been his greatest failure?
- What secrets does the man have?

Vagabond Feeding Cat – Rudy Rauben (Roger Raupp)

503

- Who is this man?
- What is special about the cat, if anything?
- Where are they?
- How did the man lose part of his finger?

THE SATYR – REVERSED

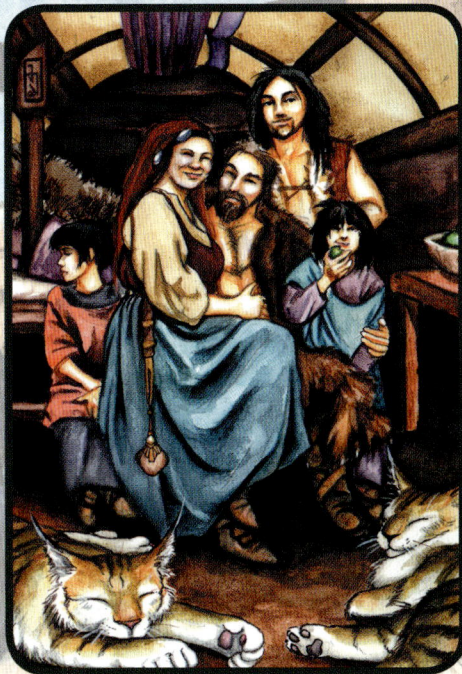

Tribal Family – Janine Johnston

504

- What is hanging from the woman's belt?
- How do the cats and the people live together?
- What is the youngster on the left thinking about or looking at?
- What makes this woman happy?

Harvest – Rudy Rauben (Roger Raupp)

505

- What is this farmer's biggest worry?
- What is the farmer's greatest hope?
- With whom and where does the farmer live?
- Whom does the farmer love the most?

Marketplace – Rudy Rauben (Roger Raupp)

506

- What can be purchased in this marketplace and nowhere else?
- What disaster is about to befall these people?
- Whom is the lower right person praying to?
- What will happen in this marketplace before day's end?

THE FISH – REVERSED

Labor and Leisure 2

507

- Who are the two people on the wall? How do they know each other?
- Who is the man in the chair?
- What secrets does this man have?
- What is this city like?

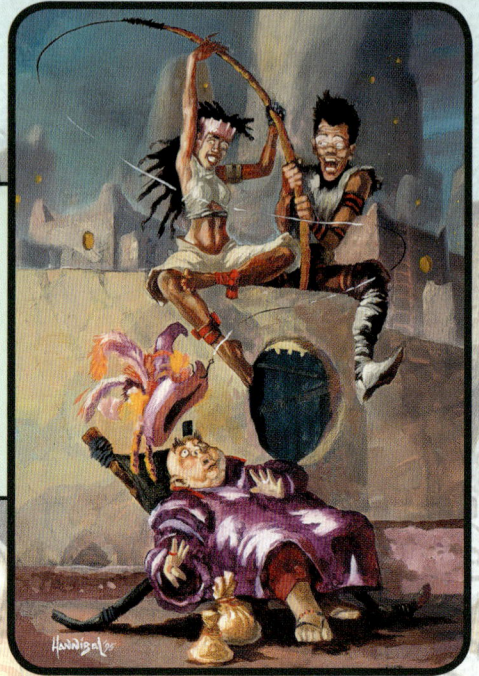

508

- What does the image on the prow of the canoe mean?
- What does the fisher's tattoo mean?
- What's his greatest accomplishment?
- What is his favorite possession?

509

- Who is the adult, and what is he reading?
- Where do these children come from?
- Who is the most gifted child in the group?
- What can that child do?
- What are the markings on the walls?

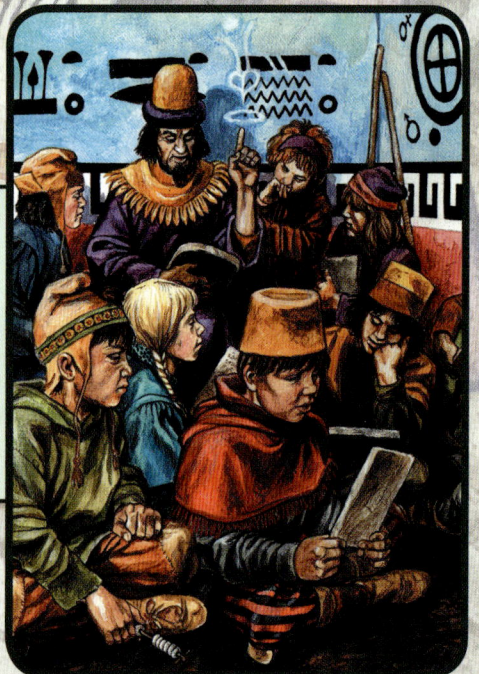

The Cockatrice – Reversed

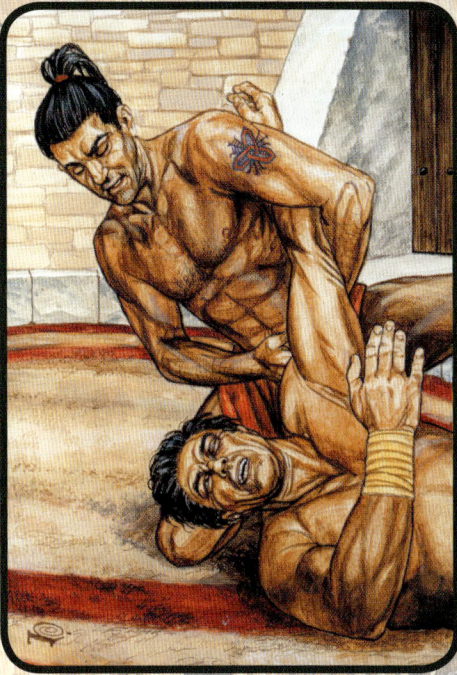

Entangling Art – Rudy Rauben (Roger Raupp)

510

- Which person has the most at stake in this struggle?
- What is the significance of the tattoo on the man's shoulder?
- Whom or what does each person most love?
- Where is this struggle taking place?

511

- What sort of game are these people playing?
- How well do the players know each other?
- Who is the person standing up, and how is that person connected to the game?
- Where is this place?

Gamblers – Doug Alexander

Artisan – Janine Johnston

512

- What is she painting?
- Does her paint or the image have any special properties?
- What does she hope to accomplish through this painting?
- Where is she?

THE DEFENDER – REVERSED

Living and Dying 1

Skin Scribes – Mark Tedin

601

- What properties do this woman's tattoos have?
- Whom does this woman most love and hate?
- What price did this woman pay for these tattoos?
- What does this woman most desire?

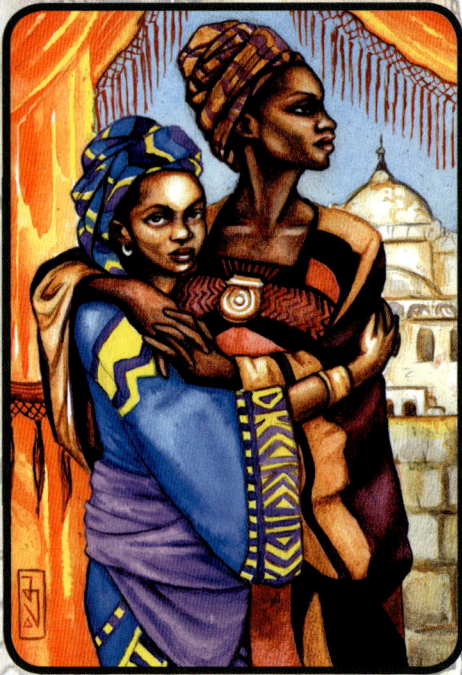

Two Women – Janine Johnston

602

- How are these two people related?
- Do the colors of their clothes signify anything?
- What is their future?
- What is the city behind them like?

Cinnamon Plague – Janine Johnston

603

- What is the relationship between these two people?
- What is affecting these people?
- What is the relationship between these people and their community?
- What secret do these people have?

TRICKERY

Woman and Bird – Janine Johnston

604

- What is the creature with this woman?
- What is the woman holding in her hand?
- Where are they?
- What is this woman's most remarkable skill or talent?

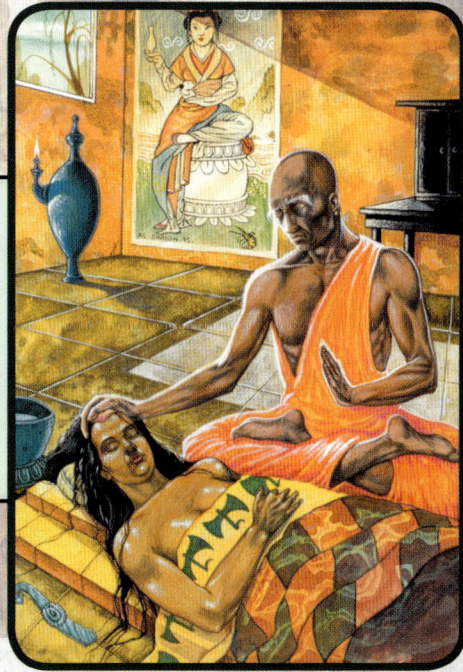

Kuan-Yin Worship – Al Davison

605

- What is this woman suffering from?
- What training in healing does this man have?
- Who is the figure in the wall hanging?
- What is in the cabinet in the background?

Green Pox – Ian Miller

606

- What disease do these people have?
- What is the skull-headed staff that the figure in the middle is carrying?
- What do these people blame their condition on?
- What significance, if any, does the tree in the background have?

Living and Dying 2

607

Ritual Bath – Rudy Rauben (Roger Raupp)

- What does this baby mean to the family and community?
- Who is the man, and what is his connection to the baby?
- What does the symbol on the man's forehead mean?
- What is the biggest challenge this baby must face?

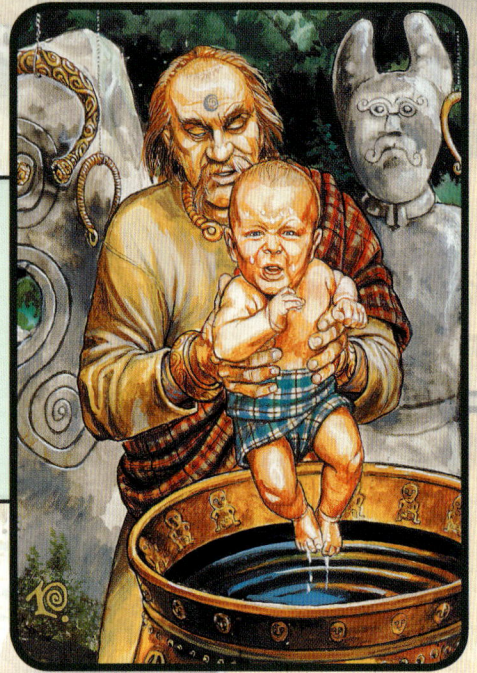

Man in Tree – Ian Miller

608

- Who is this person?
- What are the faces in the trees, or what do they represent?
- What is this place?
- Over the years, how has life changed for this person?

609

Man and Bird – Janine Johnston

- How does this man treat the bird?
- Where are they?
- What significance might his collar have?
- What is this man's best-kept secret?

THE SATYR

Dying Man and Shaman – Amy Weber

610

- Who are these two people?
- What are the animals doing?
- What is the book?
- What may happen by the time the sun rises?

611

- Who is being mummified?
- Who loved the person being mummified?
- What powers does the statue possess?
- Which of these three figures is destined to leave the others?

Anubis Worship – Tom Gianni

New Growth – Ian Miller

612

- What destroyed the plants and trees here?
- What was this place like before it was destroyed?
- What special properties does the single green plant have, if any?
- What does this plant portend, if anything?

MYTHIC BEASTS 1

701

- What bond do this woman and dragon share?
- What is the significance of the blue candles?
- Whose skull is lying on the steps?
- What destiny is laid upon this woman?

702

- What are the statues, creatures, or spirits in front of the man?
- What do the drawings on the rock wall mean?
- Does the axe have any special properties?
- What's the worst thing that could happen to the man in this scene?

703

- Does this unicorn have any special abilities?
- Who lives in the building?
- How are the people in the building connected to the unicorn?
- Is there anything special about the water?

Unicorn – Ian Miller

THE CREATOR

Satyr – Gerry Grace

704

- Why is this satyr rampaging?
- What is causing the lightning in the background?
- What was this ruin once used for?
- What transpired the last time people met at this ruin?

Phoenix – Martin McKenna

705

- What will happen when this phoenix is reborn from its own funeral pyre?
- What ancient secrets does the phoenix have?
- Who is hunting this phoenix?
- What wish will be made on the phoenix's breast feather?

Cockatrice Trapped – Janine Johnston

706

- Why is this cockatrice in a pit?
- What impact has this cockatrice had on the realm around it?
- Whom did this cockatrice last encounter, and what happened?
- What is the long-term impact of this particular cockatrice?

Mythic Beasts 2

Cockatrice – Martin McKenna

- Who died from this cockatrice's corrupting nature?
- What are the ruins like? Who built them, and why did they fall into ruin?
- Who lives in this desert now, if anybody?

Flame Wolf – Will Simpson

- Where did this flaming wolf come from?
- Is this creature seeking something?
- What impact has this creature had on the realm around it?
- What will quench this wolf's flames?

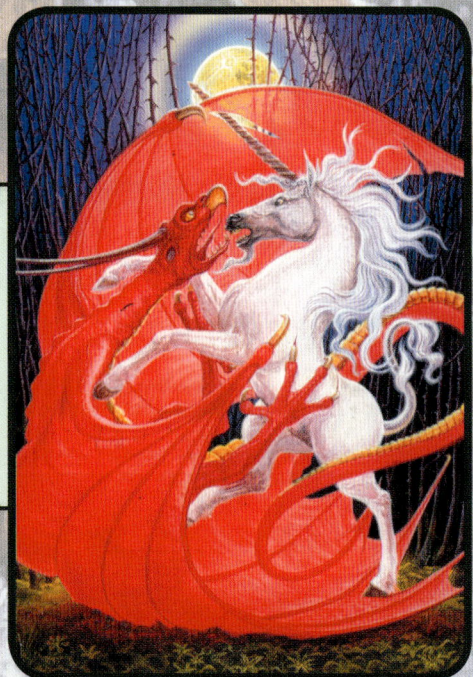

Unicorn Battle – Gerry Grace

- What led to these two creatures battling?
- Are either of these creatures championing a cause or battling of their own volition?
- Is there a significance to the full moon?
- Where is this battle occurring?

KNOWLEDGE – REVERSED

Griffin and Cockatrice – John Matson

710

- Why are this cockatrice and griffin battling?
- Who is observing this battle?
- What impact will this battle have on the nearby settlements?
- What will be left behind as an aftermath of this battle?

711

- Who is this griffin stalking?
- What or who else lives in these mountains?
- Has this griffin ever killed people?
- What is this griffin's weak spot?

Griffin – Martin McKenna

Satyr – Martin McKenna

712

- What sort of song is the satyr playing?
- Where did the satyr get its shirt?
- What else lives in these woods?
- How much contact does the satyr have with humans?

DROWNING IN ARMOR – REVERSED

RITES AND RITUALS 1

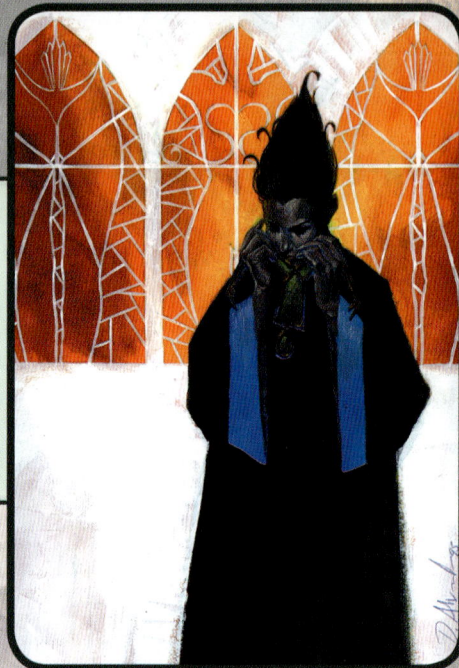

Red Priestess – Doug Alexander

801

- What is the priestess holding?
- What is her rank or status?
- What is her greatest wish?
- What are some of the beliefs or practices of her religion?

Sundial – Amy Weber

802

- What is the man doing?
- How are the animals related to him?
- What are the marks on the man's cheeks and on the animals' faces?
- What's the worst thing that could happen to the man tonight?

803

- What special properties does the bell have?
- What is the relationship between these two?
- Is there any significance to their clothing?
- What loyalties do each of these people have, and are they in conflict?

Bell Walkers – Scott Kirschner

THE COCKATRICE

Gaia Worship – Al Davison

804

- What ritual is this woman performing?
- What kind of seeds is she planting, and do they have any special properties?
- What role does this woman play in her community?
- What is the significance of this day and time?

Shaman Vision – Janine Johnston

805

- What does the bird indicate or symbolize?
- What sort of horns is this man wearing?
- What, if anything, is special about the blanket?
- What flowers and leaves is the man dropping?

Worship of Odin – Doug Keith

806

- Why is this man hanging by one foot?
- What significance do the birds have?
- Are there any special properties to the mist?
- Why is the man blindfolded?

Rites and Rituals 2

Mirror of Souls – Joe DeVelasco

- Whose faces can be seen in this pool?
- What special properties does this pool have?
- Who or what created this pool?
- Where can this pool be found?

807

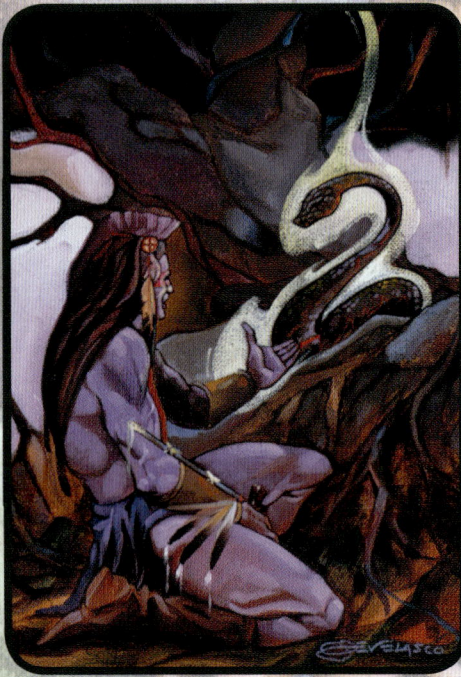

Brighid Worship – Joe DeVelasco

808

- Where did this snake come from?
- What ability do this man and snake have to communicate?
- Who is seeking this man?
- What special properties does this tree have?

Priest of the Book – Andrew Robinson

809

- What book is the priest holding, and what does the design on the front mean?
- What's the worst thing he's ever done?
- What is the significance of the candles?
- Where is he?

Nature

Coyote Worship – Joe DeVelasco

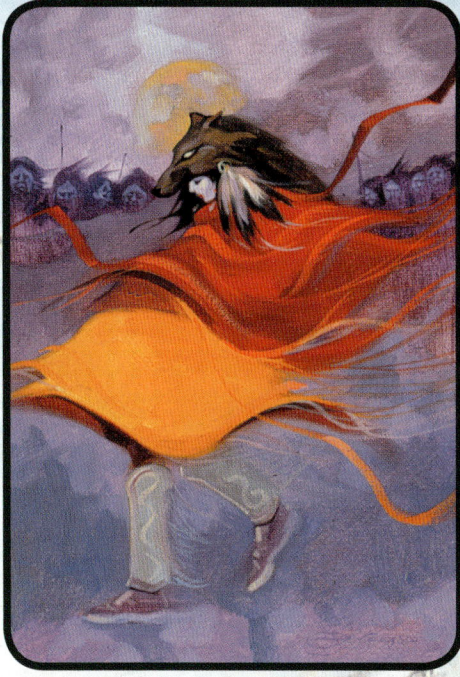

810

- What does wearing the coyote hood do?
- What relationship does this person have with their community?
- Who prepared this cloak?
- What is the significance of the day and time?

811

Quetzalcoatl Worship – Al Davison

- What role does this person play in their community?
- What special properties does the staff have?
- What building or transport is this person standing on?
- What do the stars tell this person?

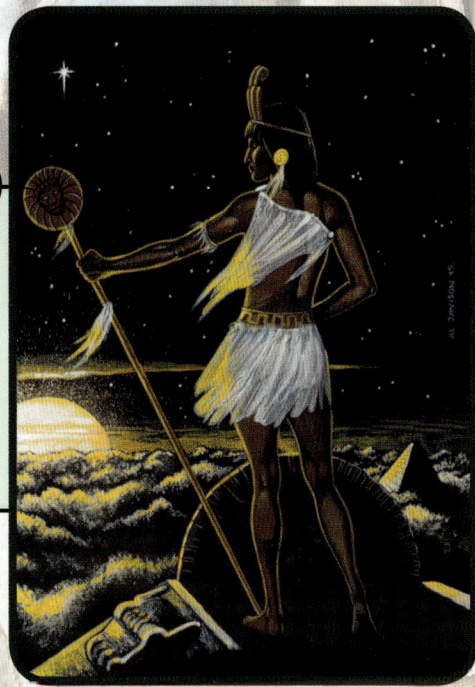

Lawless One – Andrew Robinson

812

- What is the effect of wearing these horns?
- How does the community treat this person differently from others?
- How long will it be before this man returns to his friends and family?
- What will the man recall after this experience?

Scouts and Soldiers 1

Red Lady – Doug Alexander

901

- What does the symbol on her tunic mean?
- What is special about her two swords?
- What is her biggest worry?
- Who is her most dangerous enemy?

Battlefield Soldier – Ian Miller

902

- Who won this battle and at what cost?
- Who is this warrior?
- What special properties might this warrior's armor have?
- Is the tree on the hill special?

Rogue – Janine Johnston

903

- How does this woman make her living?
- What is in her bags?
- What is the bird on her shoulder?
- What is this woman's best-hidden talent?

THE PRIESTESS

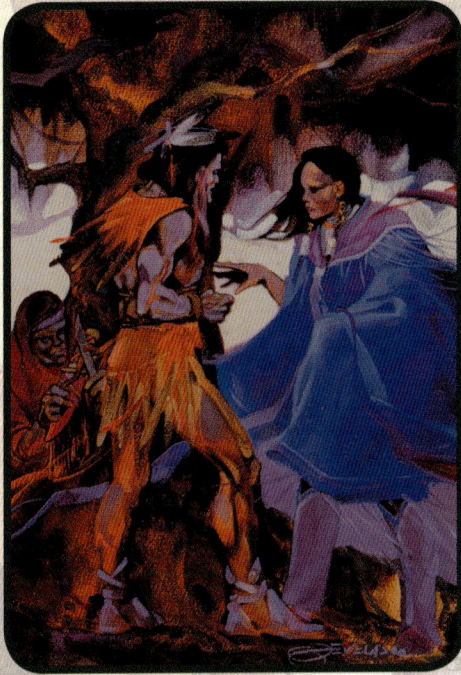

Everguard Weapons – Joe DeVelasco

904

- What are these two people talking about?
- Why is the man in the background trying to steal this man's weapon?
- What do each of these two people seek?
- Why are they meeting here and now?

905

- Why is this man charging the creature?
- What does this man fear the most?
- Where did this creature come from?
- How long will this man be journeying?

Ogun Worship – Tom Gianni

Falcon Trainer – Janine Johnston

906

- Has this bird been trained to do anything?
- What is hanging on the cord?
- What is the water behind the man?
- What is the worst thing that's ever happened to this man?

THE KING – REVERSED

Scouts and Soldiers 2

Golden Rose – Dermot Power

907

- Does this golden rose have special properties?
- What is the significance of this person's arm and face markings?
- Who gave this person the blade they carry, and what special properties does it possess?
- Who or what does this person most care for?

Huntress – Hannibal King

908

- What is this hunter hunting?
- What's the most remarkable game she's ever brought down?
- Where is she?
- What's her most prized possession?

Wind Monks – Anson Maddocks

909

- How long did this person train?
- What is the significance of the red tie?
- How far is this person from home, and when did they leave?
- Why are these two confronting this person?

Law – Reversed

910

- What group is this man affiliated with?
- How did this man come to own these clock-work creatures?
- Where does this road lead to?
- What did this man give up to leave the city?

911

- Where is this man pointing?
- Where do the stairs lead?
- What is this man's status in his community?
- Whom or what does he love the most?

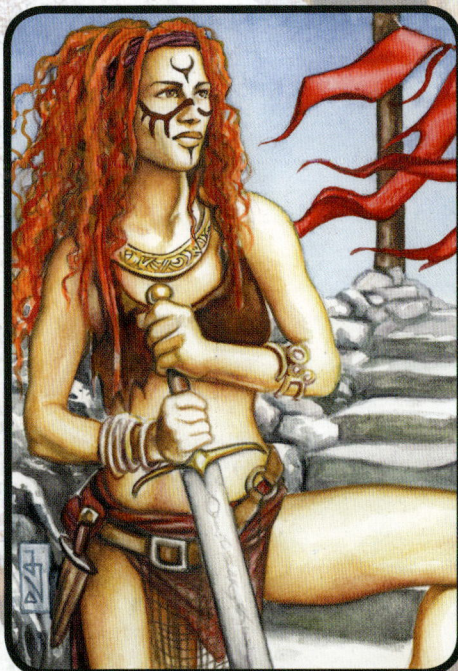

912

- What are the pennants behind the warrior?
- What do the markings on her face represent?
- What's the most heroic thing she's done?
- What does she regret?

Sea and Sand 1

Ship Upon the Waves – Janine Johnston

- Where is this ship going?
- Who is the captain of the ship?
- Who or what is in the cargo hold?
- How was the weather on this trip, and what implications did it have?
- What creatures lie in the depths below?

Goatherds – Rudy Rauben (Roger Raupp)

- How are the two goatherds related?
- What is the sundial for?
- How far away is the nearest village? Where is their home?
- Why is one goatherd crying?

Bloody Trail – Hannibal King

- Who are these people?
- What is the trail they're looking at?
- What is the bird on the woman's arm?
- Of these three, which is the most likely to betray the others? Why?

Unusual Food – Rudy Rauben (Roger Raupp)

1004

- Why are these people gathered here?
- What are they discussing?
- Is anyone here hiding something?
- Is any of the food or drink special?

1005

- What are the people like in this port?
- What's the furthest any ship has traveled after setting sail from this port?
- Who's in the rowboat?
- What is the biggest threat to this town?

Sunset Harbor – Martin McKenna

1006

- Who or what lives here or near here?
- What lives in the water?
- Is there anything special or unusual about this shore?
- What are the other lands that lie beyond the horizon?

Ocean Shore – Martin McKenna

Sea and Sand 2

Desert Wasteland – Ian Miller

- Do the rock spires have any special meaning?
- What kind of creature was the skeleton?
- Who left these posts here, and why?
- What is in the bottle?

Fish Person – Ian Miller

- Where does the fish-person live?
- Where is it going?
- What is the face in the rocks?
- What's the significance of the skull on the dagger's pommel?

Oasis – Rudy Rauben (Roger Raupp)

- Where has the traveler journeyed from, and where is he heading?
- What do the statues signify?
- What is hidden in or near the oasis?
- What's the most important or dramatic thing that has ever happened here?

Sowing Stones – Reversed

Pirates – Martin McKenna

1010

- What are these people looking at?
- Which one of them is in charge?
- Who are their worst enemies?
- What's the saddest thing that's ever happened to them?

1011

- What is the building in the cliff?
- Who built it?
- What are the statues?
- Who is on the bridge in the foreground?

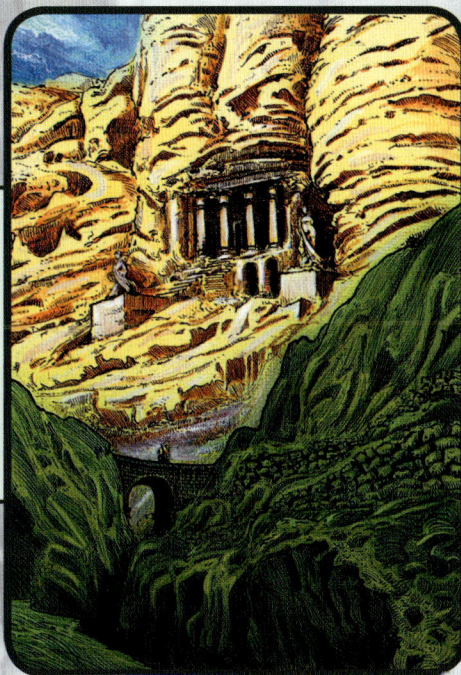

Cliff Temple – Ian Miller

1012

- Who or what lives in the city?
- What is the city's history?
- What might lie in the city's future?
- What legends (true or false) are told about this city?

Underwater City – Ian Miller

STONE AND STRONGHOLDS 1

Temple of Mercy – Janine Johnston

1101

- Is there any relationship between these two people?
- What can be found in these three pots?
- What building is this?
- How often do these people come here, and why?

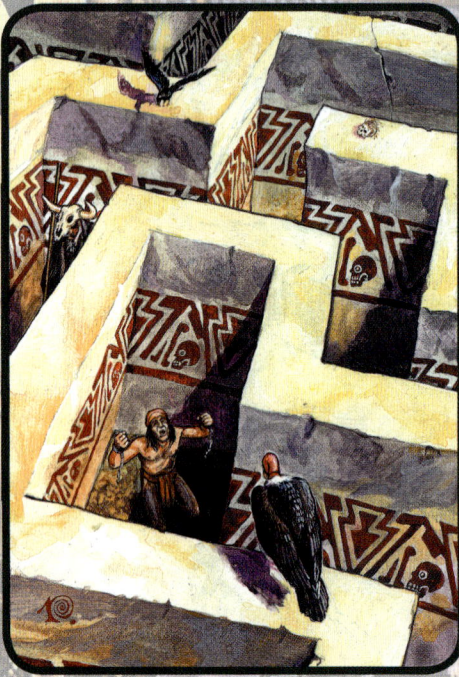

Labyrinth – Rudy Rauben (Roger Raupp)

1102

- Who put this man in the labyrinth, and why?
- Who is the wearing the bull's skull?
- Who built the labyrinth?
- Does the skull, crow, or vulture have any special significance?

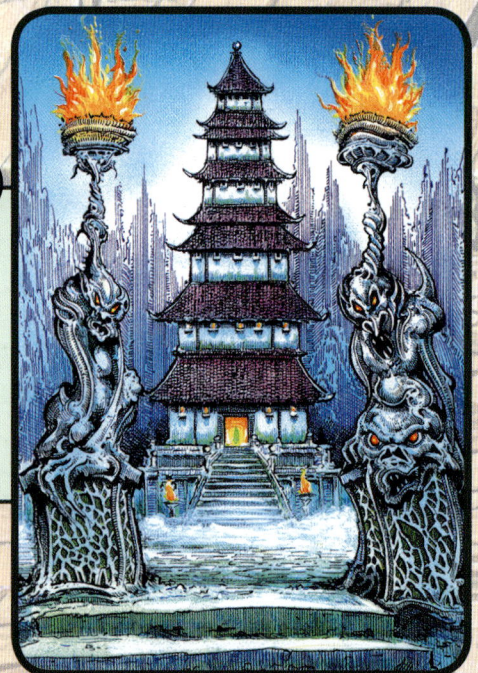

Pagoda – Ian Miller

1103

- What is this building?
- What do the statues mean or do?
- What are the spires around the building?
- Who is the figure in the doorway?

DEATH – REVERSED

Pyramid – Amy Weber

1104

- What effect does the moon have on this pyramid?
- Who built this pyramid, and why?
- What superstitions do the local residents have about this pyramid?
- How does this pyramid affect people?

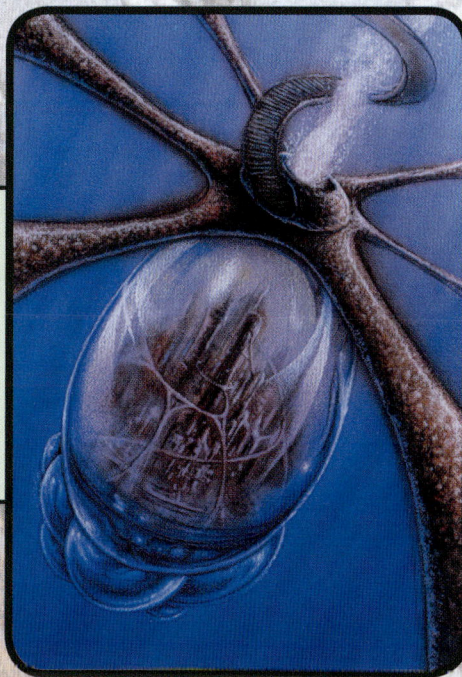

Hidden City – John Matson

1105

- How did this city come to exist in this bubble?
- What do the prophecies say about this place?
- What special properties does the spiral stairway have?
- Who is the most famous person to visit here?

Fall of the First City – Ian Miller

1106

- Who built this city, and how did it fall?
- What happened when this city sank beneath the waves?
- What are these creatures, and why are they here?
- What was the city's greatest treasure?

Stone and Strongholds 2

Child Watching Parade – Hannibal King

- Who is the child on the balcony?
- What is the parade or procession below?
- What is the animal on the railing?
- Who views the procession as something good, and who views it as something bad?

City Square – Ian Miller

- What city is this, and what is the city like?
- What is the statue in the center of the square?
- Whose skulls are in the pile?
- Whose carriage is in the background?

Undiscovered City – John Matson

- What grand purpose was this tower meant to fulfill?
- What became of the builders of this tower?
- What person arriving at this city changed its destiny?
- What lies beneath this tower's foundation?

THE LION

Ancient Tower – Ian Miller

1110

- Who built this fortress?
- Why are these strange creatures emerging from the tower?
- Whose skulls lie on the ground?
- What do the flying creatures portend?

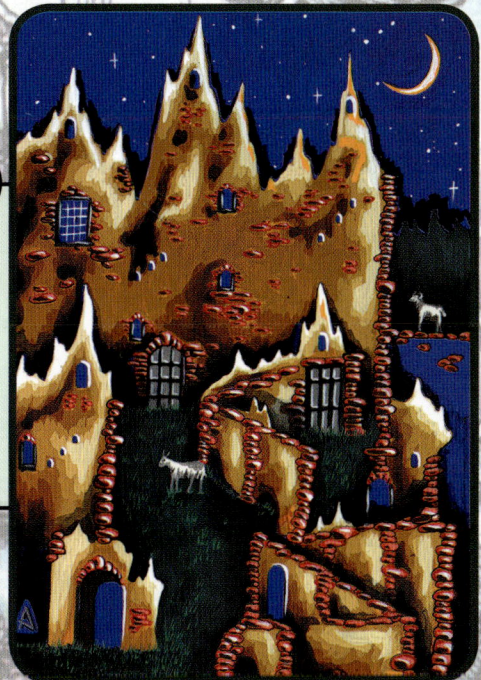

Mudbrick Village – Amy Weber

1111

- Who lives in these buildings?
- What do the people who live here think of it?
- Do the goats have any special meaning or unusual properties?
- Does the moon or stars have any special significance?

Mountain Fortress – Rudy Rauben (Roger Raupp)

1112

- Where is the warrior going?
- Who is in the palace?
- Who is lighting the lamps?
- Who is going to come down this boulevard this night?

Thresholds and Guards 1

Gate – Janine Johnston

1201

- Where does this gate lead?
- Who is the most dangerous person to travel this gate?
- When was this gate last used?
- What is the significance of this gate opening?

God of the Woods – Janine Johnston

1202

- Who is this person or being?
- What is the reason for the red leaves?
- What is this person or being thinking?
- What happened the last time this person or being was seen?

Earth Tusks – Mark Tedin

1203

- What creature did the tusks come from?
- Who is throwing weapons at this person?
- What family does this person come from?
- Why is this person sinking into the earth?
- What is the eye-like shape?

The Usurper

Fire Offering – Janine Johnston

1204

- Who are these three people, and do they trust each other?
- Who built the fire and why?
- What is the bowl and what does it do?
- Does the smoke have any special properties?

1205

Child and Snake – Chris Rush

- Who is this girl?
- Where is she going?
- What is special about the snake, if anything?
- What is the snake's weakness?

Gate Procession – Janine Johnston

1206

- Who are the people arriving through the gate?
- What is the person in black thinking?
- Are these visitors expected or welcome?
- What does their arrival signify, and is there any importance to the day they arrive?

THRESHOLDS AND GUARDS 2

1207

- What happens when the egg hatches?
- Where is this cart going?
- What are the two men discussing?
- What creature is inside this egg?

Magic Egg – Doug Keith

1208

- What is the relationship of these two people?
- What do the symbols on the stone mean?
- Is a person or creature observing this gate?
- How has this gate changed this realm?

Tree Gate – Gerry Grace

Earth Elephant – Anson Maddocks

1209

- How did this elephant break its tusk?
- Where did this gate lead to?
- Is this elephant the only one of its kind?
- What is motivating the elephant's actions?

THE CREATOR – REVERSED

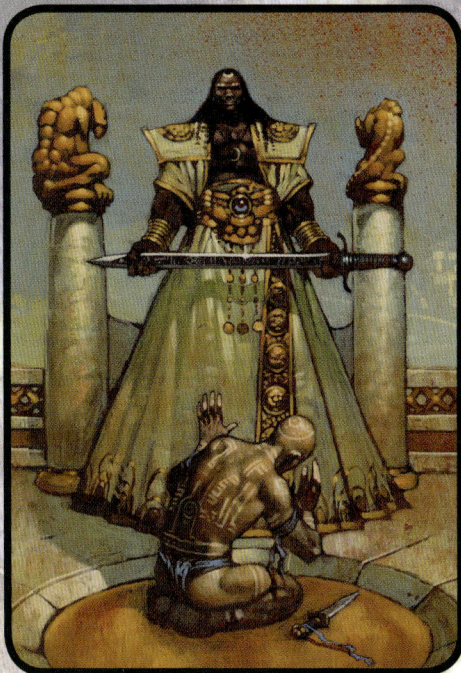

Judgment or Mercy – Dermot Power

1210

- What special properties does the blade have?
- Do the tattoos have any special properties?
- Where is this event taking place?
- Is the taller figure passing judgment or presenting a gift? Or a burden?

1211

- Why is the dagger glowing?
- What is the significance of this meeting?
- Which of these people is more dangerous?
- Which person offended the other first?

Confrontation – Scott Kirschner

Temple Statue – Doug Keith

1212

- What building is this statue in?
- Who was the artist that created this statue?
- Who does this statue honor or represent?
- What lies beyond the windows?

Wizardry and Fortune 1

Spherewalker – Doug Keith

1301

- What lies beneath this bridge?
- What will it cost these people to cross?
- Why is this creature barring their way?
- What do the keys beneath this man's beard open?

Fortune Woman – Janine Johnston

1302

- What does this woman know that you do not?
- What do these cards reveal?
- How significant are the rings to this woman?
- What secret does this woman keep?

1303

- What sort of magic is he calling up?
- Does his staff have any special power?
- Where does the stairway lead?
- From whom did this mage learn magic?

Sorceror – Martin McKenna

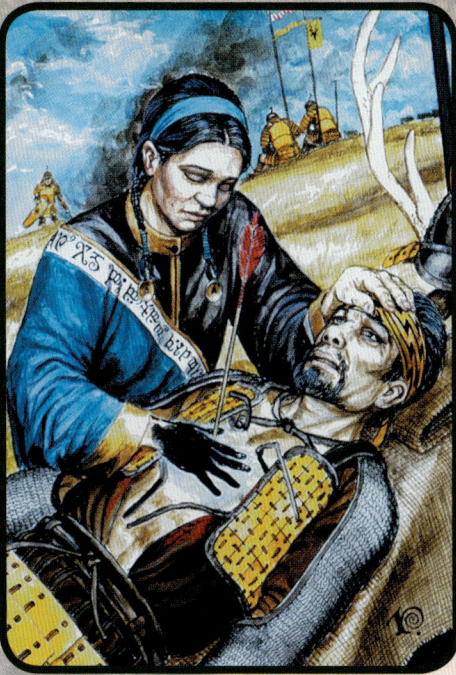

Battlefield Healing – Rudy Rauben (Roger Raupp)

1304

- Who is this man to the soldiers in the distance?
- What do the symbols on the clothes mean?
- What would this man's death cost these people?
- What is the relationship between the man and the healer?

- What is special about these feathers?
- What kind of creature is this?
- Why is the man in these mountains?
- What is this man's worst trait?

1305

Golden Feathers – Gerry Grace

Words of Creation – Doug Keith

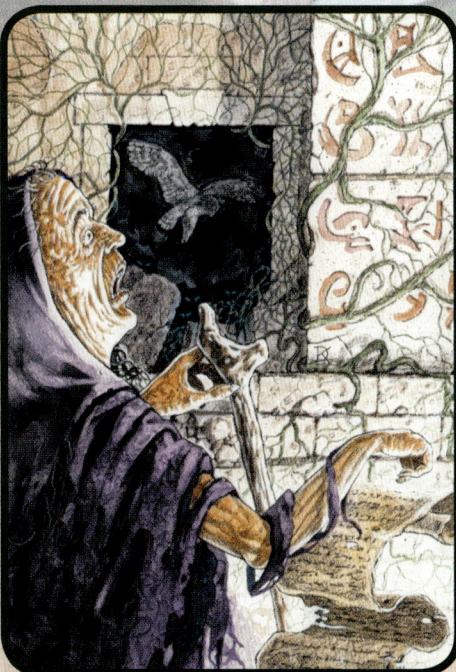

1306

- What is written on this scroll?
- What will this bird do next?
- What do the symbols on the wall mean?
- Why is this person so frail, and is it natural?

Wizardry and Fortune 2

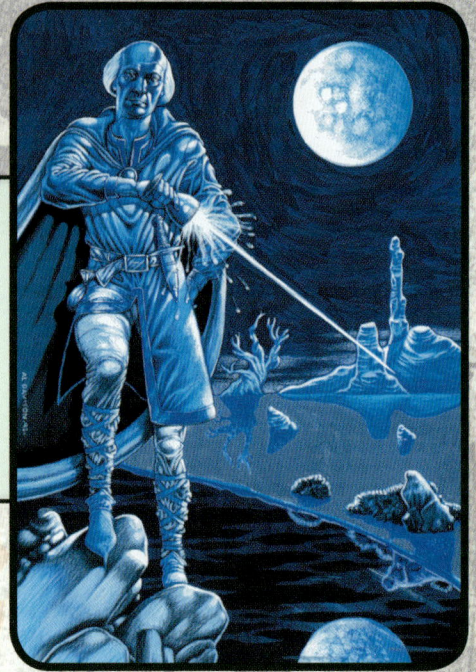

Chalice Blade – Al Davison

1307

- What does the full moon portend?
- What is about to emerge from the cup?
- What lurks in the river below?
- What lost treasure does this man seek?

Satyr Day – Mark Tedin

1308

- What is the source of this child's ability?
- How did this child's parents react to their abilities?
- Is anyone looking for children with special abilities?
- What will this child grow up to become?

Fortunate One – Al Davison

1309

- What abilities do this man's cards have?
- Who is the aggressor in this conflict?
- Where does the road they are on lead to?
- What is the relationship of the two in the foreground?

Fortune Reader – Joe DeVelasco

1310

- What knowledge is this person revealing?
- Does the smoke have any special properties?
- What difficult decision does this person need to make?
- What's the most important relationship in this person's life?

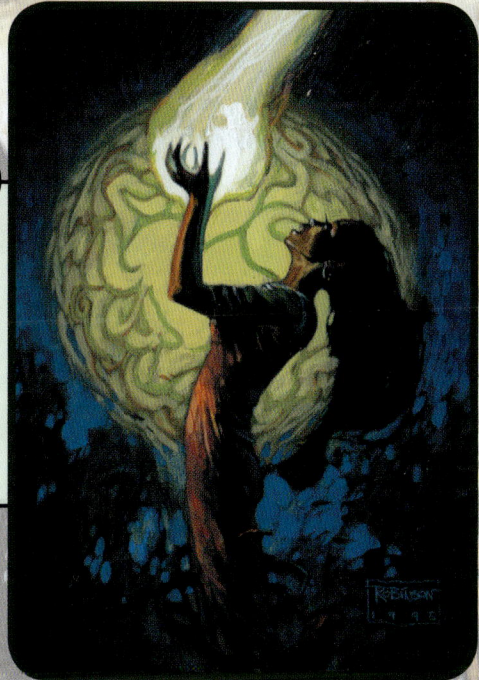

Soul Leeches – Andrew Robinson

1311

- What spell is this person casting?
- What are the shadowy forms surrounding this person?
- What is the golden orb behind this person?
- What forces are influencing this person?

Sorceress – Martin McKenna

1312

- What is the sorceress casting her spell at?
- What do the marks on her skin do or mean?
- What is the secret of her power?
- What is her greatest goal?

WONDROUS ARTIFACTS 1

- What does the ring signify?
- What does the owner of this ring seek?
- Are there any other rings like this?
- What organization is this ring affiliated with?

1402

- What special properties does this harp have?
- Who is the most famous owner of this harp?
- What is this harp made from?
- Do the strings of this harp have any special properties?

1403

- What lies beneath the surface of this mirror?
- When does this mirror appear in history?
- What battles have been fought over this mirror?
- What is the greatest tragedy reflected in this mirror's surface?

DEATH – REVERSED

True Pearl – Rob Alexander

1404

- What are the properties of this orb?
- What is the burden of owning this orb?
- Who made this orb?
- What prophecies surround this orb?

1405

- Who does this ring belong to?
- What promise was made with this ring?
- How many people have owned this ring?
- What does this ring signify?

Spirit Ring – Liz Danforth

Edge of Light and Darkness – Dermot Power

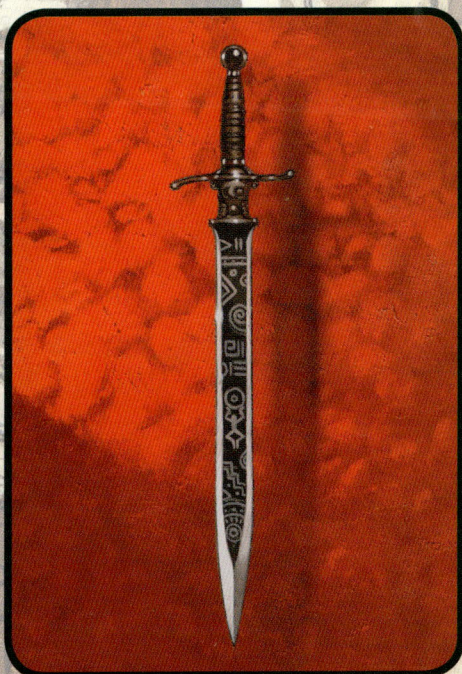

1406

- What special properties does this blade possess?
- Who was the most recent owner of this blade?
- What is the cost to the wielder of this sword?
- Where was this blade last seen?

WONDROUS ARTIFACTS 2

- What secret is this man keeping?
- What is the relationship between this man and the woman on the throne?
- What does the key around this man's neck open?
- What special properties does this orb have?

- How does this rose interact with the stars?
- What medicinal or magical properties does this rose have?
- How does this rose change at night?
- Who is seeking this rose?

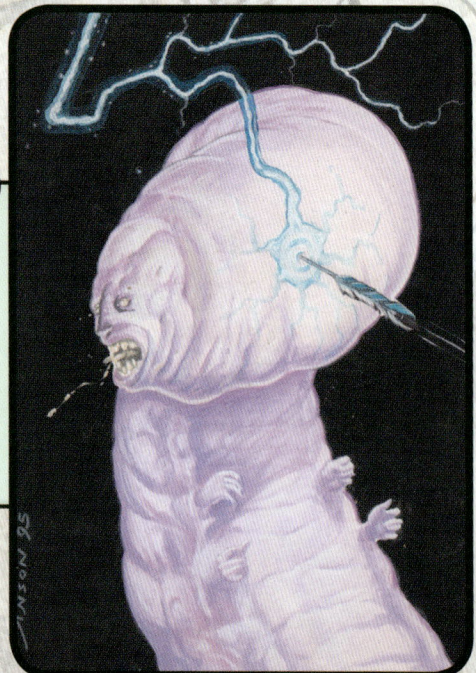

- What kind of creature is this?
- Who made this arrow and what did it cost them?
- Is the lightning natural or magical?
- How will this creature transform over time?

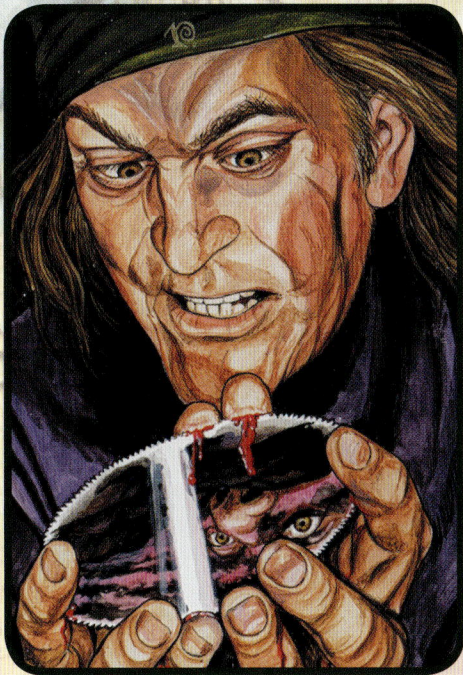

Mirror of Shadows' Price – Rudy Rauben (Roger Raupp)

1410

- What does the man see in this mirror?
- How does blood spilled on this mirror's surface change it's function?
- What does using this mirror cost the man?
- What's the most important relationship in this man's life?

1411

- What special properties does this orb possess?
- What is the significance of the symbol on this man's hat?
- Why is the man in the background transforming?
- What is the man in the foreground's greatest regret?

True Pearl's Bonds – Rudy Rauben (Roger Raupp)

Starhorn – Jeff Miracola

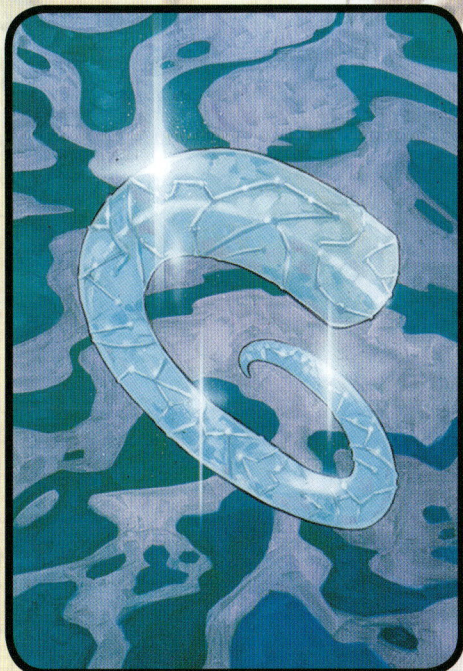

1412

- What can be heard in this glass horn?
- What do the constellations on the surface of the horn reveal?
- What momentous event has this horn changed the course of?
- What happens when this object changes hands?

TRICKERY – REVERSED

Rage and Cunning 1

1501

- Are the dragon's small wings powerful enough for it to fly?
- What skills or magical abilities does the dragon have?
- What is the dragon's goal?
- Does the dragon know any secrets?

Dragon – Ian Miller

Dragon Rebellion – Joe DeVelasco

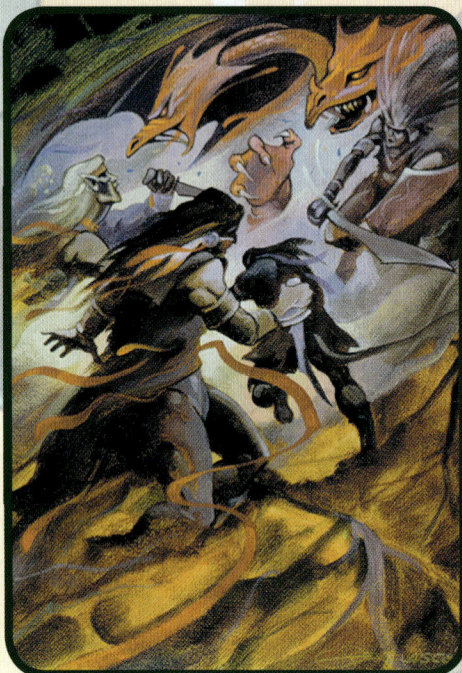

1502

- Why are these people and dragons fighting?
- Where is this conflict taking place?
- Which of these people has a secret motive?
- What special properties do these weapons have?

1503

- Where is this conflict taking place?
- Who killed this dragon?
- Where do the stairs lead to?
- What once existed at the top of the stairs that has since been destroyed?

Seventy-Seven Steps – Dermot Power

The King – Reversed

Venom Fire – Geoff Darrow

1504

- What makes this dragon different from other dragons?
- Who or what does this dragon hold in its claws?
- Where is this dragon going and what will happen when it arrives?
- Who does this dragon most despise?

1505

Fiery Tears – Gary Gianni

- What caused this dragon's fiery tears.
- Who lies slain at the dragon's feet?
- What special properties does the gold in the bags have?
- What lies at the end of the river flowing into the cave's mouth?

Dragon Capture – Al Davison

1506

- Who led the capture and defeat of this dragon?
- What special properties do the dragon's remains have?
- What else is hidden in the cave in the background?
- What long term effect will this action have on these people?

Rage and Cunning 2

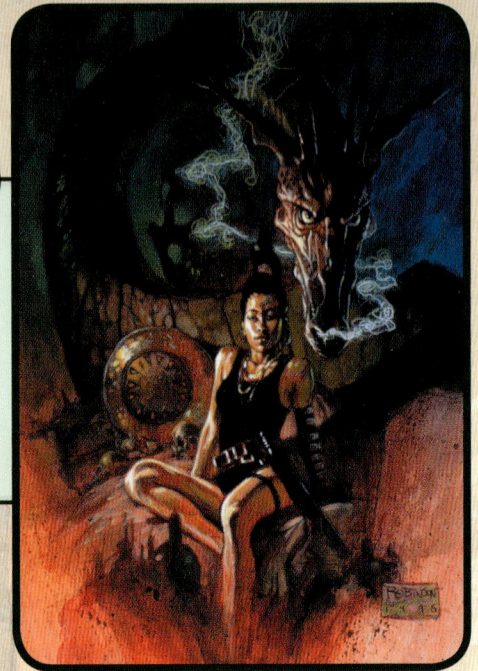

Dragon Maddened – Andrew Robinson

1507

- What is the nature of the bond between this woman and dragon?
- What special properties does the shield have?
- What does the woman most desire?
- What is in the vessels surrounding the woman?

Dragon Clash – Jeff Miracola

1508

- What are the properties of the staff this woman wields?
- What special properties do the swords have?
- What will these dragons do next if they survive?
- What conflict exists between these three people?

Dragon and the Phoenix – Al Davison

1509

- Why are this dragon and phoenix fighting?
- Who will win this battle and at what cost?
- How will the landscape of this battle site be permanently affected?
- Who is observing this battle?

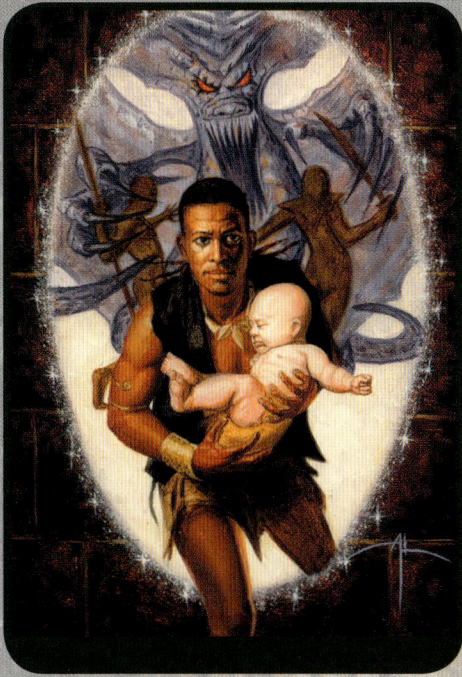

Dragonheart Child – Alan Rabinowitz

1510

- What is the relationship between this man and child?
- Who are the people holding off the dragon?
- Why is the dragon pursuing this man and child?
- Where does the gate this man is traveling through lead?

Deceiver Worm – Jerry Tiritilli

1511

- What is the relationship between these two people?
- Is the man secretly a dragon or is the dragon secretly a man?
- Who will this woman's first child become?
- Why does the woman not sense the potential danger?

Dragon Uprising – Andrew Robinson

1512

- Who are these people fighting these dragons?
- What will the cost of this battle be?
- Where is this battle occurring?
- What is the relationship between these people and do they trust each other?

Strife and Sorrow 1

1601

Sister of the Night – Gary Gianni

- What person or group is this woman's enemy?
- What oath has this woman sworn?
- How do this woman's abilities change at night?
- What is special about this woman's dagger?

Clothing on Scarecrow – Janine Johnston

1602

- Why is this man burning his clothes?
- How long will this fire burn?
- What is this man's greatest loss?
- What will this man do next?

Cutting through the Darkness – Mark Tedin

1603

- What is the nature of the blackness surrounding this woman?
- What or whom is this woman trying to reach?
- Whom did this woman leave behind?
- What do the symbols on the woman's arms and legs represent?

THE GRIFFIN

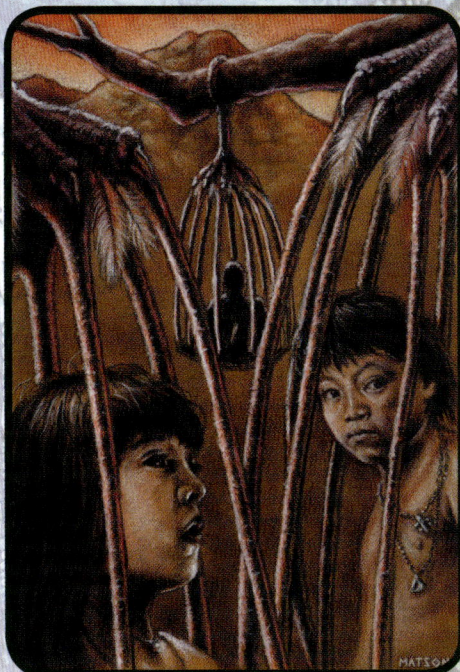

Caged Children – John Matson

1604

- Who put the children in these cages? Why?
- What significance do the boy's necklaces have?
- What are these children's homes like?
- What could be done to rescue these children?

1605

- What is at stake in this battle?
- Where did the ship come from and where will it go next?
- Which person in this battle has a secret goal?
- What will happen when this battle ends?

Sisters of Night – Gary Gianni

Weeping Oracle – Roger Coad

1606

- What terrible knowledge does this person possess?
- What will it cost a person who seeks her out?
- What is significant about the place she can be found?
- What are the properties of her tears?

Strife and Sorrow 2

Prison Cell – Ian Miller

- What does the prisoner at the window see?
- Who are these people, and how are they related, if at all?
- Who is the dog-headed person at the back?
- Who put these people in prison?

Devourer Ogre – Geoff Darrow

1608

- What is the greatest desire of this creature?
- Does the jewelry this creature wears have any special properties?
- Does this creature have a family?
- What kind of creature does the skull on the shoulder weapon come from?

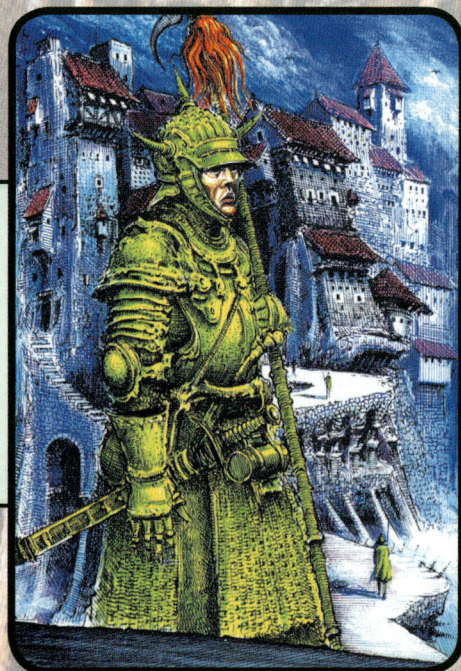

City Guard – Ian Miller

1609

- From what enemy does the soldier protect his community?
- How did he become a soldier?
- What is the most powerful or dangerous foe he has defeated?
- How do his superiors regard him?

The Cockatrice – Reversed

Conqueror's Flame – Rudy Rauben (Roger Raupp)

1610

- Why is this man the only survivor?
- What was at stake in this battle?
- What is burning in the background?
- Why did this man decide to fight?

Dragonbane Sword – Dermot Power

1611

- How does this sword affect its wielder?
- Whose skulls lie at this person's feet?
- How did this person acquire the sword?
- What price will this person pay?

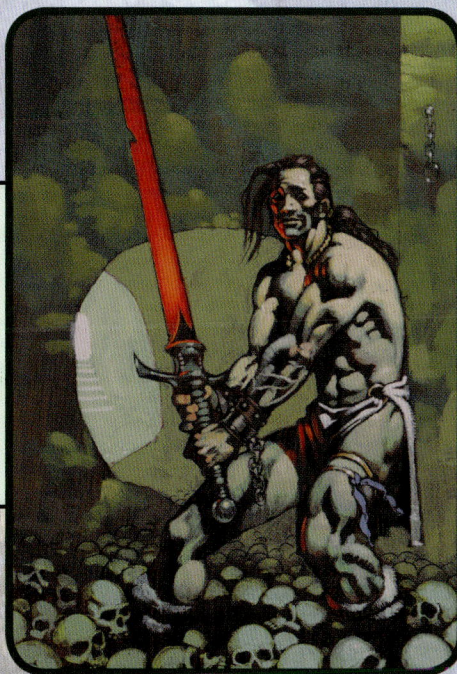

Hanging Man – John Matson

1612

- Why is this man hanging upside down?
- Who is the person watching him?
- What is the surrounding land like?
- How is the family of the hanging man involved in this scene, if at all?

THE PHOENIX – REVERSED

309

Teeth and Stealth 1

Spell Eating – Dermot Power

1701

- What abilities does this creature possess?
- What does this creature eat?
- What is the last thought of a person who encounters this creature?
- What happens when this creature infiltrates a community?

Fallen Angel – Rick Berry

1702

- What does this angel fear?
- What is this angel's greatest accomplishment?
- What debt does this angel owe?
- What is this angel's most prized possession?

Spiny Creature – Ian Miller

1703

- What is the greatest enemy of this creature?
- How many creatures are there like this?
- What event will attract or repel this creature?
- What power does this creature possess?

Infernal Machine – Ian Miller

1704

- What does this machinery do?
- Who built it?
- What powers the machinery?
- How does this machinery affect the community around it?

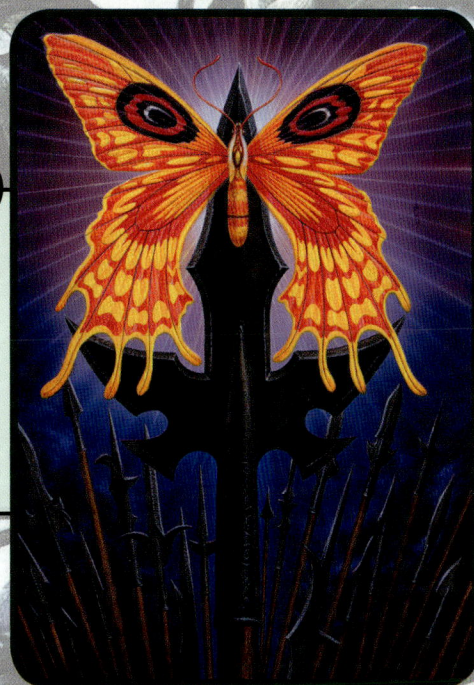

Battleflies – Gerry Grace

1705

- What is the relationship between this insect and the weapons?
- When was this creature last seen?
- How long does this creature survive?
- What effect does this creature have on people?

Needledemon – Dermot Power

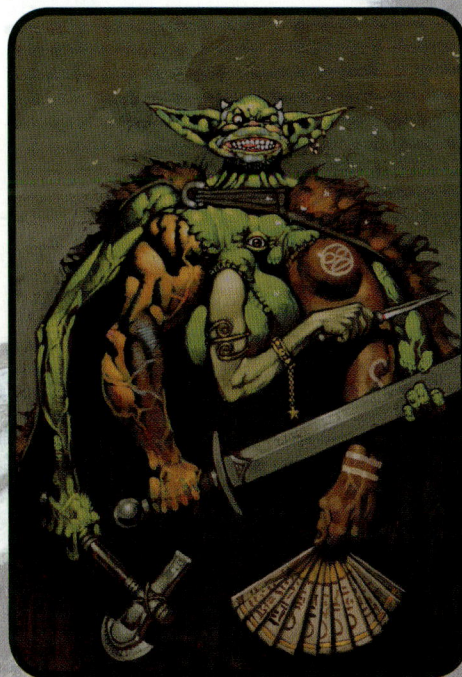

1706

- What power does this demon possess?
- What will someone pay this demon for their services?
- Where did these arms come from?
- What does this demon most desire?

TEETH AND STEALTH 2

Wraith – Rick Berry

1707

- Was this creature once human or has it always had this form?
- What effect does this creature have on those who encounter it?
- What or whom does this creature most seek?
- When will this creature find release?

Troll – Ian Miller

1708

- How many people have fallen to this troll?
- What properties do the black orbs have?
- What is the creature at the troll's feet?
- What building is this troll entering and who built it?

Pyramid Lizards – Ian Miller

1709

- What effect does this pyramid have on those who encounter it?
- What is the creature in the background?
- What properties do the lizards in this pyramid have?
- Who will mourn this man's passing?

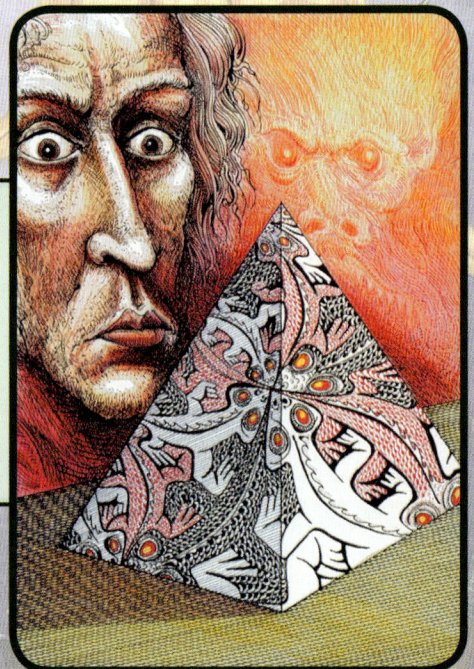

THE SOLDIER

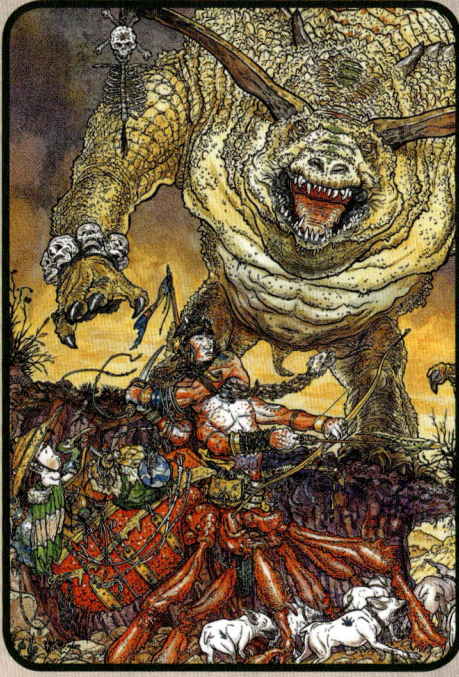

Crab Warrior – Geoff Darrow

1710

- Who is this crab warrior?
- Who controls the giant creature?
- Whose skulls are the skulls on the giant creature?
- What special properties do the pigs have?

Sneaky Adventurer – Ian Miller

1711

- What is the relation between the man and the person or creature beside him?
- What is the serpent or lizard around the man's neck?
- What significance do the pillars have?
- Who is the shadowy figure coming down the stairs in the background?

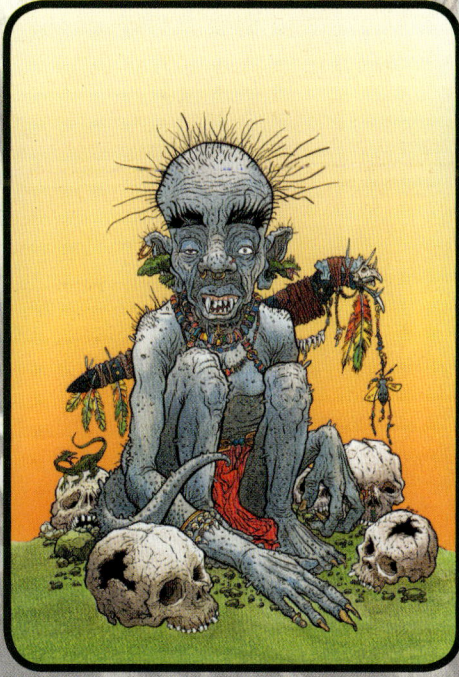

Whisper Lizards – Geoff Darrow

1712

- What is in this creature's ears?
- Whose skulls lie at this creature's feet?
- What relationship exists between this creature and the lizards?
- Where has this creature been and where is it going?

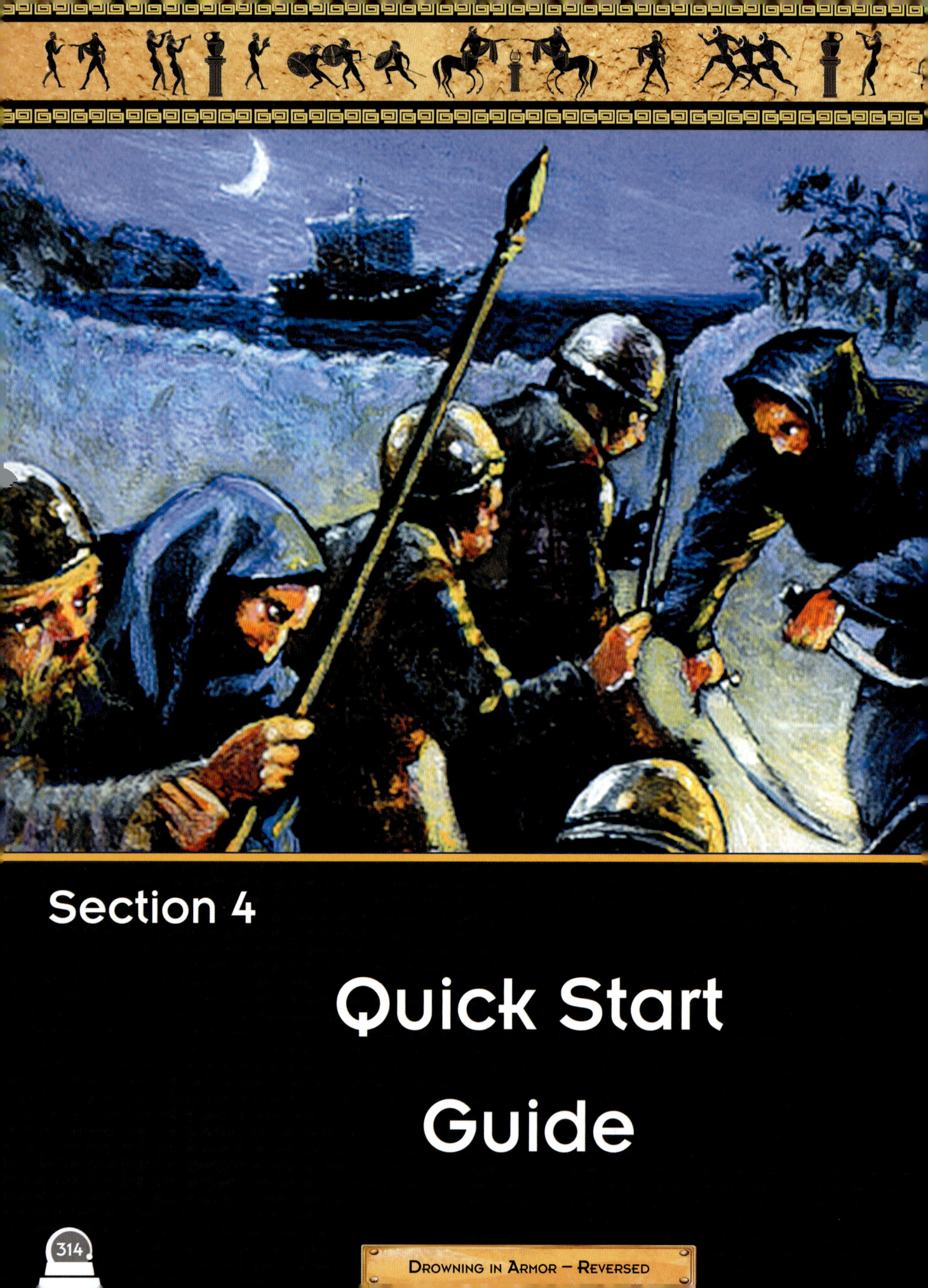

Section 4

Quick Start Guide

DROWNING IN ARMOR – REVERSED

1605. Sisters of Night — Gary Gianni

THE SATYR

910. *Order of the Silver Nail – Jerry Tiritilli*

316

THE USURPER – REVERSED

Introduction

Whether you can't wait to get started or you want to host a convention game, this section will help you get playing quickly. It is intended to be a quick summary of the most important game information, but gamemasters will still want to read through *Section 1: Playing Guide* and *Section 2: Fortune Guide* to help the players along. Gamemasters will also need a copy of **Book 2: Gamemasters** to understand how to run the EVERWAY system.

For players, this section provides twelve ready-to-run heroes, a brief summary of hero creation, and some handy charts to help them remember key information about the game. For gamemasters, the ready-to-run heroes can also serve as background characters.

To get started as quickly as possible, players can select one of the ready-to-run heroes and read the *Get Playing Quickly* section in *Chapter 8: Quick Heroes* and refer to *Chapter 9: References*. Gamemasters will need more time to prepare a quest or get familiar with one of the starting quests in **Book 2: Gamemasters**.

Additional Section Credits

Get Playing Quickly & Creating Heroes: Jesse McGatha

Ready-to-Run Heroes: Kathy Ice (Chance), Aron Tarbuck (Amber, Clarity, Shadow), Jonathan Tweet (Cleft, Fireson, Praise, Serenity, Whisper Walker), and Jenny Scott Tynes (Detritus, Opal, Puma)

Special Thanks: Kat Miller for her advice on organizing EVERWAY games and examples of her charts for convention play

SILVER ANNIVERSARY EDITION NOTES

This edition assembles all the ready-to-run heroes and reference sheets in this section to support convention play and getting started quickly.

H103. Clarity – Rick Berry.

SPRING

Chapter 8: Quick Heroes

This chapter provides a brief overview of the EVERWAY game system, action resolution, and hero creation, followed by twelve ready-to-run heroes that let you jump right into playing. Browse through the next few pages and then create a hero or pick a ready-to-run hero that appeals to you.

GET PLAYING QUICKLY

The information below quickly introduces the setting of EVERWAY, the key components of heroes, and the Three Laws of Action.

Understanding EVERWAY

EVERWAY is a mythic fantasy game. It helps you tell stories about the sort of larger-than-life people you've heard about in myths and fairy tales from all over the world. Heroes are much more powerful than the average human background character.

EVERWAY takes place in a multiverse setting, with many different worlds, called spheres, connected by gates that only spherewalkers like the heroes can traverse. In the center of this sprawling network of thousands of spheres is the realm of Roundwander on the sphere of Fourcorner. While most spheres have only two gates, Roundwander has seventy-one—the most of any realm among the spheres.

At this crossroads of the spheres, Everway is the capital city of Roundwander. Everway is an ancient cosmopolitan melting pot of peoples, cultures, and traditions. From this seat of power, influential families have governed the six provinces of the realm for thousands of years. People from other realms on Fourcorner, called Strangers, and people from other spheres, called Outsiders, dwell across the river from Everway in the makeshift town of Strangerside or in one of the provincial towns or cities.

If you are creating your own hero, you may choose to have your hero come from Roundwander or any other realm or sphere you can imagine.

Understanding Heroes

Heroes have a few important attributes:

- **Name:** Names in EVERWAY are generally words from the Tongue (the universal language) that mean something specific. For example, Brick, Shooting Star, Dismay, or Harmony are all reasonable names in an EVERWAY game.
- **Motive:** Why the hero travels the spheres. See *Chapter 9: References*.
- **Virtue:** A card from the Fortune Deck representing your hero's special strength, gift, or luck.
- **Fault:** A card from the Fortune Deck representing your hero's special weakness or vice.
- **Fate:** A card from the Fortune Deck representing your hero's destiny.
- **Elements:** Every hero has points allocated among four Elements. Each additional point in an Element roughly doubles the hero's capability in that Element. Each Element has a Specialty, an area where that hero is particularly gifted, and as such is considered to have 1 point more in that Element for actions related to their Specialty. A typical human background character has a 3 in each Element without any Specialties. The four Elements are:

  Air: Thought, focused energy, and spoken wisdom.

  Fire: Action, forceful energy, and active power.

  Earth: Might, resistant integrity, and passive power.

  Water: Feelings, receptive integrity, and silent wisdom.

- **Powers:** A hero has one or more Powers, special or supernatural abilities that help make a hero extraordinary. Each Power is linked to an Element based on its effect.
- **Magic:** Most heroes do not wield Magic. Those who do are called mages (among other names). Magic allows a hero to perform a much broader variety of supernatural manipulations than Powers can typically do.

Understanding Actions

Generally, as in other roleplaying games, the gamemaster in EVERWAY describes the circumstances the heroes find themselves in, plays the background characters, and judges the outcomes of players' actions. The players describe what their heroes do in response to the circumstances the gamemaster sets, how they interact with other heroes and the background characters, and what actions they want to take.

To decide what happens in response to the player's actions, the gamemaster uses the Three Laws of Action to determine what the outcome in each case should be, and then blends the results together to narrate the result.

- **Law of Karma:** What would most logically happen, given the circumstances, the heroes' abilities, the background character's abilities, and any location specifics.

- **Law of Drama:** What would make the best, most fun, most exciting story.

- **Law of Fortune:** What the draw of a card from the Fortune Deck suggests should happen. This can provide an unexpected new direction in the unfolding play!

CREATING HEROES

If you have the time to create a hero, this section provides a quick overview of the hero creation process. Creating heroes is a memorable part of EVERWAY, where you get to take a few images to inspire an entire origin story for your hero, in the tradition of mythic storytellers throughout time.

To begin, make sure you have a pencil and download and print a copy of the blank hero sheet from **EVERWAY.COM**. You will use this hero sheet to record your hero. Make sure you've read through the previous section, *Get Playing Quickly*, because this section builds on those concepts.

Hero creation follows six distinct stages. It is not necessary to do them in any particular order. You may revisit previously completed stages to make revisions as you understand your hero better. The most common sequence is provided below.

Vision Stage

1 The gamemaster should describe the basic premise of your game before you begin. They might ask for your input on the type of game.

Flip through *Section 3: Vision Guide* and find three to five interesting images to build your hero around. These images may represent anything about your hero that you wish. They could depict your hero, an important event or person in your hero's life, a vision your hero once had, or an item or place your hero is seeking. Think about how best to tell your hero's story in a few minutes, using these visions to illustrate important aspects of your hero.

Heroes in EVERWAY are generally humans of any size, color, gender, or shape. Heroes are mythic in proportion—larger than life and often summoned to greatness.

While you're creating your hero, you can imagine the realm they are from as well: what kind of place it was, what the people were like, and any special connections your hero has with their realm. Nearly any kind of place is possible, but check

with your gamemaster if it will be hard to tell your story along with the stories of the other heroes.

Keep in mind these three rules:

1. **The mind is sacred.** You cannot control others' minds.

2. **Interact.** Lean toward a hero who will interact more. You'll have more fun.

3. **Everything changes.** Develop a hero who has room to grow and change.

At this point you should introduce your hero to the other players. They will ask you various questions about your hero to understand your vision better and to help you get a clearer idea of who your hero is. This will help your group get closer to each other as you develop your heroes. Look for shared connections. Don't worry about going too deep, as you'll get to the Questions Stage later.

Identity Stage

2 Next you will fill in some personal details about your hero.

Name: Select a name for your hero. Hero names are usually common words in the Tongue.

Motive: Choose your hero's basic motive for traveling among the spheres. See the Motives summary in *Chapter 9: References* for options.

Virtue, Fault, and Fate: Pick one card from the Fortune Deck (see the Fortune Deck summary in *Chapter 9: References*) to represent a special gift or talent (Virtue), another for a special vice or flaw (Fault), and a third for the destiny of your hero (Fate). A Virtue typically uses a positive meaning of the card, a Fault uses a negative meaning, and the Fate uses both, representing the decision point that your hero's life is moving toward.

Powers Stage

3 You can invent magical, psychic, or unusual Powers for your hero. Any ability or possession a normal human does not have must be paid for with elemental points. You will also use these points for Elements and possibly Magic later.

Powers cost 1 point for each of the following criteria, subject to approval of your gamemaster. Your gamemaster may require 1 additional point if the Power is particularly extreme.

- **Frequent:** It is often useful in play.

- **Major:** It has a big effect on play.

- **Versatile:** It is useful in multiple ways.

Each hero may have one free 0-point Power (these meet none of the criteria above). Every Power thereafter costs at least 1 point.

Elements Stage

4 Assign unused points to the four Elements of your hero, although you may want to save some points for Magic. Your gamemaster uses these Elements to determine what your hero is capable of. Each point added to an Element roughly doubles the ability of your hero in that Element. You have 20 points to spend on Elements, Powers, and Magic combined. You must place at least 3 points and no more than 6 in each Element. A typical human has 3 points in each Element.

Select a Specialty for each Element. A Specialty is a specific skill or talent at which your hero effectively has an Element score 1 higher than your base Element.

> Your hero might also have Cross-Specialties. See p. 134 for more information.

Magic Stage

5 Magic is the ability to wield supernatural energies in order to cast spells. Most heroes do not know Magic. Your hero may have no more than 5 in Magic (or 6 if you specialize in that Magic tradition), because you must declare which Element your Magic is linked to, and your Magic score cannot be higher than its linked Element score (plus specialization).

Magic is very flexible. It can be put to many different uses in a dynamic way. You may use one of the types of Magic described in *Chapter 4: Powers & Magic*, or you may create your own. Generally speaking, whatever your hero's Magic score, their ability to create supernatural effects should be roughly equivalent to what a hero might achieve with two Elements of the same score.

You must agree with your gamemaster on the limits of what your Magic can accomplish. Your gamemaster is the arbiter of these limits in play.

Questions Stage

6 During this stage, the goal is to fully explore and develop your hero. The other players take turns asking you questions about your hero's story to help you fill in details about your hero. It is recommended to start with broad questions, then narrow the focus as you go. Other players may ask you about what additional aspects of your vision images mean. To develop shared connections, your gamemaster might ask how your hero met or is related to another player's hero. When answering all these questions, you get to decide what's right for your hero. Don't neglect questioning other players about their heroes as well. You're all trying to make the game better together.

> If you don't have time to create your own hero, the following pages contain 12 ready-to-run heroes for your use.

EVERWAY
SILVER ANNIVERSARY EDITION

NAME	MOTIVE
AMBER	**AUTHORITY**

VIRTUE
Summer
(energy)

FAULT
The Fool—
Reversed
(lack of connection)

FATE
Knowledge
(truth vs. falsehood)

POWERS 3

MAGIC 0

AIR
FOCUSED
ENERGY
FORCEFUL
WISDOM
SPOKEN
SILENT
FIRE
THOUGHT
3
etiquette
5
unarmed combat
ACTION
FEELING
MIGHT
ACTIVE
3
stealth
WATER
RECEPTIVE
PASSIVE
POWER
6
resisting unconsciousness
RESISTANT
INTEGRITY
EARTH

©2020 The Everway Company

THE SMITH – REVERSED

H101. Amber – Rick Berry   407. Cat Folk Mercenaries – Martin McKenna

VISION

Amber's people are all weretigers, which they keep secret from others. They consider themselves separate from humanity. Amber has been exiled from her village for helping humans. She now thinks she is a human with tiger powers. She feels compelled to use her powers to help people.

Weretiger: Amber can turn into a tiger or into a two-legged half tiger at will. In this tiger-woman form, she heals almost instantly from any non-magical and natural weapons, except for weapons made of or coated with gold. Her clothes change with her but things she's carrying (even in her pockets) don't.

POWERS & MAGIC

Weretiger (Water): See description above. Cost: 2 (frequent and major)

Silence of the Hunter (Water): When stalking her enemies, Amber becomes almost indetectable. Only those with special senses or strong Water (5+) can sense her. Cost: 1 (major)

Resistance to Death Magics (Earth): Magical abilities that specifically kill instantly only incapacitate Amber, but other magics harm her normally (and can kill her). Cost: 0 (free)

POSSESSIONS

- robe, tunic, sash, pants, and sandals (all of which change with Amber)
- twin short swords, in sheathes on her back.
- coins, gemstones, pelts, rare spices, incense, and other gifts.
- silver mirror

THE UNICORN – REVERSED

PLAYING AMBER

Background

In the remote mountain village in which Amber grew up, all the people are weretigers. They carefully conceal this fact from their neighbors, following strict rules of conduct to keep their secret hidden. They consider themselves distinctly separate from, if not superior to, humanity. Except for Amber, that is.

When war between clashing empires brought pillaging soldiers to the mountains, other villages suffered greatly. Amber wanted to help them, but the elders of her village said that using their tiger powers to help humans would endanger their secrecy. Amber chose to help the humans anyway, and for that act she has been exiled from her village and cut off from her family.

Wandering first on her own world and then on others, Amber has come to regard herself as a human with tiger powers rather than as a different creature altogether (though sometimes she fears she's fooling herself). Regardless, she feels compelled to use her powers to right wrongs, correct injustice, and protect the innocent. She sees her abilities as a gift from heaven, and she feels obliged to put that gift to its best use.

Questions for Development

- Having grown up in a remote village, Amber may have some strange ideas about what's right and wrong. What crimes does she consider most horrible? Are there actions that most people think are criminal that she tolerates?

- How does she prefer to deal with injustice? Through force? By revealing deceit? By helping the victims fight for themselves?

- How does she present herself to people she's met?

- Has she ever been unable to right a wrong? If so, what happened?

H101. Amber – Rick Berry

LAW

PLAYING CHANCE

Background

Born in a small village, Chance was the product of a chance encounter (if you will forgive the expression) between a local woman and a renowned warrior from another land. Chance's bastardy set him apart from the other villagers, and his strength and fighting skills, inherited from his father, only served to widen the rift. He left home at an early age and made a living for several years as a mercenary.

Despite his hard life, Chance has a poet's soul (note his strong Water score). The first time he went berserk in battle, he frightened himself quite badly. Eventually, all the fighting became too much for him, and he quit his mercenary company. Now he walks the spheres searching for a way to reconcile the two very different halves of his nature (the Warrior and the Poet). He also awaits word of his father, hoping that by meeting the man who sired him he will come to know himself a little better.

Questions for Development

- How does Chance feel about his father? How does he imagine their meeting will turn out?

- What's the worst thing that Chance has ever done, the thing that troubles his poet's soul the most?

- What virtue or quality does Chance most value (in others as well as in himself)?

- In Chance's past, who was his best friend ever?

H102. Chance – Rick Berry

EVERWAY
SILVER ANNIVERSARY EDITION

NAME	MOTIVE
CHANCE	**ADVERSITY**

VIRTUE
The Peasant
(simple strength)

FAULT
The Griffin—
Reversed
(cowardice)

FATE
War
(great effort vs. effort misspent)

POWERS 1

MAGIC 0

AIR
WISDOM
FOCUSED
ENERGY
SPOKEN
FORCEFUL
SILENT
THOUGHT
FIRE
WATER
FEELING
ACTION
ACTIVE
MIGHT
PASSIVE
RECEPTIVE
POWER
RESISTANT
INTEGRITY
EARTH

3 military tactics

6 reacting to danger

6 sensing motives

4 endurance in combat

©2020 The Everway Company

THE GRIFFIN – REVERSED

H102. Chance – Rick Berry   *902. Battlefield Soldier – Ian Miller*

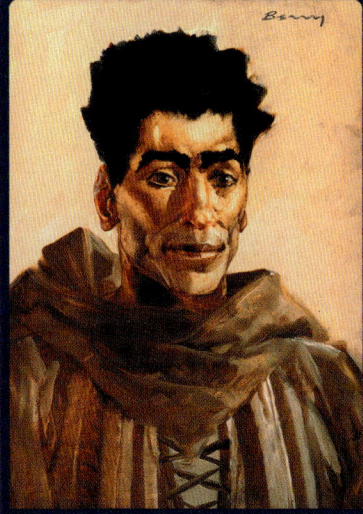

VISION

Chance is the child of a local woman and a renowned warrior from another land. He has great strength and fighting skills, which led him to join a mercenary company. The first time he went berserk in battle he frightened himself, as he has a poet's soul. He now seeks to find a balance within himself.

In combat, particularly when threatened by overwhelming odds or an unexpected foe, Chance sometimes goes berserk. His strength and endurance increase, but he becomes completely lost to reason. He becomes unpredictable, striking out at friend and foe alike.

POWERS & MAGIC

Berserk (Fire): See information above. Once a battle Chance goes berserk in is over, he regains control only with difficulty. Going berserk leaves him exhausted. Cost: 1 (frequent)

Inured to Pain (Earth): While at least as vulnerable to emotional pain as others, Chance endures physical pain easily. Cost: 0 (free)

POSSESSIONS

- steel scimitar and dagger
- spare clothes and traveling kit
- gold medallion, given to his mother by his father
- a few coins from a realm he's visited recently

EVERWAY
SILVER ANNIVERSARY EDITION

NAME	MOTIVE
CLARITY	WANDERLUST

VIRTUE
Inspiration
(creativity)

FAULT
The Defender—
Reversed
(peril)

FATE
The Smith
(productivity vs. evil effort)

POWERS
2

MAGIC
0

AIR
WISDOM
ENERGY
FOCUSED
FORCEFUL
SPOKEN
SILENT
FIRE
THOUGHT
FEELING
ACTION
WATER
POWER
ACTIVE
MIGHT
PASSIVE
RECEPTIVE
RESISTANT
EARTH
INTEGRITY

6
poetry

4
swordfighting

5
sensing others' presence

3
resisting persuasion

©2020 The Everway Company

THE PRIESTESS – REVERSED

H103. Clarity – Rick Berry

1402. Harp of the Hidden City – Janine Johnston

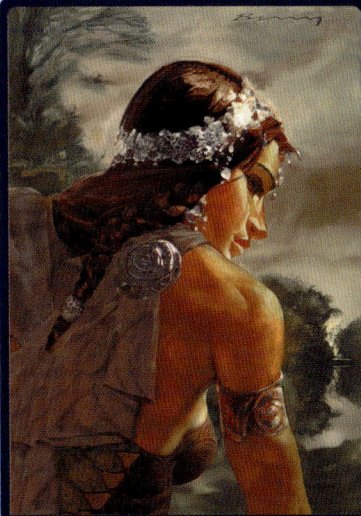

VISION

Grace, the bard who trained Clarity, told her that she was once a raven who had asked the goddess Brighid to give her the gift of song. Brighid turned Clarity into a little girl and instructed Grace to teach her to be a bard. Now she travels the spheres to learn new poems and songs and share them with others.

Clarity can recall and recite perfectly every song and story that she has ever heard or seen, and she remembers how to use every musical instrument she has ever played. She also quickly learns and retains new things that she learns from the bardic traditions.

POWERS & MAGIC

Ravenform (Water): Clarity can take on the shape of a large raven at will. Her clothes change with her, but nothing that she's carrying (even in her pockets) does. Cost 2: (frequent and major)

Perfect Memory of the Bard (Air): Clarity can remember everything that she was trained to perform or learn as a bard, including new material. Cost: 0 (free)

POSSESSIONS

- cloak, dress, high boots
- harp
- heavy knife (good for chopping)
- silver bracelets, armlets, earrings, and headband
- traveling kit in a leather pack
- gems, coins, spices, and other trade goods

SOWING STONES – REVERSED

PLAYING CLARITY

Background

Clarity remembers nothing of the time before she was traveling with Grace, the bard from whom she learned her skills. Grace told her that she was once a raven, and as a raven, Clarity had asked the goddess Brighid to give her the gift of song. Brighid, according to Grace's story, turned Clarity into a little girl and instructed Grace to teach her how to be a bard. Clarity traveled and studied with Grace for years; Grace was the closest thing to a mother Clarity ever knew.

One day, when Clarity had grown to be a young woman, she and Grace were walking through a forest. They walked between a hawthorn and an ash that had grown together, and Clarity found herself suddenly at the mouth of a cave in another world, a fearful wasteland. She went into the cave and reappeared in the forest, where Grace was waiting for her. Grace explained to Clarity that she had the power of spherewalking, a wonderful gift she must put to good use. Grace told her to travel among the worlds, learning songs and poems and sharing them with others, so that all the people of all the worlds could learn something of each other. Grace explained that as she lacked the power of spherewalking she couldn't accompany Clarity. With a fond farewell, Clarity set off alone.

Questions for Development

- How long has Clarity been traveling since she left Grace?
- What sorts of strange, frightening, and wonderful things has Clarity seen, first traveling with Grace, and now traveling on her own?
- For what purposes does she take a raven's form? For pleasure? For scouting ahead?
- Now that she's no longer with Grace, are there things Clarity is free to do that she wasn't free to do before?

H103. Clarity – Rick Berry

THE COCKATRICE

PLAYING DETRITUS

Background

Detritus was the youngest of a large royal clan. Because he was nowhere near the top of the line of succession, Detritus never aspired to leadership, preferring instead to occupy himself with scholarly pursuits. Detritus's fascination with the natural and cultural worlds blossomed early; he was often discovered by his nursemaid far from home, dissecting large insects, making sketches of plants, or digging up broken pots and tools. (It was his interest in old, broken things that earned him his name.) From a young age, Detritus was independent and never minded being on his own, though as he's grown older, he's found he craves companionship more and more.

Studying with the city's most learned master, who was also his grandfather, Detritus eagerly absorbed everything that could be taught. He developed a keen interest in dead civilizations that has never faded. At the age of nineteen, after his coming-of-age ritual, Detritus went wandering alone for five years, as is customary among his people.

When Detritus returned to his city, he found things had changed: his mother had died, and his father had bestowed leadership on his eldest living child. Detritus's eldest brother, the new leader, was interested in overcoming neighboring city-states and devoted great effort to building an army of skilled warriors. Unwilling to assist his brother in conquest, Detritus opted to extend his scholarly journeys indefinitely, exploring the spheres for the rest of his life, compiling what he hopes will be a comprehensive book about past civilizations.

He is fifty-seven years old.

Questions for Development

- What is Detritus's attitude toward romance? What sort of romantic life has he led?
- What were his relationships with his siblings like when he lived in his home city? What are they like now?
- What is Detritus's biggest fear?
- When was the last time Detritus was home? What happened there?

H104. Detritus – Rick Berry

EVERWAY
SILVER ANNIVERSARY EDITION

NAME	MOTIVE
DETRITUS	KNOWLEDGE

VIRTUE
Winter
(maturity)

FAULT
Striking the Dragon's Tail
(underestimating the challenge)

FATE
Spring
(new growth vs. stagnation)

POWERS
3

MAGIC
0

AIR
FOCUSED
SPOKEN
SILENT
WISDOM
FORCEFUL
ENERGY
FIRE
ACTIVE
THOUGHT
ACTION
FEELING
MIGHT
POWER
PASSIVE
WATER
RECEPTIVE
INTEGRITY
RESISTANT
EARTH

6 ancient lore

3 jumping

5 sensing death

3 walking long distances

©2020 The Everway Company

THE EAGLE – REVERSED

H104. Detritus – Rick Berry   1404. True Pearl – Rob Alexander

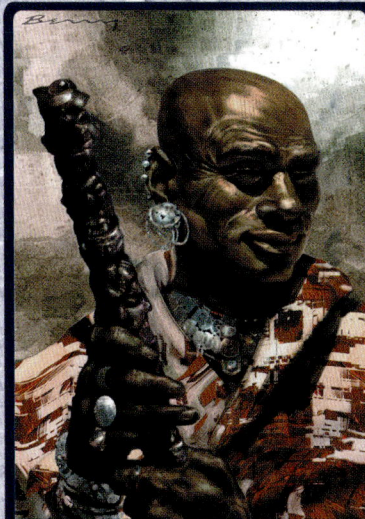

VISION

Detritus is the youngest son of a large royal clan. Detritus studied with the city's most learned master, and as an adult he has traveled the spheres compiling knowldege about ancient and dead civilizations. He carries a large pouch over his shoulders with his collected writings on the subject.

In his decades of travel (he is now fifty-seven), Detritus has collected many things, including many small items that he gives away to start conversations. One of the most intriguing objects he has found is a crystal sphere that can, at his mental command, make any manner of sound.

POWERS & MAGIC

Rune of Lurking (Water): While holding an ancient stone with a mystic rune, he can become invisible as long as he stays silent and still. Cost: 1 (frq.)

Ancient Gesture of Clarity (Air): With a complicated gesture, Detritus can dispel magical illusions. Cost: 1 (maj.)

Sphere of Sound (Air): Detritus can use this sphere within a hundred yards to make any sound, very quiet or loud. Cost: 1 (frq.)

Illuminating Clap (Fire): With a clap, Detritus can illuminate the area around him with a glow that follows him. It fades over an hour. Cost: 0 (free)

POSSESSIONS

- small pouches and strings of spices, herbs, gems, and coins from his extensive travels
- foreign jewelry, which he wears proudly, from many sources
- large pouch of bound papers and a writing brush
- small hand drum

EVERWAY
SILVER ANNIVERSARY EDITION

NAME
FIRESON

MOTIVE
ADVERSITY

VIRTUE
The Lion
(the body prevails)

FAULT
Death—
Reversed
(stasis)

FATE
The Soldier
(duty vs. blind obedience)

POWERS 3

MAGIC 0

AIR
WISDOM
FOCUSED
ENERGY
SPOKEN
FORCEFUL
SILENT
FIRE
WATER
THOUGHT
ACTION
ACTIVE
FEELING
POWER
RECEPTIVE
MIGHT
PASSIVE
INTEGRITY
RESISTANT
EARTH

3 speaking to crowds

6 fire magic

5 sensing divine energies

3 maintaining vigils

©2020 The Everway Company

THE FISH – REVERSED

H105. Fireson – Rick Berry   *101. Pyramid Priest – Rudy Rauben*

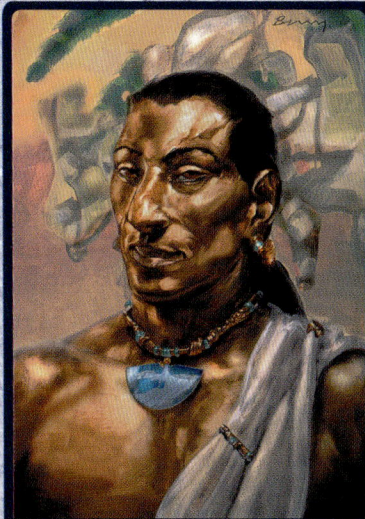

VISION

Fireson was once a priest of a fiery deity. He offended his deity, however, and was banished from his homeland. Now Fireson wanders the spheres, hoping to discover a way to regain his deity's favor. He is confident and energetic, but he can be stubborn and judgmental of those whose ways are not like his.

Fireson can channel divine energies and the energies of worshippers through powerful priestly rites. These rituals can bind oaths, improve an army's fortune, bless a land's harvest, and accomplish other mighty ends. These powerful rituals require a large number of worshippers, however.

POWERS & MAGIC

Priestly Rites (Water): Fireson can channel divine energy through priestly rites (see above). Less powerful rites, such as those to sanctify marriages or ease the dead's passage from the world of the living, require less energy and few, if any, worshippers. Cost: 2 (major and versatile)

Sweat Fire (Fire): Fireson can release flames from his skin. He can't throw the fire, and it is only as hot as a campfire, but it is still useful to deter attackers, burn enemies, start fires, provide light, and so on. Cost: 1 (major)

Friend to Fire (Fire): He can feel heat, but it doesn't burn him. Cost: 0 (free)

POSSESSIONS

- short sword
- traveling clothes and kit
- a few gems and spices to trade

THE DRAGON – REVERSED

Playing Fireson

Background

Fireson was once a priest of a fiery deity. He offended his deity, however, and was banished from his homeland. Now Fireson wanders the spheres, hoping to discover a way to regain his deity's favor and gain the right to return to his land and take the role of priest once more. He is confident and energetic (note his strong Fire score and his Virtue, The Lion), but he can be stubborn and judgmental of those whose ways are not like his (his fault is Death—Reversed). Luckily, Fireson is used to being around people of lower status and ability, and he honestly tries to be tolerant.

Questions for Development

- What deity does Fireson follow? It could be just "the Sun," but it could also be Horus, Helios, Hephaestus, and so on.
- What did Fireson do to earn the displeasure of his deity?
- What possessions does he keep as a memento of his life as priest?
- How honest is he about his past and about his fallen state?

H105. Fireson – Rick Berry

Playing Opal

Background

Opal's mother, a water priestess, was held captive by an evil wizard, a spirit in possession of a man's body. While pregnant with Opal, her mother performed a spell ensuring that her unborn child would seek revenge and murder the wizard. She died in childbirth.

The wizard held Opal captive, too, so she spent her life isolated from other people, her nursemaid her only trusted friend. It was the nurse who smuggled to Opal the bird claw gloves and opal pendant that had belonged to her mother.

As a young woman, Opal avenged her mother's death by ripping off the wizard's head with the clawed gloves. The wizard's spirit, having no body to inhabit, was rendered powerless. Opal hid the head in a large metal box and ran away as far as she could. She has since forgotten where she hid the box. Should the wizard reunite his head with his body, he would seek revenge on Opal.

Opal, free from the wizard and away from the only home she's ever known, is now wandering, looking for... for something, but she doesn't really know what.

Questions for Development

- When Opal killed the wizard, did she take any mysterious items from him? (Note: any such item can't be very powerful or it would count as one of Opal's Powers.)
- What sort of magic did the wizard use? Has it had any permanent effects on Opal?
- What is Opal's most treasured memory?
- What lessons did Opal's nursemaid teach her about life and about the world? Did the nurse have any favorite sayings or adages that Opal now repeats?

H106. Opal – Rick Berry

EVERWAY
SILVER ANNIVERSARY EDITION

NAME	MOTIVE
OPAL	**ADVERSITY**

VIRTUE — The Phoenix *(rebirth)*

FAULT — The Hermit—Reversed *(isolation)*

FATE — The Cockatrice *(corruption vs. recovery)*

POWERS: **2**

MAGIC: **0**

AIR — FOCUSED — ENERGY

WISDOM — SPOKEN — FORCEFUL

SILENT — THOUGHT — FIRE

WATER — FEELING — ACTION — ACTIVE

4 speaking well

5 climbing

6 sensing magic

3 enduring pain

MIGHT — PASSIVE — POWER

RECEPTIVE — RESISTANT — EARTH

INTEGRITY

©2020 The Everway Company

THE SMITH

H106. Opal – Rick Berry   1303. Sorcerer – Martin McKenna

VISION

Opal's mother, a water priestess, died in childbirth. She was held captive by an evil wizard, and Opal was held captive also. Her nurse-maid secretly gave Opal her mother's opal pendant and bird claw gloves, which she used as a young woman to rip off the wizard's head before running away.

The wizard was possessed by an evil spirit. After ripping his head off, she put his head in a metal box and hid it, but she no longer remembers where. Should the wizard reunite his head and body, he would seek revenge on Opal.

POWERS & MAGIC

Persuasion (Air): Opal is insightful and perceptive about human behavior. Because of her strong intuition about people, she is very effective at manipulating them. She can seduce nearly anyone and is extremely persuasive. Note: you may not use this power to manipulate other heroes. Cost: 2 (major and versatile)

Clench (Earth): When wearing her metal gloves, Opal can grasp with great strength and endurance. She could hang all night by one hand if she had to. Cost: 0 (free)

POSSESSIONS

- long metal gloves with birdlike talons. useful for fighting and climbing
- short knife (hidden in her boot) and a short sword
- opal pendant
- pouch with basic traveling necessities

THE UNICORN

EVERWAY
SILVER ANNIVERSARY EDITION

NAME	MOTIVE
SHADOW	**MYSTERY**

VIRTUE
The Dragon
(cunning)

FAULT
Autumn—Reversed
(want)

FATE
War
(great effort vs. effort misspent)

POWERS 2

MAGIC 0

AIR
FOCUSED
FORCEFUL
FIRE
ACTIVE
POWER
PASSIVE
EARTH
RESISTANT
INTEGRITY
RECEPTIVE
WATER
SILENT
WISDOM
SPOKEN
ENERGY
THOUGHT
ACTION
FEELING
MIGHT

3 disguise

5 swordfighting

6 anticipating another's actions

4 resisting magic

©2020 The Everway Company

THE CREATOR – REVERSED

H107. Shadow – Rick Berry   1211. Confrontation – Scott Kirschner

VISION

Shadow was trained and retained as a spy by a noble house. As his skills increased, his lord and lady sent him on more serious and bloodier missions. Finally, his lady asked him to perform a deed that crossed the bounds of propriety. He agreed in exchange for being released from his service.

People often try to get Shadow to help them defeat their enemies for causes they claim to be just, but Shadow holds most such people in contempt. When his heart moves him, he takes up a cause as if his own life depends on it. He has various gear for climbing, picking locks, foiling traps, and so on.

POWERS & MAGIC

Shadow Slip (Water): When wearing his "shadow gear" (a black outfit), he blends into shadows and becomes invisible. If he leaves the shadows, he becomes visible again. Maintaining his shadow slip is effortless and he can maintain it indefinitely, even asleep. Cost: 2 (frequent and major)

Weaponmaster (Fire): Shadow can use any sort of mundane, handheld weapon without training (though not necessarily siege engines, weapons that work by magic, and so on). Cost: 0 (free)

POSSESSIONS

- miscellaneous gear (see above)
- shadow gear (see "Powers")
- a narrow dagger and a long, curved, single-edged sword
- seven throwing stars
- seven yards of thin, strong chain (wrapped in silk for silence)
- a dozen hidden, large gold coins

Death

Playing Shadow

Background

Trained and retained as a spy by a noble house, Shadow (full name Shadowblade Dragonseeker of the Clan of the Spirit Mountain) lived a life of deceit and honor, etiquette and murder. As his skills increased, his lord and lady sent him on more serious and bloodier missions. Finally, his lady asked him to perform a delicate, dangerous, and ugly deed that crossed the bounds of what she could rightfully expect of him. He agreed to perform the deed on the condition that he would then be freed of his obligation to serve the nobles. He completed the mission and never returned to his home. He tells no one what this mission was.

Finally able to choose his own direction, Shadow has set out to learn about life's deeper mysteries: beauty, love, family, awe, worship, friendship, and sorrow. People often try to get him to help them defeat their enemies for causes they claim to be just, but Shadow holds most such people in contempt. He finds their squabbles petty and is sensitive and experienced enough to tell that most of them are not honest with themselves, let alone with him. When his heart moves him, Shadow takes up a cause as if his own life depends on it, but no mere words and no offer of pay can move his heart.

Questions for Development

- What person, deity, creature, or legendary hero does Shadow admire most?
- As a spy, Shadow has often traveled under other names. Does he often use names besides "Shadow"? If so, what are they?
- What was the last mission that Shadow performed for his lady?
- Since being released from service, has Shadow killed?

H107. Shadow – Rick Berry

Playing Puma

Background

Puma is a hunter, the only known survivor of an earthquake that killed her people when she was eighteen. She was hunting alone in the forest, and when she returned to her tribe's camp, she found that the ground had swallowed it up. She believes it was the great spirits' will, but she is angry at the great spirits for taking her people. She wishes they had taken her too.

Puma's people, a nomadic tribe of hunters and fishers, were faithful followers of Nature, performing ceremonial rites in her honor on holy days and dutifully protecting her creatures. They killed animals only with great remorse and thankfulness, and they moved from site to site trying to tend to all of Nature's forests, rivers, mountains, and flowers.

Now that she's alone, Puma is especially careful to carry on these responsibilities. She fears her people had fallen into Nature's disfavor and hopes, in her heart of hearts, that if she serves Nature well, the goddess will again bestow her with great blessings. Perhaps a new tribe will be born....

Puma is quick-tempered and fiercely protective of animals and children. She despises seeing the strong take advantage of the weak. She is quick-thinking and sure-footed, and she always seems to be moving. She can creep up right next to most people without their ever hearing or seeing her. It is unwise to dishonor her patron goddess in her presence.

Questions for Development

- What was Puma's childhood like? Did she have strong ties to her parents or siblings?
- Has Puma ever killed a person? If so, under what circumstances? If not, would she?
- What does Puma believe is the reason the great spirits let her live when the rest of her tribe was killed?
- How well does she get along with other people?

H108. Puma—Rick Berry

EVERWAY
SILVER ANNIVERSARY EDITION

NAME

PUMA

MOTIVE

AUTHORITY

VIRTUE The Defender *(safety)*

FAULT The Dragon—Reversed *(blind fury)*

FATE The Creator *(nurture vs. abandonment)*

POWERS 1

MAGIC 0

AIR — FOCUSED — ENERGY — FORCEFUL — FIRE

WISDOM — SPOKEN — 3 storytelling — THOUGHT — ACTION — ACTIVE — POWER

SILENT — 5 stealth — FEELING — MIGHT — 5 archery — PASSIVE

WATER — RECEPTIVE — 6 enduring the elements — RESISTANT — EARTH

INTEGRITY

©2020 The Everway Company

THE PHOENIX

EVERWAY
SILVER ANNIVERSARY EDITION

H108. Puma – Rick Berry   908. Huntress – Hannibal King

VISION

Puma is a hunter, the only known survivor of an earthquake that killed her people when she was eighteen and out hunting. Puma is quick-tempered and fiercely protective of animals and children. She despises seeing the strong take advantage of the weak.

Puma is quick-thinking and sure-footed, and she always seems to be moving. She can creep up right next to most people without their ever hearing or seeing her. It is unwise to dishonor her patron goddess, Nature, in her presence. She has a light, wood-framed pack to carry her camping gear.

POWERS & MAGIC

Speak to Animals (Air): Puma can speak to and understand all animals. This Power doesn't mean that the animals want to talk to her, however, or that they have much to say. Cost: 1 (frequent)

Cat's Leap (Fire): Puma can jump fifteen feet straight up from a standing position. Cost: 0 (free)

POSSESSIONS

- camping gear, bow and flint arrows, and warm clothes
- iron hunting knife, stone cooking knife, and iron-tipped spear
- pouches of herbs and pigments
- earrings made from things found at the seashore
- leather cords and feathers in hair

LAW – REVERSED

Berry 95

EVERWAY
SILVER ANNIVERSARY EDITION

NAME	MOTIVE
PRAISES BE	**CONQUEST**

VIRTUE	FAULT	FATE
The Eagle *(the mind prevails)*	The Defender— Reversed *(peril)*	Law *(order vs. treachery)*

POWERS **0**

MAGIC **6**

- 5 — Words of Power magic
- 3 — staff fighting
- 3 — sensing magic
- 3 — studying long hours

©2020 The Everway Company

THE FOOL

H109. Praises Be – Rick Berry　　*1301. Spherewalker – Doug Keith*

VISION

After defeating his master in a contest of magic, Praises Be concluded there was little left for his master to teach him. He set out to explore the spheres and test himself against the challenges to be found among the countless spheres.

Praises Be seeks to challenge himself and usually champions a cause to test his abilities, not to help others or to win rewards. His Earth score means he tires easily after significant magic. His Magic score is so strong that he can quickly fatigue himself into unconsciousness with powerful magic.

POWERS & MAGIC

Words of Power Magic (Air), 6: Praise's magic uses spoken words and written words to affect living things, spirits, and magic. His spells fall into three general types: spoken words, rituals, and inscriptions.

Universal Reading (Air): Praise can read "the Tongue" in any alphabet. Cost: 0 (free)

POSSESSIONS

- iron-tipped quarterstaff
- satchel of vellum sheets, inks, feather pens. string, and wax
- robes with plenty of pockets, turban, soft shoes
- traveling kit in a pack, including a bedroll, tarpaulin, tinder box, razor, knife, twine, and rope

THE LION – REVERSED

PLAYING PRAISES BE

Background

After defeating his master in a contest of magic, Praises Be concluded there was little left for his master to teach him. He set out to explore the universe and test himself against the challenges to be found among the countless spheres. When he champions a cause, it is usually to test his abilities, not to help others or to win rewards.

Praises Be is often called Praise by his friends.

Questions for Development

- Are there certain lessons that Praise did not learn from his master that he should have learned?

- As a powerful mage, Praise is likely to get many requests from people for his help. How does he feel about being called upon like this?

- How does Praise present himself to strangers? How much does he tell them about his magical powers?

- What is Praise's greatest fear?

- What is his reaction to things he does not understand?

For more information about Words of Power Magic, see p. 162.

H109. Praises Be – Rick Berry

NATURE

PRAISE'S MAGIC

Words of Power

Praise's magic uses spoken and written words to affect living things, spirits, and magic. His spells fall into three general types: spoken words, rituals, and inscriptions.

By speaking magic words, Praise can compel a spirit to obey him, kill an average person (3 Earth), or force a group of average people to back away. (Average people forced back cannot approach Praise again for about a minute, but those with strong Fire scores can approach again sooner.) He can easily force back or command animals, but they are no easier for him to kill than people are. The effects of one word of power are negated when Praise utters another word of power. For instance, if he has caused bandits to back away with a word of power, and then uses a word of power to kill one of them, the others are freed from their spell and are once again able to attack him.

Praise can inscribe objects with magic words so that the objects have magical effects. A magical inscription, however, takes a lot of time and energy to do, and it's not as powerful as a spoken word. For example, Praise could create scrolls to be used as talismans that protect their wearer from 3 Magic or weaker. (Thus, a mage with a score of 3 would not be able to cast spells on the protected person.) If the name of the wearer is worked into the inscription, it protects against 4 Magic, and if the name of the mage whose magic is to be countered is worked into the formula,

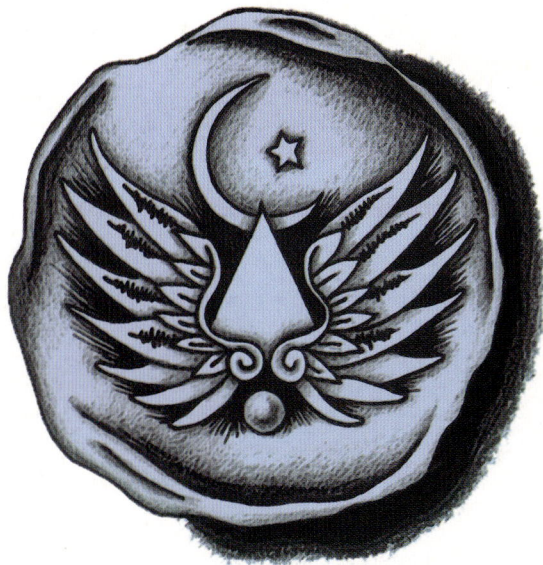

it protects up to 5 Magic (the most powerful protection Praise can offer). Praise can also work talismans to protect people against other supernatural dangers or to have other magical effects. Depending on the strength of the talisman, it takes Praise anywhere from an hour to a day to inscribe one, with more powerful talismans taking longer. Talismans' power wanes quickly.

Praise's rituals are for magical actions, such as imprisoning a powerful spirit, warding an area against magical intrusion, and other such feats. Praise's rituals last from an hour to a day, and they leave him weary.

Praise's average Earth score (3) means he tires after doing any significant magic. His Magic score is so high he can quickly fatigue himself into unconsciouslness if he casts powerful magic too quickly.

Praise's magic depends on his ability to speak words or to inscribe words and symbols.

EVERWAY
SILVER ANNIVERSARY EDITION

NAME
SERENITY FREEMANSDAUGHTER

MOTIVE
WANDERLUST

VIRTUE
Death *(change)*

FAULT
Knowledge—Reversed *(falsehood)*

FATE
The Fish *(the soul prevails vs. shallowness)*

POWERS
0

MAGIC
5

AIR
WISDOM
FOCUSED
SPOKEN
ENERGY
FORCEFUL
SILENT
THOUGHT
FIRE
WATER
FEELING
ACTION
ACTIVE
MIGHT
PASSIVE
RECEPTIVE
POWER
INTEGRITY
RESISTANT
EARTH

3 singing

5 dancing and partying

3 sensing faerie magic

4 resisting poisons

©2020 The Everway Company

INSPIRATION – REVERSED

H110. Serenity – Rick Berry   *206. Fire Dance – Janine Johnston*

VISION

Serenity is a "fourthling," meaning she is one-fourth troll. Her mother's mother, Hillshaker, was a troll who secretly taught her magic and gave Serenity her secret name: Farbright. She left her home when people began to suspect she had secret powers. Hillshaker gave her a dagger, gems, and a statue.

It is Serenity's "wild" side that gives her a penchant for boisterous parties, a tolerance for harmful substances, and a sensitivity to faerie magic. She travels extensively, trading for a living, and spending a good deal of time alone in the woods. She has a good selection of baubles and supplies for camping.

POWERS & MAGIC

Flux Magic (Fire), 5: Serenity can transform people and things. She needs no words to do her work, but she must stare at the thing to be transformed and project her energy with hand gestures. As sight is the sense connected to Fire, this magic works through her concentrated gaze.

Troll Friend (Earth): Trolls (and other earthy, magical beings) generally take a liking to Serenity. Cost: 0 (free)

POSSESSIONS
- sack of baubles
- heavy, runed bronze dagger
- sling, fishing hooks, and line
- pack with traveling and cold-weather clothes
- sack of unpolished, uncut gems
- crude, stone statuette of a pregnant woman

WAR

Playing Serenity

Background

Serenity is a "fourthling," meaning she is one-fourth troll. Her mother's mother was a troll, and Serenity learned magic from her. It was the grandmother, Hillshaker, who gave Serenity her secret name: Farbright.

Serenity learned and practiced her magic in secret, but she found it hard not to use her magic to make her life easier. After people in the household and around her family's homestead began to suspect she had magic, she left. She traveled up and down the coast of her land and up and down a few rivers, trading for a living and spending a good deal of time alone in the wilds. When her younger sister became ill, she returned home to be with her.

Now that her sister has died, Serenity has decided to leave again, but this time she intends to travel very far away. To keep Serenity safe, Hillshaker gave her a bronze dagger, some gems, and a statue of "Great Grandmother."

It is Serenity's "wild" side that gives her a penchant for boisterous parties, a tolerance for harmful substances, and a sensitivity to faerie magic.

Questions for Development

- What are some of Serenity's favorite spells to cast?

- What is troll society like, and what does Serenity think of it?

- What's the most violent or destructive thing that Serenity has ever done?

- As a mage and a trader, Serenity has had ample opportunity to cheat people. What's her attitude about using her magic to take advantage of others?

H110. Serenity – Rick Berry

THE FOOL – REVERSED

Serenity's Magic

Flux

Serenity can transform people and things. She needs no words to do her work, but she must stare at the thing to be transformed and project her energy with hand gestures. As sight is the sense connected to Fire, this magic works through her concentrated gaze.

Serenity can easily make changes in animals and objects, altering texture, color, hair covering, and other details with hardly any effort. She can also change the size and shape of inanimate objects, though this takes more effort. All these changes are temporary, and the altered things revert to normal within a day. Certain actions, such as someone naming the transformed thing or touching the thing with iron, can make it revert to its normal form sooner.

Serenity can also alter people's hair color, skin color, facial features, height, weight, and so on, but she cannot add or remove limbs, digits, or organs. She cannot transform people into animals or non-humans, nor can she change their memory, thought processes, or sense of self. She can make a person up to a foot taller or shorter and increase or decrease a person's weight by about one-fourth. Anyone with 5 Earth or stronger, however, is hard to transform, unless the character also has a strong

Water score and welcomes the change. These changes are temporary.

As Serenity's magic is linked to Fire, the least predictable of elements, her magic sometimes has unpredictable results.

Transforming things is hard work, but Serenity's strong Earth score (4) allows her to cast a fair number of spells before wearing herself out.

> For more information about Flux Magic, see p. 164.

EVERWAY
SILVER ANNIVERSARY EDITION

NAME
CLEFT

MOTIVE
MYSTERY

VIRTUE
The Lion
(the body prevails)

FAULT
The Creator—Reversed
(abandonment)

FATE
The Peasant
(simple strength vs. lack of vision)

POWERS
0

MAGIC
5

AIR
WISDOM
ENERGY
FOCUSED
FORCEFUL
FIRE
ACTIVE
POWER
PASSIVE
EARTH
RESISTANT
INTEGRITY
RECEPTIVE
WATER
SILENT
SPOKEN
THOUGHT
FEELING
ACTION
MIGHT

3 identifying herbs and plants

4 hunting

3 sensing injury and illness

5 resisting bad magic

©2020 The Everway Company

FEARING SHADOWS

H111. Cleft – Rick Berry   *305. Caribou Plains – Andrew Robinson*

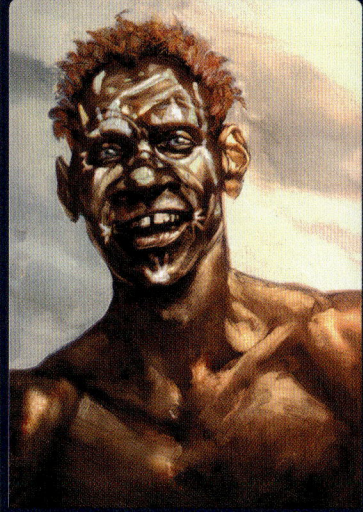

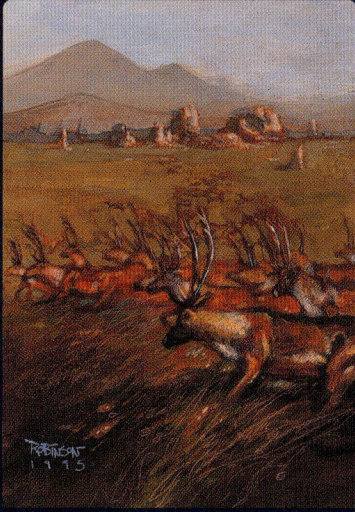

VISION

Cleft's talent for magic showed itself spontaneously, as a talent for music might. He trained in magic as one might train in the playing of instruments. When another child in the village developed magical powers like Cleft's, the village storyteller said that this child would replace Cleft's duties to the village.

When that child became an adult, Cleft left his village to roam distant lands. Years and years from now, he intends to return to his people and share with them what he's learned.

Cleft's mother told him he was a spirit living in a cleft in a stone cliff before he was born.

POWERS & MAGIC

Soil and Stone Magic (Earth), 5: Cleft draws on the fertile energy of soil and the enduring power of stone to work his magic. He is a healer, a ward against evil, and a source of strength and health.

Earth's Surety (Earth): If both of Cleft's bare feet are in direct contact with the living. level earth, he's almost impossible to knock down. Cost: 0 (free)

POSSESSIONS

- paints, clay, dust, sand, pigments, and other ritual tools
- traveling goods wrapped in a blanket
- throwing sticks, used mostly for hunting
- shells, pelts, and herbs to trade
- loincloth

PLAYING CLEFT

Background

Cleft's talent for magic showed itself spontaneously, as a talent for music might. He trained in magic as one might train in the playing of instruments. He never thought his abilities made him any more special than others, such as those who followed the tracks of game, turned arguments into smiles, or told stories that carried the listeners to Dreamtime. He did his part in the village, as did everyone.

When another child in the village developed magical powers like Cleft's, the village storyteller said that this child was Cleft's replacement, the one who would free Cleft from his obligations to his village. When the child became an adult, Cleft left the village to roam distant lands. Years and years from now, he intends to return to his people to share with them what he's learned.

Cleft's name comes from his mother's story that he was a spirit living in a cleft in a stone cliff before he entered her womb to be born a human.

Questions for Development

- What is the strangest thing that Cleft has seen so far in his travels?

- Whom does he miss the most from back home?

- What trait, virtue, or talent does Cleft admire most in others?

- When does he expect in return for using his magic to help others?

CLEFT'S MAGIC

Soil and Stone

Cleft draws on the fertile energy of soil and the enduring power of stone to work his magic. He is a healer, a ward against evil, and a source of strength and health.

As touch is the sense connected to Earth, Cleft's magic works through touch, especially through the hands. He also uses the bounty of the earth—plants, herbs, dust, and clay—to work his strongest healing magic.

In a single day, under his direct and constant care, a simple wound heals as if two weeks have gone by. If Cleft tends a wounded person daily but not constantly, the person recovers twice as fast as normal. His touch can ease pain, stop bleeding, and keep a wound clean. With great and constant effort, he can prevent a mortally wounded person from dying and nurse that person back to health. Depending on the wound, it can take days to weeks of care to heal the person to the point where death is no longer a threat.

Cleft's touch and care can also (in increasing order of difficulty) cure diseases, neutralize poisons, temporarily lift curses, and banish malignant spirits. Particularly deadly or profound diseases (such as leprosy), potent poisons (such as that of the cockatrice, 6 Poison (*lethal*), powerful

curses, and mighty spirits can resist his magic.

Cleft can promote health and prevent harm by blessing people, crops, wagons, and so on. He can improve a person's resistance to a particular danger (such as poison, Words of Power magic, or cold), and such a blessing lasts three days and nights. (He paints a hand on the person to be protected to focus his protective power there.) He can, through a long ritual, bless fields to encourage bountiful crops. He can even give some protection to a large, unified body of people, such as an army, though only through a long and tiring ritual.

For more information about Soil and Stone Magic, see p. 166.

EVERWAY
SILVER ANNIVERSARY EDITION

NAME	MOTIVE
WHISPER WALKER	**BEAUTY**

VIRTUE — The Hermit *(wisdom)*

FAULT — Drowning in Armor *(protective measures turn dangerous)*

FATE — The Phoenix *(rebirth vs. destruction)*

POWERS **0**

MAGIC **4**

AIR — FOCUSED — ENERGY

WISDOM — SPOKEN — SILENT

3 historical insight

FORCEFUL — FIRE

4 spirit battles

ACTION — ACTIVE

THOUGHT — FEELING — MIGHT

5 speaking with spirits

WATER — RECEPTIVE — INTEGRITY

PASSIVE — POWER

4 "Soul's Wall of Stone"

RESISTANT — EARTH

©2020 The Everway Company

360

KNOWLEDGE – REVERSED

H112. Whisper Walker – Rick Berry   1311. Soul Leeches – Andrew Robinson

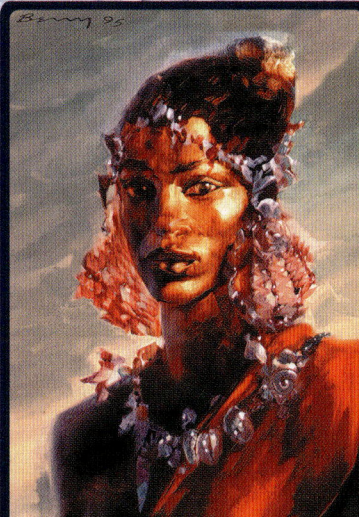

VISION

When Whisper Walker was a child, a village ceremony went horribly wrong, and several malign spirits took possession of her. The village's medicine woman drove the spirits away, but when they fled, one carried a dark egg or stone that was "part" of her away. Since then, she has been sensitive to spirits.

Under the medine woman's guidance, she became an accomplished spirit woman. Now that she is an adult, she has decided to explore the many worlds the spirits have told her about. She told her family that she is seeking the "egg" the spirits took from her, but she really just wants to travel the spheres.

POWERS & MAGIC

Open Chalice Magic (Water), 4: Whisper Walker can sense energies and unusual auras of all kinds. Whisper Walker can open herself to spirits, call them into herself, and let them act through her.

Vision of the Departed Spirit (Water): Whisper Walker can tell by sight whether a person is awake, unconscious, or dreaming. Cost: 0 (free)

POSSESSIONS

- magical herbs and incense
- ritual items in a cloth bag: wooden chalice, ceramic pitcher, small metal mirror, and so on
- curved dagger
- several changes of clothes
- traveling kit: twine for starting fires, knife, bedroll, and so on

THE KING – REVERSED

PLAYING WHISPER

Background

When Whisper Walker was a child, a village ceremony went horribly wrong, and several malign spirits took possession of her. The village's medicine woman drove the spirits away, but when they fled, the medicine woman saw that one was carrying an object of some sort. It looked like a large, dark egg or stone, and the medicine woman said that it was some "part" of Whisper Walker.

Since then, Whisper Walker has been sensitive to the world of spirits. Under the medicine woman's guidance, she has developed into an accomplished spirit woman herself.

Whisper Walker's name was given to her at her puberty ceremony. It refers to the belief that the gods and goddesses created people by speaking and created the spirits by whispering. Thus her name means "she who walks among spirits." She has other names given to her by family members and the village leaders: Cub, Gentle River, Bright Eyes, Mother's Joy, and Hope. She may sometimes choose to use these names, though she prefers "Whisper Walker."

Now that Whisper Walker is a woman, she has decided to explore the many worlds the spirits have told her about. She told her family that she is seeking the "egg" that the spirits took from her, but in her heart she knows that she really just wants to travel beyond the horizon and see new and wonderful things.

Questions for Development

- How does Whisper Walker feel about average people, who cannot sense the energies and spirits that she lives among?
- What's the scariest encounter that Whisper Walker has ever had with a spirit?
- In what way may she be unprepared to meet people from different cultures?
- What does she especially dream of seeing or doing now that she is traveling?

THE DRAGON – REVERSED

Whisper's Magic

Open Chalice

Whisper Walker can sense energies of all kinds, though particularly subtle energies may be difficult or impossible for her to identify. Negative energies disturb her, and very powerful negative energies can weaken her or even knock her out.

Whisper Walker can see unusual auras of any kind, noticing supernatural disturbances and extremes. She can tell an item is magical, a person is a mage (or is otherwise magical), an area is imbued with some sort of energy, and so on. She cannot tell if someone is lying or detect general personality traits. Only extremes of some sort are visible to her.

Whisper Walker can open herself to spirits, call them into herself, and let them act through her. (While a spirit is "possessing" her, the gamemaster runs Whisper Walker.) She can usually reassert herself at will. She can also communicate with spirits that others cannot see or hear. Powerful spirits are likely to overcome her and may resist giving up possession of her body. The most powerful spirits may not even "fit" in her; contact with spirits of this kind can hurt or damage her. Whisper Walker's magic puts her in a dangerous position: she is advanced enough to accept spirits without always being powerful enough to control them.

Whisper Walker's magic lets her communicate with animals, but the communication is always nonverbal. (Her magic is linked to Water, not Air, so it is silent, rather than spoken.)

Whisper Walker has a special ability that she calls "Soul's Wall of Stone." It is her technique for erecting a psychic barrier to prevent intrusion. (In game terms, it's simply her Earth Specialty, giving her an effective score of 5 to resist magical intrusions.)

Whisper Walker has incense and herbs that she uses in her rituals. Some herbs she burns or crumbles into dust. Others she steeps, forming a drink. If she has time to prepare a ritual, she is more likely to meet with success.

For more information about Open Chalice Magic, see p. 168.

205. Scroll Library – Martin McKenna

Autumn

Chapter 9: References

This chapter contains quick reference sheets you may photocopy for personal use during play. These are meant to remind players and gamemasters who are new to EVERWAY of important concepts explained in detail elsewhere in this book.

References

The Peasant – Jeff Miracola

Motives 366

901. Red Lady – Doug Alexander

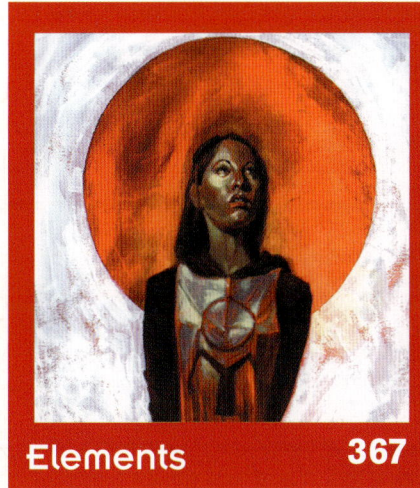

Elements 367

1512. Dragon Uprising – Andrew Robinson

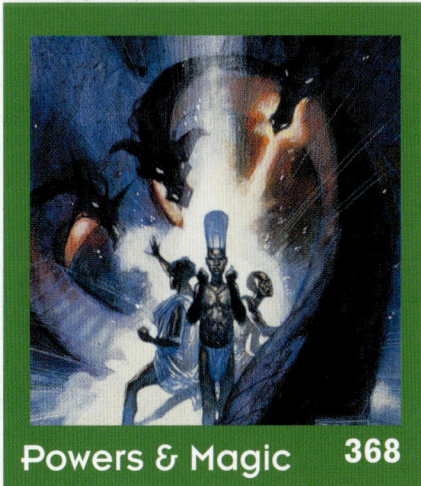

Powers & Magic 368

1310. Fortune Reader – Joe DeVelasco

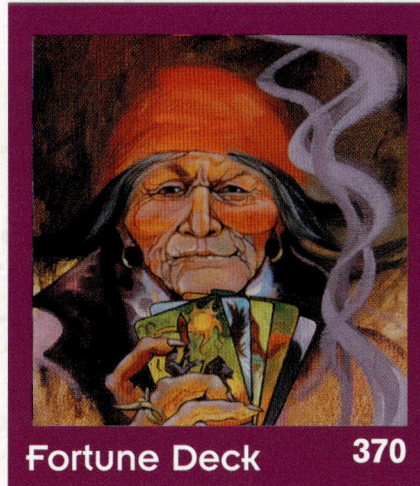

Fortune Deck 370

WANDERLUST — SUN

The hero wanders the spheres with little or no care for a purpose. Wherever the sun rises and sets is called "home," though no one place is for long.

MYSTERY — MOON

The hero seeks no mundane goals but wishes to confront mysteries on other worlds. They seek a secret or subtle understanding.

KNOWLEDGE — MERCURY

The hero seeks knowledge to be found in new realms and new worlds. The knowledge sought may be mundane or hermetic.

BEAUTY — VENUS

The hero seeks to share or to experience that which is beautiful: art, music, romance, poetry, aphrodisia, and more.

CONQUEST — MARS

The hero lives for challenges and loves to exert power. The hero may be a master of martial abilities.

AUTHORITY — JUPITER

The hero is the hands, the eyes, the mouth, or the sword of some authority, such as a deity, ruler, or holy order.

ADVERSITY — SATURN

The hero is under some compulsion to walk the spheres. Such a hero may have a saturnine disposition.

THE THREE LAWS OF ACTION

There are three laws of action that the gamemaster uses to resolve any situation while playing the game. The gamemaster may use any one or all of these to determine the result of each action a hero takes.

The Law of Karma

The most likely result based on a hero's Elements, Specialties, Powers, Magic and tactics determine the outcome of a hero's action.

The Law of Drama

The needs of the plot determine the outcome of a hero's action.

The Law of Fortune

A draw from the Fortune Deck determines the outcome of a hero's action.

THE SOLDIER – REVERSED

THE ELEMENTS

	Air	Fire	Earth	Water
1	dim	feeble	sickly	oblivious
2	simplistic	lethargic	frail	insensitive
3	average	average	average	average
4	bright	energetic	robust	perceptive
5	brilliant	vital	tough	sensitive
6	ingenious	mighty	enduring	empathic
7	legendary	legendary	legendary	legendary
8	prescient	boundless	indomitable	mystical
9	inscrutable	unstoppable	indestructible	transcendent
10	divine	divine	divine	divine

You have 20 elemental points to spend on your hero's Elements, Powers, and Magic.

OVERLOOKING THE DIAMOND – REVERSED

POWERS

You can invent any sort of magical, psychic, or unusual Powers for your hero (including magical items or pets), but you must "pay" for them with elemental points at hero creation.

Powers are limited in scope and have specific effects. If you wish your hero to wield magic, which implies a more general knowledge and ability, you may want to spend these points on Magic instead.

Cost of Powers

The more useful a Power is, the more Element points it will cost.

To determine how many Element points a Power costs, assign 1 point each for:

- **Frequent:** Power will often be useful in play.

- **Major:** Power will have a big effect on play.

- **Versatile:** Power will be useful in a variety of ways.

Some Powers may be doubly Major or Versatile. You may have one 0-point power for free, but each one after that costs a minimum of 1. See p. 151–157 for a list of example Powers.

MAGIC

A hero's magic score must be linked to one of the hero's Elements, and their Magic level cannot be greater than that linked Element (Element plus 1 if they choose a specialization in the linked Magic).

MAGIC LEVEL

If a hero's Magic score is... the hero will be:

1 An Apprentice: A beginner, capable of both modest tricks and catastrophic mistakes.

2 A Weak Mage: Capable of a decent spell or two; has an understanding of magic as a science.

3 An Average Mage: A humble practitioner with some impressive powers in their area of specialization but not one to tackle great magical challenges. A town of a thousand people might have one such mage.

4 A Gifted Mage: A talented spellcaster with a good grounding in magic and some real promise. A city of ten thousand people might have such a mage.

5 A Powerful Mage: Well above the average; capable of facing powerful magical threats. A kingdom of a hundred thousand people might have one such mage.

6 A Mighty Mage: The mightiest living mage that most people have ever heard of; a master of magic. A realm of a million people might have one such mage.

Semicircle Test

A mage of a specific Magic level should be able to achieve the same effect as a hero with two Elements at the same level. Magic is very broad, and you can invent almost any type of magic tradition you want. You may want to consider one of the following example traditions of magic to get started quickly.

WORDS OF POWER
P.162

AIR MAGIC

This form of magic uses spoken and written words to affect living things, spirits, and magical forces. The mage can inscribe charms with magic words and symbols, but the charms don't have the same effect as a directly spoken word. This form of magic is very versatile. It is especially useful for binding spirits, sealing portals, warding chambers, compelling lesser creatures to obey, and striking down opponents with power words.

As sound is the sense connected to Air, this magic works through words.

FLUX
P.164

FIRE MAGIC

Flux magic transforms things, as fire can transform wood to ash, sand to glass, water to steam, and ore to iron. Like flames, the effects of this magic last only a short time, usually about a day.

As sight is the sense connected to Fire, this magic works through the concentrated gaze of the mage.

OPEN CHALICE
P.168

WATER MAGIC

The mage is receptive to energies, powers, and spirits. For example, the mage can sense strong emotions in a location where they were experienced, allow spirits to speak through them, sense energies that are ruling or affecting a realm, and so on. The mage can see auras of increasing subtlety as this magical power increases, but interpreting those auras can be tricky.

As taste and smell are the physical senses ruled by Water, this magic sometimes uses magic drinks, smoke, incense, or other aids.

SOIL AND STONE
P.166

EARTH MAGIC

The mage can draw on the fertile energy of soil and the enduring power of stone. The mage is a healer, a ward against evil, and a source of strength and health.

As touch is the sense connected to Earth, this magic works through physical contact, especially with the hands.

AUTUMN

SEASONS

Meaning: Plenty
Reversed: Want
Correspondence: Earth

FERTILITY

DEITIES

Meaning: Growth
Reversed: Decline
Correspondence: Earth/Water

THE COCKATRICE

BEASTS

Meaning: Corruption
Reversed: Recovery
Correspondence: Earth/Water

THE FISH

ANIMALS

Meaning: The Soul Prevails
Reversed: Shallowness
Correspondence: Water

THE CREATOR

DUALITY

Meaning: Nurture
Reversed: Abandonment
Correspondence: Earth/Water/Moon

THE FOOL

ESTATES

Meaning: Freedom
Reversed: Lack of Connection
Correspondence: Fire/Water/Sun

DEATH

DEITIES

Meaning: Change
Reversed: Stasis
Correspondence: Water

THE GRIFFIN

BEASTS

Meaning: Valor
Reversed: Cowardice
Correspondence: Air/Fire

THE DEFENDER

DUALITY

Meaning: Safety
Reversed: Peril
Correspondence: Air/Fire/Sun

THE HERMIT

ESTATES

Meaning: Wisdom
Reversed: Isolation
Correspondence: Air/Water/Mercury

THE DRAGON

BEASTS

Meaning: Cunning
Reversed: Blind Fury
Correspondence: Air/Earth

INSPIRATION

DEITIES

Meaning: Creativity
Reversed: Lack of Imagination
Correspondence: Fire/Water

DROWNING IN ARMOR

FOLLIES

Meaning: Safeguards Turn Dangerous
Reversed: True Prudence
Correspondence: Water/Saturn

THE KING

ESTATES

Meaning: Authority
Reversed: Tyranny
Correspondence: Air/Fire/Earth/Water/Jupiter

THE EAGLE

ANIMALS

Meaning: The Mind Prevails
Reversed: Thoughtlessness
Correspondence: Air

KNOWLEDGE

DEITIES

Meaning: Truth
Reversed: Falsehood
Correspondence: Air

FEARING SHADOWS

FOLLIES

Meaning: Unnecessary Fear
Reversed: Recognizing Safety
Correspondence: Fire/Mars

LAW

DEITIES

Meaning: Order
Reversed: Treachery
Correspondence: Air/Earth

TRICKERY – REVERSED

The Lion

ANIMALS

Meaning: The Body Prevails
Reversed: Weakness
Correspondence: Fire/Earth

Nature

DEITIES

Meaning: Life Energy
Reversed: Energy Sapped
Correspondence: Earth

Overlooking the Diamond

FOLLIES

Meaning: Failing to See Opportunity
Reversed: Recognizing Opportunity
Correspondence: Air/Mercury

The Peasant

ESTATES

Meaning: Simple Strength
Reversed: Lack of Vision
Correspondence: Air/Earth/Venus

The Phoenix

BEASTS

Meaning: Rebirth
Reversed: Destruction
Correspondence: Fire/Water

The Priestess

ESTATES

Meaning: Understanding Mysteries
Reversed: Impracticality
Correspondence: Earth/Water/Moon

The Satyr

BEASTS

Meaning: Indulgence
Reversed: Moderation
Correspondence: Fire/Earth

The Smith

ESTATES

Meaning: Productivity
Reversed: Evil Effort
Correspondence: Air/Fire/Mars

The Soldier

ESTATES

Meaning: Duty
Reversed: Blind Obedience
Correspondence: Fire/Earth/Saturn

Sowing Stones

FOLLIES

Meaning: Fruitless Labor
Reversed: Ceasing Fruitless Labor
Correspondence: Earth/Venus

Spring

SEASONS

Meaning: New Growth
Reversed: Stagnation
Correspondence: Air

Striking the Dragon's Tail

FOLLIES

Meaning: Underestimating the Challenge
Reversed: Recognizing the Larger Problem
Correspondence: Air/Fire/Earth/Water/Jupiter

Summer

SEASONS

Meaning: Energy
Reversed: Exhaustion
Correspondence: Fire

Trickery

DEITIES

Meaning: Deceit
Reversed: Subterfuge Revealed
Correspondence: Air/Fire

The Unicorn

BEASTS

Meaning: Purity
Reversed: Temptation
Correspondence: Air/Water

The Usurper

VOID

Meaning: Varies
Reversed: Varies
Correspondence: Varies

War

DEITIES

Meaning: Great Effort
Reversed: Effort Misspent
Correspondence: Fire

Winter

SEASONS

Meaning: Maturity
Reversed: Inexperience
Correspondence: Water

FERTILITY – REVERSED

371

NATURE

THE SATYR – REVERSED

THE EAGLE

Lackey • Chris Tuck • Chris W. Harvey • Christopher A. Hoffmann • Christopher Abrenica • Christopher Robichaud • Christopher Stieha • Chuck Childers • Clemens Euli • Cleo Schmitz • Cliff Hensley • Cliff Winnig • Colin Suess • Collin G Brooke • Colm McCarthy • Cory "Rook" Williamsen • Creative Play and Podcast Netw • Crispy T • D. Greg • Dak F Powers • Dan Kassiday • Daniel Gregory • Daniel K. Lundsby • Daniel P Washington • Darla Burrow • Darlis Nordhagen-Smith • Darren Hennessey • Darryll B. Carter • Darvin L. Martin • Dave Brookshaw • David "Dynamitochondria" Lawson • David Astley • David Buswell-Wible • David Coleman • David Dorward • David Dunham • David Jose • David Liu • David Rubin • David Thorp • David Weisberger • Derek Deren • Dermot Power • Dorian Indûr Blackburn • Douglas G. King • Drew Chase • Drew Wendorf • E. The Vagabond • Edgar Gonzalez • Edouard Contesse • Edvard Blumentanz • Edward MacGregor • Elan Goldmann • Eleanor Hingley and Robin Farndon • Emmanuel "Ketzol" LANDAIS AKA Vengeance Smith • Emory Susar • Eric (Erikku) Storm (Arashi) • Eric Coates • Eric Minton • Erich McNaughton • Erik Ogan • Ethan Trovillion • Eva S. • Evan Franke • Evan Sass • Evan Torner • everwayan. blogspot.com • Forêt Gwénael • Fran Thomson • Frank Cord Lohmann • Frank Michael Lazar • Fred Herman • Frederic Menage • Frederic Weil • Gabe & Zach Auschrat • Gabriel Kung Fu • Galen Pejeau • Game Dave • Gareth 'drownedsummer' Dunstan • Gary Anastasio • Gary Schaper • Gaylan Lewallen • Genevieve Slunka • George Moralidis • Giuseppe D'Aristotile • GK & Julia Coleman • Glen R. Taylor • Glenn Overby II • Gord Sellar • Gordon C Landis • Gray Richardson • Gwenael Granal • Hannah Teson • Hans Axel von Fersen • He-Zin Kwon • Hedgehog • Heiko Ludwig • Herman Duyker • Hyperlexic • Ignacio Granados Jiménez • Itay "LoCriti" Horev • J Coleman (BX) • J. James Craig • J. Wick • Jack Gulick • Jacob Moore • James Allen • Jamie Smith • Jamie Wheeler • Jason & Kai Wodicka • Jason Dryan • Jason George • Jason Kottler • Jason Schindler • Jason Schupp • Jean-Christophe Cubertafon • Jeannine Chang • Jeff Berry • Jensen Bruns • Jeremy "Bolthy" Zimmerman • Jeromy M French • Jesse Koennecke • Jesse Meyer • Jesse Morgan • Jim Holthaus • Jim Stutz • Joel Pearce • John Ahlschwede • John C. Tompkins • John Desmarais • John Fiala • John Hawkins • John Hoyland • John Kasab • John Kuzma • John M. Portley • John Nienart • John S Novak, III • John WS Marvin • Jonas Courteau • Jonas Schiött • Jonathan "Buddha" Davis • Jonathan C. Dietrich • Jonathan Evans • Jonathan Fish • Jonathan Grimm • Jonathon Burgess • José Luiz "Tzimiscedracul" Cardoso • Joseph A. Russell • Josh Harrison • Josh Reynolds • Joshua Hudner • Joshua Macy • Juergen Walker • Justin Hamilton • Justin Melvin • Karl Olaf Knutson • Karsing Fung • Kathy Ice • Kelcey Calderon • Kell Shaw • Kelly Carson • Ken Finlayson • Kerry J Smith- Ally • Kevin Elmore • Kevin Putnam • Kim Dong-Ryul • Kirsten M. Corby • Kris Gould • Kris Green • Kryptyk Physh • Kurtis Conrad • L. A. Parker • Laurie Koudstaal • Leokii • Lisa Padol • Lorrraine aka Rain of Terra • Louis B Schoener • Louis Sylvester • Luis K. Penn • M. Sean Molley • M. Shanmugasundaram • Mailanka • Malc Arnold • Mamading Ceesay • Marc Kevin Hall • Marc Lummis • Marcus Katz • Marguerite Beveridge • Mark - EIC of Gamersledge • Mark Hunter • Mark Pankhurst • Mark Piper • Mark Scrudder • Mark, Kamala, Aurelia, Hugh, and Eamon Wyler • Markus Raab • Martin J. Manco • Marty Chodorek • Matt A. Borselli • Matt Gregory • Matt Townsend • Matt Whalley • Matthew & Elizabeth Parmeter • Matthew Broome • Matthew D Shaver • Matthew Ross • Menno Smit • Michael Croft & Ginger Stampley • Michael Croitoriu • Michael Crowley • Michael Cule • Michael Daisey • Michael Feldhusen • Michael J Kruckvich • Michael Kirkbridd • Michael Maneval • Michael McVeigh • Michael Osburn • Michael Phillips • Michael Pietrelli • Michael Scott Mears • Mike Carey • Mike Lehmann • Mike Matchett • Mike Mearls • Mike Simpson • Mikhail Bonch-Osmolovskiy • Mr. Miércoles • Murray Dahm

• Myles Corcoran • N. Barmore • Nathan Rockwood • Neil Smith • Neil Thompson • Nick Bower • Nicola Went • NJ Glassford • Noa Terra H~ • Norikatu Konisi • Oliver V. • Olof Dahl • Ols Jonas Petter Olsson • OneWithNothing • Pat & Sue Waters • Patrick 'Winterfuchs' Fittkau • Patrick Higgins • Patrick McDonough • Patryk Adamski, Ruemere • Paul "LostLegolas" Leone • Paul Alexander Butler • Paul Hughes • Paul King • Paul Siegel • Paul Weimer • Peter the Beard • Phelddagrif • Phil Masters • Philip W Rogers Jr • Piers Beckley • Quinn Richter • Quirin Eimer • R Zemlicka • Rabbit and Brandes Stoddard • Rachel Brodsky & Andrew Finch • Rakesh Malik • Random Jones • Randy Carnahan • Rennie "Wild Sword" Araucto • Rev. Keith Johnson • Rich Harrison • Richard "Vidiian" Greene • Richard Hletko • Richard T. Balsley • Rick Marbles • Rick Neal • Rikard Elfgren • Rob Barrett • Rob Lightner • Robert Dempsey • Robert James • Robert Slaughter • Rolfe Bergström • Rory Hughes • Ross A. Isaacs • Rukh • Russ Luzetski • Ryan Williams • Ryker Wallace • Sabina Walter • Sam Brookover • Sandler L. Bryson • Sarah Boffoli • Sarah Callaghan • Sarah Dshamila Günther • Saskia "Nyo" Reiss • Scott Acker • Scott Bennett • Scott Freyburger • Scott Havens • Scott Hungerford • Sean "Kadino" Sweeney • Sean "Imp Familiar" Carroll • Sean Dawson • Sean Sherman • Sebastián Brugnoli • Shane Cubis • Shepherd Jim Best • Silvio Herrera Gea • Simon Dalcher • Spenser I • Stefon Mears • Stéphane Rochat • Stephen • Stephen Cumiskey • Steve "Anarin" Martin • Steve Mumford • Steven Barrett • Steven Danielson • Steven Joel Zeve • Steven Torres-Roman • Steven Watkins • Steven Wilson • Steven Zalek • Stuart Chaplin • Stuart Dollar • SwiftOne • T. Kurt Bond • Teemu Kivikangas • TGabor • Thalji • The Holden-Brown Family • The Last Epicurean • Thomas Haakinen • Thomas McManus • Thomas Walter • Tillerz • Tim Czarnecki • Tim Ellis • Tim Flannigan • Tim Pen • Timothy Carroll • Tobiasz Cwynar • Tod Ruckdeschel • Tom LaPorta • Tor Kjetil Edland • Travis Bryant • Travis Foster • Tristan Chenier • Unsung Tempest • Utah Prevo's • Vandaal • Vincent Boscher • Vincent Carpe • Vincent Craplet • Waco Gle • Wade G. Sullivan • Wally DeBarger • Wayne Rossi • William Hilton • WizeManBOB • Wooz • Xylemicarious • Zed Lopez

ARCHIVISTS (DIGITAL BOOKS)

Aaron Billingham • Adam & Looie Krump • Ananda Patterson • Brian Laliberte • Bruce Baugh • Bruce Curd • Bryce Leland Carlson • Chris Michael Jahn • Chris Taggart • Christopher Allen • Christopher Young • Chuck Cooley • CJ LaRoe • Colin Fredericks • Darth Mauno • David B. Semmes • David Millians • David Stephenson • DocChronos • Doom Chupacabra • Ed Ingold • Ewald Große-Wilde • Félix Gauthier-Mamaril • Frederic Ferro • Friedrich Roehrer-Ertl • Gabriel Sorrel • Giorgio Tentella • Grant B. • Hao Zhang • Hidetoshi HAYAKAWA • J. Delamotte • James Meredith • Jason Brandt • jason e. bean • Javier Quintero • Jay Sparks • Jaymi Elford • JC Hay • Jo "Lawjick" Louie • Jochen Linnemann • John "johnkzin" Rudd • John Gabriel • Joseph Geary • Jukka Särkijärvi • Julia Pluta • Katrina Hennessy • Keith Richmond • Kira • Kyle Benson • Maddy Eid • Mark Jessup • Mark Sabalauskas • Melani Weber • Meri and Allan Samuelson • Meri, Rosie, Chris, and Bimi Sims • Michael Hill • Michael Sahyun • Michael Schwartz • Mildra The Monk • Mitch Albala • Myke "fnord" Thomas • Neal Dalton • Objectionable Content • Paul 'The Bastard' Douglas • Paul "FatPob" Goldstone • Paul Hayes • Perry Clark • Physicphy • Pierre "Rôliste" Rose • Pyxie • Ralf Achenbach • Rich Warren • Richard DiTullio • Robert "Jefepato" Dall • Robert Carnel • Rorke Haining • Ryan Thames • S. Ben Melhuish • S. Bingman • ScrappySPJ • Seana McGuinness • Steve Arensberg • Steve Crawford • Steveotep • Tamanegi Sunaga • Trans Rights! • Trentin C Bergeron • Twila Oxley Price • Wright Johnson • Yann Abaz

EVERWAY

SILVER ANNIVERSARY EDITION

NAME	MOTIVE

VIRTUE	FAULT	FATE

POWERS

MAGIC

AIR

ENERGY

WISDOM

FIRE

WATER

POWER

EARTH

INTEGRITY

FOCUSED

FORCEFUL

Spoken

Silent

Receptive

Resistant

Active

Passive

THOUGHT

ACTION

FEELING

MIGHT

VISION

VISION

VISION

POWERS & MAGIC

POSSESSIONS

Anchorview Road

Sentinel Aqueduct

Quarry Gate

North Wall District

Arcane District

Platinum Court

Keeper

Arcane Hill

Library of All Worlds

Library District

Antiquities District

Scratch

Crookstaff Hill

Crookstaff

Mask

King's Tower

Tower Park

Gaming Houses

Salt District

Tower District

Rose Gate

Carter

Healer

West Wall District

Butcher District

Martial District

Watcher

Canal District

Merchant District

Grand Canal

Central Sewer

Arenas

Crow

Ja

Market District

Harbormaster

Wharf District

Water District

Fleet

North

Harbor Gate

Sunset Harbor

Fleet Bridge

Fleet Island